PRAISE FOR

ENOUGH ROPE

"... Doss' twisty, curvy plot dishes out the goods: scandalous secrets, including blackmail and extramarital affairs. ... The lengthy list of suspects is impressive, and readers won't find it easy pinpointing the killer's identity. ... A murder mystery that sneaks up, takes hold and refuses to let go."

– KIRKUS INDIE

"Wow. I love finding new authors, and P. L. Doss is quite a find. Her story is exciting and her characters are well defined." **– MADDERLY,** Barnes & Noble

"... An exceptional debut that becomes more and more complex as the evidence builds and the tale unfolds. ... The author has seamlessly woven together themes of fallible human nature, deceit, greed, betrayal, and family secrets. ... The characters are wonderfully drawn, especially Halloran and Hollis, but the minor members of the cast are also well characterized. ... The author has masterfully woven together a well-crafted tale."

– GALI, OnlineBookClub.org

"*Enough Rope* is a labyrinthine tale of murder, lust, revenge, and secret histories. ... Will keep your interest until the explosive conclusion." **– STAR,** Goodreads

"From page one I got up in this mystery with Hollis Joplin and Tom Halloran. It seemed that with every page I turned the mystery of the murders became more complex and the plot thickened. I could not put this book down at all. Any spare moment I got, I was reading this book – even at stoplights to and from work. ... This was a thrilling and wonderfully written murder mystery read, and I would highly recommend it to anyone who enjoys mysteries."

– GIRL OF 1000 WONDERS

"Doss has constructed an intricate, swervy plot to titillate the most discriminating of mystery lovers."

– DRAKE CHANDLER, Amazon

PRAISE FOR

BLOOD WILL TELL

"P.L. Doss has done it again! Her second novel with Joplin and Halloran as the main characters is as much of a page turner as *Enough Rope*, her first novel. I love her attention to detail, writing style and many twists and turns as well as the character and relationship development in her novels! If you are a fan of crime dramas you will NOT be disappointed with this book!"

– BIGCANOELOVER, Amazon

"This is without doubt, the best murder mystery I have read for quite a while."

– TRACEY TRANTER, Goodreads

"Kudos to Ms. Doss for a thoroughly absorbing mystery, full of fascinating family dynamics."

– PAYTONPUPPY, Barnes & Noble

"I thoroughly enjoyed this crime drama. The writing built suspense and the plot was intricate enough that the final solution was not easily gleaned until revealed. The characters are well developed, believable and engaging. I look forward to more from this author."

– VIXENREINDEER22, Amazon

"The author skillfully draws in the reader and then ratchets up the suspense. A great read."

– TREE HOUSE READER, Amazon

"Absolutely engrossed me from page one to the end! The story line, while complex, was written and tied together beautifully! The ending was a shock to me. Never saw it coming at all! Love the characters. I must go and get the first book to get all caught up now!" **– BEV,** Goodreads

"Gripping and hard to put down, *Blood Will Tell* is definitely worth reading. Was hooked from the very first page and looked forward to finding out 'who dunnit' and why. … HIGHLY recommend." **– DENISE,** Goodreads

PRAISE FOR
THE DEVIL'S BIDDING

"This is a brilliant read. Wonderful well written plot and story line that had me engaged from the start. ... Great suspense and action with wonderful world building. Can't wait to read what the author brings out next."

— BILLIE WICHKAN, Goodreads

"Awesome! A real page turner with amazing plot twists and characters you'll love or loathe but cry out for more! Can't wait for the next book!" **— LEGALLIZ,** Amazon

"A clever whodunnit with many layers ..."

— SAM HARPER, Goodreads

"... the story line kept me engaged and the ending was explosive. ...this novel was entertaining, informative, suspenseful, and thought provoking. This is a new-to-me author and I am looking forward to reading more of her books." **— LYNGUY1,** Barnes & Noble

"This book...was soooo good! ... I wholeheartedly appreciate seeing a different view of a criminal investigation which this book definitely provided. ...The character dynamics were interesting and I loved how Joplin and Halloran interacted. ...I think I want to go back and read the other books as well now so I can get the full story from the beginning." **— SEJLA KAZAFEROVIC,** Goodreads

"I really enjoy the knowledgeable forensic background of the book and I feel attached to the characters. I've read all three in the series and couldn't put them down."

"Doss manages to be topical, culturally relevant AND entertaining in each of her novels. While the story about a young woman's mysterious murder pulls you in, and the dialogue and banter between the main, recurring series' characters … is always entertaining (and can remind you of your own relationships), Doss' criminal justice background and all of her research regarding forensics and murder investigations shines through."

SOUTHERN CROSS

A Joplin/Halloran Mystery

P. L. DOSS

**Mayfair
Press**

SOUTHERN CROSS
Copyright ©2024 by P.L. Doss

Published in the United States of America by Mayfair Press.

Paperback ISBN: 978-0-9890934-7-7
Ebook ISBN: 978-0-9890934-6-0

This book is dedicated to my
husband, William Donovan,
who makes me laugh several
times a day, every day.
Especially when I'm writing.

And to Mary K. Donovan, who
devoted her life and career to
getting kids to love books.
Old souls never die.

**SO WE CHEATED AND WE LIED AND WE TESTED
AND WE NEVER FAILED TO FAIL ...**

FROM "SOUTHERN CROSS" BY
CROSBY, STILLS, AND NASH

PROLOGUE

THE IMPACT OF hitting the water brought the man back to consciousness, but he felt groggy and couldn't remember what had happened. He couldn't see anything either, and his head throbbed. The water was dark and cold. His lungs began to burn and panic flooded through him, causing him to flail his arms futilely. He realized he would die if he didn't get to the water's surface. A surge of adrenalin helped him pump his legs, and he fought to control his arm movements. But even as he moved upward, his lungs betrayed him, convulsing in a desperate effort to fill with air. Instead, they filled with water.

The renewed terror that hit him as the sensation of breathing in water registered in his mind made the man panic even more. His thrashing became wilder, then it slowly subsided as he became weaker. A feeling of calm, almost comfort, flowed through his body, replacing the fear. He felt himself drifting, knowing he was dying, but not caring. The current moved him past dead tree branches that scraped against his face until one held him fast, as if in a final embrace.

1

JOPLIN WISHED HE'D never even told Carrie about the invitation from the Hallorans to spend the August 19th weekend with them at Wolfscratch. Not that it would have made any difference. Carrie would have heard about it from Maggie Halloran anyway.

It wasn't because he didn't want to spend that much time with Tom, even though he still had a career-long bias against lawyers. The four of them had become good friends despite that, especially since it had been almost two years since Tom tried to involve himself in a homicide investigation. As a death investigator with the Milton County ME's Office, Joplin drew a fine line between law enforcement and civilians who didn't know a corpse from a *corpus delicti*.

The bottom line was that he was simply trying to protect Carrie. There were just too many things that could happen out in the wilderness. No lions and tigers, he admitted, but there were plenty of black bears.

And snakes. He'd talked a lot about snakes while telling her about the invitation. Nothing, however, had seemed to dampen her enthusiasm for a weekend away from the heat and humidity of August in Atlanta.

"But you're six months pregnant!" he'd finally said, knowing that was a mistake, even as the words escaped from his mouth. Especially since Carrie was cooking and had a knife in her hand.

"Pregnancy isn't a disease, Hollis," she'd said, her expression reminding him of his fourth-grade teacher, Mrs. Wilkie, who couldn't take a joke. "I'm still working full-time, remember?"

"I know that, Carrie," he'd said quickly. "And a fine job you're doin', lass," he added, hoping the pseudo-Irish accent would work its usual magic.

She had continued to stare at him as she finished chopping some garlic, uncharmed by the accent or the winning smile on his face. Her long, almost-black hair was in a loose ponytail, and her equally dark eyes had fairly crackled with umbrage. She was wearing a coral sundress that complemented her bronzy skin; it also molded itself around her growing baby bump. She looked like a Hebrew goddess, although Joplin knew that was a total contradiction. Whatever, he decided; he'd never been more attracted to her, nor more in love. Or more intent on protecting her from whatever might threaten her or their baby. He'd opened his mouth to say that when she cut him off, eyes still glaring.

"So, if I can perform three autopsies a day, I think I can handle a little hiking and swimming at a beautiful resort in the mountains."

"I'll call Tom right now and give him the good news," Joplin had said, still smiling. He'd now been married to Carrie for a year and a half and knew when she might be about to switch gears.

That had been five days ago. Any hopes that his boss, Chief Investigator Sarah Petersen, would refuse to modify his work schedule for the weekend had been dashed as soon as he'd made the request.

"I think that's a great idea, Hollis," she'd said, her chiseled, Kennedy-esque features forming a smile. "You've hardly taken any leave since Carrie found out she was pregnant, and this will be good for both of you. It's so wicked hot here, you're lucky to be able to go to the mountains. Do the Hallorans have a house up there?"

"No, it belongs to Healey and Caldwell, Tom's law firm. Another partner had booked it to entertain some new clients, but he had to cancel and offered it to Tom."

"Well, I envy you. Coming from Boston, I love the Atlanta winters, but the summers are miserable. Especially in August."

Only the cats, Quincy and Banshee, had been on Joplin's side. Carrie had arranged for their neighbor, Maya Turnbull, to feed them over the weekend, but Quincy had looked up at Joplin in disbelief as they walked out of the new house in Garden Hills with their bags. And Banshee's wailing had serenaded them as they loaded up Joplin's car.

"They'll be fine," Carrie had said, refusing to turn around.

So here they were, on an already-hot Friday morning in Maggie Halloran's Lexus SUV, driving the sixty-six miles from Atlanta to Wolfscratch, a sprawling, 8,000-acre community in Rutledge County. The resort had three golf courses, two swim clubs, stocked lakes, and myriad hiking trails. It didn't have quite the cachet of Highlands, North Carolina or Lake Hartwell in Northeast Georgia, but it was much closer to Atlanta and had its fair share of spectacular houses with lake or mountain views. The one they were heading to had neither, but it did have a gorgeous pool, according to Carrie, who'd checked it out on Zillow.

"I packed a picnic lunch for our hike to the Upper Falls," said Maggie. "And I made a reservation at Maison for tonight. It's a cozy little Southern bistro just outside the North Gate that Tom and I love."

"So, have you stayed at the firm's property a lot?" Joplin asked as they turned off Georgia 400 onto Highway 369 at Exit 18.

"Not really. Maybe three or four times. Various partners usually arrange golf weekends to entertain clients there, and Tom's not one of them."

"Golf takes too much time," Tom said. "And I'm not good at letting a potential client win just to get new business."

"Why am I not surprised by that, Tom?" asked Joplin.

"We've spent some time at Wolfscratch because my Aunt Moira and her husband have a house there," Maggie said quickly. "They used to own and run a large horse stable nearby, but they're retired now. So, Tom and I and the kids and my parents have come up here for weekends several times in the past two years."

"Is she your mother's or your father's sister?" Carrie asked.

"My mother's," Maggie said, turning around from the front passenger seat to smile at them. "And I'm afraid she knows we'll be up here this weekend. She'll probably insist we all come by for a drink, but Tom and I can just run over to see them if you'd rather not go."

"Well, your mother is one of my favorite people," Joplin said. An image of Colleen O'Connell, surrounded by her children and grandchildren at their house on Cherokee Road in Buckhead, popped into his mind. She was an older, smaller version of Maggie, with short auburn hair and large green eyes. Like Maggie, she was also an excellent cook who loved to entertain, and the O'Connells had often included him and Carrie in family gatherings. "So, I'm sure we'll like your aunt. Right, Carrie?"

"Of course," she said. "We'd love to meet her."

"Well, if you're expecting someone like Colleen, you're in for a surprise," Tom said. "The Callaghan sisters are nothing like each other."

"Tom!" Maggie said.

Tom glanced at her, then turned back to the road. "You can't just drag them over to meet Moira and Ryan without a heads-up, Maggie. Remember *my* first visit with them?"

"I'd rather not."

"I don't mean to butt in," Joplin said, "but maybe a little heads-up would be a good idea, Maggie. Besides, I grew up in a small town around what Southerners like to call 'characters,' so I might have a higher threshold for eccentricity than Tom. But what are we talking about here? Does your aunt wear purple hats or keep a goat in the house? Or is it something more extreme? My mother's mother was the Emily Dickinson of Austell, Georgia. She liked to sit with people who were dying, right up to the very end, to see if they talked to Jesus or had a vision of hell. My other grandmother called her the 'Angel of Death.'"

"That's pretty shocking, Hollis," said Tom.

"See, I told you, Maggie. People from Chicago just don't appreciate eccentricity like we do in the South."

"No, I mean, I had no idea you'd ever even heard of Emily Dickinson."

Joplin just smiled and said, "One of the conditions Carrie placed on my marrying her was being able to read on a sixth-grade level."

"He's graduated to a ninth-grade level after a year with me," Carrie added, grinning. "Remember, I was an English Lit under-grad, so I've given him a lot of intense tutoring. Dickinson was on the list."

"Our child will be born with a library card in her hand," Joplin said.

"I stand corrected," said Tom.

"So, now do I get to hear about your aunt, Maggie? "

"She's a remarkable person," Maggie said, then swatted Tom on the shoulder when he gave a snarky laugh. "It's just that she sort of…dominates any room she's in."

"Even with *your* husband in the room?" Joplin asked, thinking of the first time he'd met Tom Halloran. Joplin had known of Tom's reputation as a hot-shot attorney with wealthy clients who left their estates to young wives half their age. He'd also seen him being interviewed on TV when court battles over those estates made headlines. But he'd been unprepared for the impression Halloran made in person. It hadn't just been the man's height, almost palpable arrogance, or even his steely blue eyes. It was more Tom's determination three years earlier to convince Joplin that his friend, Elliot Carter, had not killed himself, no matter how things looked. No matter what obstacles he might encounter. No matter what he had to do.

"Let's just say that, for the sake of family harmony," Tom said now, in a tone that seemed to end any further discussion of Maggie's aunt, "I've learned to pick my battles when it comes to Moira Fitzgerald."

The conversation turned to the gorgeous countryside around them, at least where it wasn't being overtaken by new housing developments with names like "Rosemount Ridge" or "The Paddocks." Despite Atlanta's distance, the area was fast becoming a bedroom community, with plans to widen Georgia 400 yet again. But there were still several farms with cows and horses dotting the landscape.

Just past a sign that directed them to the Mount Tabor Baptist Church, Tom turned onto Old Federal Road, and the area seemed much more rural. As they approached a small bridge that spanned an even smaller creek, Joplin saw a sign on the right that read, "Trail of Tears."

"My God!" he said. "Is this the beginning of the route where they marched the Cherokee out of Georgia?"

"Yes," said Maggie, turning around again to face them. "I always feel a twinge of sadness when I see those signs. They're everywhere up here. But I think it's important that we not forget about what happened, don't you?"

"I do," Joplin said, trying to keep the images he'd seen in history books of the forced removal of almost sixteen thousand Cherokee men, women, and children from their native lands out of his brain. An estimated four thousand had died before they reached the new Indian Territory in Oklahoma.

At times like this, he wished he weren't cursed with an eidetic memory that allowed him to recall everything he'd ever seen. It was an asset in his role as the "eyes and ears" of the forensic pathologists who would perform autopsies on the bodies he examined at death scenes. But it had caused him more sleepless nights than he could count and problems with close relationships.

And now, it was giving him a strange sense of foreboding about their weekend getaway to the mountains.

2

THE HOUSE ON Blue Ridge Lane was even more spectacular than the photos Carrie had found on Zillow.

It was a sprawling Craftsman-style bungalow with lots of
stone, dark brown cedar shingles, and large casement windows
under gabled eaves. A three-car garage was off to the right, but
Tom parked in the middle of the driveway, just outside the
front door, with its covered entry and short columns. As they
all got out of the car, Joplin admired the lush landscaping surrounding the house.

"It must be nice being one of Healey and Caldwell's clients,"
he said. "Even nicer to be one of its partners, Tom."

"Hey, I worked very hard to achieve that, Hollis."

"I know that, and I'm lucky to be invited here. Especially
since it's almost ten degrees cooler up here and half as muggy."

"Then how about helping me with the bags? I think the ser-
vants are off for the weekend."

Joplin grabbed his and Carrie's weekend bags from the way-
back and followed Tom through the arched double doors into

the house. The entry hall led past a dining room and staircase on the left and an enormous open area with a vaulted ceiling. A gourmet kitchen was on the right, with a great room on the left. Couches and high-backed chairs were grouped around a tall stone fireplace, while an area outside the wall of windows at the end of the room held another covered dining area.

"This is magnificent," Carrie said. She walked past him into the great room, carrying her purse and an insulated tote bag. "The pictures didn't do it justice. I didn't realize a Craftsman-style house could look so elegant and rustic at the same time. And the view is amazing!"

"We can take a little tour once we get settled in," Maggie said. "Tom, why don't you show Hollis and Carrie their room while I put up these groceries?" she added, holding up two Fresh Market bags.

"I need to refrigerate the appetizers I brought, too," said Carrie. "I'll be right with you, Tom."

Joplin followed Tom through the great room and past a set of descending stairs to a small hall.

"There's a powder room just there to the right," Tom said, motioning with his head, then led Joplin into a beautifully appointed bedroom. "Maggie said to put you on this floor so Carrie won't have to go up and down too many stairs."

"For God's sake, don't let Carrie overhear you," Joplin whispered. "She'll go up and down both sets of stairs at least three times just to prove she can."

"That bad, huh?" Tom said.

"You better believe it," said Joplin, setting the bags down near the king-sized bed that would have to try much harder to fill the room. "If she tells me one more time that 'pregnancy isn't a disease,' I'll get earplugs."

"Maggie went on a pretty drastic organic food regimen when she was pregnant with Tommy. And red meat was forbidden. I had to sneak around just to have a steak now and then, but I felt so guilty I never really enjoyed it."

"Wow! I had no idea that lawyers ever felt guilty."

"Payback for my snide remark about Emily Dickinson, right?"

"Of course."

"Well, I guess I deserved it. Anyway, the good news is that this sort of behavior seems to be more typical of a first pregnancy. The second one is easier."

"Something to look forward to," Joplin said.

"What's something to look forward to?"

Joplin whirled around to see Carrie standing at the door. "Our hike," he said quickly. "Tom says the Upper Falls area is stunning. And then we can come back and lounge around the pool."

Carrie's eyes narrowed, but she looked around the bedroom, smiled, and rushed to the large window.

"God, I forgot about the pool! Hollis, come see it."

He did and was blown away by the vision of a stunning, rectangular pool surrounded by lounge chairs and Hibiscus plants and bordered on one side by cedar trees. It was a far cry from their neighborhood pool in Garden Hills teeming with kids, babies, and bored parents on their cell phones.

He took a chance and said, "How 'bout we skip the hike and go straight to the lounging by the pool?"

"No way," Carrie scoffed. "I need some exercise."

✦ ✦ ✦ ✦

THE PICNIC LUNCH was distributed among their four back-packs. Joplin's held two cans of beer and some soft drinks inside an insulated bag, while Tom Halloran's was full of food. Maggie's had the plastic plates, utensils, napkins, and several bottles of water. Carrie was allowed only the tablecloth, but when she started to complain, Maggie shushed her. To Joplin's surprise and unabashed amazement, Carrie shushed. He chalked it up to the fact that Maggie had given birth twice and therefore had more standing than he did, but made a mental note to interrogate her on the subject in the near future.

They parked at the beginning of a trail off Wildwood Parkway that held space for about ten cars. The temperature had risen in the past hour, but it was still cooler than Atlanta, and they walked at a leisurely pace along a gravel jeep trail. Joplin wished he had hiking boots like the ones Hallorans and Carrie wore, but his Nikes were okay. About a quarter-mile up the trail, they came to an old log cabin that Maggie explained had been transplanted from another area. Two picnic tables were off to the right, and a family with three young children had taken one of them. A creek burbled nearby, adding to the rustic atmosphere.

Joplin had begun to think he'd overestimated any hiking risks to Carrie until they came to a wide creek with a narrow bridge and one railing that allowed only single-file crossings. The Hallorans forged ahead and didn't even look back as they hopped on it. Carrie quickly followed as Joplin hovered behind her, terrified she would lose her balance and fall to the rocks below, smashing herself and their unborn child. He held his breath as she pranced—actually *pranced*—to the other side, then moved quickly to walk next to Maggie. He reluctantly followed as they picked their way over dangerous tree roots, remaining alert for copperheads. They reached the Lower Falls ten minutes later, but Joplin's heart was in his throat the entire time. He took a deep, cleansing breath and admitted it was a lovely sight, with water cascading down from a large rock formation above them. Patches of water sparkled in the sun, and a fine mist cooled his face.

"This is wonderful!" Carrie said happily, holding out her arms. She looked adorable in her khaki shorts and blue tank top. The hiking boots seemed to make her legs look even longer.

"Why don't we just have our picnic here?" Joplin said. "It's lovely."

"We could," said Maggie, "but the Upper Falls has picnic tables. It would be much more comfortable than sitting on a big rock."

Carrie took out her phone and began to snap some pictures. "Of course, it would," she said. "And I wouldn't miss seeing them anyway." She took a few more photos, including one of Joplin with the water behind him, then headed for the much wider wooden bridge that spanned this part of the creek.

"Sure you don't want to rest a bit and have some water?" Maggie asked her.

"Thanks, but I'll be fine till we get there," she said, glaring at Joplin.

"I didn't say anything!" he insisted, but she marched past him and headed back up the trail.

"Somebody's in trouble," said Tom, grinning at him.

It was another thirty minutes before they reached the Upper Falls. Joplin could hear the roar of the water well before they got there. They were all pretty sweaty by then, but it was cooler up here. The picnic area had five tables, all empty. He assumed that other potential picnickers had wisely stayed inside or gone to the resort's clubhouse for lunch due to the heat and humidity. There were also no cars in the parking area. They followed the sound of the water to the edge of a cliff, and a breathtaking view of cascading water awaited them. It pounded into a pool studded with large, smooth boulders, then rushed down to another pond just below the first one.

"Wow!" said Carrie, pulling out her phone again. "This is even prettier than the Lower Falls."

"It's a good thing we didn't let Hollis talk us out of coming up here," Tom said.

Maggie made a face at him and took off her backpack. Reaching into it, she retrieved a small Canon camera then set the bag down. Adjusting the lens, she swept the camera over the falls and the pool below, then began taking pictures. Joplin was sure they'd be amazing, since Maggie was a nationally-known photographer. Several clicks sounded in succession as she made shots, then stopped abruptly. Joplin turned to look at her and saw her staring down at a spot below them. The expression on Maggie's face was puzzled. She put the camera up to her eye again, adjusted the lens setting, and then turned to him.

"I don't want to spoil our picnic, but I think there's a body down there," she said.

3

JOPLIN TOOK THE camera from Maggie, aimed it where she directed, and adjusted the lens. What had looked like a piece of dark clothing or a discarded cloth bag to the naked eye was the back of a shirt on a man with his face in profile. He was nestled in some tree branches caught by two large boulders where the water was more shallow, just before it lowered into the second pool. He looked dead, but Joplin didn't want to take any chances.

"Maggie, call 911," he said. "Tom, let's go down and see if he's alive." He turned away as Maggie began to tap in the numbers.

"I think I should go, too," said Carrie. "He might need medical attention, and we don't know how long the EMTs will be."

"Let me check first, okay? The path down there is pretty steep."

Carrie frowned at this, but didn't insist.

Joplin reached the water first. "Why don't you take a few pictures while I check him out," he said, handing Tom Maggie's camera and his wallet and phone, then sitting on a nearby rock to take off his shoes and socks.

"No sense both of us getting wet."

"Sure," said Tom, pocketing the wallet and phone. "But be careful. I can help if you need me."

Joplin nodded, then waded into the area where the man's body lay. The sickly-sweet smell of decomposition hit him two feet from the creek's bank. By the time he reached the body, the water was waist-high, but it was crystal clear, and he could see down to the man's shoes. He waved away some green bottle flies that had landed on the face, which had abrasions, maybe from the tree branches. Joplin saw dozens of larvae and eggs in the eyes, nose, mouth, and ears. He was about to check for rigor or livor mortis to get a better idea of the post-mortem interval, then remembered that this was Rutledge County, not Milton, and he had no jurisdiction. It was important not to disturb the scene in any way.

A siren off in the distance drew his attention away from the body. Before he looked back, Joplin examined the surrounding area, unsure what he was looking for. The man's death could have been accidental or from natural causes. Or both. He could have tripped and plunged into the water or had a heart attack and fallen into the water. But by habit and training, Joplin was on alert for any anomaly that would point to something more sinister. An autopsy could prove—or disprove—either possibility, but whatever he could pick up from the scene might be important. Rutledge County had a coroner system instead of a medical examiner system. He hoped whoever was sent to examine the body was in law enforcement or at least had some training in death investigation, because his gut was telling him this was no accident.

Unfortunately, the scene itself wasn't telling Joplin much of anything. He did notice what looked like an empty liquor bottle on the creek's opposite bank, but it might have been there for days or weeks.

"Tom, can you get a shot of that liquor bottle over there?" he said, pointing across the creek.

"Sure."

"The Wolfscratch EMTs are here," Maggie called down.

Joplin looked up to see Carrie standing next to her. He shook his head to let her know there was nothing she could do. Seconds later, he saw two men wearing dark blue uniforms hurrying down the path to the water, both carrying pieces of equipment.

"No need to rush," he called out. "I'm afraid he's dead."

"I think we better check, sir," said the bigger one on the left.

"He's a death investigator with the Milton County ME's Office," Tom Halloran said. "I think you can take his word for it."

"There's been a lot of insect activity," Joplin said. "Bottle flies and maggots. I don't think he's been in the water very long, but the heat and humidity probably sped up the decomposition process. He's pretty ripe."

The man nodded, then turned to his partner and said, "I'll let Rutledge EMS know so they can call the coroner."

"You recognize him?" Joplin asked the other man as he returned to the creek's bank.

"No, but a lot of people live here, so that doesn't mean anything."

"Who contacted you?"

"Rutledge called us since we could get here faster if someone needed resuscitation or immediate treatment, but they're on the way. We can't transport anyone to a hospital. Or the morgue," he added.

"You know the coroner?"

The man shrugged. "Not really. I mean, I know *who* he is. Name's Harold Danforth. Owns Danforth Funeral Home over to Nolan, the county seat. But most of the dead people we see here in Wolfscratch die of natural causes at home. Usually in bed." He shrugged again. "We got a lot of older people livin' here. Retired people, you know?"

Joplin nodded. He was glad the coroner was a funeral director because he would at least have a working knowledge of death and the human body. But the name rang a distant bell that somehow had a negative association for him. Another siren cut off his thoughts as he was trying to place it.

"That'll be Rutledge," said the Wolfscratch EMT. With a nod to Joplin, he turned and walked back up the hill.

"Tri-State Crematory," Joplin said suddenly, as images of Fox reporter Dan Ronan breaking the story on February 15, 2002 flashed through his mind. Various front-page headlines followed this in the *Atlanta Journal-Constitution,* then an article on February 20th in which Harold Danforth was interviewed. And another one just two months ago.

"That's the uncremated bodies scandal, right?" said Tom. "Where they found bodies all over the property of a crematory business?"

"Yep. Three hundred thirty-nine bodies, to be exact, in Noble, Georgia. Not too far from here. Tommy Ray Brent Marsh, AKA Brent Marsh, who'd taken over the business from his father, got behind on the job, and the bodies started piling up. Literally. I was a rookie cop, but my partner and I helped canvass some of the mortuaries up in the northern part of Milton County to see if they'd used Tri-State and could identify photos of the less decomposed bodies."

"I had just joined Healey and Caldwell that fall and was working my tail off, so I didn't keep up with the case, but there was a lot of discussion in the Estate division about the Georgia Supreme Court's ruling that dead bodies have no monetary value."

"Which got the theft by deception charges against Marsh eliminated," said Joplin. "He pled guilty to the other charges and got twelve years in prison, but a lot of people thought it was way too little. Especially the families who got boxes filled with cement dust instead of the cremains of their relatives. I'm sure they felt the same about his apology at a press conference when he was released this past June."

"Yeah, but didn't the families end up getting a pretty big settlement when they filed a class-action suit against Marsh, Tri-State, and the funeral directors who sent bodies to the crematory?"

"They did," said Joplin. "And Harold Danforth, now the coroner of Rutledge County, was one of them."

Tom smiled at him. "Given your eidetic memory, Hollis, I believe you," he said. "But I'm sensing a certain level of animosity in your tone. Granted, the directors didn't do their due diligence concerning conditions at the crematory, and, as I recall, the formaldehyde from the embalmed bodies was deemed a toxic hazard to the community, but couldn't they also be seen as victims of Marsh's negligence?"

"Spoken like the lawyer you are, Tom," said Joplin. The appearance of two more EMTs, dressed in khaki uniforms and supporting a portable gurney between them as they made it to the water's edge, kept Joplin from saying more. He introduced himself, gesturing toward the body as he explained again how they had found it and determined that the man was dead.

"Well, we gotta wait for the coroner to pronounce him," said the taller of the two. "He may want to ask you a few questions, so I hope you don't mind hangin' around here for a bit."

"Not at all," Joplin said, and Tom nodded in agreement.

But it wasn't Harold Danforth who showed up ten minutes later. The man approaching them looked to be around thirty, with short, dark hair already thinning on top and prominent, wide-set eyes that gave him a frog-like appearance. He was overweight and slightly out of breath as he reached their group. Joplin glanced at the clip-on ID attached to the navy windbreaker he was wearing that announced he was Deputy Coroner Bo Danforth, then dropped to the black bag he was carrying.

Ignoring Joplin and Halloran, Danforth stared at the body in the water, then at the two Rutledge County EMTs, and said, "Whatta we got here?"

The same man who'd talked to Joplin said, "These people found the body and called us. Wolfscratch Fire Department got here first and was told the man was dead when they checked on him. So Wolfscratch radioed that to us, and I called you. Well, I mean, I called the coroner's office."

Bo Danforth glanced at the body again, then down to the EMT's dry pant legs. "Doesn't look like you verified that, Jimmy."

Jimmy glanced at his partner, then pointed at Joplin. "Mr. Joplin here told us he's a death investigator for the Milton County ME's Office," he said, sounding defensive. "He said the body was already decomposing. So, I took his word for it."

Danforth finally looked at Joplin. It was a searching look that held both challenge and wariness, then settled into smugness.

"That doesn't mean I have to," he said, but instead of wading into the water, he turned back to Jimmy. "Go check it out."

The EMT stared at Danforth for several seconds, then slowly waded into the water without bothering to take off his shoes. Joplin was disgusted by the deputy coroner's manner toward the man, but had run up against good old boys like this too often to be offended. Instead, he smiled and looked down at the ground. Tom, however, wasn't having it.

"Isn't that *your* job?" he asked pointedly. "I guess the county doesn't pay you much, but they're still not getting their money's worth."

Danforth turned beet red and glared at Halloran. "Who are you?" he spat out.

"A taxpayer," he said. "And fortunately, I don't live in this county."

Bo Danforth's wide-set eyes goggled at Halloran, then narrowed abruptly. He pointed a finger and said, "I know who you are. You're Tom Halloran, that hot-shot lawyer who's on TV a lot. Well, this isn't Atlanta, and you have no business telling me how to do my job."

Tom folded his arms and somehow made his six-foot, four-inch frame look even taller, something Joplin had seen him do before. "If you were doing your job, I wouldn't have to," he said. "This could be a crime scene; you should examine the body. Or you should listen to what my friend has observed so far."

"Crime scene?" Danforth sneered. "This was an accident, plain and simple. Anyone can see that. We call it HUI up here in North Georgia—Hiking Under the Influence." He turned toward the water and pointed. "You see that liquor bottle on the other side of the creek? That's what killed this man, plain and simple. That and his own stupidity."

Joplin couldn't believe the man's arrogance, but said only, "Are you going to request an autopsy?"

Danforth's eyes narrowed again. "Why would I do that, when I just told you what killed him?"

"He's wearing tan slacks, a button-down shirt, and loafers. Not your typical hiking clothes."

"So what? Wolfscratch gets a lot of tourists this time of year. They wear all kinds of things. Or maybe he just came up here to look at the Falls."

Joplin put another smile on his face. "At night? The body has already started to smell, and bottle fly larvae are also present, which shows a postmortem lapse of at least twelve hours. Maybe less in this heat. So, we're talking about eleven or twelve last night. He must have had a car to get here, or someone drove him."

Deputy Coroner Bo Danforth drew himself up to his full height of five feet, eight inches and glared at Joplin.

Then he turned and glared at Tom, too, for good measure. "We don't have any control over what folks at Wolfscratch do in their spare time," he said. "We stay out of their business, and you should stay out of ours." And without glancing back at Jimmy, still standing beside the body, he yelled, "Load him up and take him to the morgue, boys!"

4

"**Y**OU MIND CHECKING his pockets for ID?" Joplin asked the EMTs after they'd placed the man in a body bag and onto the gurney.

"I guess we could do that," Jimmy said. "Just don't say we did," he added, giving Joplin a conspiratorial grin.

"Not me. I sure don't want to get you into any trouble. It's just that—"

Jimmy held up a gloved hand. "At this point, I don't really care. That asshole has jerked my chain one time too many. I like this job, but I'm about ready to quit and move to another county to get away from him. His father, the *real* coroner, is respected around here, but Bo's a jerk. And more and more, lately, he's been sending Bo to scenes." He unzipped the bag and felt in the left-side pants pocket, but found nothing. The right-side pocket held a waterlogged wallet, which Jimmy opened, then pulled out a driver's license and handed it to Joplin.

Joplin quickly read the information on the license and handed it back to Jacob. "Thanks," was all he said.

"No problem," the EMT said as he slid the license back into the wallet, put it back into the man's pocket, and zipped it up again. Nodding to Joplin, he helped his partner collapse the wheels on the gurney and trudged up the path.

"You happen to have a handkerchief on you, Tom?" Joplin asked when they were out of sight.

"I do," Halloran answered, pulling it out of his shorts pocket and handing it to Joplin. "May I ask why?"

"I want to take that liquor bottle with us, and I don't want to mess up any prints on it."

"You really think this might be a murder scene, don't you?"

"Let's just say that if I were called out to a scene like this in Milton County, I'd treat it like a homicide until the evidence showed otherwise. I don't know who this man is other than his name, Eric Jaeger. But his death deserves more attention than Deputy Coroner Danforth is willing to give it."

"I agree, Hollis, but what can you do about it?"

"I'm not sure. But I'm gonna find out."

✛ ✛ ✛ ✛

MAGGIE AND CARRIE were waiting for them when they reached the top of the cliff.

"I got the impression that the coroner doesn't think the death looks suspicious," Carrie said. "He wouldn't talk to us, but the Rutledge EMTs did when they brought the body up."

"That would be *Deputy* Coroner Bo Danforth," replied Joplin, "and I don't think he would have found JFK's death suspicious."

"Is that why you're carrying an empty Jim Beam bottle in a handkerchief?"

"You got it, Dr. Salinger. The man pissed me off so much I decided to collect some evidence myself. Potential evidence, anyway. You have a paper bag in with the lunch stuff, Maggie?"

"Well, I think I have one that will hold that, but it's not paper."

"It'll do for now anyway." Joplin waited while Maggie rummaged around in her backpack, then he carefully placed the bottle into the Ziploc bag she gave him.

"I'm not sure that'll pass chain of custody protocols," Tom said. "Just saying."

"Doesn't have to. This is just for me. Hopefully, Eric Jaeger—that's the dead man's name—will have his fingerprints on record. Anyone else's might belong to the person he was with last night."

Carrie frowned and cocked her head. "Are you maybe over-thinking this, Hollis? I mean, I have a great deal of respect for your gut feelings, but..."

"I probably am, but this is just something I need to do, okay? I won't do anything until we get back to Atlanta and I can take this to the lab. But it's not going to ruin the weekend. I promise."

"Okay, then," said Maggie. "Let's eat."

✦ ✦ ✦ ✦

IT WAS A somewhat dispirited group that made its way down the mountain. They had all tried to get back into a festive "getaway" mode during their picnic lunch, but as Joplin had often observed, death had a way of putting a damper on things.

Nevertheless, Maggie, consummate hostess that she was, had insisted that everyone change into bathing suits and better moods, then gather outside at the pool once they returned to the house on Blue Ridge Lane.

"We've got a whole weekend ahead of us to relax and have fun," she'd said.

The beautiful setting began to work its magic once they were all stretched out on chaise lounges by the side of the pool. They didn't discuss the body at the Upper Falls by tacit agreement. Before changing into his trunks, Joplin had swapped the Ziploc bag for a paper one to help preserve any prints on the Jim Beam bottle, then placed it in the guest bedroom closet, determined not to think about it until he was back in Atlanta. The sun was bright in a clear blue sky, but they stayed cool with frequent dips in the pool and an ice chest full of bottled water. They had all brought books, but only Tom attempted to read his, *A Gentleman in Moscow*, by Amor Towles. As Maggie and Carrie chatted quietly, their voices becoming soothing murmurs, Joplin gave up on his own book, *Danger Road: A True Story of Death and Redemption*. Deciding it was too pretty a day to read about the murders of three drug dealers in Florida, he closed his eyes and drifted off.

"Cocktail time," he heard Maggie say. Joplin opened his eyes to see her standing over him, holding a frosted Pilsner glass and a bottle of Yuengling.

"My favorite time of day," he said, grinning.

"It used to be mine, too," Carrie said, looking down at her baby bump. "Instead of a library card, this baby better come out holding a Martini glass for me."

✚ ✚ ✚ ✚

MAISON OCCUPIED A rustic farmhouse just outside the North Gate. The gravel parking area was almost filled as Tom pulled into it, a good sign in Joplin's opinion. Several diners were seated at tables on a deck off to the left, obviously enjoying themselves. Another good sign. Inside, a blast of noise— more people enjoying themselves at high-topped tables crowded in front of a large bar—hit them as they walked over to the hostess stand. A lovely, petite woman with dark, blunt-cut hair greeted them.

"Tom and Maggie!" she said. "I got excited when I saw your names on the reservation list for tonight. We haven't seen you since the beginning of the summer."

"Believe me, we wish we could get up here more often," said Maggie. "Carole, these are our friends, Carrie and Hollis Joplin. And this is one of Maison's owners, Carole Lincoln," she added, turning to them.

Hands were shaken, menus were gathered, and the four of them were led through a high-ceilinged room full of even more chattering, eating diners to a table near a back window. Several amazing oil paintings hung on the walls. Carole assured them a server would be with them soon, but took their drink orders herself.

"Wow," Joplin said. "It's not what you know, it's who you know, right, Tom? Not that I'm complaining."

"Carole's just an excellent host," said Tom. "Besides, you get the same treatment at Davio's."

The conversation turned to entrée recommendations by the Hallorans. When the drinks arrived, and their server—a young, pretty girl with long, curly hair who Joplin later found out was Carole's daughter, Alaina—had taken their orders, Maggie said, "Is anyone up for taking a pontoon boat out on the lake tomorrow?"

"That sounds great," said Carrie. "I want to run in the morning, so can we make it sometime in the afternoon?"

"Sure. We don't have to be at my aunt's for drinks until five-thirty."

Tom made a face and was about to say something when a man called out his name. They turned to see a handsome, middle-aged couple walking toward their table. The man was tall and fit, with thick, graying hair; the woman was slender, long-legged, and bottle-blonde. She looked like an older version of all the girls who wouldn't date Joplin in high school. Together, they looked like they'd just filmed a Cialis commercial. Or just stepped off a yacht, Joplin decided.

"Jack, Betsey," Tom said as he and Joplin stood up. Maggie hugged the woman as Tom made the necessary introductions, then Betsey Cunningham insisted they sit down.

"We came with another couple," she said, gesturing to a table on the other side of the room, "but we just had to come over and say hello. It's been *too long*! I think a year, at least, since we've seen you. I wish I'd known y'all were coming up this weekend."

"It was a last-minute thing," said Maggie, smiling. "We'll be sure to get in touch next time."

Betsey smiled back, showing off perfectly white teeth. "Are you staying with Ryan and Moira?"

"No, we're staying at the firm's house."

Betsey moved closer to her and dropped her voice to a stage whisper. "Then maybe you haven't heard about the dead body they found at the Upper Falls."

"A dead body?" Maggie said, opening her eyes wider.

"I don't think they want to hear about that, honey," said Jack, frowning.

"I guess not," said Betsey, looking disappointed. "I mean, y'all have crimes happening every day in Atlanta, but it's the most excitement we've had up here in a long time."

"So, it wasn't an accident?" Joplin asked casually.

She turned to look at him, then tucked a piece of hair behind her ear. "Well, I don't really know, now you mention it. I guess I just assumed. I heard about it from Jane Southerland—her husband's the president of the POA up here—and she said no one knew who he was or what he was doing in Wolfscratch."

Mercifully, Alaina arrived with a large tray that held their salads.

"Let's let these people have their dinner, Betsey," Jack Cunningham said quickly.

"Of course," she said, beaming at them. And with another hug for Maggie and a wink for Joplin, she whirled around and took her husband's arm.

"Word travels fast up here in the mountains," Joplin said after their salads had been served.

"Especially with Betsey around," said Maggie. "They're good friends of my aunt and uncle, and I've known them almost all my life, but I always feel like I'm playing Twenty Questions when I'm around her."

They'd all agreed not to discuss the body at the Falls during dinner, so the conversation moved back to how they would spend the next day, then to the great food and ambiance they were enjoying. But a pall had come over the evening that not even another round of drinks could lift.

✚ ✚ ✚ ✚

IN HIS DREAMS, Joplin walked through a dilapidated compound of buildings surrounded by trees. Bodies in varying stages of decomposition were strewn around it: some still in hospital gowns, some wrapped in sheets, others packed in cardboard boxes. Caskets were stacked up against a crematorium, and a body was half-in, half-out of the opening. He walked behind the buildings and came across others reduced to their various body parts—a skull here, a leg bone there—probably by animals. Joplin went further into the forest and saw more bodies: Men dressed in long shirts, leggings, and moccasins, their heads shaved, with only a scalplock remaining under a Mohawk headdress. The women wore long, wrapped skirts, their hair hanging loosely. Children, even babies in papooses, surrounded them. Their eyes were all open, staring at him in accusation. Joplin hurried on and came to a large creek with a waterfall. Eric Jaeger sat on a bench, legs crossed, looking like he'd been waiting for him. He still looked dead, with his half-open eyes filled with maggots, but his head turned toward Joplin as he came closer.

"Don't leave me here," he said. "It's not where I'm supposed to be."

5

THE PROBLEM WITH having relatives—especially in-laws—who didn't live in the same city but were not far away, Tom Halloran decided as he drove the four of them to the Fitzgeralds' house, was that you still had to visit them more often than you wanted to. Most of his own family still lived in Chicago, reducing time spent together to once or twice a year. But Maggie's extended family was close-knit. They got together for holidays, birthdays, anniversaries, graduations—the list was endless. He had hoped they could have their weekend at Wolfscratch to themselves, but with her parents keeping the children, he knew that wasn't possible.

"We're almost there," Halloran said as they went further up Cliffview, which scaled Spearfinger, one of three mountains inside Wolfscratch.

"Well, wherever they live up here, the view must be spectacular," said Carrie.

"Oh, it is. You can see all the way to Atlanta from the back of their house at night, when the skyline is lit up."

Halloran hoped they wouldn't be around to see it that night since it was only 5:30, but with Moira, one never knew what might happen. Maggie and Carrie already had that evening's meal prepped, but that would mean nothing if Moira decided they should stay for dinner. Not that it wouldn't be spectacular—it would be. But it wouldn't be what they'd planned, which ticked him off. Trying to swallow his resentment for Maggie's sake, Halloran pulled into the circular drive and parked in front of an enormous Craftsman that would dwarf the firm's house on Blue Ridge Lane.

"Damn!" said Hollis. "You sure this isn't Tyler Perry's house, Tom?"

"I wish," he answered, prompting a jab from Maggie.

"It's actually a smaller version of their house at Fox Run, their stables," she said. "They built this the year before they retired."

"Well, they must have gotten a pretty penny for the original," said Hollis.

"Don't be gauche," Carrie said.

"Okay," said Hollis. "I'll stop as soon as I figure out what 'gauche' means."

Before Carrie could respond, the house's double doors burst open, and Maggie's aunt came out onto the wide porch, making a grand entrance. Or exit, in this particular case. Despite his irritation at her command performance, Halloran had to admire her style. Moira Fitzgerald was the picture of casual elegance in a long black and white skirt and a white tank top that showed off tanned, muscular arms. Her dark hair was cut into a chin-length bob accented by a widow's peak, with a gray streak extending from both sides. She clapped her hands like an excited child and beamed at them all.

"Welcome!" she said, walking down a few of the porch's steps. "I'm Moira, and you must be Carrie and Hollis," she added when they had gotten out of the car.

"We are!" Carrie said brightly, taking her outstretched hand.

"Nice of you to have us," Hollis said, and Halloran hoped he'd mean that by the end of their visit.

Once he and Maggie had been air-kissed and clucked over, Moira led them back up the porch steps and into the house, her perfume trailing behind her. She ushered them through the high-ceilinged entry hall into the even higher-ceilinged great room. It hadn't changed since the last time Halloran had been there, still filled to bursting with overstuffed chairs and sofas, Persian rugs, and paintings that covered every available space on the walls. Luckily, a massive stone fireplace and a back wall made entirely of windows kept the room from looking like a museum.

Feeling even more resentful at being ordered over for drinks, Halloran noted that the only thing different in the room was Betsey Cunningham sitting on one of the two pale yellow sofas, vibrant pink Cosmopolitan in hand. She waved it at them, smiling broadly, and said, "We started without you!"

Moira turned to them and said, "Betsey called me this morning and said she'd run into y'all at Maison last night, so I insisted she and Jack join us."

"I'm so glad," Maggie said quickly, moving toward the sofa. She elbowed Halloran discreetly as she went past him.

"Where's Ryan?" he asked.

"Out on the terrace," Moira said. "The bar's set up out there, but Betsey and I decided it was too hot. Why don't you take drink orders, Tom, and see if you can get him and Jack back inside?"

"I'll help you," said Hollis. He turned to Carrie. "Honey, what would you like?"

"Just some tonic water. With a slice of lime."

"Maggie?" Halloran asked.

"That Cosmo looks good," she said, gesturing toward Betsey's drink.

"Back in a jiffy," Halloran said, but he planned to stay out on the terrace once he'd gotten the drinks. He whispered this to Hollis as they walked through the huge kitchen, breakfast room, and screened porch to the terrace.

"My God," said Hollis as he looked out at the view when they were outside. "You weren't kidding."

"Tom!" said Ryan Fitzgerald from the other side of the covered terrace, which featured another stone fireplace and a combination grill and gas stove. A teak bar, complete with barstools, was off to the right. Ryan, a ruddy-faced man with shaggy brown hair and bright blue eyes, was almost as tall as Halloran, but broader across the shoulders. He wore a navy linen shirt with the sleeves rolled up and white shorts. "I've got some 18-year-old Glenmorangie with your name on it."

"Then I guess I better drink some of it," Halloran said with more cheer than he felt. "This is Hollis Joplin, Ryan—a friend from Atlanta. And you already know Jack," he added, turning to Hollis.

Hands were shaken, and drink orders taken. Halloran grabbed Maggie's and Carrie's drinks and some cocktail napkins and carried them back to the great room, where Moira was holding court. Maggie was a wearing a fixed smile, but Carrie seemed genuinely amused by Moira's story about an encounter with a Trump supporter wearing a MAGA hat in the Clubhouse dining room.

"I mean, it's not the man's *politics* that bothered me—Ryan and I have made big contributions to Trump's campaign—but a baseball cap in the *dining room*?"

"For God's sake, Moira, it was Dan Kowalski," Betsey chimed in. "He's from New Jersey."

Maggie grimaced, took the Cosmo from him, and said, "Betsey, I know a lot of very nice people from New Jersey. I'm sure you do, too."

"Well, I wish he'd go back there," said Moira, ending the discussion. She smiled up at Halloran as he gave Carrie her tonic water. "You're the only Yankee I've ever liked, Tom, and that's the truth."

"Probably because I'm from the Midwest, Moira, but I'll take that as a compliment anyway," Halloran said, used to Moira's bias toward people she considered "outsiders." He gave Maggie a look he hoped she would interpret correctly, then said, "I've got to go grab a drink Ryan's fixing for me, but I'll be back."

"Bring Carrie's handsome husband back with you," drawled Betsey Cunningham.

"You bet," said Halloran.

✦ ✦ ✦ ✦

WHEN HALLORAN RETURNED to the terrace, Hollis, Jack Cunningham, and Ryan had moved to some oversized wicker chairs surrounding a square coffee table in front of the fireplace. Ryan motioned toward a drink on the table and said, "You need to catch up, Tom. We're almost ready for another."

"I'll do my best," he said, sitting down. He took a long sip of his drink, savoring the peaty burn of the single-malt Scotch. "I'm supposed to rejoin the ladies and bring Hollis with me, but I might enjoy the nice mountain air for a bit. I think Moira was about to rehash the Civil War. Or the 'War of Northern Aggression,' as she calls it. Luckily, I'm her favorite Yankee, but that might not last long."

"Tell me about it," Ryan said, shaking his head. "I moved to Georgia over forty years ago from Denver, but that doesn't mean a thing. The Callaghan family has owned property here for two hundred years. My children are Southerners, but I'm not, in her mind."

"Well, I *am* Southern, but I come from a long line of share-croppers," said Hollis. "Not sure what the hierarchy is among Yankees, Westerners, and rednecks, though."

"I've done a lot of thinking on the subject," said Jack, who appeared to be more than one drink ahead of him, "and it depends on whether you think *Gone with the Wind* is a national treasure or a disgrace to literature."

"What the hell are you talking about, Jack?" Ryan said.

"Think about it, Ryan." Jack paused and seemed to be suppressing a small belch. "Ever since that movie *Twelve Years a Slave* came out, the media has had a field day attacking the Confederate flag and movies like *Gone with the Wind*."

"So?"

"So, you and I both have wives who are card-carrying members of the Daughters of the Confederacy, ole buddy. S'cuse me: the *United* Daughters of the Confederacy. And you'd think they woulda gotten over all that by now, but I've noticed that Betsey brings up *Gone with the Wind* whenever we meet someone new. It's a reference point for a big ole group of South-erners."

Halloran laughed, thinking it was a joke, then realized Jack wasn't smiling.

"You think it's funny, don't you, Tom? And I don't blame you, but I'm not kidding. Some people just can't let the past go, especially since half of America thinks we're yahoos down here. Every time there's a tornado in the South, the TV crews show trailer parks and people who didn't get past the seventh grade with cigarettes hanging out of their mouths. And Betsey doesn't have many good memories as a freshman at Ohio State. They treated her like some hick, teasing her about her accent and all the beauty pageants she'd been in. She transferred to Old Dominion the next year."

Halloran thought of a former client, now dead, who'd been one of the loveliest, most authentic people he'd ever known. Also, a former beauty queen, who'd even looked a little like Betsy. He was about to mention Libba Woodridge when the women came out onto the terrace.

"We thought you and Hollis were coming back inside, Tom," Betsey said, a pout on her face. Her glass was now empty.

"My fault," said Hollis, standing up. "I've been enjoying the view," he added, his hand sweeping out toward the panorama behind the house. "Let me get you a refill. How about you, Moira? What are you drinking?"

Looking somewhat mollified, Betsey gave him her glass and an indulgent smile, saying, "Chivalry certainly isn't dead. Thank you."

Moira also handed hers to him and said, "Scotch rocks."

Ryan suddenly seemed to remember he was the host and jumped up to usher Maggie and Carrie to chairs and ask if they wanted refills. A few minutes later, they had re-grouped around the coffee table. All the lanterns on the deck slowly blazed to life, adding to the cozy atmosphere. Whatever tensions had possessed either foursome now dissipated as the air began to cool down and tempers were eased by alcohol. The conversation became pleasantly superficial, avoiding any mention of Trump, Yankees, or, thankfully, the body at the Falls.

Halloran surreptitiously glanced at his watch, wondering if they could make a getaway in the next twenty minutes. His hopes were dashed when the door from the screened porch burst open, and Maggie's cousin Tullie suddenly appeared. She was wearing white jeans and a denim shirt, her long, curly red hair tied back into a low ponytail by a blue bandana.

"Tullie?" said Hollis.

"I was hoping I'd find you here, Hollis," she said.

6

HALLORAN TURNED TO stare at Hollis, then back at Tullie. "You know each other?" he asked.

"Oh, *hell*, yes, Tom," she said in her usual brash manner. "Longer'n you have, I bet."

"What a wonderful surprise," Moira said, standing up and going over to her daughter. She gave her a quick hug, which Halloran noticed that Tullie barely reciprocated.

"I never connected you to *this* Fitzgerald family when Tom and Maggie invited us up here," said Hollis, still looking surprised.

Tullie strode over to the bar, poured herself a healthy slug of Jack Daniels, added a few ice cubes, and turned back to Hollis. "Why not? I'm not *refined* enough?"

"Tullie!" said her mother.

"N-no, of course not," Hollis stammered.

Halloran was fascinated. In the two years he'd known Hollis Joplin, he'd never seen the man at a loss for words. He hadn't had this much fun at an in-law gathering since Maggie's grandfather got roaring drunk at a family wedding and admitted father- ing a child with a Boston waitress when he was at Harvard.

"You found a body yesterday," said Tullie, eyes boring into Joplin. "Eric Jaeger. He was one of my parolees."

"*You're* the one who found the body?" Betsey said, frowning. "Why didn't you tell us last night?"

"Actually," said Maggie, always the peacemaker, "I'm the one who spotted the body when we reached the Falls. I told Hollis about it. And we really didn't want to talk about it at dinner, Betsey. I'm sure you understand."

Betsey didn't look like she understood at all, in Halloran's opinion.

"And that *shithead* of a coroner's deputy didn't think it was a suspicious death," Tullie said, blowing the who-didn't-say-any- thing-about-the-body issue out of the water.

"I don't allow language like that in my house," Moira said stiffly.

"We're *outside*, Mother," Tullie said, then took a hefty sip of her drink. "I'm using my outside voice, like you always taught us."

"Why don't we go *inside,* and I'll tell you what I observed," said Hollis, going over to her and nodding toward the door.

"Nooo!" wailed Betsey. "We want to know what's going on."

"Maggie and Carrie and I can tell you all about it," Hallo- ran said and caught a grateful look from Hollis before they left the group.

✦ ✦ ✦ ✦

"HOW DID YOU know I'd be at your parents' house?" was the first thing Joplin said when they reached the enormous den.

"I got a call from a buddy of mine with the Rutledge Sheriff's Office," Tullie said, plunking herself down on a vast, camel-back leather sofa. She rattled the ice around in her glass and brushed a wayward strand of hair off her forehead. "He'd heard about the body from one of the EMTs. And that a death investigator and an attorney from Atlanta had discovered it and weren't happy with how that asshole Bo Danforth had handled things. The EMT had written down your name and Tom's for some reason. When Will—my buddy—ran Jaeger's name through NCIC, he saw a parole violation warrant on him, found out I was supervising him, and called me. Knowing my mother, I figured y'all had been invited for drinks, but if not, she'd probably know where you and Tom were staying."

"Yeah," said Joplin, "it's like we were microchipped when we came through the North Gate."

Tullie gave a laughing snort. "Tell me about it, Hollis. I check my car for tracking devices every time I visit my parents. But why'd you have a problem with Bo's assessment of the death? Besides him just being an all-around incompetent jerk, I mean."

Joplin filled her in on his reasons for thinking the death might not have been accidental: the fact that Jaeger hadn't been dressed for hiking, but no car was found, the empty liquor bottle, and the probable time of death. Then he asked a question of his own. "Why'd you violate him?" he said, employing a term that most parolees and probationers used when their supervisors requested a violation warrant.

"He had a drug trafficking conviction and tested positive for cocaine at his last report. His judge wanted him brought back to court for any positive screens. Funny thing was, he was a meth dealer, so the cocaine surprised me. But he always insisted he never used meth because he needed to keep his mind clear to run the lab."

"Maybe, but you and I know dealers have to sample their product, and users end up dealing to support their habit, so I wouldn't have put much stock in that, Tullie. And maybe cocaine was easier to get, since most of the meth labs up here have been shut down in the past few years."

Tullie nodded, but didn't respond right away. Then she said, "I'm gonna talk to the judge in Milton County who sentenced Jaeger and try to get an order for an autopsy."

"Well, I agree with you that one should be done, but aren't there any family members who can request an autopsy?"

"Jaeger's father is in prison—for killing his mother when Jaeger was fifteen. He had no siblings, and the aunt who took him in died two years ago. Nothing will happen if I don't do something, because I'm sure Bo Danforth couldn't care less. The man's useless."

"Obviously, you know him."

She made a face. "I grew up in this county. As my mother would say, the Danforths are a 'prominent family,' and Bo and I went to the same private school. It was a Christian academy—you know the type, Hollis. That was sometimes a code back then for 'segregated.' My mother also didn't want Aidan and me to rub elbows with too many rural folks, and there weren't any Catholic schools in the area."

"I got the impression Harold Danforth has a good reputation," Joplin said. "Why would he make Bo his deputy? Is that even allowed?"

"It's not an elected position, like his, and no one objected," said Tullie, shrugging. "And family comes first around here.

In Austell, where you come from, too, right? Besides, from what I've heard, he'd been fired from two previous jobs, and Mayellen, his mama, wanted him to have some job stability. Go figure," she added, a disgusted look on her face. "Anyway, if I get the autopsy order and have the body sent to Milton, could you make sure it gets priority at the ME's Office?"

Joplin grinned. "I can do better than that. My wife can do the autopsy. She's a deputy ME in Milton."

"That pretty lady sitting next to you on the terrace?"

"Don't let her looks fool you, Tullie. She's on the cutting edge when it comes to autopsies."

Tullie heaved herself up from the sofa and headed for a nearby bar cart. Adding more Jack to her drink, she looked back at Joplin and said, "I'd forgotten how much you like stupid puns, Hollis. I pity your wife."

"She's laughing all the way to the bank, Tullie," Joplin said, grinning. "I grossed $60,000 last year."

✛ ✛ ✛ ✛

AFTER ONE MORE drink, they'd been able to make their escape from the Fitzgeralds and the Cunninghams, mainly because Tullie had replaced them on the discussion menu. Halloran had kept his word and detailed their discovery of the body at the Upper Falls. With Tullie's admission that Eric Jaeger was one of her parolees—something, Halloran was sure, that even Wolfscratch's resident oracle, Jane Southerland, didn't know—the two older couples were off and running, chasing new news as the Joplins and Hallorans eased out of the house.

Now, after a wonderful dinner back at the Blue Ridge Lane house, they were once again lounging around the pool, this time with tiki lamps and Italian lighting instead of a blazing overhead sun.

"That was the best time I've ever had at your aunt's house," Halloran said, the excellent St. Emilion at dinner, on top of the pre-dinner drinks, loosening his tongue.

"I was blown away by the house itself," Hollis said quickly. "And your aunt and uncle are incredible hosts, Maggie."

"Thank you, Hollis. But there's no need to cover for Tom. We're honest with each other about family members. He knows I can't stand his sister, Kathleen."

"Did you ever date Tullie?" Carrie asked, holding her glass of Perrier in both hands and twirling it slowly. A bad sign, in Halloran's opinion.

"Tullie? No, of course not!"

"Why 'of course not?'" Carrie said. "She's gorgeous. And it sounds like you two know each other very well."

"I met her right before I left the Homicide Unit," Hollis said. "She was just out of college, so she was like a kid sister to me. A real tomboy, too. And she can drink me under the table. No self-respecting Southern man could put up with that in a wife," he added, trotting out the killer grin.

Carrie gave a long sigh. "My next question would be how, exactly, do you know she can drink you under the table, Hollis, but I'll stop there."

"Anybody for Cards Against Humanity?" Halloran asked, playing defense. It wasn't like Carrie to be jealous or even suspicious of Hollis, but she was six months pregnant, which might be a game-changer.

Carrie stood up and smiled at Halloran and Maggie. "It's been a fun day, but I'm bushed, so I think I'll turn in. That doesn't mean the rest of you have to end the evening, though." She moved towards them, gave each a hug, then blew Hollis a kiss and walked into the house.

"Maybe I'd better turn in, too," Hollis said, still staring at the door where Carrie had gone back inside.

"Give her a little bit of time," Maggie said. "It *has* been a long day, and she might need a few minutes by herself."

Hollis nodded slowly, then turned to Maggie. "Listen, I wasn't putting Tullie down or anything. She's a great kid. I mean 'woman.' She's great. Really."

Maggie smiled at him and shook her head. "You don't need to say that. I knew what you meant. I adore Tullie and think she's one of the best people I know. She's one of a kind. Has been since she was a little thing. And the bane of her mother's existence, if you want to know."

"I noticed a little coolness on Tullie's part when they hugged."

"Well, she's entitled to that. Not my mother, but a lot of Irish-American mothers favor their sons. Aidan Fitzgerald hung the moon, as far as Moira is concerned. Tullie's had a lifetime of that, topped off by Moira's decision to turn Fox Run Stables over to him when she and Ryan retired."

"Did Ryan have a say in that?" Hollis asked.

"Not really. The money to start the business came from my grandfather, and Moira never let Ryan forget that, although Ryan's knowledge of horseflesh and his business acumen made it successful. He's made sure to take care of Tullie in other ways, though."

"Now tell me," Halloran said, "how you found out Tullie could drink you under the table."

Joplin gave a long sigh. "It's a long story. And it involves an escort service working out of a strip mall in Sandy Springs, one of her parolees, whom we suspected of killing a stripper, some counterfeit money, and a goat."

Halloran closed his eyes, took one last, long sip of his drink, and stood up. "That might be more than I can deal with tonight. I agree with Carrie. It *has* been a long day, and that's a story for another time."

7

ON MONDAY AT 11 a.m., Joplin, who had the day shift, got a phone call from Tullie Fitzgerald.

"I got the order from Judge Mabry," she said, not bothering to identify herself.

"And good morning to you, too, Tullie," he said. "How are you on this bright, sunshiny day? I'm fine, just in case you were wondering."

"Did you talk to your wife about doing the autopsy, Hollis?" was all she said.

"I did, and she's happy to do it. Dr. Minton's on board, too," Joplin added, referring to the Chief ME.

"I also took that liquor bottle to the CSU lab director and logged it in. And I wrote up a report of what I observed at the Falls."

If he'd expected any thanks, Joplin would have been disappointed. Luckily, he'd learned to accept Tullie's less-than-effusive attitude over the years.

"I faxed a copy of the order to my buddy at the Rutledge Sheriff's Office so they can notify the coroner's office to transport the body today," she said. "I'm afraid Bo will think of some cheap way to dispose of it once he finds out there's no family to claim it. Would you let me know when you get it?"

Joplin couldn't help but think of the Tri-State Crematory. He knew it had been demolished after Brent Marsh had gone to prison, but wondered whether another company had filled the void. Making a mental note to find out, he said, "Sure thing. Fax me a copy of the order, too, if you would."

"I owe you, Hollis," Tullie said, shocking the hell out of him.

"No, you don't. I've got my own concerns about the whole thing."

He could almost hear Tullie shrugging. "Have it your way, then. I'll fax the order." And without saying "goodbye," she clicked off.

Joplin stared at his phone for several seconds, then heaved himself up from his desk and went to update Carrie. Any problem she might have had about his knowing Tullie Fitzgerald had dissipated by Sunday morning. They had all enjoyed a sumptuous, calorie-laden buffet brunch at the Wolfscratch Clubhouse, followed by a three-mile walk, then packed up the car for the drive home. Carrie had seemed relaxed and content, talking about what a good time they'd had and suggesting they all return to Wolfscratch during leaf season.

Her office door was open, but she wasn't inside. Joplin recalibrated, took the stairs to the basement level, and headed for the autopsy room. Carrie was working on a male corpse at the third table, but looked up as he entered the room. Her face shield caught the glare from an overhead light, and he couldn't see her expression.

"Hi, sweetie," he said. "Tullie just called and is faxing the judge's order for the autopsy. We should get the body in a few hours. You think you could get to it this afternoon?"

"I think so. I've got one more autopsy after this one, and then I'm free. You up for Golden Buddha tonight?"

"I was thinking the same thing. I'll even order it."

✦ ✦ ✦ ✦

JUDGE MABRY'S ORDER had come through the Unit's fax machine when Joplin returned to his desk. It outlined the drug trafficking conviction in Milton County in 2010, the parole violation warrant issued on July 29, 2016 for a positive drug screen, and the reason for the requested autopsy. Judge Mabry had given "suspicious circumstances" for that, then listed the anomalies Joplin had observed. He was heading for Sarah Petersen's office when his cell phone rang.

"That bastard Bo sent Jaeger's body off to be cremated!" Tullie sputtered into his ear. "Will called me from the coroner's office after handing Harold Danforth the autopsy order."

"When was this?" Joplin asked.

"Just a few minutes ago."

"No, I mean, when was the body transported, Tullie?"

"First thing this morning! Will said Harold apologized, that he'd been busy with a group of family members planning a funeral when Bo ran it by him. Said he didn't know there was any problem with the scene or he would have intervened. Then he offered to call Judge Mabry and explain. As if that would fix everything!"

"What's the name of the place?"

"Peach State Cremation. It's in LaFayette."

Joplin looked at his watch. "It's only been a few hours, so I doubt they've processed the body, but have your buddy Will contact the crematory and make sure they don't. I'll head up there right now with a transport van."

"I owe you another," Tullie said tersely.

"Don't get mushy on me, Tullie," he said, then headed for Sarah Petersen's office.

✛ ✛ ✛ ✛

"VIV SHOULD BE back from a vehicular scene soon, so you're good to go," Sarah said once he'd explained the situation. "You want Daryl or Sam to drive you up there?"

Joplin shook his head. "I'll be fine. I can get someone at the crematory to help me load the body. I want to get up there as soon as possible. This whole thing just doesn't feel right. My gut's been giving me fits since we found this guy."

"Your gut is legendary, Hollis," his boss said, smiling her full-teeth Kennedy smile. "Who am it to doubt it?"

8

THE TOWN OF LaFayette—pronounced LuhFAYette by Georgians, which Joplin was sure must piss off both non-Georgians and compatriots of the Marquis De LaFayette, after whom it was named—was the county seat of Walker County. The trip there took almost two hours and was anything but scenic once he got off 575 North. It took him another fifteen minutes to find the Peach State Crematory, going down dusty, often gravelly, side roads that MapQuest recommended.

Joplin pulled into the parking lot of a large, homey-looking brick building with a wide front porch and circled the van to the back, where he assumed the bodies were unloaded. There were no windows on that side, only double doors in the middle of the building. He got out and pushed a button on an intercom system to the right of the doors.

"Can I help you?" a woman's voice asked.

"I'm Hollis Joplin with the Milton County ME's Office, here to pick up the body of Eric Jaeger."

There was a long pause, then a buzzer sounded, and one of the double doors popped open. Joplin entered a garage-like vestibule with a wide glass door that swung open as he approached it. A tall, middle-aged woman with a chin-length hairdo that looked sprayed into place greeted him with a tentative smile.

Joplin handed her a copy of Judge Mabry's order. "Did you get a call from a Rutledge County sheriff's deputy?" he asked.

"I believe we did," she said, drawling out the last word. "But you'll need to talk to my husband."

"Is he the owner?"

Her chin rose a little. "We both are. But he handles things like this." She gestured toward a door behind her. Joplin followed her through a room that held a desk, a chair, a PC, and another wide door off to the right that he suspected led to a "cold room" to store bodies. They moved down a narrow hall that ended in yet another door. The woman opened it and said, "Wade, the man from the Milton ME's Office is here." She handed him the order.

A large, beefy-looking man with slicked-back hair stood up from behind a cluttered desk and took the paper from her, then offered his other hand to Joplin with a smile much more assured than his wife's had been. "Wade Cantrell. And you're...?"

"Hollis Joplin. I'm a death investigator with the Milton County ME's Office. I'm here to pick up the body of Eric Jaeger, and I've got a two-hour drive back, so..."

"Of course, of course." Cantrell set the order down on his desk without looking at it. "Mind if I see some identification first?"

Joplin shook his head and pointed to the ID tag clipped to his navy "Milton County ME's Office" windbreaker.

"No, I mean a badge or something." Still with the wide smile.

Smiling back, Joplin pulled out the case holding his badge and opened it. "That do it for you?" he asked, more politely than he felt.

Cantrell shrugged. "Of course. You want to get your gurney from the van, or do you need help?"

"I'll be fine," Joplin said. He turned and left the building the way he'd come in, looking back at the double doors as he walked to the van and, this time, spotting the camera aimed at the parking lot. It made sense; the ME's Office had a similar camera to monitor body transports. But something about the crematory—and its owners—seemed off. They'd been notified that he was coming up to get Eric Jaeger's body; obviously, they'd also seen him park the clearly marked ME's van out back. Why the charade over his identification? Was it a delaying tactic?

Deciding he'd better get a move-on if so, Joplin quickly retrieved the gurney, leaving the van's back door open.

✦ ✦ ✦ ✦

TEN MINUTES LATER, Joplin was back in the van, Eric Jaeger's corpse in a black body bag strapped to the gurney. Jaeger was still dressed in the same clothes he'd been wearing when he was pulled from the Upper Falls in Wolfscratch. They were still damp and smelled like they'd been in the body bag since Friday. The body itself smelled much worse after three days of decomposition, even though Joplin assumed it had also been kept in cold storage at Danforth's mortuary. There had been no further delaying ploys from the Cantrells. In fact, they'd seemed almost anxious to have him gone when he'd returned with the gurney and checked to make sure the body was Eric Jaeger's. Wade Cantrell had even helped him load it into the van.

"Maybe my legendary gut isn't what it used to be," Joplin said aloud. Then again, why should it be? It had only been two years since he'd almost been eviscerated and forced to wear a colostomy bag before getting his colon resectioned. "What do you think, Eric?"

When there was no answer, he followed MapQuest's directions to return to 575 South. But while stopped at a red light on North Main Street, Joplin saw a sign with various nearby towns listed. One of them was for Noble, Georgia, just a few miles up Highway 27. Although he knew that the Tri-State Crematory had been torn down years ago, he felt an inexplicable need to see the site itself.

Eight minutes later, Joplin was on Old Delk Road, searching for anything telling him where the crematory had been. A memorial had been created at the Tennessee-Georgia Memorial Park Cemetery in Rossville, where the unidentified bodies had finally been buried, but he thought something would still be at the site.

Reluctantly, Joplin pulled into the next driveway he saw to turn the van around. An elderly woman sat on the front porch, fanning herself with a cardboard fan. He hadn't seen a fan like that since he was a small boy, going to his grandmother's church on hot, summer Sunday and Wednesday nights. On impulse, Joplin got out and walked up the short path to the house. The woman stared at him impassively.

"Sorry to bother you, ma'am," he said. "I'm wondering if you could tell me where the Tri-State Crematory used to be."

"You a reporter?" she asked, resting the fan on her lap. Her hands were gnarled by arthritis, but her blue eyes were bright with curiosity. "Used to be a lot of them coming up here, but that was a long time ago."

"No, ma'am, I'm a death investigator with the Milton County Medical Examiner's Office."

She gave a short, barking laugh and shook her head, which was crowned with wispy white hair. "Well, you're a little late, then. Ain't no bodies there anymore. They tore it all up."

"I know. I was just up this way and thought I'd look at the place where it used to be."

"Miss Clara signed the whole property over to the state after Ray Brent went to prison. She still lives in the area—Ray Brent, too, now that he's out of prison—but they pretty much keep to themselves. Don't blame 'em, I guess." The old woman gave a long sigh. "They were good people, did a lot for the community. All of 'em, even Ray Brent, till he lost his mind. He was the high school's star football player," she added, her eyes turning upward, as if she were lost in memory. Looking back at Joplin, she said, "They were one of only a few Black families who lived in this area for years and years, and we were happy to have 'em." She tilted her head, then said, "That surprise you?"

"Not really, ma'am. I'd heard that about the people here in Noble when the story came out. I also grew up in a small town. Austell, Georgia. It had its fair share of racists, but my grandmother wasn't one of them, and she raised me."

The woman nodded, then began fanning herself again. "She still alive?"

"No, ma'am. She passed about ten years ago."

"Guess you've seen a lot of death in your job. A lot of dead people."

"I have," said Joplin.

She put the fan down and looked up at him, searching his face. "Then, tell me something, young man."

"Of course. If I can, I mean," Joplin wasn't sure what she might ask him.

"Do they stay dead?"

9

"**WHAT DID SHE** mean by that?" Carrie asked as she adjusted her Plexiglass visor. She and Tim Meara, the ME's photographer, and Sam Johnson, the senior forensic tech, were grouped around Eric Jaeger's body on the far-end steel table in the autopsy room.

Joplin shrugged. "I really don't know. I mean, I asked her, but she just laughed and said she was an old woman with old eyes and couldn't trust her memory sometimes. My grandmother got like that a few years before she died. Told me she kept seeing relatives who'd died years before at church or the grocery store."

"Mine did, too," Sam said, nodding solemnly.

"Yeah, my mother thinks she sees my little brother in crowds to this day," Carrie said. "But he still looks five, so she knows it couldn't be him."

"Do you ever see him?" Joplin asked. Carrie didn't talk about her brother much. He'd died of Tay-Sachs disease and had been the reason she'd gone into medicine. But it was still difficult for her. They'd had genetic testing done before trying to conceive, even though Joplin wasn't Jewish and the disease required a recessive gene from each parent to occur. Carrie had also insisted on having the fetus tested at four months. Luckily, Tay-Sachs wasn't detected.

She gave him a small, wistful smile and said, "No, never."

"Is that because Jews don't believe in the afterlife?"

"Wow!" said Tim. "Maybe I should convert to Judaism. We Catholics have hell or purgatory to look forward to if we've been bad, and I haven't been to confession in ten years."

Carrie ignored that and said, "I refuse to go over this with you again, Hollis."

"I know, I know," Joplin said. "It's not that you don't believe there's life after death; you just don't *know*. So, you keep the memory of loved ones alive by naming children after them."

"Exactly."

"So, you gonna name your baby after someone who's passed?" Sam asked.

"Yes!" Joplin and Carrie said simultaneously.

"That's real nice," said Sam. "Can I ask who?"

"No!" they said.

The subject of their baby's name was not an easy one for either of them. Joplin had wanted to give Carrie the first choice, but her brother's name had been David Seth Salinger, and neither name lent itself to being feminized. Carrie had then suggested they use his grandmother's name for their baby girl and wait to use "David" or "Seth" for a boy. Made sense, in Joplin's opinion, since she'd raised him, but her name had been "Addie Belle," which had surprised Carrie, and not in a good way.

Since Joplin's mother was probably still alive—he hadn't seen her since he was nine, when she'd left him with his paternal grandmother to run off with a golf pro after his father died of alcoholism—her name wasn't in the running. It was just as well, he'd told Carrie, because her name was "LaWanda Lucille." So, even if she turned up dead and they took off the "La," Joplin was sure no Buckhead girl worth her salt would want to be saddled with "Wanda."

They'd tossed the name "Addie" around but hadn't made any decision so far. Joplin was in favor of scoping out more dead family members on each side. Carrie had simply glared at him when he'd suggested that, at which point, he'd decided he would never really understand women, no matter how long he lived.

So, no, they didn't want to talk about the baby's name, thank you very much.

Sam raised both hands, palms up, and said, "No problem."

Joplin cleared his throat and said, "Well, I've got some paperwork to do, so I'll let y'all get on with it."

Carrie nodded and turned back to Jaeger's body. "Let's get some photos, Tim."

"Sure thing," he said.

✛ ✛ ✛ ✛

JOPLIN HAD FINISHED his report on transporting Eric Jaeger's remains and was pondering whether to make a covert call to his Aunt Aline for other dead relatives' names when his office phone rang.

"You got a visitor, Hollis," said Sherika, her voice low. "Someone named Tullie Fitzgerald. I can tell her you're busy."

"But I'm not busy," he told her.

"Well, maybe you *should* be, Hollis. I don't think Carrie would want her to visit you."

Joplin sighed. Sherika was the receptionist, but she actually ran the place, even though there was an official office manager. Nothing escaped her notice; she knew what was going on inside the ME's Office at all times, both personally and professionally. It was frightening, but oddly reassuring; besides being one of the most competent people Joplin knew, Sherika was fiercely protective of them all.

"She's not my girlfriend, Sherika," he said. "She's a community supervision officer, and Carrie's met her. In fact, Carrie's doing the post on one of Tullie's parolees right now, so I suspect that's why she's here."

"If you say so, Hollis," she said, making it clear she didn't believe him. "I'll send her on back to the IU."

Joplin put the phone back in its cradle and rubbed his forehead. It was only 3:30 in the afternoon, but it felt like he'd pulled a double shift. The weekend at Wolfscratch had ended up being pleasant, yet he felt like he'd been on a busman's holiday, never really relaxing. But when the door to the Investigative Unit opened, Joplin jumped up and put a smile on his face.

"Tullie!" he said heartily, hoping she hadn't overheard Sherika's whispered comments to him. "I bet you came to get a heads-up on Jaeger's autopsy."

His hopes were dashed when she said, "No, I came to ask you to leave your beautiful, pregnant wife and run away with me to Las Vegas."

The sigh was even longer this time. "I take it you overheard Sherika talking to me," Joplin said.

"Then you take it right," Tullie said. "Next time, I won't wear my hussy clothes and carry my man-catcher purse."

Joplin smiled and shook his head, noting the very professional-looking black jacket, gray slacks, and white shirt Tullie was wearing; even her hair was pulled back into a low, subdued ponytail. But there was no taming of its vivid color or her full lips and khaki-colored eyes.

"I'm sorry," he said. "Sherika is sort of a den mother around here."

"Oh, don't apologize! We could use someone like her at our office. Especially when parolees make their first report after being released. But to answer your question, I was hoping I could *attend* the autopsy. Don't worry. I won't faint or throw up or anything. I've seen one before."

Joplin looked at his watch. "Well, she started it about an hour ago, but we can go downstairs and check with her. See how far along she is," he added, hoping Carrie wouldn't see that as an intrusion.

Fortunately—for him, if not for Tullie—Carrie was pulling Jaeger's face back up to the middle of his skull as they entered the autopsy room. Although his rib cage was still splayed apart and the organs excised, this meant the procedure was almost finished.

Carrie looked up and smiled at them through her visor. She usually didn't like people interrupting her during an autopsy, and Joplin wasn't sure if she'd be thrilled to see Tullie under any circumstances. But smiling was good, he decided.

As if she'd read his mind, Carrie said, "Nice to see you again, Tullie. Although probably not under these circumstances."

Tullie stared down at Jaeger's body. "I guess I should have called first before barging in here," she said, then looked at Carrie. "What happened to his face?"

"I think he got scraped by some tree branches, and bottle flies had gotten to him," Joplin said. "The eye sockets, nose, and mouth were filled with maggots."

"I cleaned them all out after I examined him, but there was some tissue damage," Carrie said. "Unfortunately, being in a body bag and even a cooler at the crematory didn't stop them from feeding. Which means the entomologist might not be able to help much with time of death. But would you like to hear what I've found out so far about Mr. Jaeger's death?"

Tullie took a deep breath and then seemed to collect herself. "Yes, if you don't mind," she said.

"Not at all. I'm glad you came by, because I have something interesting to show you." Carrie turned to Sam and said, "Can you help me turn him over on his side?"

"Sure thing."

"You'd be able to see this better in the photos Tim took, but it will give you a pretty good idea of why I'm declaring his death a homicide." Carrie pointed to two faint bruises just under the scapular bones. They were about three inches wide and five inches high. "These were made by someone's hands. Mr. Jaeger didn't fall off the cliff into the water; he was pushed. He was struck hard enough to leave bruises, but didn't live long enough afterward for them to be fully formed. I've taken measurements, but they could belong to either a man or a woman. He was also struck on the side of his head, just behind his right ear."

Tullie nodded slowly, then said, "Well, your findings certainly justify the autopsy order. It might also be interesting to learn when he got that tattoo on his right shoulder. His file contains a description of any distinguishing marks on his body, including tattoos, and there weren't any listed."

Joplin moved closer to get a better look. "Is that what I think it is?"

"If you think it's a crude rendition of the Southern Cross medal, yes," said Tullie.

"I thought it was some kind of Nazi symbol," Carrie said. "It gave me the creeps." She nodded at Sam, and they returned the body to its original position.

"Well, it *is* a symbol of white supremacy," said Joplin. "And it does resemble the German Iron Cross, which Hitler updated in 1939, that included a swastika in the center of it. But the Southern Cross was a medal of honor dreamed up several decades after the Civil War by the United Daughters of the Confederacy to honor their veterans. In 1899, to be exact."

Carrie cocked her head to one side. "How do you know all this, Hollis?"

"From going with my grandmother to put flowers on various relatives' graves once a month when I was growing up. Most graveyards in the South have Civil War veterans buried in them. Especially in small towns and rural areas like Austell, where I grew up. Replicas of the medal are often on their tombstones, and free-standing stone replicas are scattered around. Of course, all of them were added later, long after the war was over. When I was older and saw documentaries about World War II, I was struck by the similarity to the German Iron Cross myself, so I did some research."

"I had a similar experience growing up in North Georgia," Tullie said. "Seeing the Cross on tombstones. But I also had a more.....personal knowledge of it."

Images from their evening at the Fitzgeralds' house flashed in Joplin's mind. "You mean because your mother is a member of the United Daughters of the Confederacy?" he asked.

"Card-carrying," she said. "One of her most prized possessions is the medal awarded posthumously to my great-great-grandfather, Colonel Daniel Byrne Callaghan, who fought at Antietam."

They all took several seconds to process this revelation. Carrie was the first to break the silence. "So, why do you think your parolee had this tattoo on his back, Tullie?"

Tullie shook her head. "I have no idea. But, whatever the reason, it can't be a good one. And it may have involved him in something that got him killed."

10

A **VISIT FROM DAVID** Healey, managing partner of Healey and Caldwell, was at best annoying and sometimes verged on maddening. Today was no different. Halloran looked up from his desk as Healey burst into his office. Joan followed closely behind him, her lips pursed.

"Why didn't you bother to inform either Alston or me that you were involved in a murder up at Wolfscratch over the weekend?" Healey spat at him.

"I'm sorry, Mr. Halloran," Joan said quickly. "I didn't have a chance to buzz you."

"No problem, Joan," Halloran said mildly. To Healey, he said, "Why don't you have a seat, David? I always confess to murder more easily when someone isn't looming over me." He had the satisfaction of hearing Joan chuckle as she pulled the door behind her, knowing that would bother David Healey even more.

"This isn't a joke," he responded angrily. "I just got off the phone with a reporter from the *AJC*, who wanted me to comment on a body found at Wolfscratch. By *you* and that Hollis Joplin. The reporter also asked if the dead person had been a guest at the house owned by this firm!"

Halloran was tempted to agitate Healey even more by asking if he'd forgotten to take his meds that day, but decided against it. "The reporter was just trying to get under your skin, David," he said instead. "Obviously, it worked."

Healey glared at him. "Are you going to tell me what happened, or do I need to involve Alston? This could be extremely bad publicity for the firm."

"If you feel the need for Alston to reinforce your authority, by all means, call him," Halloran said, referring to the firm's senior name partner. "But I doubt that discovering a dead body and doing my civic duty by contacting the local EMTs will result in any bad publicity. And I can assure you that there was no connection to the firm's house at Wolfscratch. We found the body at the Upper Falls, at least five miles away from it."

"Was it anybody you knew or who might have any connection to this firm?" Healey asked, only slightly mollified.

"I doubt it, unless it was on a *pro bono* basis. The man's name was Eric Jaeger, and he'd recently been paroled from prison for a drug trafficking conviction." Too late, Halloran realized that he'd given Healey a chance to bring up the Will Henry case.

"Well, *you* handled a *pro bono* criminal case for this firm a few years ago, in case you've forgotten."

"And maybe you've forgotten that Cate Caldwell and I helped overturn that conviction and got quite a bit of *favorable* publicity for the firm. National publicity, in fact, because of Will Henry's celebrity status."

David Healey stood up. His face broke into a condescending smile, and he said, "You also almost got your wife killed in the process, in case *you've* forgotten." And having delivered that salvo, he marched out of the office.

Fortunately, Halloran only had a few seconds to let that sink in before his cell phone rang.

"You have a few minutes?" Hollis Joplin asked him.

"Of course, but first, you should know that David Healey just left my office in a snit because the *AJC* called about the body we found at Wolfscratch. Word's gotten around."

"Well, I guess that was to be expected, Tom."

"Maybe. But the reporter also knew that Healey and Caldwell own a house there. I may need to discuss how that information was released to the press with someone at the Property Owners' Association in Wolfscratch."

"Do what you think is best, Tom, but that piece of information could have come from any number of people living in Wolfscratch. Your firm has a large profile there, what with your clients being entertained on the golf courses and at the Clubhouse. And Maggie's aunt and uncle live there. Which brings me to the reason I called you."

Halloran listened intently as Hollis told him about Tullie's judge signing an order for the Milton County ME's Office to perform an autopsy on Jaeger. He wasn't surprised about Carrie's determination that his death had been a homicide. However, hearing about the tattoo on Jaeger's back was unsettling, especially when Hollis brought up the discussion about *Gone with the Wind* and the United Daughters of the Confederacy on the Fitzgerald's deck on Saturday night.

"Are you implying that there might be some connection between Eric Jaeger's murder and Maggie's aunt and uncle?" he asked.

"Not really," Hollis said.

"*Not really*? What does that mean?"

"That it could just be a coincidence that Maggie's aunt is a member of the United Daughters of the Confederacy and her cousin's parolee was found dead at Wolfscratch. Or that said parolee has a tattoo of a medal designed by the UDOC. According to Tullie, one of Moira Fitzgerald's prized possessions is a Southern Cross medal given to her family for her great-great-grandfather's service in the Civil War."

Halloran sighed. "I get the point, but that's stretching it a bit. What did Tullie have to say about that?"

"Not much, but I could tell it bothered her. Especially in light of the homicide ruling. I didn't want to press her on it."

"And here I was concerned about the *AJC* finding out that my firm owns a house up there." Holloran gave another long sigh. "Maybe Maggie can shed some light on this. Or Colleen, for that matter. Although I still can't see how in the world Moira Fitzgerald and Eric Jaeger would have any connection. Besides that medal, I mean."

"Neither can I, Tom, but with the *AJC* on the story, it might be a good idea to check it out. You know I'm sort of a news junkie, and this story—a body found at an affluent mountain resort by a member of a prominent Atlanta law firm—is something the media will jump on. Not to mention that you and I have been in the public eye several times in the past few years. Maggie, too, for that matter."

"Not you, too!" Halloran said. "David Healey brought up Maggie's brush with death when he was complaining about the call from the paper."

"It hasn't even been two years, Tom. And that story was front and center in the *AJC* for days. Especially since it was a distraction from the bigger story that one of their editors was a stone-cold killer. It won't take much for any good investigative reporter to discover that your in-laws are residents of Wolfscratch. Just talk to Maggie about it."

✦ ✦ ✦ ✦

"BUT I WAS the one who dragged *you* into helping with Will Henry's appeal, Tom," Maggie said heatedly after Halloran had recapped his visit from Healey and the phone call from Hollis Joplin. "I can't believe David said that to your face!"

They were having drinks on the back terrace of their house in Ansley Park. The weather had cooled slightly, and Maggie had let Tommy and Megan watch *Ren and Stimpy* since they'd finished their homework. Also, of course, so that the adults could talk in peace.

"Well, I did insinuate once that he might have killed Elliot and Ann Carter. I don't think he's forgotten that."

"You had every right to think that. At the time, anyway. But I also can't understand why Hollis said Moira and Ryan might be mixed up in Eric Jaeger's murder."

"He didn't actually say that," said Halloran. "He just thinks we should get ahead of the press on it."

"But how would the press ever find out that Jaeger had a Southern Cross tattoo on his body? Or that my aunt is a member of the United Daughters of the Confederacy?"

"Good point. I didn't think to ask him that. Now I will."

Maggie sipped her wine, then said, "Well, I will admit that that damned medal *is* one of Moira's prized possessions. The whole Civil War connection always embarrassed my mother, but Moira, like my grandmother, revered that part of our family's history."

Halloran recounted the conversation between the men on the Fitzgeralds' deck, then asked, "Do you agree with the *Gone with the Wind* litmus test that Jack Cunningham talked about?"

"No, I don't. Just because a lot of people in the South, especially Atlantans, like the book doesn't make them racists, for God's sake. I mean, the book won the 1937 Pulitzer Prize! To this day, it's second only to the Bible in terms of popularity."

"I bet that's a hard choice for most Southerners," Halloran said dryly. "This is still the Bible Belt."

Maggie sighed, then set her glass down on the wicker coffee table. "You didn't grow up in Atlanta like I did, Tom. Margaret Mitchell was *huge*! The movie played at the Fox Theater every ten years—I saw it when I was fourteen. And the news shows always ran clips about the worldwide search for the perfect actress to play Scarlett and all the glamour surrounding the 1939 premiere at the Loew's Grand Theater with Vivian Leigh and Clark Gable. Mitchell was Atlanta's claim to fame at the time. There was all this hype about an unknown writer whose book took the nation by storm. Add to that Margaret Mitchell's reclusiveness, the long wait for her second novel, which never happened, and her tragic death by a drunk driver on Peachtree Street, and she became legendary."

"But did you ever read the book?"

"Of course I did," Maggie said, looking offended. "All 1,000-some pages of it. It was like reading a historical romance novel, and I loved it. But later, in college, I took a Southern Lit course and discovered all that 'history' about plantation owners and their families being like chivalric lords and ladies was a crock. My professor—who was Southern, by the way—told us there was a concerted effort by writers during and after Reconstruction to re-write history, casting Northerners and 'vengeful slaves' as the perpetrators of the Civil War. They all supported what they called the 'Lost Cause.'"

"How did they gloss over the Confederate attack on Fort Sumter, which started the war?" Halloran asked. "Or that seven Southern states seceded from the Union before that even happened?"

Maggie shrugged. "I guess they thought the best defense was a good offense. Believers in the Lost Cause insisted that it was a matter of 'States' Rights' and that members of the Confederacy were simply trying to preserve their way of life. The South was still mostly agrarian then, despite the Industrial Revolution. It was centered around plantations and cultivating crops like cotton and tobacco. Unfortunately, that way of life couldn't exist without cheap slave labor. And enslaved people who gave birth to *more* enslaved people. They were the primary commodity, so to speak."

"But Margaret Mitchell's book wasn't published until 1936. A lot had changed by then."

"Yes, and she's considered part of the Southern Renaissance movement. It was much more critical of the Civil War in describing the character of the South and Southerners. Critics then saw her creation of Scarlett as an embodiment of the South, clinging to the past and driven to rebuild it. They thought it was brilliant. But my professor thought Mitchell wasn't on the same level as other writers in that group, like Faulkner and Thomas Wolfe."

Halloran grinned and said, "Well, one of *my* favorite Southern writers sure loved her: Pat Conroy. He wrote a preface to a new reprint of the book in 1996 that I saw on the internet, where he talked about his mother reading the entire book to him and his siblings when they were growing up. Conroy said he saw it through her eyes, even though his own books deplored the racism he saw all around him. A few years later, *The New York Times* wrote an article about the ongoing negotiations between Conroy and the trustees who controlled the rights to the book. They wanted him to write the sequel to *Gone with the Wind*."

"I didn't know that."

Halloran nodded, sipping his drink. "Probably because the negotiations fell through. The Mitchell estate trustees had heard a rumor that Conroy was going to kill off Scarlett and write the sequel from Rhett's perspective. So, they laid down rules forbidding that and any homosexuality or miscegenation in the sequel, since Conroy hinted that things like that would be in his version. He saw that as censorship and an insult to his artistic sensibilities. Told them that if they didn't back off, the first sentence of the book would be, "After they made love, Rhett turned to Ashley Wilkes and said, 'Ashley, have I ever told you that my grandmother was black?'"

Maggie started laughing and almost choked on her wine. "I love that!" she said. "Good for him! Although I would have loved to read the sequel he planned."

"Think I should tell Moira that story?"

"Only if you have a death wish," Maggie said. "She'd be mad enough to drown puppies and have a hissy fit, as we say in the South."

Halloran smiled and said, "Bless her heart."

JOPLIN HAD THE evening shift on Tuesday, so by 7:30 that morning, he was out in the driveway, warming up for his run. He'd fed the cats after Carrie left for work and was going through his stretching routine. It was already hot, but not as humid as it would be in just a few hours.

Joplin had taken up jogging since they'd left the condo and its convenient gym. He'd decided against returning to the YMCA at Peachtree Presbyterian he'd used before he and Carrie moved into the condo. It had felt like a step backward, and Joplin wondered if he were becoming too used to a life he couldn't afford before marrying her. Although Carrie's salary as a deputy medical examiner was a pittance compared to what she could earn in the private sector, it still eclipsed his. She also had access to a trust fund her grandfather had left her.

It still bothered Joplin. He insisted on paying whatever he could, including part of the mortgage, although that didn't make him feel better. But he also didn't want to keep Carrie from enjoying things she could afford just to salve his male ego. So, he'd agreed to buy the house on Winslow Drive because she loved it and wanted to raise their child there.

If there's no solution, there's no problem, right? he thought.

Right.

Joplin finished his last set of stretches and set off down Winslow Drive, heading to Frankie Allen Park. He turned right onto Peachtree Way, picking up a little speed before turning left onto Acorn Ave. After crossing West Wesley, he passed by the Garden Hills community pool, smiling at the thought that next summer, they could bring their baby girl there on their days off.

Hopefully, the poor thing would have a name by then.

Deciding not to go down that rabbit hole, Joplin turned onto Brentwood Terrace, then jogged the few hundred feet into the park. A faint breeze ruffled the trees near the stone entrance, and as he headed to Bagley Ave, Joplin tried to focus on the plants and grass and other people walking and jogging. Not on what had been there almost a hundred years ago.

Before buying the house, Joplin, an architectural buff, had researched the neighborhood, looking for insight into its character. He'd found more than he wished, none of it uplifting. And his eidetic memory cursed him with the ability to recall all of it, in detail, every time he took this particular jogging route.

Frankie Allen Park had once been called Bagley Park. Before that, it had been Macedonia Park, where four hundred African-American families, many of them sharecroppers and maids, had lived since the late 1900s. Developer John Ownes created a subdivision for them in 1921. Four years later, Atlanta lawyer Phillips Campbell McDuffie surrounded it with Garden Hills, a white subdivision, developing the area between Peachtree and Piedmont Roads, with Pharr Road as its northern border and

Lindbergh Road as its southern border. And everyone lived there together in peace and harmony.

Until, of course, they didn't.

In the 1940s, Joplin had discovered, an academic report for the Cultural Landscape Foundation noted that the white residents of Garden Hills began to resent that the Black residents of Macedonia Park lived so close to them, even though they'd occupied the land long before Phillips McDuffie came along. Coincidentally, Fulton County was expanding its parks and recreation program. So, the Garden Hillers had petitioned the Fulton County Commission to "condemn and remove" Macedonia Park because, due to its lack of "sewerage," it was a "health menace" to the neighborhood, especially the students at North Fulton Grammar School. But the Garden Hillers also insisted that "...for the wellbeing of the negroes themselves, they should be moved to some section where they could have proper sanitation."

Joplin had learned that the Commission then began buying up whatever properties they could in Macedonia Park, which took eight years and grossly underpaid the owners, if they paid them at all. They simply condemned the other properties and then razed them to the ground. So, Fulton County gained a new park, the second largest in the county, which they graciously named after one of the former Black residents of Macedonia Park, William Bagley. But the boys were all white when a baseball league for local youths was established there. In 1980, even that connection to Macedonia Park was destroyed when the park was renamed Frankie Allen Park for a popular (white) Buckhead Baseball umpire.

However, the residents of Garden Hills were left with one reminder of the little African-American community they'd

helped to destroy: the graveyard of the Mt. Olive Method-
ist Church. The Garden Hills Women's Club had bought the
church in the 1950s, but in 2009, the county sold the graveyard
for unpaid taxes, even though the law specifically exempted
churches from property taxes. Fortunately, when a developer
petitioned the county to remove the graves, a lawyer with the
Buckhead Heritage Society filed a lawsuit on behalf of a Bagley
descendant whose parents had been forced to move. The developer's petition was denied.

Score one for the downtrodden masses, Joplin thought as he
jogged onto Bagley Ave.

He'd never shared what he'd learned with Carrie. The
housing market had roared back in the past two years, leaving
very few neighborhoods in the city that even her trust fund
could afford. Even so, they'd had to pay well above the asking
price and write—at their agent's suggestion—a letter to the
owners detailing why they wanted to live there, which included
Carrie's pregnancy. So, he'd remained silent, but he still felt
guilty.

Joplin ran past stately trees and jogging paths, the baseball
field with its empty stands, and the inviting creek flowing past
park benches. Yet all the while, he was picturing the tiny houses
of Macedonia Park, its two grocery stores and two restaurants, and its little church. By the time he reached the graveyard, his mind's eye saw further back into the past to the North
Georgia mountains and the Cherokee villages that had also
been destroyed. In Garden Hills, there were still graves to prove
that formerly enslaved people and their descendants had lived
in this area. In and around Wolfscratch, however, only signs
marked the Trail of Tears to show that the Cherokee had once
owned the land taken from them.

Joplin's eyes moved around the ground where the remaining headstones and unmarked slabs were scattered. In 2015, he'd learned, the Buckhead Heritage Society had cleaned up and repositioned the ones not destroyed by vandals over the years. He wondered if they'd also recently planted the begonias beside each one. He hadn't seen them a week ago.

Another slight breeze moved through the trees surrounding the graveyard, and Joplin felt chilled despite the rising August heat. He wondered why he kept punishing himself by coming so often to this graveyard, but knew the answer already. His gut also told him that he hadn't seen the last of Wolfscratch either, and the next time he did, it probably wouldn't be for a relaxing weekend.

12

AROUND 11 A.M., Halloran had a break between clients and decided to research the United Daughters of the Confederacy. Maggie had promised to talk to her mother about Moira's membership in the group, but his curiosity was piqued. What he found both fascinated and alarmed him.

What intrigued Halloran was that the two women who founded it in 1894, Caroline Meriwether Goodlet and Lucian H. Rains, were able to accomplish so much in the twenty-four years before women even got the right to vote. What alarmed him was *what* they accomplished and how their efforts rewrote the history of the Civil War, at least in the South.

Established initially to care for Confederate veterans and their families, Halloran read, the UDOC soon extended its scope to adorning cemeteries and church graveyards where veterans were buried, with Confederate markers and memorials. Among these were images of the Southern Cross of Honor Hollis had talked about, carved on tombstones and stone and iron replicas among the graves. The Daughters then focused on raising money to build monuments to the Confederacy and lobbied local governments to place them in prominent parks and near state capitol buildings.

But perhaps the UDOC's most alarming achievement was perpetuating the Lost Cause myth through Southern schools. The group had thousands of members in each state of the former Confederacy and even outside it, with enough power to ensure that only school textbooks that presented their view of the Civil War would be acceptable. They also created a youth group called the Children of the Confederacy, which met regularly and included all the tenets of the Lost Cause in their indoctrination.

Halloran had to stop reading for a few minutes as remembered photos of Hitler's Youth League paraded through his mind, showing young boys saluting the Nazi flag in their brown-shirted uniforms. He closed his eyes, trying to dispel them. When that failed, he returned to the article he'd been reading.

It didn't get any better, unfortunately. Halloran learned the UDOC also made a huge effort to publish the memoirs of strong, yet "genteel" women who claimed to have observed first-hand the horrific aggression of the North, the heroism of their men, and the fidelity of enslaved people to the South and its way of life. They all recounted Union atrocities and insisted that "their" slaves were happy and well cared for, and only Northern slave owners mistreated enslaved people.

Luckily, when Halloran started reading about the UDOC's support of the Ku Klux Klan—they sponsored its first parade in Atlanta in 1915—his cell phone rang. The screen showed that it was Maggie.

"Thanks," he said. "I needed a break from reading about the United Daughters of the Confederacy. Please tell me you found out your aunt decided to cancel her membership and join the ACLU."

"I wish. My mother said Moira's even been trying to get her to attend meetings with her. She told her something to the effect that 'things are beginning to heat up lately,' and the group needs everyone's help."

"What did she mean by that?"

"Well, Mom said she was excited over the UDOC's recent success in a lawsuit they brought against Vanderbilt University when it changed the name of a dorm, Confederate Memorial Hall. The Daughters had funded the building in 1935 and claimed breach of contract. They were awarded $1.2 million, today's equivalent of the original $50,000 donated."

"Not bad," said Halloran.

"Yes, but Moira agrees with the Daughters that trying to change the hall's name is only the beginning of a push to undo everything they've managed to achieve since the War of Northern Aggression, as they call it. Particularly since the Black Lives Matter movement has gained momentum."

"You mean like a push to take down all the Confederate memorials they helped fund and get erected? Did you know there are over 450 of them, with 170 of them in Georgia?"

Maggie sighed and said, "No, but I can believe it."

"Then there's the fact that Donald Trump expressed a lot of negativity toward the BLM movement during his campaign this past year. And the other night, Moira mentioned she and Ryan had donated a lot to his campaign, which surprised me."

"Why? All the polls say he's attracted a lot of educated suburban women like Moira. They had a significant presence at the RNC convention last month."

"Don't remind me."

Halloran considered himself a moderate Republican, the cliched "socially liberal, fiscally conservative" type. He'd voted for George W. Bush twice and John McCain in the 2008 election, despite Sarah Palin's being on the ticket. He considered McCain a true statesman and was sick to his stomach when Trump labeled him a "loser" because he'd been a POW during the Vietnam War. Like many of his friends and the GOP "old guard," Halloran had been appalled by the negative, name-calling, hit-below-the-belt campaign that Trump had run. The candidate had even directed a thinly veiled threat on his rival's life at a rally in Wilmington, NC, suggesting that "Second Amendment people" take action against Hillary Clinton or they would lose their right to bear arms. Several social media responses supported this, one person even threatening to "John Wilkes Booth her ass."

Halloran had never expected Trump to win the nomination. But win it he did, even though both Bushes, John McCain, and John Kasich had declined to attend the convention or endorse Trump. A wise decision, given the "Celebrity Apprentice" atmosphere, Melania's plagiarized speech, and all the Confederate flags waved around. Ted Cruz, whose wife had been maligned by Trump, had even urged the delegates to "vote your conscience" instead of following the party's rules to give the front-runner their votes.

Soon, Halloran would have to face another dilemma: He couldn't—wouldn't—vote for Donald Trump in November, but neither could he vote for Hillary Clinton. Her shenanigans at the Rose Law Firm, uncovered during the Whitewater investigation, and her heavy-handed management of the White House travel department during her husband's presidency, repelled him. Even Maggie, who was a staunch Democrat, had doubts about Clinton.

"Have you thought any more about becoming a Libertarian?" he asked her now.

"It would just split the vote," she said. "And Hillary's the lesser of two evils, in my opinion. Besides, Trump doesn't have the proverbial snowball's chance in hell of winning, Tom."

"I hope you're right, Maggie."

"Trust me," she said.

13

O **N THURSDAY MORNING,** August 25th, Tullie stood at the office door of her boss, the chief of Milton County Community Supervision.

Vince Randall looked up from a thick stack of paperwork. His short, cropped hair, dark eyes, and skin contrasted with the crisp, white Oxford shirt he was wearing. As a concession to the heat, his navy blazer hung from the back of his chair and his sleeves were rolled up. Randall had more than a passing resemblance to Barack Obama. He'd been promoted to chief four years ago, prompting some P.O. IIIs who'd been around longer to bring up the race card. The ones who knew him well didn't subscribe to this; the others, for the most part, got past it after he'd had the job just a few months. Randall had been a tough, highly competent officer; he was an even better chief, raising standards, but supporting all his people, whatever their color.

Out of earshot, many of the officers called him "Prez." If Randall knew that, he never let on. But at the first office Christmas party, six months after his promotion, he'd worn a suit and tie that was pure Obama: tailored black suit with a white shirt and a striped, gray tie. He was also carrying a cell phone loudly playing "Hail to the Chief." After that, the officers still didn't call him "Prez" to his face, but everybody relaxed, and there were no more complaints about his promotion.

"What's going on, Tullie?"

"You got a minute?"

"Always. Take a seat."

Tullie sat in one of the chairs in front of Randall's desk. She crossed one leg over another, then picked at a piece of lint on her own navy blazer. She stared out the large window that looked down on Alpharetta's square for several seconds. There wasn't much else to look at in Randall's office besides his framed diplomas, two ficus trees, and a large map of Milton County. He'd gotten divorced a few years before he made chief, but even before that, Randall had never kept photos of his family around. He advised new officers to do the same, given the violent nature of the crimes that many of their parolees and probationers had committed.

"It's Eric Jaeger," she said. "I got a call from a friend with the Rutledge County Sheriff's Office, Will Sykes. He said no detective's been assigned to the case, and no one's talking about it. Like word's been passed down that it's off the grid."

Randall sat back and clasped his hands over his belt buckle. "What do you think that means?"

Tullie shrugged. "It could mean anything, but Will thinks they don't plan to investigate Jaeger's murder. He thinks the coroner's behind this, probably because I pushed for an autopsy here in Milton County."

"Does the coroner have that much clout in Rutledge?"

"Evidently."

Randall sat up, put his forearms back on his desk, and didn't respond immediately. Then he said, "I don't mind making a few phone calls to some people who might get things back on track up there. But besides the fact that proper procedures aren't being followed—which is enough by itself—tell me why this case is so important to you, Tullie."

Tullie took a deep breath and let it out slowly, thinking carefully about what to say. "I've been asking myself that same question, and I'm not sure I know the answer. I guess it comes down to the fact that somebody should care about his death. His murder. Eric Jaeger was no innocent. He'd had run-ins with the law since he was a teenager, and he spent seven years in prison for dealing drugs. But I was surprised when he got the positive drug screen, then failed to report. He had a good job, so I really thought he was beginning to turn things around. And you know I'm no bleeding heart."

Randall nodded solemnly. "Gospel truth," he said.

"So, I need to know what happened. Eric had been clean since he got out seven months ago. He told me the time in prison convinced him he never wanted to go back. He was also upset when his aunt, who had taken him in as a teenager, died and he couldn't go to her funeral. As I said, I thought he wanted to change his life."

"Want and *do* are two different things, Tullie."

Tullie bit her lip, then her chin came up. "I know that, Chief. And I keep my expectations low. But this guy seemed intent on taking charge of his life. Taking responsibility for it. But in the last month, something changed. I could see it at his last report. I just couldn't figure out what it was. He was...agitated. Maybe even scared of something. But he wouldn't open up."

"Are you maybe overthinking this? Couldn't that have been because he knew he would test dirty?"

"It's possible," she admitted. "But I just don't believe that. I think Eric got caught up in something that ultimately got him killed. And I want to know what that was and who killed him." Her chin came up again. "I also want to know why he had that Southern Cross tattoo on his back."

Randall studied her for a few seconds, making her feel like he could see right into her mind. Then he blinked and said, "Okay, good enough for me. I'll make those calls."

✦ ✦ ✦ ✦

BY LATE THURSDAY afternoon, Tullie made the first of two phone calls. Hollis Joplin answered his cell on the second ring. Without even saying who she was, she said, "I need your help again."

"Change a tire? Pick up your clothes from the cleaners? Paint your house? I'm at your service, Tullie."

"It's a little more complicated than that, Hollis."

She heard Joplin sigh. "Somehow, I knew that," he said. "Don't tell me: It has something to do with Eric Jaeger."

"See? I knew you were the right guy. Nothing gets past you."

"Right guy for what?"

"To investigate Jaeger's murder. Rutledge County is stone-walling the whole thing. To paraphrase my buddy, Will, 'Ain't nobody gonna do nothin' about anything.'"

She heard Joplin whistle. "That bad, huh?"

"It gets worse. Chief Randall called Chief Landon, with Community Supervision in Rutledge, to get some idea of what goes on up there. The bottom line is that the DA is pretty much a wimp, and the sheriff and coroner are in lock-step when it comes to investigating suspicious deaths."

"How can that be, Tullie? This sounds like something out of the Old West!"

"Actually, more like the Old South. It also fits the expression, 'All politics are local.'"

"Please tell me the judges there at least follow the law."

"I could tell you that, but it would only be half-true," Tullie admitted. "According to what my chief heard, Judge Danby was a good judge until he started having early Alzheimer's symptoms a few years ago. He's not running for re-election next year, but no one's seen fit to remove him or even suggest he retire. So, he pretty much gives the DA full rein and rules accordingly when he hears the very few cases that make it to court. Most of them are plea-bargained. The only other judge, Judge Roker, follows the rule of law, but again, he can only monitor and rule on cases that manage to get before him. The major reason he got elected two years ago was that the local newspaper endorsed him. Seems the editor, who also owns the paper, is the only one to push back against the 'Unholy Three,' as they call the DA, the sheriff, and the coroner."

She could almost see Hollis rolling his eyes and shaking his head. "And you want me to wade into a cesspool like that?" he asked.

Tullie paused a few seconds, then took the plunge. "Not officially. Think of it as a kind of undercover job. Chief Randall has asked Judge Mabry, who sentenced Jaeger, to appoint you as a special investigator on the murder case. You'd report your findings to me, which I'll write up as a sort of post-sentence report, as opposed to a pre-sentence report, which we usually do, and—"

"I get it," Joplin said. "Clever. And Judge Mabry agreed to that?"

"Judge Mabry isn't called 'The Wicked Witch of West Law' for no reason," Tullie said. "She heard the case and sentenced Jaeger, so he's under her jurisdiction, even though he's dead. Besides, the judge is a little pissed about the whole thing herself. If a sheriff in Milton County ignored the murder of a parolee, she'd throw him in jail for contempt. And since my job is to report and advise her and any other judge in this county about parolees and probationers I supervise, she's basically giving me the green light to investigate Jaeger's death. Only I'm not a trained investigator, so—"

"That's where I come in."

"Exactly."

There was a long silence as Hollis appeared to be thinking this over. Finally, he said, "First of all, I'd need to run this past *my* chief. Just because she didn't mind my going up to transport Jaeger's body here doesn't mean she'd okay something like this. And even if she did, I'd still need to fit it in during my time off."

"I can understand that."

"Secondly, it seems to me I'd be about as welcome in Rutledge County as a porcupine at a nudist colony, Tullie. I've already pissed off the deputy coroner, and they weren't too friendly to me at the crematory when I went to pick up Jaeger's body. How can I work 'undercover' at this point?"

Tullie sighed. She hadn't figured that part out herself. "You'll think of something, Hollis. You were a homicide detective for seven years. So, even though you're a death investigator now, you still knew how to smoke out Elliot Carter's killer and the guy who killed that investigative reporter a few years ago. Besides, you won't be doing this alone."

"What does that mean?"

"Well, I'll be working with you, but I also hope Tom Halloran will partner with us. I'm meeting with him and Maggie around six tonight."

Tullie heard Hollis make a sputtering sound. "Halloran? Why Halloran?" he asked.

"Because you've worked with him before," she said, puzzled by his response. "And he was with you when you found Jaeger's body. I figured he could talk to people up at Wolfscratch. Find out who might know something."

"You mean because he's a lawyer and fits in up there?"

Tullie realized she'd stepped in it. She hadn't known Hollis was sensitive about coming from a working-class family. She'd always admired that he'd put himself through Georgia State University and had even gotten a master's degree in criminal justice a few years ago. Maybe she'd read him wrong. Or maybe he and Tom weren't such great friends. But then, why had the two couples spent the weekend together at Wolfscratch?

"It's just a simple division of labor, Hollis," she told him. "Tom wouldn't know how to look into what Jaeger's been doing since he disappeared or sniff out why Harold and Bo Danforth have so much power in Rutledge County. That's your area of expertise. *Unless*," she added, emphasizing the word, "you'd rather spend more time with Betsey Cunningham. I could tell you were just her type."

After a long pause, Hollis said, "I can see your point. But if I'm going to be working with Halloran, there have to be some ground rules. I want to be at that meeting tonight. And since Carrie did the autopsy for you, I think she should be included, too."

Tullie was intrigued by that request. She was also very pragmatic. "You got it," she said. "See you in a few hours."

14

THE HALLORANS' TWO-STORY Federalist-style house on 17th Street in Ansley Park was a handsome mini-mansion, in Joplin's opinion. It sat in stately fashion at the top of a sloping driveway, surrounded by azalea and hydrangea bushes and several Japanese maples. Joplin and Carrie got out of Carrie's Audi and walked the brick pathway to the front door, which was opened by Tommy and Megan Halloran.

"Did you bring your gun, Mr. Hollis?" Tommy asked. He'd grown at least two inches since Joplin had last seen him at their Fourth of July barbeque.

"You're not supposed to ask him questions like that," Megan said, looking and sounding like a miniature Maggie. "Remember what Mommy said."

"That's okay, sweetie," Joplin said to her. "Tommy, I didn't bring it. But when you're eighteen, I'll take you out to a shooting range and teach you how to shoot."

"Hollis!" Carrie said.

"But only with your parents' permission," Joplin added quickly.

"Awesome!" said Tommy.

"Now, can we come in?" Joplin asked.

Before Tommy could answer, Maggie appeared in the entry hall. "Sorry," she said, seeming a little flustered. "Please come in. Tom and Tullie are in the den." She hugged Carrie, then added, "Go on back there while I get these two settled."

After muttered protests from Tommy, Maggie led them away. Joplin and Carrie walked back to the den, which overlooked a brick terrace and a lush, plant-filled yard. Tom Halloran, sitting next to Tullie on one of the large sofas facing each other on either side of the fireplace, stood up as they entered.

"Speak of the devil," he said, looking at Joplin. Then he walked over to Carrie and hugged her.

"I thought my ears were burning," said Joplin. He stared at Tullie. "Did you start the meeting without us?"

"Just catching up on family stuff," she said, smiling brightly.

Joplin looked over at Tom, then back to Tullie, not entirely buying it, but he decided not to say anything.

"Anyone for a drink?" Tom asked. "I just got home, and it's been a long week." After taking their drink orders, he headed for the kitchen, passing Maggie carrying a large platter of cold shrimp and crab claws.

"I've never had a chance to feel hungry in this house, Maggie," Joplin said.

She set the platter down on the coffee table between the sofas and smiled at him. "I'd be mortified if you had. Now, please sit down and eat some of this. You, too, Tullie. You're thin as a rail."

"I can get that from my mother, Maggie," Tullie said. "Speaking of whom, she called me last night and tried to pump me for information about 'that dead person Tom and Hollis discovered,' as she put it."

"What'd you tell her?" Joplin asked. He waited for Carrie to serve herself on one of the little plates Maggie had provided, then got himself a heaping plate of the seafood.

"I told her I couldn't talk about any of my parolees. Something I've *been* telling her for years, not that it's ever stopped her from asking."

"Were you able to ask *her* about her involvement with the Daughters of the Confederacy?"

Tullie didn't answer until she'd accepted a drink from Tom and taken a long sip. "I didn't really have any context for a question like that, since I couldn't tell her about the tattoo on Jaeger's back."

"I was able to find out a little about that from my mother," Maggie said, then told them about Moira's recent attempts to get Colleen to join the group and its success in suing Vanderbilt University.

Tom finished serving the drinks as she talked, then sat beside Tullie. "I was blown away by that $1.2 million verdict," he said. "But even more so by the way the Daughters have been able to promote this 'Lost Cause' version of the Civil War for the past 150 years. And to learn there are still around 20,000 or so active members."

"Why are you surprised, Tom?" Joplin asked. "Until last year, when Governor Deal abolished it, Georgia still celebrated Confederate Memorial Day on the fourth Monday of April to honor the Confederate soldiers who died in the war. But it's still a state holiday, even though it isn't named that anymore. That hasn't kept other states, like Texas, Mississippi, Alabama, Florida, and both Carolinas, from continuing to celebrate it, though."

Tom took a sip of his drink and sighed. "Yeah, I know. Moving here from Chicago, I always found that strange. Like most law firms and other businesses, Healey and Caldwell never took the day off, so I ended up just ignoring the whole thing."

"Pretty hard to ignore if you're Black," Tullie said. "I used to volunteer for the skeleton crew we had to maintain despite the holiday, but I was still embarrassed around Black co-workers."

"Same here," said Joplin. "The ME's Office was always open, and so were police departments, of course."

"Well, we're here tonight because a murder victim had a Confederate symbol tattooed on his back," said Carrie, looking around the room at each of them. "We can't do anything about the past, but what can we do about what might be happening right now? Tullie says Eric Jaeger didn't have that tattoo when he was released on parole. So, I think the first thing to investigate is when he got it. And *why*."

Joplin took a deep breath and said, "Finding out exactly when Jaeger got the tattoo might take some time. As for the 'why,' it identifies him as a member of a white supremacy group, which is my best guess. But I hope I'm wrong."

Tullie took a big gulp of her drink and said, "Unfortunately, that's what I think, too. And it's scaring me shitless."

"That doesn't necessarily mean your mother and father are involved with any domestic terrorist groups, Tullie," Maggie said.

"I know that, and deep down, I can't believe it. But there's something you need to know, Hollis. Something I told Tom and Maggie about before you got here. Tom insisted I needed to tell you about it, but I wasn't sure."

Joplin looked at Tom, then Maggie, then back at Tullie. "Well, that's a first. Keeping things from me is a distinctly Halloran trait. Which is why I insisted on this meeting. And I could tell as soon as I came in that it was *déjà vu* all over again."

"That's my fault, Hollis, not Tom's," Tullie said. "But when I tell you what happened, I hope you'll understand."

"I'm all ears, Tullie," he said.

She took another slug of her drink, then a deep breath. "A few days after Eric Jaeger's last report to me—before I got the urine test results—I thought I saw him with my brother, Aidan, in a Home Depot parking lot in Alpharetta. In Aidan's truck. They didn't see me because I was in a friend's car. I was going to confront Jaeger about it at his next report, only he didn't show."

Joplin said, "Now *that* I didn't see coming. And I guess I can understand why you were reluctant to tell me about it. Does your chief know this?"

Tullie shook her head. "No, but after tonight, I'll need to tell him." She gave a long sigh, then said, "I'm still not sure it was Jaeger in Aidan's truck, so I didn't want to implicate my brother in anything."

Frowning, Joplin said, "Okay, so you didn't get to talk to Jaeger about that, but I'm assuming you've asked Aidan."

Tullie just shook her head and took another sip of her drink, leaving Joplin dumbfounded.

"Maybe I should jump in here and talk about family dynamics a bit," Maggie said, staring at Tullie. Joplin saw Tullie give an almost imperceptible nod. "Hollis, you remember I told you that Moira gave Aidan the family business—the Fox Run Stables—when she and Ryan decided to retire?"

"Yes, I do," he answered, wondering where this was leading.

"It was a total surprise to Tullie. She didn't even know her parents had decided to retire, and the next thing she knew, Moira just casually mentioned at a family dinner that Aidan now owned the business. She also announced that she and Ryan were moving into Wolfscratch. Tullie told us she really didn't want to manage Fox Run, that she was happy where she was, but—"

"But they could have at least asked me," Tullie said calmly. "I can take it from here, Maggie." She turned to Joplin. "Aidan and I are fraternal twins. We did everything together." She shrugged, then said, "I guess that's why I was such a tomboy growing up. Anyway, we were close, and it was like he and I—and even my dad—were allies in some kind of battle. One that we didn't understand. At least, Aidan and I didn't understand. But we had each other's backs. We both worked at Fox Run after school and in the summers. And we both had to deal with all of our mother's expectations of us. So, we agreed that as soon as we finished college, we would get as far away from the whole thing as we could."

"But that changed?" Joplin said, encouraging her.

"Yes. It did. Even worse, Aidan changed. This was 2008, and the crash happened three months after we graduated. He'd started as a rookie reporter at the *Savannah Morning News,* but was let go. I was a first-year law student at UGA, hell-bent on becoming a prosecutor."

"I can see that," Joplin said, nodding. "What happened?"

Tullie shrugged. "As I said, this was 2008. Fox Run lost half its business by the end of October. People couldn't afford to board horses or train them or even have their teenage daughters take lessons and participate in dressage and jumping events. At the same time, all of us at UGA law heard that firms were letting their new hires and even a lot of two-year associates go."

"It took Healey and Caldwell almost four years to recover from the crash," Halloran said.

"I didn't feel I could justify staying in law school when I had no idea if I could find a job after graduation," Tullie continued, "even though that upset my parents. They insisted the tuition wasn't a problem. Anyway, the upshot was that Aidan and I went back home to live and help with Fox Run. We filled in for the trainers my parents had to let go, mucked out the stables, exercised the horses still boarding there—you name it. Two years later, things began to stabilize, so when the state hiring freeze was lifted, I applied for a job as a parole officer with the Department of Corrections—this was before probation and parole were combined to form the Department of Community Supervision–just to get a foot into law enforcement. And move out of Fox Run."

"But I take it Aidan stayed on," Joplin said.

Tullie slowly nodded her head. "At first, he claimed it was to make sure the business was back on track—not what it had been, of course, but things were loosening up. But then a year went by, then another year, and he started distancing himself from me. Telling me not to hassle him about moving on, he was happy where he was. And he was just, like, sucking up to my parents all the time, especially my mother. Then, a year ago came the big announcement about their retirement. Fox Run was in good shape by then, and they'd begun building the house at Wolfscratch six months earlier, so I should have known something was up. But it never occurred to me that they'd give Fox Run outright to my brother. My mother tried to say it was a 'wedding present' for Aidan and his new wife." She turned to Carrie and added, "He'd married his college sweetheart, Brooke, six month before. But then she finally admitted that she was afraid that if she left the business to both of us in her will, I'd somehow make Aidan sell it. She wanted it to stay in the family and felt that was the only way. I was stunned. And then, Aidan wouldn't even talk to me about it. That was more of a betrayal than what my parents did."

"Have you and Aidan discussed it since then?" Carrie asked.

Tullie nodded and said, "A lot of good that did." He was extremely defensive. Said he'd 'earned' it, working his ass off getting the place back on track. That Dad's marketing ideas were outdated, and Mother didn't want to spend the money to 'move into the future,' as he put it."

"Did he tell you what he meant by that?" Joplin asked.

"No, in fact, he ended the conversation. We'd met at Marlow's Tavern at Avalon, and he just got up and left. Stuck me with the bill, too."

"Well, that sucks," Joplin said.

"Big time," said Tullie.

✚ ✚ ✚ ✚

"WHY DIDN'T YOU tell them the rest of it?" Tom asked when Hollis and Carrie had left. He handed Tullie another drink.

Tullie shrugged. "Blood is still thicker than water, Tom. And I don't want to implicate my brother in anything just yet. But if he's on the wrong side of the law, that'll be in the report to Judge Mabry."

"It'll have to be," said Tom. "I'm an officer of the court in this situation, just as you are. And as I told you earlier, I don't like keeping things from Hollis. It's been a problem in the past."

"Then for my sake, for the *family's* sake," she said, raising her glass toward Maggie, "find out what's going on at Fox Run. And Wolfscratch," she added.

15

ON SATURDAY MORNING, August 27th, Tom Halloran went for his usual run, heading out from his house on 17th Street to The Prado, then across Piedmont to the park. He wanted to clear his head before heading to Wolfscratch for the weekend. Maggie had managed to get them invited to Moira and Ryan's house by asking her mother to mention to Moira that they hadn't been able to relax much the previous weekend, what with finding the body and all.

"Piece of cake," she'd told him, adding that Colleen was happy to have Tommy and Megan again. "I also told Moira, when she called me, that we'd love to see what Aidan has done to Fox Run and visit with him and Brooke. So, we're invited there for brunch tomorrow."

"Good work," he'd said. "Remind me to double your salary."

"Two times nothing is still nothing," Maggie had said. "And this is for my family. But thanks for the thought."

As he passed the Driving Club, then headed into Piedmont Park at the 14th Street entrance, Halloran couldn't help but think, as he did every time he ran here, about finding Elliot

Carter's body hanging from a tree near the Playscapes. It had only been three years, yet so much had happened that it all seemed a lifetime ago.

One thing was that his relationship with Hollis Joplin had gotten more complex. They'd been through a lot together, joining forces on three cases and almost getting killed in the process. Halloran knew he could trust Hollis with his life and thought Hollis felt the same, but that was the only area in which they trusted each other completely. Part of this, he knew, had to do with an innate distrust between law enforcement and the legal profession. Also, Hollis considered him a "civilian" who had no business injecting himself into criminal investigations, even when those investigations involved Halloran's clients, like Libba Woodridge. But when he wanted information from Halloran that involved attorney-client privilege, Hollis resented his refusal to share that information.

Somehow, they'd learned to navigate those waters, usually able to stop short of putting each other to a test of wills or professional ethics. The fact that Maggie and Carrie were good friends certainly helped; sometimes, the women had even been back channels of information he and Hollis couldn't share. But Halloran knew there would be tension between them each time they collaborated on a case. And this case involved withheld information from the get-go.

Not only had Tullie seen Eric Jaeger in Aidan's truck—and there was no uncertainty about that, despite what she'd told Joplin—she had also seen Jaeger counting out money to him. A few minutes later, Aidan had lunged at him, grabbing him by his shirt. Jaeger had forced her brother's hands off of him and then thrust his right index finger into his face, glaring at him. Then, Aidan had thrown up his hands several times and vehemently shaken his head. Jaeger had just stared at him, but

Tullie had told Halloran that the expression on his face showed a lot of anger.

Halloran turned left to follow the lake and thought over the rest of what Tullie had said. It was clear to him that she was worried about more than the fact that Aiden and Eric Jaeger were somehow connected.

"Jaeger's a convicted drug dealer," she'd said. "All I can think is that my brother is buying drugs from him and maybe worse— even *selling* drugs to some of the kids who ride at Fox Run. And their friends, for crap's sake."

"You don't know that, Tullie," Maggie had insisted.

"Well, what else am I supposed to think, goddammit!" she'd said. "I *don't* think Jaeger was buying a horse from my brother, for fuck's sake. And there was a lot of heat going on in that truck. Aidan was furious with Jaeger for some reason. And then Jaeger turns up dead a few weeks later. It's not looking good, is all I'm saying."

"Then why not just ask Aidan," Halloran had asked.

Tullie had given a long, dramatic sigh, then set her glass down carefully on the coffee table. "Because I don't fucking know him anymore, Tom," she said, shaking her head. "I can't tell when he's lying to me these days. And Eric Jaeger is dead. Murdered. So, I'm pretty sure something was going on."

Halloran was rounding the tennis center when it occurred to him that if Aidan's own sister—his twin—couldn't tell when he was lying, how could she expect him to know? How was he supposed to figure out if Aidan Fitzgerald was using drugs or involved in dealing them? Although his years as a trial lawyer had given him a heightened sense of when people were lying to him—most of the time—he wasn't sure what questions to ask or where to look for answers. But it was too late to back out now. He'd agreed to be part of this investigation because of Maggie. It was her family who might be involved in some type of criminal activity, maybe even murder. And even though Moira and Ryan weren't Halloran's favorite people, they were Tullie's parents, and he had a great deal of affection for Tullie.

As he headed toward Magnolia Hall, Halloran decided to play everything by ear. He and Maggie were heading up to Wolfscratch around eleven that morning, then going to Monteluce Winery in Dahlonega with the Fitzgeralds for lunch. Maggie planned on finding a way to bring up the United Daughters of the Confederacy sometime during the day, which might prove fruitful. And he was sure they would ask for any updates on Eric Jaeger, since the story had been in the news. Halloran couldn't reveal anything about the autopsy or the undercover murder investigation, but he could try to draw them out by asking what the Wolfscratch rumor mill was grinding out.

Because Wolfscratch, for all its resort-like atmosphere, was at heart just a small town. And every small town had its secrets.

✤ ✤ ✤ ✤

THEY STOPPED AT the IGA three miles from Wolfscratch to buy flowers and wine for the Fitzgeralds. It was surprisingly well-stocked for a rural chain store, rivaling most supermarkets in Atlanta or even a Total Wine store. Halloran headed for the wine section. He grabbed two bottles of Quilt Cabernet, one of Ryan's favorites, then joined Maggie in the checkout area. She was carrying a huge bouquet of blue hydrangeas.

"Anything else?" he asked, eyebrows raised.

"No," she said. "I told Moira lunch at Monteluce is on us. I just hope she's not making a big deal out of dinner tonight."

"Surely you jest," Halloran said. "As long as she hasn't invited half of Wolfscratch, I'll be happy."

✦ ✦ ✦ ✦

IT WASN'T UNTIL Halloran had reached the driver's side of his car that he saw a large, upside-down pineapple on its hood, evidently placed in the middle of the windshield so it wouldn't roll off.

"Now, where did that come from?" Maggie asked, nodding toward the pineapple.

Halloran shrugged as he fished in his pants pocket for the keys. "It probably fell out of someone's bag when they were unloading groceries, and someone saw it and put it on the hood so it would be found."

Maggie grinned at him and shook her head. "But upside-down, Tom? I don't think so." She set the hydrangeas on the roof of the car and pulled her iPhone out of her purse. After tapping the camera app, she took a picture of the pineapple.

"Is that for posterity, or do you have hopes of solving the mystery?" Halloran asked.

"I'm not sure. Right now, it just appeals to my sense of the absurd."

"Good, because we have enough on our agenda just trying to find out if Aidan—or your aunt and her fellow Daughters of the Confederacy—are connected to Eric Jaeger."

"Yes, dear," Maggie said. "But I'm keeping the pineapple."

16

THE FIRST THING Joplin did on Saturday morning, after feeding the cats and turning on the coffee maker, was to call Will Sykes, Tullie's deputy friend in Rutledge County. After verifying the information Tullie had given him and arranging to meet at a barbeque place near his house at noon, he asked if Sykes had a reliable—and discreet—contact in the Wolfscratch Public Safety Department. The deputy gave Joplin the name of Gary Summers and the phone number where he could be reached.

Summers answered on the second ring. Joplin explained who he was and asked to meet with him that afternoon. When that request was met with silence, Joplin suggested that he contact Will Sykes if he felt uncomfortable about a meeting.

More silence followed, then Summers said, "I'll talk to Will first, then call you back, okay?"

"Sure thing," Joplin said, sensing this wouldn't be as easy as he thought. When he hung up, he immediately called Tullie and asked how hard it would be to get a subpoena for the security footage at both gates at Wolfscratch from Thursday morning through midnight on Friday.

"I can call Judge Mabry at home right now and find out," she said. "I take it you're hoping Jaeger will be on it, and maybe the person who took him up to the Falls. Crap, why didn't I think of that? This investigation might be over before it begins."

"Not necessarily. If the murder was premeditated, the person who brought Jaeger in—and we're assuming that person is the killer, but that's not necessarily true—might have had Jaeger get down on the floorboards of the car so he wouldn't be seen. And you didn't think of checking the security footage because you're not a trained investigator, as you've even admitted. Which is why I'm spending my Saturday in North Georgia for the second time in a week."

Joplin heard Tullie sigh, then she said, "Could you aim a little of that frustration I hear at the corruption in Rutledge County, Hollis? If they weren't stonewalling a murder investigation, this wouldn't be necessary. And if I could have done this by myself, I would have. I mean, I have a lot of experience doing PSIs–Pre-Sentence Investigations–but that's just compiling information for a judge. The evidence has already been gathered."

"Sorry, Tullie," Joplin responded, regretting what he'd said. "I'm an asshole, and you didn't deserve that. Could you let me know what the judge says?"

"Of course," she said, sounding a little mollified. "I'll get back to you as soon as I can."

"Why are you an asshole, and what didn't Tullie deserve?" Carrie asked, coming into the kitchen. The sleeveless white nightgown with smocking at the top that she was wearing accentuated her baby bump. Carrie still looked sleepy, and her unbrushed hair framed her face in a wild tangle. Joplin thought she had never looked more beautiful.

He pulled out one of the bar stools around the kitchen island and said, "Sit down while I make you a cup of tea, and I'll tell you. And you'll probably have the same reaction Tullie did because you women all stick together when confronted with male assholeness."

"Try not to be redundant so early in the morning, Hollis," she said, managing to make getting up on a barstool while pregnant look graceful.

✦ ✦ ✦ ✦

BIGUN'S BARBEQUE WAS in Talking Rock, just off I-515. It was a one-story, simulated log cabin with wooden poles rising from short stone columns to support a roof over the front porch. A happy-looking pig was pictured on the upper façade, between the words "Bigun's" and "Barbeque." It reminded Joplin of Wallace Barbeque in Austell, his grandmother's favorite place to eat, with a similar pig on its sign, albeit with racing wheels. He hoped the food would be as good.

Will Sykes, who had told him he'd be in a booth at the very back of the restaurant, nodded as Joplin approached. He was wearing jeans and a black Nike polo shirt. Even sitting down, Sykes looked tall, and his ram-rod posture and buzz cut indicated a military background. He didn't offer to shake hands, and Joplin assumed Sykes was trying not to call attention to the fact that they didn't know each other. He'd assured Joplin that his colleagues didn't frequent Bigun's because it was too far from the Sheriff's Office, but Joplin was still uneasy about meeting in such a public place. Deciding he'd have to trust the deputy's judgment, he scooted into the booth and nodded.

"Thanks again for meeting me," Joplin said in a low voice.

"No problem," Sykes said, then looked up as a harried-looking, middle-aged waitress with a notepad and a pencil behind her ear approached them. "Hey, Jackie, how's it goin'?"

"Like every other Saturday, Will," she said, taking the pencil from behind her ear and holding it over the pad. "Busier than a one-legged man in a butt-kicking contest. What'll you have today?"

They didn't even have menus, but Sykes said, "I'll have the Big n Sloppy with a side of Redneck Lasagna, collards, and some sweet tea."

"I'll have the same," Joplin said quickly, sensing that Jackie would have no patience for anyone who needed to look at a menu.

She nodded and hurried away without telling them they'd made excellent choices, which raised Joplin's rating of Bigun's Barbeque. He hated servers who did that.

"So, how do you know Tullie?" Sykes asked him.

A challenging undertone in his question made Joplin think that the two had been involved at some point. Maybe still were, for all he knew. But whatever their relationship, Tullie trusted him, and Joplin would have to as well. So, he gave Sykes a thumbnail sketch of his background and how and when he and Tullie had met. A look of recognition crossed the deputy's face when Joplin mentioned the ME's Office.

"So, you're one of the guys who found Eric Jaeger's body," he said. "Tullie didn't mention that. Man, you sure pissed Bo Danforth off right good!"

"Well, he pissed me off, too. He didn't do his job. "

"Yep," Sykes said, nodding. "You got that right." He looked up as Jackie approached them, carrying a large pitcher of tea.

"Food'll be right up," she said as she filled their glasses.

"Good," the deputy said, then smiled. "This is a buddy of mine from my Army days, Jackie. Ronnie Fulsom. He wanted some barbeque, and I told him Bigun's is the best and has the prettiest waitresses."

"You lie like an old bear rug, Will Sykes," Jackie said, but a hint of a smile crossed her face. "Nice to meet you, Ronnie," she added before she hurried away.

"Just a little cover story for our meeting," Sykes said. "Everybody in the restaurant will know about my good friend, Ronnie, before we finish lunch."

"Good idea," Joplin said, then turned the conversation back to Bo Danforth. "I was surprised to learn that Harold Danforth made his own son a deputy coroner." He took a sip of his tea. It was sweet enough to stand a spoon in, just the way he used to like it before Carrie had convinced him otherwise. "I know Harold from some training we took together some years back. He seemed like a pretty decent guy. Does he monitor Bo at all?"

"Not so's you'd know. Most times, he sends Bo out on the low-level stuff—car accidents and such. We get any drug-related or violent deaths, Harold goes to the scene himself. I guess he musta thought Jaeger's death was an accident—not worth his time. This time of year, we do have a lot of boating and hiking accidents at Wolfscratch. But from what the EMT guys said, that didn't seem to be the case with Eric Jaeger."

"Did your sheriff let Harold know what they said?"

"That's not something he would tell me," Sykes said, looking steadily at him.

Joplin didn't know if the deputy was trying to get some kind of unspoken message across to him, so he nodded and said, "Thanks for vetting me with Gary Summers. He called back, and I'm going to pick up the security footage from both gates later this afternoon. First, I plan to go to the newspaper office and see what they'll tell me about your political problem here. I figure they won't let the wrong people know I'm investigating Jaeger's murder. But I also need to tell you about something found on Jaeger's body at the autopsy."

Joplin was about to tell Sykes about the tattoo when Jackie appeared with their lunch. "There's hot sauce on the table, y'all," she said. "You need anything else? More tea?"

"We're fine, Jackie, thanks," Sykes said.

The Big n Sloppy turned out to be a pork sandwich with sweet barbeque sauce; the Redneck Lasagna was macaroni and cheese with Brunswick stew on top. Joplin was thrilled. He knew Carrie would disapprove—she'd been trying to get him to eat more healthily since they'd married—but, *damn*, it looked good!

"You gonna eat it or write a letter home about it?" Will Sykes asked, his mouth full.

"Sorry. My wife is pregnant and won't allow food like this in the house."

"Then, I guess you better destroy the evidence."

"Excellent idea," Joplin said and shoveled a massive bite of Redneck Lasagna into his mouth.

They ate in contented silence for several minutes, then Sykes said, "I think you were gonna tell me about something found on Eric Jaeger's body, just before Jackie brought the food."

Joplin set his Big n Sloppy down on his plate, wiped his mouth, and told the deputy about the Southern Cross tattooed on Jaeger's back. He said nothing about Moira Fitzgerald's involvement with the United Daughters of the Confederacy or Tullie's fear that her mother might somehow be connected to her parolee's death. But just the mention of the tattoo made Will Sykes set his own sandwich down and shake his head.

"Then we might have something bigger goin' on than a murder investigation," he said finally.

"What do you mean?"

Sykes leaned toward Joplin and spoke in a lower voice. "About six months ago, I arrested a good ole boy in a beat-up truck for a DUI. He was so drunk he couldn't even get out of the truck when I pulled him over, much less do a field sobriety test. I cuffed him and put him in the back of my car, then called for backup. We searched his truck and found two AK-47 rifles and an M16 in the compartment under the bed of his trunk."

Joplin gave a low whistle. "That's not good."

"What's even worse is when I got him back to the SO and another deputy helped me get him into a cell to sleep it off, we searched him. In the process, his shirt rode up, and there was a tattoo of a Southern Cross medal on his back. I didn't know what to make of it then, but I started asking around. Turns out the guy was part of a militia."

Joplin stared at him. "A militia? I mean, I figured it was associated with a white supremacy group, but a full-blown militia? You're kidding me."

Sykes shook his head. "Wish I was. Militias like the Oathkeepers and the Three Percenters are like the police forces for white supremacists. Some are part and parcel with a particular supremacy group, and I found out we have our own here in North Georgia. It's called The Cause."

"The Cause? You mean as in 'the Lost Cause?' The failed Confederacy?"

"Yep. According to one of my sources, every member of the militia has a replica of the Southern Cross medal tattooed somewhere on their bodies."

17

MOIRA FITZGERALD GREETED them with as much enthusiasm as the weekend before. She held her arms out to Maggie as she climbed the steps to the house, then enfolded her and the blue hydrangeas in a big hug. Halloran followed, carrying the wine and the pineapple. Moira raised a perfectly shaped eyebrow as she stared at the pineapple.

"You look like you're going to a luau instead of a winery, Tom," she said.

Maggie laughed and said, "We found it on the hood of our car. Upside down. We have no idea who put it there or why, for that matter."

Ryan appeared at the door just then and walked out onto the front porch. "Hello, hello! Welcome back. And I see you come bearing gifts."

"Well, the flowers and wine were intentional, but the pineapple wasn't our idea."

"It was on the hood of their car, Ryan," Moira said. "Upside down."

"Well, aren't you the lucky ones."

"What do you mean?" asked Maggie.

"It means," said Moira, "that you've been invited to a wife-swapping event."

✦ ✦ ✦ ✦

THEY TALKED ABOUT the Wolfscratch Swingers' Club all the way to Monteluce as they drove on gravel roads that MapQuest insisted upon. According to the Fitzgeralds, the club had been around for a long time. Maybe since the Nineties, Ryan informed them. Or even before that, Moira had said, citing an unnamed source. It now had about two hundred members, some full-time, others who hooked up sporadically.

"And I do mean 'hook up,'" Moira said, raising her eyebrows for emphasis. "I've heard about threesomes, foursomes, orgies—you name it."

"And don't forget the watersports," Ryan interjected.

"Watersports?" Maggie asked, barely able to say the word.

"Several of the members have pontoon boats," Ryan said, "and a group will go out at night on Lake Etowah in the summer—sometimes two or three boats—and everybody skinny-dips. There's lots of booze, food, and more booze, and it gets pretty wild. From what I've heard anyway," he added quickly.

"They tried to get something going on with the nudist camp just up the road from Wolfscratch, but nothing came of that," Moira said. "Apparently, the camp is full of purists. They just like being in nature during warm weather without their clothes on."

"There's a nudist camp up here, too?" Halloran asked. He was still recovering from the pineapple-swingers' club revelation.

"North Georgia isn't just for hikers, Tom," said Moira coyly.

By the time they reached Monteluce, a sprawling Tuscan-style resort in Dahlonega that had privately-owned houses, rental houses, hilly vineyards, and the winery and restaurant, the Hallorans had heard more than enough about the Wolfscratch Swingers' Club. Moira and Ryan had provided so many details that Halloran wondered if they were members. The thought made him a little queasy, and from the expression on Maggie's face, he was sure she was thinking the same thing.

The parking lot was packed, so Ryan let them out in front of the stone steps leading up to the restaurant. They were ushered into the main dining room, with its high ceilings and wall of windows overlooking the vineyard. The view wasn't as magnificent in late summer as it had been for an October wedding they'd once attended, but it was still lovely. To get off the subject of wife-swapping, Halloran chattered on about the view until Ryan joined them.

"Let's order," was the first thing he said, sitting down. "I'm starving. And thirsty, too. Thank God they have beer here!"

"What kind would you like?" said their server, who seemed to appear from nowhere.

"A Stella Artois," said Ryan.

"Same here," said Halloran.

"Let's get a bottle of the Chardonnay, Moira," Maggie said quickly. Halloran was sure she could drink the whole bottle herself after their conversation in the car.

They all turned to their menus, but before they could look at them, Betsey Cunningham loomed over Halloran's shoulder and hugged him. "What a nice surprise!" she said, pulling back to beam at him and Maggie. "I never imagined I'd see you three times in one week."

Halloran and Ryan started to stand up, but Betsey waved them back to their seats. It was like a replay of their dinner at Maison the week before, with Ryan playing Hollis Joplin's role, and he wasn't sure it was a coincidence.

"Would you like to join us, Betsey?" Moira asked. "Is Jack with you?"

"Yes, but we're with two other couples from Atlanta to tour the winery. I just came over to say hello."

"Too bad," said Moira. "Tom and Maggie got a pineapple invitation, and we've been discussing it."

"Nooo!" Betsey drawled, smiling down at Moira, and in that moment, Halloran was certain that she was a card-carrying member of the Wolfscratch Swingers' Club.

And maybe Moira was, too.

18

AFTER LEAVING BIGUN'S, Joplin sat in his car and called Andrew McAllister, the owner and editor of the *Rutledge Gazette*, briefly explaining who he was and what he was doing. McAllister didn't respond to his request to meet with him for several seconds.

"I'd be happy to talk to you, Mr. Jenkins. That new winery I've been hearing about sounds promising, and I'd be glad to give it some space in the paper, but I'm on my way out the door. You mind meeting me at my house? I've got a plumber coming, so I thought I'd work from home this afternoon."

"I don't mind at all," Joplin said, playing along. Either someone was in the *Gazette* office whom McAllister didn't want to know that Joplin had contacted him, or the editor thought it was bugged.

"I appreciate it. I'd hate to miss an update on the winery for this week's paper. The address is 912 Red Fern Road. Just off Old Henderson."

"I'll find it and meet you there."

"Good. See you soon, then."

Joplin plugged the address into MapQuest and saw it was about twenty minutes away. Figuring that would give McAllister enough time to get home, he pressed the audio icon and set off. It was a straight shot south on State Road 515 out of Talking Rock. He turned off on Juniper Road fifteen minutes later, then took a right onto Red Fern. Updated cottage-style houses and several newer two-story houses bordered the street. McAllister's house was one of the newer ones, a brick Colonial with black shutters set back from the road.

No plumber's truck was in the driveway, which didn't surprise Joplin. He turned into it and parked, then walked up a brick pathway to the front door. It opened before he could knock, and a tall, lanky man in his thirties wearing khaki pants, a starched shirt, and leather suspenders greeted him. McAllister looked like a small-town newspaper editor straight out of central casting.

"You must be Investigator Joplin," he said, offering his hand. "Sorry about dragging you out here, but I'm uncomfortable discussing sensitive issues on the newspaper's premises."

"I figured that's why you wanted to meet here when you called me 'Mr. Jenkins.' Now you can just call me Hollis."

"And I'm Andy. Come on in."

McAllister led him through a narrow entry hall to a small study that served as a home office. Joplin flashed back to another editor's entry hall and office the year before. But he recovered quickly, having a reasonable expectation that this editor wouldn't drug him and try to kill him. McAllister motioned Joplin to a chair next to the desk.

"Have a seat and tell me what this is all about," he said, sitting down. "I heard that a body had been discovered at the Upper

Falls in Wolfscratch, but I was told it was an accident. Still news for our little paper, but I guess it might be more than that."

"It is. But first, I need you to know that this is off the record. I'll be happy to share some of what we know, but right now, I need information from you, Andy. And coming from a small Southern town myself, I know that the editor of a county newspaper knows a lot more than ever gets published."

McAllister smiled and nodded. "You could say that. And I'm fine with being off the record, although I don't know what I could tell you. I don't even know the name of the dead man."

"It's Eric Jaeger. Several months ago, he was released on parole after completing seven years on a drug-dealing conviction. Meth, to be exact."

"Actually, I remember the name. We ran a story on the lab he helped run. How the hell did he end up in Wolfscratch?"

"That's what we're trying to find out," Joplin said. He told the editor as much as he thought necessary: Bo Danforth's incompetency, the subsequent homicide ruling in Milton County, the stonewalling of any further investigation by the sheriff, and Judge Mabry's order. McAllister reacted by alternately nodding and shaking his head as he listened.

"That's quite a story," he said, when Joplin finished. "And nothing you've said surprises me. The DA and Sheriff Odum pretty much control things in Rutledge County, not to mention the coroner."

"Well, your paper managed to help get a new judge elected despite that, from what I've heard. So, you must have some influence on your readers."

"Yes, but I don't know how long that'll last," McAllister said. "To tell you the truth, I've been tempted to sell the paper in the past year. There's already a damned good regional paper here called *Smoke Signals* that's won all kinds of awards. And I've got a family to consider. I don't mean to sound paranoid, Hollis, but the sheriff and the DA are out to get me. The mayor, too, I think."

"And you think they're bugging your office."

"Yes. I know my cell phone's okay, and I have someone who sweeps my office for bugs regularly, but I don't like to take chances."

"I don't blame you under the circumstances. And I know you're a busy man, so I'll cut to the chase: Do you know anything about a white supremacy group called 'The Cause?'"

McAllister stared at him. "How do you know about them?"

"A deputy named Will Sykes, who also knows what I'm doing up here, told me when I said Eric Jaeger had a Southern Cross medal tattooed on his back. He also told me he knows of at least one deputy connected to them. And maybe the sheriff himself."

The editor took several seconds to process that, then said, "I'm not really surprised, but what proof does he have?"

Joplin repeated what Will Sykes had told him, then said, "The next day, the guy he arrested wasn't in the lock-up, and when Sykes asked about him, he was told the Georgia Bureau of Investigation came and took custody of him. But Sykes felt something was off, and when he tried to pull up the incident report he'd filed, it had been deleted. There was no entry about the GBI taking the case or the arrestee, and the weapons he'd confiscated were gone. When Sykes talked to the deputy who'd helped him search the truck, the man just shook his head and told Sykes he should forget about it. Said it was above their pay grade, and the sheriff was handling it."

They were interrupted by a knock on the door, which quickly opened to reveal a pretty woman with honey-blonde hair and blue eyes. She was wearing a tank top, shorts, and black Nike running shoes.

"Oh," she said when she saw Joplin. "Sorry to interrupt. I didn't know you were meeting with someone, Andy."

Joplin stood up, good Southern boy that he was, and said, "Hollis Joplin, Mrs. McAllister. I sort of barged in on your husband."

"Call me Jenna, please," she said, holding out her hand.

"Hollis is investigating a murder at Wolfscratch," McAllister said, then added, "I don't keep things from my wife, Hollis. Everything that impacts me impacts her. But she knows what 'off the record' means."

"No problem," said Joplin. "My wife and I have the same type of relationship."

"Well, I'll let you two get on with your discussion." She turned to McAllister and said, "I'm off to pick up the kids from swim class, Andy." And with a wave to both of them, she was out the door.

McAllister cleared his throat and said, "What I'm about to tell you also has to be off the record. I'm in no position to write a story about this for the paper, and I don't want my source to be in danger."

"Understood."

"I have a stringer who lives in a pretty isolated part of Rutledge County. He's a Civil War reenactor with the GDRA—the Georgia Division Reenactors Association."

"You're kidding. I didn't realize they were that organized. The reenactors, I mean. I thought it was like a weekend hobby."

"I wish I were kidding," said McAllister. "Membership in these groups has dwindled somewhat, but it's starting to pick up, according to Jesse Waldrup—the stringer I mentioned. He says it *is* just a hobby for him; he started doing it in Tennessee, where he's from. Jesse's sort of a loner, but he said it gave him what little social life he has. Anyway, he's participated in reenactments of the Battle of Resaca and the Battle of Tunnel Hill here in North Georgia for the past few years. Tunnel Hill's coming up again in September, so Jesse's been training on weekends, and he agreed to go on what's called a 'total immersion event' with a group of guys that he says are pretty hardcore. He spent a week with them in the woods in Gordon County, living in tents, wearing only Confederate clothing, and just eating what they could kill or find on the land. He came back pretty shaken up."

"Let me guess," Joplin said. "They invited him to join a militia called The Cause."

McAllister nodded slowly. "Jesse let them think he was interested. Said he'd give it some thought, but he couldn't wait to get out of that place."

"Do you think he'd talk to me?"

"I'll ask him, but I have no idea what he'll say. He only told me about it because he said he might have to quit the paper. Move away."

Joplin cocked his head, his eyes narrowing. "He was that afraid? Did they threaten him in some way?"

"Let's just say he got the impression that he could say no to joining the militia, but if the wrong people got wind of The Cause, they'd know it came from him."

Joplin's mind flashed to Eric Jaeger's body on the autopsy table. Had Jaeger talked to the wrong people? Was that why he'd been murdered? Suddenly, finding a body at the Upper Falls at Wolfscratch took on an even more sinister meaning.

"Tell Waldrup I'll guarantee his safety," he said. "Professionally and personally."

✚ ✚ ✚ ✚

AFTER PICKING UP the security footage from Gary Summers at Wolfscratch's main gate, Joplin called Tullie and filled her in on his conversations with Will Sykes and Andrew McAllister. He'd texted her earlier that a warrant for the footage wouldn't be necessary, but this was his first chance to talk to her. Not surprisingly, Tullie was stunned by the information that the tattoo on Jaeger's back connected him to a white supremacy group with its own militia.

"Shit, Hollis. This is getting worse by the minute," she said after a long pause.

"It still doesn't mean your family is mixed up in it," Joplin told her. "We need to take this one step at a time, Tullie. Let's go through the security footage together this afternoon. Jaeger's face was so ravaged by trees and bottle flies, I'm not sure I'd recognize him. Then, tomorrow, I'll see if McAllister has contacted Jesse Waldrup. And don't forget: Tom and Maggie are on the job, too."

"Yeah," Tullie said glumly. "They might even have the worst part of it."

19.

THIRTY MINUTES LATER, Joplin met Tullie in the parking lot of the Milton County courthouse, where the central office of the county Department of Community Supervision was housed. He grabbed his notebook and the security flash drives when he saw her car.

Tullie parked her dark blue Jeep Cherokee next to his, and they both got out at the same time. She was dressed more casually today in black leggings and a long, lightweight blue sweater over a white tank top. Her hair was pulled up into a high ponytail. The only make-up she seemed to have on was pink lip gloss.

"You look about fifteen today," Joplin said.

"I wish," she said. "I did a boot camp training session this morning and got my ass kicked. The Big 3-0 is not too far away."

"Well, I'll trade you. The Big 4-0 is closer than I want to admit. I'm going to be the oldest first-time father in my kid's kindergarten class."

"You'll do just fine," Tullie said, patting him on the arm.

A security guard let them into the building when Tullie flashed her badge. They rode an elevator to the seventh floor, then she led him to a conference room with a big-screen TV on the far wall. Joplin sat in a chair facing the laptop Tullie had put on the table and opened his notebook while she loaded the flash drive from the North gate at Wolfscratch.

"Only visitors and residents go through the Main gate," she said. "They can use the North gate, too, but contractors, moving vans, and service people *have* to use it, so I thought we'd start there."

"Hopefully, Jaeger will be among the footage," he said. "Do you know what kind of car or truck he had?"

Tullie shook her head. "He told me he bought a used truck so he could work construction, but I don't know the make."

"Well, just keep your eyes peeled. Jaeger could also be a passenger in someone else's vehicle. Including one of the residents or someone who works at Wolfscratch and has a permanent pass."

"Okay, I'll do my best."

Tullie was silent while several contractors and local service trucks passed through the gate closest to the small, rustic building where the security guard was stationed. Each driver stopped to get a pass, which was to be displayed on the front windshield and used to open the gate when they left. When they had all gone through, she ran the tape back, then focused on the other two other gates, which could be opened by transponders on residents' or employees' windshields. When a silver BMW convertible approached it, Tullie smiled and said, "That's Marianne Carlsberg—she started Ladies of the Lake, and my mom is a member."

"Ladies of the Lake?"

"It's one of the clubs at Wolfscratch. They go out on pontoon boats from the Lake Etowah marina and have wine and cheese." Tullie didn't talk for a few minutes as she watched a few more trucks pass through, then pointed at a blue Jaguar and said, "You remember Jack Cunningham, don't you?"

"Oh, yes," Joplin said, nodding. "And his lovely wife, Betsey."

"Right." Tullie watched several more minutes of footage without seeing Eric Jaeger. "Alright, that's it. We've gone through this gate's Thursday afternoon footage."

"I didn't realize how much traffic goes into Wolfscratch," Joplin said. "And this is just the North gate. We haven't even gotten to the Main gate yet."

"Well, it's a big community, Hollis. So big it has its own satellite post office. And there are a lot of visitors, too. People from all over the country rent houses here. This is still peak season because, unlike Georgia, many states' school systems don't start until after Labor Day. And you don't ever want to be here during leaf season. It's ridiculous!"

"Did your parents know that before they built a house in Wolfscratch?"

"Of course. They've been friends with several of the residents over the years. But Wolfscratch has a lot to offer that trumps all that. It's not only a fantastic setting and a wildlife preserve, it also has wonderful amenities, like a wellness center, a beach club, and three golf courses designed by Joe Lee. And it's home to some of the most educated, artistic, and talented people you'd ever want to meet. There are over forty book clubs and clubs for artists, writers, photographers—you name it. Native Americans used to call it 'The Enchanted Land,' and anyone can see why, Hollis."

"Wow!" Joplin said. "Have you thought about signing on as a PR rep for Wolfscratch? Last week, you seemed to think it was more of an overgrown small town with big eyes and ears."

Tullie nodded, looking a little embarrassed. "I know, I know. I guess I haven't really gotten over my parents just up and leaving Fox Run like that. After almost forty years." She sighed and said, "But this isn't about me. Let's get back to the footage."

Thursday evening's tape showed more cars than trucks and vans, but there were still several. Tullie recognized only two residents out of the many who went through the gate within an hour's time. There was also a steady stream of people evidently visiting friends or renting houses for the weekend, because all of them getting visitors' passes.

"We're right about 8 p.m. now," said Tullie. "That's another contractor's truck, and—" She stopped talking and stared at the frame. Finally, she said, "Freeze that, Hollis."

"What is it?"

Tullie focused intently on a man driving a black Ford pickup. He wore a ball cap that covered most of his hair and had angular facial features. Finally, she sat back in her chair and shook her head.

"You know him?" Joplin asked.

"No. I thought it was Eric Jaeger for a minute, but it's not. Looks a lot like him, but...no."

Before they could view any more footage, Joplin's phone rang. "BJ here, Hollis," said the head of the Milton County CSU lab's director.

"It's Saturday, BJ. Don't you ever go home?"

"Home is where the heart is, as they say, Hollis. So, here I am. Do you want to know whose fingerprints are on that Jim Beam bottle you brought me or not? I finally had a chance to get to it."

"Sorry," Joplin said. "Of course I do. And I appreciate you calling me."

"The prints belong to a man named Jacob Gunter. He's in the system for a number of past convictions, mainly for drug possession and a few DUIs."

Joplin sighed and said, "Then I guess the bottle's totally unrelated to the body I found."

"Not necessarily," BJ said. "I'm sending you a copy of his latest mugshot and one of Eric Jaeger's. Hang on."

Two jpegs attached to a text appeared on his phone a few seconds later. Joplin opened both and then showed them to Tullie.

Her mouth opened as she stared at the photos. "The one on the left is Jaeger," she said. "And the other one—"

"—is the man in the black pickup you thought might be Jaeger. And they look almost identical."

Tullie nodded slowly. "So, whose body is at the ME's Office?"

20

CARRIE SAT ON the couch, flicking the fishing pole cat toy back and forth between Quincy and Banshee. It was their favorite game, although it had taken Banshee a while to appreciate it as much as Quincy did. Blaine Reynolds, Banshee's former owner and Hollis' former girlfriend, had evidently not had much time to play with the cat. According to what Hollis had told Carrie, her job as an investigative reporter for the *Atlanta Journal-Constitution* had been demanding, often keeping her out late or out of town altogether.

And then Blaine had been murdered.

The baby kicked suddenly, and Carrie's left hand rose to the top of her rounded belly. Not for the first time, she thought of the baby Blaine had been carrying when she'd died, then the one that would have been Hollis' baby before that. She wondered what kind of mother Blaine would have been. The decision to put her career on hold for the second child weighed in her favor, but it had also led to Blaine's death. Carrie wondered if she could have done the same thing if she'd gotten pregnant during medical school or her residency. As it was, now she was free to take extended maternity leave and then work a shortened schedule for as long as she wanted. And if it were up to her mother, that shortened schedule would become a permanent leave of absence.

Harriet Salinger had always been very supportive of Carrie's medical career. At least, when she'd planned to devote herself to researching pediatric diseases. A plan forged because her younger brother died of Tay-Sachs disease at age five. But everything changed when Carrie began a thirty-day intern rotation at the Milton County ME's Office. Not right away, of course. And not until she'd almost lost Hollis and realized she didn't want to spend the rest of her life in a research lab.

Carrie and her mother had eaten lunch at Seasons 52 earlier in the day, and the subject of What Would Happen After the Baby Was Born was once again brought up. She had listened patiently as her mother went over all the reasons why she should be a stay-at-home mom. Or at least consider working someplace less "dangerous." The patience resulted from her parents' ultimate acceptance of both her decision to switch careers and her choice of Hollis Joplin as a husband. Given that Hollis wasn't Jewish and had also been married before, it had taken a lot of acceptance on their part. There was also that incident where a serial killer had kidnapped and almost killed her.

Carrie was sure her parents loved Hollis, and they knew he would make a wonderful father. Ironically, they were also grateful that he *wasn't* Jewish, at least from a genetic perspective. Although anyone could be a carrier of Tay-Sachs, Jews of Eastern European ancestry, Ashkenazi Jews, had a higher incidence of the chromosomal abnormality—a lack of a specific protein called hexosaminidase A. Carrie and her parents were all carriers. Fortunately, Hollis wasn't, but she'd insisted on genetic testing early in their marriage, even though the probability that he could be was very low.

"You weren't a stay-at-home mom," Carrie had said softly, knowing she was bringing up painful memories.

Harriet had looked down at her plate, as if she might find just the right response mixed in with the grilled salmon on a bed of sauteed zucchini. She seemed tiny compared to Carrie, who'd inherited her height from her father's side of the family. Yet Carrie knew her mother commanded respect and admiration from everyone who knew her.

"Not after David died, no," her mother had said, looking off to her left as if remembering. "I had to reinvent myself."

"You went back to school and got an MBA at Emory. And even Daddy admits you were the force behind making Salinger Furniture what it is today—and franchising it to six other states. So, I thought you understood why I needed to reinvent myself, too, when Hollis almost died."

"I did. I still do. It's just that…children change your priorities. I worked in the Buckhead store before you were born, managing personnel and accounting. But afterward…I don't know. I just didn't want to leave you, even though your Bubbie Ida said she could take care of you. I didn't want to miss anything, you know?"

Carrie had reached out and taken her mother's hand. "I *do* know," she'd said. "And maybe I'll feel the same way, Mom. My plan right now is to take three months off, then work half-days for another three months. Then, I'll take stock and decide what's next. Dr. Minter has told me I can set my own hours for as long as I want. That's not something most women get to do, so I'm pretty lucky."

Her mother had put her free hand over Carrie's and smiled. "You are," she'd said. "Don't think I don't realize that. And I'll help you any way I can. You know that." Then she'd sighed and patted Carrie's hand. "So, now I need to back off and let you figure things out. And respect your decision, whatever it is."

Quincy suddenly leaped onto the couch and stared at her, his blue eyes reproachful. Carrie realized she'd stopped playing fishing pole and stroked his gray-white fur, murmuring apologies. She was about to return to the game when her cell phone rang. It was Hollis.

"I was just thinking about you," she said warmly. "Are you on your way home, I hope?"

"Almost," he said. "I just got a call from BJ Reardon. The fingerprints on the Jim Beam bottle I brought back from Wolfscratch weren't Eric Jaeger's. They belong to a man named Jacob Gunter."

"Well, there was no guarantee the bottle was connected to the body we found, Hollis."

"I know, but the mug shot BJ sent me matches a man in the security footage from Wolfscratch. A man who looks like he could be Jaeger's brother, if not his twin."

"Are you saying the body I autopsied belonged to this man, Gunter, and not Eric Jaeger?"

"Not yet, but it's a real possibility. Did you happen to take prints from that body?"

"Of course. It's standard procedure, even when the body's been positively identified. Which I thought was the case here. The prints are on a card attached to the autopsy file."

"That's good news. Saves me from having to print him myself. But I need to run get them and take them to CSU, so I'll be a little later than I thought. How about I pick up something from the Buckhead Diner on my way home?"

"It's a deal. Especially if you get an order of the Maytag Blue Cheese Chips. They're full of fat and calories, but I've had a terrible craving for them lately. Am I being a bad mother?"

"The baby will love them. See you soon."

Carrie smiled, picked up the fishing pole, and then danced it around the cats. But her smile faded as she thought about the implications of a misidentified body in the morgue. She was sure this wouldn't be the first time something like that had happened, but it was still troubling. If the body didn't belong to Eric Jaeger, how had everyone involved, including Tullie Fitzgerald, failed to realize that? Granted, the facial features had been somewhat distorted by decomposition and tree branches, but when the Southern Cross tattoo was discovered, why hadn't Tullie questioned whether the body was Jaeger's instead of assuming he'd gotten it once he left prison?

And if the body she'd autopsied did belong to Jacob Gunter, where was Eric Jaeger?

✦ ✦ ✦ ✦

JOPLIN AND TULLIE stared down at the body in the cold storage drawer. Since no family member had claimed it, the plan had been for Milton County's indigent burial fund to cough up the money for a simple interment on rural property owned by the county. Fortunately for the county, the paperwork hadn't been completed. Now that the body had been officially identified as Jacob Gunter through the prints Carrie had taken, the

ME's Office would try to locate *his* family members. Hopefully, someone among them would claim his body.

And maybe shed some light on what Gunter was doing in Wolfscratch the previous weekend and how he had Eric Jaeger's wallet on him. Which might also lead to the reason for his murder.

Tullie shook her head and let out a long sigh. "Now that I know this isn't Eric, I can't understand how I thought it was," she said. "I mean, it *looks* like him, but I see a lot of differences, too. The shape of his head and the way his hair is cut. I don't think Eric was this muscular either, although I certainly never saw him with his shirt off."

"You weren't looking for any differences, Tullie," Joplin said. "You were told the body at the Falls was Eric Jaeger's, and that's what you saw. That's what you were meant to see. The question is: Why? Why did the killer want you—and probably a lot more people—to think Jaeger was dead?"

"I can't even begin to answer that," she said. "But if that were the goal of this whole charade, then it has to mean that Eric was a part of it. He *wanted* people—especially me and the Department of Corrections—to think he was dead. It had to have been planned, Hollis. Getting this look-alike into Wolfscratch, planting Eric's wallet on him, and then sending him to the crematory without any real investigation of his death."

"But that means knowing that Bo Danforth would be on call that Friday to guarantee foul play wouldn't be suspected."

Tullie sighed again and nodded slowly. "Too many variables to be workable. Or you have to assume there was some kind of conspiracy that would involve a lot of people."

"Okay, then, let's simplify it. No conspiracy, no group of people. For reasons of his own, Eric Jaeger saw the resemblance between himself and Jacob Gunter and decided to kill him and switch identities. He didn't know Bo Danforth was an idiot, but he figured the picture on his license looked enough like Gunter to fool a county coroner."

"Yes, but how did he lure Gunter to the Upper Falls? And how did he get into Wolfscratch? Or out of it? We didn't see Jaeger on any of the footage we looked at, including the rest of the North and Main gate footage. He might have driven Gunter's truck from the Upper Falls, but we never saw it leave Wolfscratch, with or without Jaeger. So, what the fuck happened to it?"

"All good questions, Tullie, I admit. Which means we have to re-think notifying Gunter's family until we know more. It could very well be that since Gunter had Eric Jaeger's ID on him, Jaeger is now passing himself off as Gunter. I think we need to proceed very carefully. I'll contact Will Sykes and see what he knows about Gunter. And I'll call Gary Summers at Wolfscratch and have him be on the lookout for Gunter's truck."

"Good idea. And I'll need to update Judge Mabry on this newest wrinkle. Since the body isn't Eric Jaeger's, she might not want us to continue the investigation."

"I hadn't thought about that angle," Joplin said. "Was the bench warrant on Jaeger canceled when we thought he was dead?"

"I don't know," Tullie said. "I'll check." She looked down at Jacob Gunter's face and shook her head. "I have a bad feeling about this, Hollis. Eric must have been involved in something big for all this to happen. And it's all on my watch."

"Last time I checked, the recidivism rate for convicted felons was still around forty percent," Joplin said. "Maybe higher for drug dealers. You did your job, and when Jaeger tested positive for cocaine and absconded, you took out a warrant."

"Yeah, I know," she said.

It looked like she wanted to say more, but she didn't. And Joplin was left with the uneasy feeling he'd had at the Hallorans' house the night before that he wasn't getting all the information he should have gotten. Information that Tom Halloran probably already had in his possession by virtue of his relationship with Tullie.

21

THE DRIVE TO Fox Run on Sunday took less than fifteen minutes. Once out of the North gate, they drove two miles, then crossed Highway 136 onto a gravel road that took them past a property with heavy iron gates. The grounds were well-kept, with a picturesque creek that ran the length of what they could see.

"That's the nudist colony I told you about," Moira said. "Or maybe not a colony, just a high-end campground."

"Have you ever been in there?" Halloran asked.

"No, they're pretty strict when it comes to letting in outsiders," Ryan replied as Halloran turned left onto State Road 52 East. He and Maggie thought of it as the "apple road," since it was lined on each side with apple farms.

"You have to be *nominated* by an existing member before you can even apply," Moira said, making air quotes around the word "nominated." Before he could ask what that meant, she switched the subject, intent on filling them in on everything they might ever want to know about Aidan and his lovely bride, Brooke. And some things they might not need—or want—to know.

"She went off the Pill six months ago," Moira said, lowering her voice, Halloran guessed, so no one outside the car could hear her. "But so far, nothing. I mean, *nothing.* Not even a late period. And they're *so* in love and *so* ready to share that love with a child. It's a shame, really. And not just for them. I'm ready to be a *grandmother*, for god sakes! And it's not likely that Tullie will have children any time soon, much less get married."

Once again, Halloran marveled at how Moira Fitzgerald saw everything through her own Moira prism. It was as if nobody else's wants, needs, or opinions mattered. He wondered if she knew how other people—her children, especially—saw her, then immediately discarded the thought. It was obvious that she didn't.

Maggie had gotten her to talk about the United Daughters of the Confederacy at dinner the night before, simply by expressing an interest in the group. Moira had chattered on about many things Halloran already knew from his research. Still, he was struck by her complete devotion to the UDOC and her acceptance of all its beliefs about the Confederacy. Especially the Lost Cause. The only thing new that they'd learned was that a meeting of the local Georgia chapter was coming up in September. When Maggie had asked if she could attend, Moira was thrilled, immediately making plans to include her.

Mercifully, the turn-off to the stables suddenly appeared, and Halloran drove through the wrought-iron gate with the Fox Run name and horse logo embedded in it. Although this was Georgia horse country, with several other stables in the area, Fox Run was head and shoulders above all of them. The imposing main house, looking as if it had been transported from

Berkshire County in England, was set on a hill overlooking the stables and paddocks. A large pond basked in the August sunlight to the left of the house. To its right were open and covered show areas where competitions took place.

"Oh, Ryan, I miss it every time I see it," Moira said, a slight catch in her voice. "But Aidan's done such a wonderful job! Don't you think so, Tom? Isn't it beautiful?"

"It always was," Halloran said. "But I can see some additions. That's a new building next to the big indoor arena, right?"

"Yes, and it's fabulous!" Moira said. "There's a full bar and tables for lunch and tea—he modeled it on the Royal Ascot Racing Club. And with a tent outside, it expands into a wedding venue. It's just genius, if you ask me. That's where we'll be having lunch today. "

"But I didn't bring my top hat," Halloran said.

"And I didn't wear my fascinator," said Maggie.

"Oh, you two!" Moira said indulgently.

✦ ✦ ✦ ✦

AIDAN HAD AGED in the fifteen months since Halloran had seen him. He was still handsome and fit, with broad shoulders like his father's and green eyes like his mother's. But a watchful look was in his eyes now, coupled with a tiredness in his whole demeanor that hadn't been there at his wedding. Though, of course, it wouldn't have been. That had been a happy day for everyone, especially Aidan. He was marrying the love of his life, which he'd said to everyone at the rehearsal dinner, holding his glass up to his almost-bride. And his best friend, he'd added.

After giving Aidan the requisite handshake, hug, and slap on the back, Halloran turned to Brooke. She was lovely as ever, but a little too thin and a little too blonde. White blonde, which was a few shades lighter than at her wedding. But her smile was still sweet, and she didn't have Aidan's watchful look or tiredness.

Not really best friends these days, Halloran thought as he hugged her. *Or she would be carrying part of whatever burden her husband was experiencing.*

Maggie took her turn hugging Aidan, then Brooke. She caught Halloran's eye and gave him a look that told him she saw the same thing he did. He and Maggie, at least, were still best friends.

"Well, I hope y'all are *hungry*!" Brooke said, beaming at them. "'Cause I've been cooking since *yesterday!*"

"We *are*!" Maggie said, matching Brooke's tone.

Halloran prepared himself for an afternoon of Southern charm, rich food, and drawls that always seemed to become more potent with alcohol and family stories. Hopefully, he'd learn more than the people gathered together in this elegant setting meant to reveal.

✚ ✚ ✚ ✚

WINE HAD LOOSENED the tongues of everyone except Aidan Fitzgerald by the time dessert, an enormous coconut cake, was served. Not that he wasn't drinking, Halloran observed. In fact, Aidan ignored his cake and poured another glass of an excellent white Burgundy. But he was either content to listen to the others' chatter or too preoccupied to participate.

Brooke, an accomplished dressage performer, was singing the praises of her latest acquisition, a ten-year-old Hanoverian gelding, interrupted now and then by questions from Moira. Maggie seemed to be listening intently as Ryan, clearly proud of his son, listed upcoming projects at Fox Run. They included a bed-and-breakfast to be built on the premises and the clearing of an acre of land that Aidan had recently bought from a neighboring farm to be used as a sustainable kitchen garden.

"Moira and I would never have thought of doing things on such a grand scale," Ryan said. "We thought Aidan might be biting off more than he could chew when he created all *this*," he added, sweeping his arm to encompass the bar and dining room. "But it's already paid off. Right, son?"

Aidan smiled at his father and nodded. "Big time, Dad."

"Your mother says you and Brooke are taking off for St. Kitts next weekend," said Ryan. "I'd be happy to stop by every day and check on things. Even stay here while you're gone, if that would help," he added, almost wistfully. "It's Labor Day weekend, but we don't have much going on. Not during the day anyway."

Halloran saw Aidan's expression change to alarm, if only for a second, and then it was gone, replaced quickly by another smile. "Dad, I really appreciate that, but it turns out I can't go to St. Kitts. Brooke has her eye on another jumper, and next Saturday is the only day the owner can meet with me. You know how that is; I need to negotiate the price in person. But I wouldn't mind a backup since you won't be too busy. You could play wet blanket, and he might come down a little. You game?"

"You bet I am!" Ryan seemed to sit up a little straighter with this invitation from his son, obviously pleased to be asked for his help. Halloran saw how easily Aidan was able to shape his father's actions and attitude. But Halloran himself wasn't diverted from what seemed to be Aidan's intention: to keep his father from spending time alone at Fox Run and to stipulate a time when it was okay for him to be there.

But why? he wondered. Was it to keep Ryan from snooping, maybe looking at Fox Run's accounting books? Or to ensure he didn't see the people coming to the stables on business with Aidan at other times?

Or both.

It could be, of course, for another reason altogether. But whatever it was, Halloran was certain that Aidan was hiding something. It might have nothing to do with Eric Jaeger or any kind of drug deal he was involved in, especially since Jaeger was dead. But Jaeger's death opened up another, more serious possibility, which Halloran knew must be adding to Tullie's fears.

"What's this I hear about you two not going to St. Kitts?" Moira said, turning to look at Aidan. Her expression was a mixture of concern and displeasure. "You've planned this trip for a while."

Aidan lifted his wine glass and took a long sip before answering her. "Some things came up," he said finally. "Brooke understands, Mom. I need to talk to a man about a horse, as they say." He gave Moira the same quick smile he'd given his father, only more intense. "It's a Dutch Warmblood named Black Jack that she's wanted for a long time. So, she's taking a friend with her to St. Kitts instead. Caroline Hastings."

"Oh," said Moira, sounding mollified, but clearly not pleased. There were grandchildren to be conceived and sooner, rather than later. Halloran realized that that must have been what the Caribbean vacation was all about, at least in Moira's mind. He could almost see her weighing the choices, both dear to her heart: new horseflesh or a child named after her, should it be a girl. "Well, if Brooke is fine with it, then who am I to complain?" she added, her face brightening. "And Caroline is always fun to be around." She turned to Brooke and said, "You're staying at Belle Mont Farm, of course," referring to a luxury resort in the mountainous St. Paul's area. He and Maggie had stayed at the Marriott the one time they'd been there. It was lovely but didn't have quite the cachet Belle Mont Farm did. And Halloran was certain that Brooke, like her mother-in-law, expected cachet. Lots of it.

"Of course," Brooke answered. "And after a week of pampering, I get to come home to Black Jack."

"Well, if the price is right," Aidan said.

"Then I guess I better be here to help make sure it is," said Ryan heartily.

"Couldn't do it without you, Dad."

Halloran was reminded of what Tullie had told them on Friday night about Aidan's "sucking up" to their parents. It certainly wasn't overt, but it was there. He gazed at Aidan, keeping a smile on his face and swirling his Chablis as he looked for any signs of drug abuse.

Halloran's brother, Johnny, had started using cocaine after their father's suicide. He'd been suspended from Boston College, and Halloran had left South Bend to help him pack up and return to Chicago. Johnny had been defiant, insisting that he didn't have a problem, but he'd lost a lot of weight. On the trip back to Chicago, he disappeared into the restroom every time they'd stop for gas, then talked a blue streak about how he would get reinstated at BC. He'd also sniffed and blown his nose repeatedly. Halloran was sure his brother had been using, but his priority had been to get Johnny home and then get him treatment. Any confrontation would only have added another layer of stress for both of them, and he'd been afraid that Johnny would simply bolt from the car at the first opportunity. Later events proved him right on both counts.

Halloran didn't see any similar signs of cocaine use in Aidan, but there were a lot of other drugs he could be using, of course. What he knew about methamphetamine use wasn't much; he'd need to ask Tullie about that. Or Hollis, for that matter. But Aidan wasn't using it unless it manifested in an outwardly laid-back attitude and watchful eyes. There was, however, another tack he could take to see what his connection to Eric Jaeger might be.

"Did your dad tell you about our finding a body at the Upper Falls last weekend?" he asked Aidan.

Halloran saw the wariness in Aidan's eyes intensify, but only momentarily. He shook his head and said, "Are you kidding? It's all anybody's been talking about up here. After Dad called me, I heard about it from two 'concerned families' whose daughters train here. As if a thing like that could present some kind of danger to them." He picked up his glass and finished off the wine, then quickly poured himself another one. A little too quickly, in Halloran's opinion.

"Have you heard that the victim was one of your sister's parolees?" Halloran asked. "Can you believe that?"

"Yeah, small world, isn't it?" Aidan said. "I'm sure that must've hit Tullie hard. I really need to call her."

"She was pretty upset," Halloran agreed. "She stopped by while we were having drinks at your parents' house last Saturday. When they ran the man's name, a deputy friend of hers called and found an outstanding parole violation warrant issued by a Milton County judge." He paused, then said, "His name was Eric Jaeger."

Aidan showed no reaction to the name, either because he was more prepared or because he didn't recognize it. Maybe Jaeger had used another name in whatever dealings he had with Aidan. At any rate, Halloran didn't think he should push the conversation further. He took one last sip of his wine, then set the glass firmly on the table and said, "I need to stretch my legs. How about a tour of the stables?"

✦ ✦ ✦ ✦

THE STABLES WERE anything but utilitarian, like everything else about Fox Run. Halloran counted twenty stalls under a vaulted, raftered ceiling, each made of rich wood with polished brass fittings. Closer inspection revealed nameplates for each animal that announced that horses of distinction, such as Bailey's Bailiwick, Atherton's Rival, and Suleiman II, were housed there. On the shiny concrete floors, sturdy but elegant benches sat in wait for owners or riders to meet with trainers to discuss progress and strategies.

In five of the stalls, horses greeted them with bright eyes and inquisitive whinnies. Ryan and Moira hurried over to them, calling them by name as they stroked glossy manes.

"Come and meet Cupid's Quiver, Tom and Maggie," Moira ordered. "Isn't he a beauty?" she added, clearly delighted with the chestnut stallion.

Halloran tried to say the right things. Growing up in a Chicago suburb hadn't given him much access to horses.

Maggie, at least, had enjoyed riding at Fox Run as a child and young teenager. She oohed and aahed in a manner enthusiastic enough to satisfy Moira, then did it again when Ryan insisted she meet Gulliver's Traveler, an enormous roan-colored horse at least a foot taller than his neighbor.

A young girl in her mid-teens, with long legs encased in jodhpurs and polished riding boots, suddenly burst into the stable, a scowl on her face. She seemed surprised at seeing them, as if they were somehow intruders on her private territory.

"What's going on, Madison?" Aidan said quickly, moving toward her. "Is there some problem?"

"Yeah," she said. "It's that shit trainer you hired. I won't work with him anymore."

"What happened?"

She brushed some strawberry-blonde hair off her forehead and shook her head, as if she still couldn't believe what the trainer had done. "He told me my half-pass technique needed some work. That I wasn't holding the outer rein correctly. That's a bunch of *crap*, Aidan!"

Aidan put his arm around the girl, nodding as he said, "Don't worry about it, Maddie. I'll talk to him."

"You better," she said, but the scowl had left her face.

Halloran glanced at Moira and Brooke to see what their reaction was. Moira was smiling, but Brooke's eyes had narrowed and were fastened on the teenager. He wasn't sure whether it was because of Maddie's proprietary manner toward Aidan or Aidan's arm around her. Or maybe both. But Brooke's reaction might explain the apparent distance in their marriage and her complacency over her husband's absence on the trip to St. Kitts.

"Why don't we go check out the arena," Ryan said, with a quick look at Aidan. "Tell your parents I said hello, Madison."

But Madison didn't answer him; she was busy supplying Aidan with a list of other things wrong with the trainer. Without even knowing him, Halloran hoped the man had other talents that might save his job. Working with spoiled, entitled teenagers apparently wasn't one of them.

22

JOPLIN HAD THE day shift on Sunday. He'd called Gary the night before, requesting him to put a BOLO on Jacob Gunter's truck. But as soon as he got to his cubicle, he said hello to Val, then contacted Will Sykes, leaving a message about Jacob Gunter and asking him to call. He also contacted Andrew McAllister, who was surprised by the news and disturbed by what it could mean.

"I knew Jacob Gunter," he said. "He did some work on my house before I fired him for drinking on the job. And I'm sure Bo Danforth would have recognized him, even though he probably wouldn't have recognized Eric Jaeger. This doesn't make sense."

"Well, Bo never got that close to the body," Joplin said. "He didn't want to get his feet wet."

"That still leaves the fact that people were supposed to believe that Jaeger was dead. So, where is he? And," McAllister added, "did he kill Jacob Gunter?"

"Good questions. I'll let you know if I find out."

When he hung up, the phone rang immediately; a uniformed cop requested his presence at an apparent suicide scene in Buckhead. Grabbing his black bag, Joplin told Val where he was going, then left the Investigative Unit, walking past the empty reception area. Sundays at the ME's Office always seemed a little forlorn to Joplin. *Only a skeleton crew,* he thought to himself, smiling at the unintended pun. But it was true. A lone morgue attendant was downstairs and a pathologist was on call, but it still seemed too quiet. Especially without Sherika.

The address Joplin had been given was on Lenox Road, where condominiums—mostly townhouses, but a smattering of high-rises—lined the street. He drove past the complex where Carrie had lived before they were married—and where she'd been abducted by a serial killer—then turned into a narrow street lined on each side by brick townhouses. A police car was directly in front of the sixth unit on the left, its lights still flashing. An unmarked sedan with a portable red light on its dashboard was next to it. Joplin parked beside it and got out. A small crowd had gathered opposite the unit. He saw a blur of faces with pinched, worried expressions and arms crossed protectively.

A uniform stood at the entrance to the victim's townhouse, but ushered Joplin in and told him the body was in the master bedroom on the second floor. Ike Simmons was waiting for him at the top of the stairs. Joplin had a sudden flashback to the Libba Woodridge crime scene three years earlier; he and Ike had looked at each other from the same perspective on another staircase. He fervently hoped he wouldn't see as much blood at this scene.

"How was your Saturday in North Georgia?" Simmons asked. He wore his usual jacket and tie, but the tie was loosened because of the heat, "Find any more bodies?"

"I guess word gets around, huh?" Joplin replied. He and Ike had been partners for seven years in the Homicide Unit before Joplin joined the ME's Office. Someone in the Crime Scene Unit must have told him about the liquor bottle Joplin had brought in.

"Actually, I called Carrie today about a trial comin' up where she's testifying, and she filled me in on your weekend at Wolfscratch and your trip up north yesterday. I guess if you have to find a body on your day off, that's not a bad place to be. She said the victim was one of Tullie Fitzgerald's parolees."

"Yeah, well, the body in question turned out to be someone else," Joplin said, hoping Ike wouldn't follow up on that. He didn't feel like discussing the situation, even with his old partner.

"I was thinkin' of takin' Alfrieda and the kids up there during leaf season," said Ike, maybe picking up on Joplin's reticence on the subject.

"I think that's a great idea, Ike. And the kids would love it. When you get tired of leaf-watching and apple-picking, you can rent a pontoon boat on Lake Etowah."

"Sounds good. You've talked me into it."

"So, what do we have here?" Joplin asked, nodding toward the back of the townhouse.

"Kathryn Hampshire, aged fifty-two. She was supposed to meet her daughter for brunch today, but when she didn't show up or answer her phone, the daughter came here to check on her. Found her in bed with a plastic bag on her head and some open pill bottles on the night table. Ambien and Tramadol. Daughter said she'd been depressed lately over a pendin' divorce from her second husband and was seein' a therapist, but she just can't believe her mother would kill herself."

"She leave a note?"

"If she did, it's not here now," Ike said, referring to the fact that family members often disposed of suicide notes before the police were called. Suicide still had a stigma attached to it, even in 2016. "And the daughter—Margaret Keating is her name—pulled the plastic bag off her mother, thinking she might still be alive. She also tried CPR before calling 911."

"Well, that's understandable, even though the scene's been messed with. She still here?"

"Just left a few minutes ago. Husband picked her up. She was in pretty bad shape."

Joplin nodded, then looked past Ike Simmons to the stairs leading to the second floor. "I'll get started then."

"I'm gonna hang around for a bit. Talk to some of the neighbors outside. Just to be on the safe side."

"Good idea," Joplin said as he headed for the stairs.

✚ ✚ ✚ ✚

KATHRYN HAMPSHIRE'S BODY lay propped up by two pillows on a queen-sized bed in a spacious master bedroom. Her arms lay on top of the coverlet, and her head drooped to one side. Her face was cyanotic; her eyes closed. She was wearing a sleeveless, white cotton nightgown. The room was tastefully furnished in muted pastels of green and cream, with similarly muted prints of landscapes on the walls. As evidenced by the neatly stacked books on the bedside table, which also accommodated a Chinese lamp, reading glasses, and two open pill bottles, Kathryn had been a reader. A copy of *The Nightingale* was splayed face-down on the coverlet. Joplin wondered if she had been reading it before taking the pills and then tying the plastic bag over her head. As Simmons had told him, the bag had been pulled off and now lay next to the book.

Joplin took several photos of the scene, then gloved up and placed the plastic bag in a paper one to preserve any fingerprints. He also bagged the hands, then gently lifted each eyelid. Next, he checked for lividity and rigor mortis. Both were advanced. Although the woman's back and upper arms were only faintly mottled, her forearms, buttocks, and legs were purple. He had to break the rigor first to see this, as it had extended the length of her body. Joplin then pulled up the nightgown, made a small slit in the area of her liver, and inserted a thermometer. He'd already checked the room's ambient temperature by reading the upstairs' air conditioning monitor in the hall outside the bedroom.

After packing everything into his bag, Joplin took one more look at Kathryn Hampshire's body and headed back downstairs. Ike Simmons was waiting for him in the entry hall.

"You see any problems?" he asked, eyebrows lifted.

"I'd hang on to this one a little longer, Ike. Maybe bring the estranged husband in for questioning. Although it can happen, the facial cyanosis doesn't seem to fit suffocation by a plastic bag. And there are more ocular petechiae than I expected to see. Let's see what the autopsy turns up, okay?"

Simmons shrugged. "Fine with me. I think the daughter would push for that anyway. Let me know when the post is, and I'll be there."

"Will do."

Joplin's phone rang as he was putting on his seat belt. Jesse Waldrup, sounding reluctant, agreed to meet him in the parking lot of a Chick-fil-A off Exit 19 on I-575 in Canton. After describing his truck and getting a description of Joplin's car, he clicked off without saying goodbye. Evidently, Waldrup was still pretty spooked, Joplin decided, as he checked the time on his cell. It was almost one o'clock.

A box of chicken nuggets and waffle fries would hit the spot.

✠ ✠ ✠ ✠

JESSE WALDRUP WAS a medium-height, wiry-looking man in his late twenties with short-cropped sandy hair. He slipped out of his gray Ford pickup and slid into the passenger seat of Joplin's car after a quick look around.

"Thanks for meeting me," Joplin said.

"I don't want to be doing this," Waldrup said. "But Andy thinks it might be important. And he's been good to me in a lot of ways. I barely finished high school and had a bunch of dead-end jobs. Then I moved down here and hired on to the paper. I was just hauling newspapers around to stores and drop-off points for the delivery guys for him at first. Then, I started reading them and asking him how he got the stories. So, he gave me a few assignments, sending me to talk to people who might have stories for him. That's how I became a stringer," he added, sounding like he still couldn't believe in his good luck. "It's a real job. I get to interview people, find out their stories, and see if something would make a good article. I mean, I owe him. It's also why I thought I had to tell him what happened. Why I might need to disappear."

"I can understand that. And I don't want to put you in any danger. I can provide protection, like I told McAllister. This is about a murder investigation. Did he tell you?"

"Yeah, he did. And right now, I think I'm okay, but you've got to keep me out of it. You can't tell people about the camp they took me to or about The Cause. They'll know it came from me."

"I'll be very discreet. But is there someplace out of town you can stay for a week or two?"

Waldrup glanced sideways, then said, "I have a sister in Nashville. I can give her a call, go visit her. She's always asking me to come up, and it's been a while."

"Good idea. Now tell me what happened at that camp in the woods."

✚ ✚ ✚ ✚

IT WAS A harrowing story about days spent drilling with weapons Waldrup had never encountered in any Civil War reenactment, subsisting on little food and a lot of whiskey. He was exhausted every day and given little time to rest or ask any questions, something straight out of a cult induction playbook, in Joplin's opinion. Instead of stories about past reenactments, talk around the campfire focused on how to "take back the South" and start a "new" Civil War that would redeem the Lost Cause and the Confederacy. Phrases like "white extinction" and "the great replacement" were frequently used, and both Catholics and Jews were cited as groups fostering the ideas behind them. Waldrup repeatedly heard that Catholics, in particular, were responsible for the high birth rates among minorities as a way to expand their own religious and financial power in America.

"I was startin' to believe them at first," he said, shaking his head slowly and looking off to his left, as if he were hearing the words again. "Tell you the truth, I've only known a few Catholics in my life, and I've never even met a Jew. So, I figured maybe these guys were right about them. I mean, what do I know? But the trash talk got worse, and they started saying we needed to *do* something. To put the Blacks back in their rightful place, instead of letting them take our jobs or get all that welfare money when they wouldn't even work." Waldrup was silent for a moment, then said, "They talked about the Klan. Said it had done a lot of good in its day, and we could, too. But we wouldn't wear sheets over our heads and hide. We'd identify ourselves as patriots. *Real* patriots, who weren't afraid to stand up for what was right and take our country back."

"And how are they going to do that?" Joplin asked, not wanting to hear the answer.

"By killing people," Waldrup said, turning to look at him. "They talked about 'tactical warfare' and 'engaging the enemy on his turf'—going to peace rallies and protests and pushing back, what they called 'having a presence.' They want people to be afraid. But I knew that all those guns weren't just for show. They looked like military-grade weapons to me. Something made to kill a lot of people, you know? And they won't be happy until they use them."

✛ ✛ ✛ ✛

TULLIE CALLED AS Joplin was pulling into the ME's parking lot.

"Jacob Gunter had two misdemeanor DUI convictions, one for marijuana, but no felony arrests or convictions," she told him, "and no outstanding warrants. Judge Mabry reinstated the warrant for Jaeger, and we can try to track him down. But anything more than that would be on shaky legal ground. Jacob Gunter wasn't my parolee, so the judge has no jurisdiction over him."

"Which means we have to turn the body and the case back over to Rutledge County," Joplin said, unhappy with the turn of events. He hadn't wanted to take on the investigation, but was too far into it to let it go. Especially after talking to Jesse Waldrup.

"Yes, but I don't see how the sheriff—his name is Odum—and the DA can blow off Gunter's death, now that it's been ruled a homicide and Eric Jaeger's identification was planted on him. They'll *have* to open an investigation."

"Unless they're mixed up in it." Joplin told Tullie about his meeting with Waldrup and the chilling description of his week with The Cause militia.

"Jesus, Hollis, you're scaring the shit out of me."

"Join the club. Waldrup thinks these wackos have something in the works. Something that will involve using all the weapons they've stockpiled."

"Which brings me to Judge Mabry's next directive," Tullie said after several seconds of silence. "I updated her on what you learned from Will Sykes and the newspaper editor about the white supremacy group. She wants us to turn over everything we've discovered to the GBI. Immediately. And when I tell her about this, she'll want it done even sooner. She says this is way beyond the scope of a murder investigation."

Joplin sighed. "Well, I can't say I disagree with her. This is above my pay grade, for sure. But she'll have to request their help. I'm not on the list of people who can do that," he added, referring to the fact that only officials like sheriffs, police chiefs, DAs, Superior Court judges, and the Governor could enlist aid from the GBI. "They'll most likely want Homeland Security and the ATF involved, too."

"I'll call her right now," Tullie said.

"Wait," Joplin said. "Are you gonna tell me about your brother? What did Tom and Maggie find out this weekend? And did you tell them the real identity of the body we found?"

There was a long silence before Tullie said, "I did tell them about Jacob Gunter, and they were just as shocked as you and I were. As for Aidan, they didn't uncover anything incriminating. Just…troubling. Like, Aidan isn't going on a planned vacation with his wife next weekend. Says he's got to stick around to buy some horse Brooke wants. Tom said Brooke seemed okay with that, but she got slightly bent out of shape over a teenage rider who was too clingy with Aidan. And Aidan seemed to be on what Tom called 'high alert' during the time they spent there."

Joplin let out a breath. "Well, I can see what you mean by 'nothing really incriminating,' Tullie, but Tom's a sharp observer, and some red flags evidently went up for him. I also don't think either of you is telling me what got you so worried that your brother and Jaeger might be up to no good." When Tullie started to protest, Joplin said, "It's not me you need to convince. The GBI will want to talk to me ASAP, but you'll be in their sights, too. And your chief, if you talked to him like you said you would. They need to find Jaeger, and, officially, you know more about him than anyone. I imagine they'll also contact the prison to see who Jaeger was chummy with during his incarceration. My advice is to tell them everything you know. Let them sort it out. This situation is bigger than your relationship with your brother, Tullie. Or your mother.

One person is already dead, and if what Jesse Waldrup told me is true—and I think it is—there might be a lot more deaths."

"Got it," Tullie said, her voice tight.

✚ ✚ ✚ ✚

DESPITE JOPLIN'S CONCESSION to Judge Mabry's orders, his subconscious couldn't let go of the case. That night, his dreams were filled with scattered images from the Upper Falls in Wolfscratch, the camp that Waldrup had described, and the trip to the crematorium to collect what he thought was Eric Jaeger's body. But the final set of images belonged to a country road near the old Tri-State Crematory owned by the Marsh family. And to an old woman who had said something he didn't understand when she'd asked him if he'd seen a lot of dead people in his job.

"But do they stay dead?" she'd responded when he told her his job involved seeing dead people every day.

Just before dawn, Joplin woke up, trying to remember something he'd thought was important in his dream. It was just the germ of an idea and didn't seem to have any connection to The Cause or Eric Jaeger's disappearance. But as Joplin tried to empty his mind and get back to sleep, more images filled the void, urging him to arrange them in some kind of visual order, like an enormous jigsaw puzzle.

He finally gave up all hope of sleeping and went to the kitchen to make coffee. Quincy and Banshee leaped softly off the bed to keep him company. And maybe score an early breakfast.

His cell phone rang at precisely seven a.m., with a request from Assistant Special Agent in Charge Kevin Masterson that he be at the Georgia Bureau of Investigation regional office in Cleveland, Georgia by nine a.m. The ASAC added that this request was in response to a call received by Director Winslow from Judge Laura Mabry. He also requested that Joplin bring any paperwork or materials related to his investigation of Eric Jaeger, including, but not limited to, the autopsy report on Jacob Gunter, his notes about interviews with Rutledge County Sheriff's Deputy Will Sykes, Andrew McAllister, and Jesse Waldrup, and the security tapes from Wolfscratch.

Joplin wasn't fooled by the word "request."

23

JOPLIN SHOWERED AND dressed in fifteen minutes, then made Carrie some Earl Grey tea. She was already sitting up in bed when he returned to their bedroom and smiled as he handed her the mug.

"Since it's your day off, I assume you've heard from the GBI," she said.

"Yeah, they didn't waste any time. Makes me think they might have heard some rumors about The Cause before now." He leaned down and gave her a lingering kiss. "I need to be at the regional headquarters in Cleveland by nine, and I have to stop by the office to get a copy of Gunter's autopsy report, so I better get going, but I'll call you when I'm on my way home."

"I'd appreciate that. And please tell the SAC up there that if there are any questions about the autopsy, I'll be happy to answer them. My first autopsy isn't scheduled until one this afternoon because of the case detective's schedule."

"I will," said Joplin. "Take care of our baby today." He kissed the top of her head for good measure and headed out of the bedroom.

"Always," he heard her say as he headed to the kitchen.

✦ ✦ ✦ ✦

JOPLIN REACHED THE GBI regional office on Cobb Vantress Drive with five minutes to spare, but that was because he'd used his portable red light after he exited 400. It was an unpretentious red brick and gray siding building. An empty flagpole rose from a grassy island in the parking lot. ASAC Kevin Masterson greeted him as he went through the door, a bureaucratic smile on his face. He was about six feet, with a rangy build, brown hair cut short, and gray eyes that looked predatory.

Or maybe he just missed breakfast, Joplin thought, but he kept that to himself and transferred one of the messenger bags he was carrying to his left arm as he shook the man's proffered hand.

"We're all in the conference room," Masterson said, turning abruptly toward a hall behind him.

Joplin followed, wondering who Masterson meant by "all" and sensing that he was being told he was somehow late to the party. Which once more confirmed his belief that joining the Feds or the GBI would have been a poor fit for him. Joplin preferred the relative autonomy that working in the Homicide Unit or at the ME's Office had given him. They were paramilitary enough for him.

Thank you, Jesus! he thought, then thought it again as Masterson opened the door into a large conference room holding about twenty people around the equally large table. Masterson ushered him to the seat in front of him at the end of the long table. It was closest to the door, which was its only advantage, as it enabled all eyes to be on him from all sides of the room.

Joplin listened carefully as Masterson introduced the people at the table, taking in all the "Special Agent" designations before their names from the GBI and the ATF, then the Homeland Security Investigators. Last to be introduced was Masterson's boss, SAC George Pendleton, an older man with almost white hair and alert blue eyes. He seemed to take himself less seriously than Masterson and, therefore, looked more commanding to Joplin.

"Thank you for coming here today," Pendleton said, nodding to Joplin. "And on such short notice. I've known Judge Mabry for almost twenty years, and when she tells me something concerns her, I listen. So, after she told me what you've managed to uncover, I was concerned, too." He lifted his arm and gestured to the rest of the room. "They are, too. I'd like you to take us through everything that happened and everything you saw and heard, if you would. Use whatever notes and materials you have with you. I want to hear it in your own words first. And then we'll probably have some questions for you. Is that alright with you?"

"It is, sir, thank you," Joplin said, then started from the very beginning with the weekend trip to Wolfscratch.

✦ ✦ ✦ ✦

CARRIE WENT FOR a long walk before the morning began to heat up. In the past, she would have gone to work at the usual time, even though her first autopsy wasn't scheduled till one that afternoon. But the pregnancy had changed her. Now, it seemed more important to keep up her walking schedule and everything that went with it as she prepared for this new life to come into her world. And walking this route was one of the things that would continue after the baby came. Carrie would make sure of it, pushing her little girl in the stroller her mother had recently bought. They would go up to the old graveyard and linger awhile, just as she did now.

An hour later, Carrie had showered and put on a floral sundress to run errands before heading to the ME's Office. The dress was smocked, making her look bigger than usual. Or maybe she *was* bigger. Obstetrics wasn't her field, so she'd needed to read up on the various stages of pregnancy and the impact on both mother and child. Medical books simply didn't do that. Carrie's current favorite was *The Only Pregnancy Book You'll Ever Need*. It had warned her that weight gain took a big jump between the fifth and sixth months as the fetus' growth sped up. Maybe that was why she'd been hungrier than usual. And *eaten* more than usual lately.

But all of it—weight gain, no alcohol, and constant heartburn—was worth it, even though Carrie knew she complained too much to Hollis. But he seemed to handle it okay. He gave her back rubs when she was tired and told her she was beautiful when she worried about gaining weight. He also talked to the baby, telling her she had a crazy mother who worried too much and didn't seem to know how gorgeous she was. Then, Hollis would put an ear to her belly and insist that the baby responded to him, telling him that she'd decided to kick Mommy whenever she complained.

Carrie took a deep breath as she parked in front of the Baby Bundle shop on Peachtree in Buckhead. The invitations to her first baby shower had been sent the week before, and she still hadn't registered there. Or at Macy's and Bloomingdale's, either. She wished she could ignore the whole process; registering for gifts seemed so tacky, no matter how "convenient" people told her it was for the guests. It just seemed so transactional: Baby gifts in exchange for a lovely lunch at a lovely restaurant. Like the bridal showers and the wedding reception her friends and family planned when she and Hollis married. Hollis had taken it all in stride; he'd been married before.

Slowly, she let the breath out. *Just think about the baby,* Carrie told herself. That was all that mattered. She was having a healthy baby with a husband who loved her and whom she loved dearly. She also had supportive parents and co-workers who were willing to help her in any way.

And a group of friends who needed her to register at three different stores so the baby shower they were giving her would be a success.

Carrie took another deep breath and hurried into the Baby Bundle.

✚ ✚ ✚ ✚

HOLLIS CALLED HER just after she'd left Bloomingdale's and gotten back in her car. It was 12:30 p.m., but he sounded exhausted, like he'd run a half-marathon in muggy heat.

"I'll tell you what went on when I see you tonight," he said. "Right now, I just want to get on the road and get home. But

I need to ask if it would be okay to invite the Hallorans and Tullie Fitzgerald over tomorrow night to discuss everything that's happened. You don't have to do a thing, Carrie. I'll get some pizzas or Chinese food or something."

Carrie smiled and shook her head. As if she would ever have the Hallorans or Tullie Fitzgerald—maybe *especially* Tullie—over for a meal without cooking it herself. To Hollis, however, she said, "That's fine. Just get home and relax a bit. We'll talk about it later."

"Thanks, sweetie," he said, sounding relieved. "See you when you get home."

24

JOPLIN KNEW THAT meeting at their house wouldn't prevent Tullie and the Hallorans from keeping him out of the loop on certain things—he was convinced there was more going on with Aidan Fitzgerald than he'd been told—but at least he and Carrie wouldn't be late to the party this time.

Besides, two could play that game, he decided as he opened the front door.

Carrie had found a white lasagna in the freezer she'd made a month ago and had announced earlier she was serving that instead of take-out. Maggie was carrying a salad she'd insisted on bringing. Tullie brought two bottles of red wine. Since it was a weeknight, they settled in at the dining room table, foregoing appetizers and small talk.

"Wonderful house," Tullie said, raising her glass as the salad was passed around.

"Carrie was the decorator," Joplin said.

"I figured," said Tullie. "I went to your house on Mathiesen for a Christmas party a while back. The décor was distinctly *apres divorce*, as I recall."

"His Naugahyde period," said Carrie, smiling. "I remember it well."

"Does anyone want to hear about my meeting at the GBI's regional office in Cleveland?" Joplin asked, hoping to get control of the conversation.

"I do," said Maggie, and Joplin blessed her for that.

"Luckily, I had the day off because I spent most of it there and traveling up and back. It was a full-court press—Special Agents from the GBI, the ATF, and even an investigator with Homeland Security. Turned out they'd gotten wind of The Cause from a few sources, but hadn't been called in to investigate by an appropriate entity until Judge Mabry contacted them, so they were all over me like—"

"—ticks on a sleeping dog," Tullie finished.

"On the way over here, Tullie told us a little about The Cause and Judge Mabry insisting that you turn everything over to the GBI," Tom said, "but there wasn't time to fill us in."

Especially if you were filling her in on whatever you'd found out about Aidan that she didn't tell me, Joplin thought. But he smiled and said, "Then, I'll be happy to do that."

His retelling lasted through the salad and the lasagna, with no breaks for questions since Joplin held up a hand every time someone started to ask one. When he finished, everyone except Tullie gave him open-mouthed stares. Even Carrie, since he hadn't gone into as much scary detail when he'd talked to her about his meetings with Will Sykes, Andrew McAllister, and Jesse Waldrup.

"Well," Maggie said after several seconds of silence, "I don't know if Margaret Mitchell would be turning over in her grave about this, but she might be a little surprised."

"And maybe thrilled to pieces," Tullie said, "given what the United Daughters of the Confederacy have been able to accomplish since the Civil War. And now they've got a presidential candidate who might support them."

"You said the various agents at this meeting had heard about The Cause?" Tom asked. "I'm sure they didn't reveal any of their sources, but did you get a sense of where the information came from or what type of source?"

Joplin shook his head. "Not really. The source—or sources—might have been anonymous. People alarmed enough to contact law enforcement, but too scared to come out in the open."

"I guess I can understand that," Tullie said.

Tom looked at her sharply, but didn't say anything.

"But I also think they know more than they're telling me," Joplin said. "And they're very concerned. The Homeland Security agent brought up the arrest and conviction in 2011 in Gainesville, Georgia of four men—members of the Georgia chapter of the Three Percenters militia group—who plotted to kill several high-up government employees, politicians, business people, and media members, using guns and ricin. The men—all in their sixties and seventies, by the way—evidently had the connections to do it, and traces of ricin were found on a beaker in one member's home. I remember seeing the story on the news that week, and the reporter said that Federal investigators had infiltrated the group and had them under surveillance for about seven months."

"I remember reading about that, too," Tom said.

"So do I," said Tullie. "Did you ask if they'd been able to infiltrate The Cause?"

Joplin nodded. "Yeah, but Pendleton said they couldn't discuss that and moved the discussion on to something else. So, I think the group I met yesterday has been investigating—and maybe already infiltrated—The Cause, which is a big relief. I also think the ATF has been closely monitoring sales of military-grade weapons and ammo, probably focusing on Daniel Defense."

"Is that a person?" Maggie asked.

"Yes and no. Marty Daniel is the founder and CEO of the company, which is in Savannah. It's been around since 2000, becoming one of the biggest private gun manufacturers in the U.S. It sells to individuals and government agencies. Even foreign governments. It's also no surprise that it's a big Republican Party supporter—financially and vocally. Guess who the company endorsed '100%' for the Republican presidential nominee because of his stance on gun ownership?"

"Dare I say Donald Trump?" Carrie said.

"You got it. If he's elected, their profile will get even bigger. And, like Trump, it loves social media. When the NFL rejected an ad they submitted for the 2014 Super Bowl because of its regulations against promoting 'firearms, ammunition or other weapons,' Daniel Defense put it on its website, with a blurb that it was 'the greatest Super Bowl ad that never was.'"

Nobody said anything for several seconds, then Maggie and Tullie started clearing plates off the table. When Carrie attempted to help, they both glared at her. Joplin got up to bring out the dessert, but they glared at him, too. He poured himself another glass of red wine and offered the bottle to Halloran.

"I've got court in the morning," Tom said, taking the bottle, "but, damn, this conversation is pretty scary, Hollis."

"Alcohol is our friend during times like this, Tom. You're Irish. Didn't you get the memo?"

Tom sighed. "Yes, but I saw what it did to my father and a lot of other relatives, so I've tried to stay in the 'moderate drinker' range."

"So have I, for the same reason, but with less success. What's your secret?"

"Sheer terror," said Tom. "And Maggie. She has an equal number of relatives who've been victims of that particular disease."

"Good thing Tullie can hold her liquor, then."

Tom raised his glass in salute. "You bet. And God help anyone who tells her differently."

✦ ✦ ✦ ✦

THE WOMEN RETURNED to the dining room bearing lemon squares that Joplin knew hadn't been in the freezer. He was pretty sure the lasagna hadn't been in there either, but had wisely refrained from saying anything when Carrie had popped it into the oven earlier. Pregnancy had made her lovelier than ever, but it had also increased her need to do everything her way. *Happy wife, happy life,* he thought as Maggie passed the dessert around the table. Besides, he and Carrie were simply anal about different things. He needed to dot every i and cross every t about his cases; she was the same way about her autopsies. And food. And anything to do with their baby. So, who was he to complain about any of those things? Especially the food, because it was always outstanding.

"So, has the GBI contacted *you*, Tullie?" Joplin asked after demolishing his lemon square in two bites. Damn, they were good! He might need to have another, just to make Carrie feel good.

Tullie put down her fork and focused on him. "I just knew you were going to ask me that, Hollis. And, yes, they have. I'm not getting the full-court press like you, though. Prez and I are meeting with the Deputy SAC in his office tomorrow morning at nine sharp."

"Prez?" asked Maggie.

Tullie sighed. "It's a long story. The short version is that he has a passing resemblance to Barack Obama. Anyway, I've been gathering all my paperwork on Eric Jaeger and trying to figure out what questions he might have."

"One he might not know to ask is whether your brother has any connection to Jaeger," Joplin said pointedly.

"I know, I know," she responded, ducking her head. "And I'm gonna come clean. I already have with my chief."

"And how about me?" Joplin asked.

Tullie's chin came up, and her eyes glittered briefly, but she nodded and said, "You, too, Hollis. And Carrie," she added. "Right now."

Joplin listened as she talked about not only seeing Jaeger and her brother in Aidan's truck, but also seeing Jaeger count out money and give it to him. Then she described the heated exchange that seemed to be taking place between them and her fears that the transaction might have involved some kind of drug deal. Or something even worse, now that the body at

Wolfscratch had been identified as Jacob Gunter, and Jaeger was in the wind.

"I'm assuming Tom and Maggie knew all that, right?" he said, when she was finished and was satisfied to see them all look a little crestfallen.

"I take all the blame," Tullie said quickly, but Joplin held up a hand.

"Family is family," he said. "I understand that, believe me. But if you—or Tom," he added, looking directly at his some-time partner, "ever keep me out of the loop on something again, forget asking for my help."

No one said anything for several seconds, then Maggie raised her hand. "Does that include me, Hollis?"

Joplin was momentarily taken aback. "Well," he said, "I don't know. Probably not," he added, thinking of all the times she'd helped him over the past two years.

"Definitely not," Carrie said, looking at him as if he'd lost his mind. "Maggie is our friend, Hollis. And friends always help friends."

Joplin stared at her. "Yes, but they should trust *their* friends, Carrie, right?"

She blinked and patted her stomach. "Yes, and I think they will from now on."

Joplin stared at them for several seconds, then said, "Okay, then. Let's move on."

25

I CALLED CENTRAL STATE Prison, where Eric served his sentence," Tullie said, "and got some information from the Deputy Warden about his time there. His buddies in his cell pod, visitors, phone calls, letters. Things like that. They'd already sent me a conduct report on Eric before his release, which was good and the basis of his early parole. But Ted Lafferty, the Deputy Warden, pulled his file so he could give me a little more."

"What visitors?" Joplin asked.

"Just his lawyer a few times after his conviction. I guess to discuss an appeal, but that never happened. And his Aunt Sally once a month until she died in 2014. Those two were the only ones to send him letters. No girlfriends or male friends or any other relatives."

"Was he a member of any gang, say, a white supremacy gang?" Tom asked. "I mean, wasn't he in there for several years?"

"Over seven of a fifteen-year sentence," Tullie responded. "So, yes, I specifically asked Lafferty about that. He said the COs—

the correctional officers—wrote up that Eric was approached by members of the Ghostface Gangsters, a white supremacy group originating in Georgia that focuses on cocaine and methamphetamine distribution on the outside. According to Lafferty, they try to recruit members soon after they're incarcerated, but he said the COs told him Eric steered clear of them. "

"But wasn't Jaeger convicted of distributing meth?" Joplin asked.

Tullie shrugged. "Yeah, he was. But, except for a few people on his cell block, he was pretty much a loner at Central. He joined a 12-step group, used the gym on a daily basis, and took some classes in carpentry and building maintenance. That's basically the profile of an inmate trying to keep his nose clean and make early parole."

"So, who were the ones in his cell block that he did associate with?" asked Joplin.

"Well, he got along well with his cellmate, a young guy named Kyle Mason, in for being part of a state-wide chop-shop operation. And Eric and Kyle were chummy with an older inmate named Johnny Waycross, who was doing time for several credit card fraud convictions."

"That seems like an odd mix," Maggie said.

"Maybe," Tullie said. "But what they did have in common was they were each part of groups on the outside that sold or distributed illegal or illegally obtained merchandise. They were salesmen of sorts for criminal organizations. What *was* odd was Eric's friendship or connection—whatever you'd call it—with an inmate named Ray Brent Marsh."

"That name sounds familiar, but I don't know why," Maggie said.

Joplin only half-listened as Tom explained to Maggie about the Tri-State Crematory, the scandal Brent Marsh had brought down on his family and the State of Georgia, the pain felt by the relatives of the unburied people there, and the horror experienced by anyone who read about it. Instead, he was once again back on that country road in Noble, listening to an old woman ramble on about the Marsh family.

"They were good people, did a lot for the community," she'd told him. "Even Ray Brent, before he lost his mind. I mean, that's all we could think of when heard about it. He just plumb lost his mind."

Had Marsh gotten some of his sanity back in prison? Joplin wondered. *Was he on medication? Did anyone—maybe Eric Jaeger— discover why he'd left all those bodies out to rot on the crematory grounds instead of doing his job? And did any of that have something to do with Jacob Gunter's death and Jaeger's disappearance? Or what Tullie saw happening between Jaeger and Aidan Fitzgerald?*

Joplin suddenly realized Tom had finished talking, and everyone was staring at him. He cleared his throat and said, "Jaeger's possible friendship with Brent Marsh might change the whole narrative, but I'm not sure how yet. Or it might simply be some kind of offshoot or parallel thing that had nothing to do with The Cause and what they might be planning to do."

Tullie squinted and cocked her head. "And *I'm* not sure what anything *you* just said means, Hollis."

Joplin rubbed his forehead with his middle finger, carefully choosing his words. "From the time we discovered what we thought was Jaeger's body, certain aspects of this case kept pulling me back to Brent Marsh and the Tri-State Crematory scandal. For instance, the Rutledge County coroner is Harold Danforth. His funeral home used Tri-State and was one of several other mortuaries, along with Tri-State and Brent Marsh, sued by the victims' families. Then Harold's incompetent son, the deputy coroner, refused to flag the body for autopsy or even have it officially identified. Next, the body was sent off to a new crematory not far from the old Tri-State crematory. And the people there gave me a hard time when I went to pick it up. And then, the body turned out to belong to Jacob Gunter, not Jaeger. But now, the *biggest* coincidence in all this—and y'all know how I hate coincidences—is that Marsh was friends with Eric Jaeger while they were both at Central State Prison. And Marsh was released just a few months ago in June, which might somehow fit in with everything that's happened."

"How so?" Tullie asked. "I mean, I get that there are a few too many 'coincidences' going on, but what would Marsh's release from prison have to do with Gunter's murder and Eric Jaeger's disappearance?"

Joplin shook his head and gave a long sigh. "I don't know. But chronologically, it happened not long before you saw Jaeger and your brother together and before Jaeger's dirty drug screen. That drug screen seemed to lead to his going AWOL and a parole violation warrant being issued. And all of *that*, I think, led to Gunter's murder. Everyone—especially you, Tullie—was supposed to think it was Jaeger who died at the Falls."

"But why?" asked Tom. "And what could it possibly have to do with The Cause?"

"I don't have any answers—yet. And the whole thread with Brent Marsh might not be connected to The Cause at all. The only real connection is Harold Danforth, who seems to be in an unholy alliance with Sheriff Odum and the DA. And the sheriff seems to be connected to The Cause." He paused, then said, "There is one other connection to the Tri-State scandal.

I thought of it while sitting in that conference room yesterday, surrounded by GBI agents: The GBI was in charge of the investigation."

"That's right," said Tom. "And if any agency could've uncovered why Marsh didn't cremate all those bodies, it would have been the GBI. But, evidently, they didn't."

"Ken Poston, Marsh's attorney, said he was a victim of mercury poisoning from cremating bodies over the years that had dental fillings using mercury dental amalgam. The GBI must have checked that out, but I don't recall seeing anything in the news about it."

"I think we're getting too hung up on any connection Brent Marsh might have to this case," Carrie said. "Let's move on."

They spent the last half hour of the dinner meeting throwing around ideas on what, if anything, they should do next, given Judge Mabry's restrictions. Carrie favored backing off entirely and turning over the new information about Jaeger's connections in prison to the GBI. Maggie supported her, while Tom was surprisingly silent. Tullie expressed conflicting emotions, caught between her judge's explicit orders and her need to know what happened to Eric Jaeger. She promised to let everyone know about the interview with the GBI, and Joplin said he intended to discuss the situation with Sarah Petersen the following day.

✦ ✦ ✦ ✦

WHEN EVERYONE HAD left, Joplin and Carrie sat curled up on the sofa with both cats snuggled against them. Joplin's arm encircled her baby bump in a protective hold. As if reading his mind, Carrie said, "It scares me to death to think of bringing our child into a world with this much hate in it, Hollis."

Joplin kissed the top of her head, breathing in the lemon scent of her shampoo. "I think that's been a fear expressed by most human beings since time immemorial," he said. "Probably because there's never been a time this planet *wasn't* filled with danger. But I think having a child is an expression of hope that things might change, even in a world that spawns greed and hatred and cruelty."

"Well," said Carrie, yawning. "It's too late to change my mind now. But if that's your way of saying we should name our daughter 'Hope,' forget it. I knew a girl named Hope in the eighth grade, and she was the meanest person I ever knew. At least at the time."

Carrie yawned again. Joplin disentangled himself from her and the cats and stood up, pulling her gently with him. "No 'Hope' for you then, missy," he said, unable to help himself, then added, "Sorry," when she groaned.

Banshee followed Carrie into the bedroom, but Quincy went with Joplin to the kitchen on the off chance that a late snack might be involved. When it became clear that Joplin was simply stacking a few more dishes in the dishwasher and wiping down the granite countertops, Quincy, too, headed for the bedroom. Joplin made a mental note to buy some Chick-fil-A nuggets for the cat the next day. He realized it had been a long time since he'd done that. Carrie had improved everyone's diets for the better in the past two years. And while Joplin understood— and appreciated—that, his ancient lizard brain, which required lots of meat and fat for hunting and gathering—was still scrambling to catch up. He suspected Quincy, his sole companion for many years, was in the same evolutionary time warp.

Joplin finally turned out the kitchen lights and headed for the bedroom. He wasn't sure whether he'd succeeded in calming Carrie's fears about bringing a child into the world during these violent, unpredictable times—hell, the argument hadn't convinced *him*—or whether she just wanted to end the conversation. Carrie was much more pragmatic than he was; he'd always known that. She was also better educated, more analytical, and knew the names of philosophers he'd never heard of. But Joplin was sure he had more angst than almost anyone on the planet, Carrie included. And that angst and an intuitive gut that belonged in the evolutionary Hall of Fame would protect his family.

Moonlight was filtering into the bedroom through the plantation shutters. Joplin slipped into the bathroom, brushed his teeth, then stripped to his boxers. The cats were curled up at the foot of the bed, both snoring softly. He inched into his side of it, hoping not to disturb Carrie, but she turned over to face him, only inches away. Cupping his face with her free hand, she gave him a long, lingering kiss.

"I read somewhere that primates use sex to drain the adrenaline from their systems after a fight-or-flight situation has passed," she said, her hand now much further south than his face.

"Are you saying our little dinner party was the equivalent of a lion attacking a group of monkeys or a prehistoric beast charging some cavemen?"

"Well, maybe not that bad, but the conversation was very unsettling."

Joplin pulled her closer and once more breathed in the soft, sweet smell of her and said, "Then, Sugar Pie, I'm your primate."

26

AS USUAL, SARAH Petersen was already in her office with the blinds and door open when Joplin arrived at 7:45 a.m. He pointed a finger up as he passed and received a quick nod in reply. After dropping his bag and getting a cup of coffee from the break room, Joplin doubled back and sat in one of the chairs in front of the chief's desk. He'd briefed her yesterday about his meeting with the GBI, but now he needed her advice.

Petersen raised one eyebrow and tilted her head to the side. "Tell me."

When he'd finished informing her of the details that Tullie had left out about her brother's meeting with Jaeger and Jaeger's friendship with Ray Brent Marsh in prison, Petersen ran her hand through her blond hair and set her piercing blue eyes on him.

"Wicked complicated, Hollis," she said.

"Tell me about it."

"This whole thing started out as a favor for a colleague, and now you've stumbled upon a redneck militia with a cache of guns, and the GBI is involved. The safest thing to do is nothing, but we both know you don't want to do that. I wouldn't either," she added. "But my job is to serve the interests of this office, which includes following judges' orders and not overstepping our investigative authority. However," she continued, "there's still a body in our morgue, which gives us a little wiggle room. To a certain extent, anyway. At least until Rutledge County claims it. And there can often be unexpected delays."

Joplin put his hand on his heart and said, "Are you suggesting that we misplace paperwork or have a sudden transportation problem, Chief?"

Petersen glared at him. "Of course not. But there are often things over which we have no control, Hollis."

"Don't I know it."

Sarah Petersen put her hands together and scrunched her mouth into a thinking position. "So, here's what we're going to do."

"What's that?" Joplin asked when she didn't immediately answer.

"We're going to run a possible scenario by Doc and see if he'll sign off on it. That way, everyone's ass is covered, if he agrees. And I trust his judgment completely."

She made a quick phone call, and two minutes later, they were in Dr. Minton's large corner office.

Lewis Minton, wearing, as usual, a white lab coat and a loud tie, swiveled his chair around. His thick gray hair contrasted with his almost unlined face, and his dark brown eyes fastened on them. "Hollis," he said, smiling. "How's the father-to-be these days?"

"Already worried about teenage boys flocking around my daughter, Doc. Other than that, I can't complain. Carrie's the one with heartburn and an ever-growing baby bump."

"I remember it well," Minton said. "Sit down, both of you, and tell me what's going on."

Joplin remained silent as Sarah explained the situation and the legal/bureaucratic issues involved. Dr. Minton listened intently, his eyes on her and his fingers steepled on his desk. He took his time responding, carefully considering everything she'd said.

"Hollis," he finally said, eyes now on Joplin, but hands still steepled. "Are you sure you wouldn't rather go back to the Homicide Unit?"

Joplin was a little taken aback. "I'm positive, Doc. I love it here. It's the best job I've ever had."

Minton nodded slowly. "And you're one of the best death investigators I've ever known. But in the past three years, you've gone outside your job description a bit. Always with my support, of course, because of the various circumstances involved—the ruckus Tom Halloran raised over his friend's death in Piedmont Park, the dead woman who was Halloran's client but wasn't really dead, and the former Marine Corps general who wanted you to investigate his daughter's death because you'd once dated her." When Joplin started to protest, Minton raised a hand and said, "I know, I know. These are all good reasons for you to go out on a limb, even though each situation almost got you killed. But, Hollis, this is a little different." Minton thumped his desk. "No, a *lot* different. This time, you want to sneak around a Superior Court judge's order, investigate a murder that rightfully belongs to Rutledge County, and possibly insert yourself into a multi-agency investigation. Does that about sum it up, son?"

Joplin sighed. "I guess it does, sir."

Minton turned to Sarah Petersen. "How about you, Chief?"

"You've made it wicked clear, sir."

"Okay, then, we're all on the same page. So, here's what we're going to do. "

✚ ✚ ✚ ✚

TWENTY MINUTES LATER, Joplin was in Carrie's office. She was just getting into her lab coat, her hair pulled back into a low ponytail. She smiled brightly, then gave him a big kiss, smelling of Coco Mademoiselle. "I thought you were off at a scene when I saw that you weren't in your cubicle."

Joplin put his hands in his pockets and leaned against the door jamb as Carrie moved behind her desk and sat down. "Actually, I'm here to ask your permission for something."

Carrie slumped a little in her chair. "You got Dr. Minton involved in this mess, didn't you?"

Joplin moved quickly to one of the chairs in front of Carrie's desk. "Yes, but unless you sign off on this, he's shutting everything down, Carrie. And I won't do anything else on the case. I promise."

Carrie shook her head vigorously. "That's what you promised me before you almost got yourself killed the *last* time, Hollis. And I only agreed to *that* scenario because I wanted Blaine Reynolds' murderer caught as badly as you did. And because Ike was your backup. Who's going to be watching your back on this one? Tullie Fitzgerald?"

"She's actually pretty good at that, going by some previous cases we worked together several years ago. But as we discussed last night, Judge Mabry has given us strict instructions not to compromise the GBI's case. We can look for Jaeger because she reinstated Tullie's warrant, but that's it. And according to Sarah and Doc, we can spend a little time looking into Jacob Gunter's death until Rutledge County claims the body. Which probably won't be anytime soon, since it's unlikely they're going to investigate his homicide."

Carrie sighed and stared at him. "And neither of them sees that as interfering with the GBI's case? Give me a break. Hollis."

"I've said I won't do anything further, if you don't want me to, Carrie, and I mean it. But hear me out. Tullie has every right to go to Central State to learn more about Jaeger's time there, and Tom and Maggie can follow up on what they learned from the visit to Wolfscratch and Fox Run. With your permission, I plan to go back to Walker County and see if I can talk to either Ray Brent Marsh or his mother, as well as that old woman I met up there. I think she knows something that she doesn't really understand. But a lot of investigating can be done right here."

"What do you mean?"

"We can push harder to get Gunter's tox report expedited. And I can call Will Sykes again and try to narrow down where Gunter might have gotten that tattoo and had his last meal. And you and I and Sarah can go over his body with a fine-toothed comb, so to speak, and see what else might turn up."

"Why Sarah?"

"Because she worked her way through college as a morgue assistant at the Boston ME's Office and even helped train anatomy students during her post-graduate studies, remember? And she'll bring fresh eyes to the table."

"Are you questioning the thoroughness of my autopsy, Hollis?"

Joplin swiped a hand through his hair, rethinking the decision to pursue the hot mess Tullie had dropped in his lap. Or at least suggesting that his boss join them in the autopsy room. Carrie's hormones were definitely working overtime these days. "No, for God's sake!" he said. "I know your work. But you were autopsying what you thought was Eric Jaeger's body. You don't need to open Gunter up again, but let's focus on that tattoo. Take some high-res photos of it and maybe find out who inked it. And I can ask Maggie to review the photos she took at the crime scene and see if we missed anything. There's a lot we can do without violating Judge Mabry's order or tipping off Rutledge and compromising the GBI's case."

Carrie didn't respond immediately, and Joplin didn't know if that was a good or bad sign. He saw her lift her right hand to the bulge under her lab coat, as if protecting their unborn child. Then she took a deep breath and said, "I'm fine with re-examining Gunter's body, but if Tullie goes to Central State, she should go alone. If you go with her, the Rutledge sheriff might hear about it, which could send out a big alert. Same thing with that deputy. Even if he asks, don't go up there to see him; just talk on the phone. As for any attempt to meet with Brent Marsh or his mother, although I totally respect your gut, I think the connection to this case is a big stretch. So, I also don't think you need to talk to that woman who asked if the people you've seen stay dead."

Joplin nodded, then stood up and inclined his head in a semi-bow. "As you wish, Buttercup."

Carrie's eyes narrowed. "Wait a minute—isn't that a quote from *The Princess Bride*?"

"Yes, and here's another one: 'This is true love. Do you think that happens every day?'"

27

TULLIE FITZGERALD AND her chief, Vince Randall, stood in the parking lot of the GBI regional office in Cleveland, Georgia Wednesday morning and spoke quickly and quietly, not wanting to attract unwanted attention. Tullie, wearing a skirt and jacket for the first time in she didn't know when, was subdued, feeling as if she'd been called into the principal's office at her old high school. Which had happened more times than she'd wished, usually because a teacher had overheard her using "inappropriate language."

"You did okay, Tullie," Randall assured her. "You told the truth, and you did so in a very respectful, cooperative way. "

"Not my usual style is what you're saying, right, Chief?" she said.

Randall loosened the tie of his gray suit and shook his head. "No, that's *not* what I'm saying. It was tough in there—for me, too. Because the buck stops with me, you know? So, if you hadn't handled things the way you did, my ass would've been on the line. But you did, so it's not. Now, let's get out of here and go have some lunch. We can talk some more about this while we eat."

Tullie googled the nearest Mexican restaurant, which luckily had good ratings. Ten minutes later, they were sitting in a booth at Cancun Express and had ordered steak fajitas for two and a large guacamole. Although Tullie would rather have had a large Corona on tap, she settled for a Diet Coke, since they were both on duty.

"So, what was your takeaway from the meeting?" she asked Randall.

Randall raised his eyebrows. "The same as yours, I hope," he said. "You can pursue—in a limited way—executing the violation warrant out for Eric Jaeger, per Judge Mabry."

"Yes, of course," Tullie responded, head bobbing. "But what, exactly, does that mean? SAC Pendleton suggested I go to Central State to get more information on Jaeger's connections there, so that word won't get back to The Cause or the militia that the GBI is interested in them. So, does that mean I can follow up on the outside and contact them? Specifically, Brent Marsh, since Hollis Joplin was so struck by Jaeger's making a friend of him?"

"That's a good question. When you brought up Marsh, Pendleton mentioned that the GBI had handled the Tri-State investigation. I remembered seeing photos of the site with a dozen agents in GBI jackets working it."

"Yeah, Hollis Joplin brought that up last night when we all got together. We discussed whether the GBI had ever discovered why Marsh never cremated all those bodies."

"Well, to be on the safe side, I'd contact the ASAC about that. He gave you his card."

"Okay," Tullie said, "But I think he was hitting on me."

"Really?" Randall said, looking shocked. "Masterson?"

Tullie wished she hadn't said anything. "A little. Maybe. But probably not."

"Then don't call him," her chief said, glowering. "You don't have to put up with that. And let me know if *he* calls *you*."

"Alright," Tullie said, having no intention of doing it. She'd been handling situations like that since she started working for the Department of Corrections, despite all the mandatory sexual harassment training it had sponsored. In her opinion, reporting someone wasn't worth the effort and often caused more problems. However, she had supported another female officer who'd blown the whistle on a supervisor several months ago, backing up her testimony when she'd witnessed it. "So, if I don't ask for clarification, what do you suggest?"

Randall stopped glowering and thought about it. "I'd do what Pendleton suggested. And if something needs an outside follow-up, let *me* run it by the ASAC, not you."

"I appreciate that, sir," Tullie said, lowering her eyelashes. She wasn't sure what had brought on Randall's protective attitude, but she wanted to keep pursuing Jaeger as long as possible. So, she held the eyelashes down for a few more seconds.

And hated herself for it.

✛ ✛ ✛ ✛

WHEN JOPLIN GOT to the autopsy room, Sarah and Carrie were both gowned and gloved. They'd skipped the plexiglass visors, since they were just examining Jacob Gunter's body.

Joplin was only observing, so he didn't need any extra coverage. Given the talent in the room, he felt pretty useless.

"Youse guys need any heavy lifting, I'm your man," Joplin said. He resisted the urge to scratch under his armpits.

Carrie shot him a look, but Sarah just ignored him. So much for manly humor.

"By the way," Carrie said, grabbing two magnifying glasses from behind her and handing one to Sarah, "I asked the lab to expedite the tox report, and I went over Gunter's stomach contents. I remembered he'd eaten Mexican food, but not the specifics. Looked like a chicken burrito with sour cream, beans and rice, and guacamole, salsa, and chips. He'd also had some beer, but I remember the contents smelled strongly of whiskey, too. Hopefully, we'll know soon."

"Thanks for checking on that," Joplin said. "I'll talk to Will Sykes and find out what Mexican restaurants are in the area."

The large y-shaped incision stood out on Gunter's pale body. Joplin stared down at him, wondering again what circumstances had led to his murder. Had Eric Jaeger been the intended victim, or was he meant to be the beneficiary of a new identity? Either way, Jaeger must have been the killer—in self-defense or to step into Jacob Gunter's shoes. If their little group hadn't stumbled upon the body, everyone would have assumed that Jaeger, a convicted felon with a parole violation warrant on his head, was dead. Case closed. Did that mean Jaeger was part of The Cause, or was the motive something altogether different, involving Aidan Fitzgerald?

"Are you with us, Hollis?" he heard Carrie say, pulling himself back to the present.

"Yes, sorry. I was just going over some possible motives for Gunter's death now that we know Jaeger's probably alive. And if he is, he was also involved in the killing, either in self-defense or to escape from something."

"I can see that," Sarah said as she bent over to examine an abrasion over Gunter's left eyebrow. "He might have been brought to the Falls under false pretenses, and Gunter—or someone else—forced him to exchange clothes at gunpoint. Although it would make more sense if it were the other way around. Why would Jacob Gunter want to assume the identity of a parolee on the run?"

"Good point," said Joplin.

Sarah grabbed a digital camera from the counter behind her and handed it to Joplin. "Here," she said, "make yourself useful. Take a close-up of this."

Joplin took two shots, then said, "So, are you saying there was a third person up there with them? A mystery man—or woman—who lured Jaeger there? Because we know Gunter drove through the North gate in his truck."

"Don't know. We may never know. I'm just saying that we don't know what, at this point, Jaeger's role was in this whole thing. Everything's speculation. The only thing tangible is this body, and so far, it's not telling us much."

Carrie, meanwhile, had already begun to hover over the body with her magnifying glass, scanning the lower torso, legs, and feet for any anomalies. She waited while Sarah did the same thing with the upper half, including a careful examination of the scalp. Finally, at Sarah's signal, they turned Gunter over.

The tattooed replica of the Southern Cross was still enmeshed in the blood that had settled on the body's dorsal side, but its boundaries appeared somehow clearer. Or maybe Joplin was simply seeing it more clearly. Sarah bent over Gunter again, aiming the magnifying glass at the tattoo for several minutes.

Then she reached out with her left hand and lightly brushed the skin. Her fingers stopped over an area at the top of the medal, where the word "Cross" was inked.

"There's something embedded under the 'o' here."

Carrie handed her a small, slim knife, and they both watched as Sarah made a quick incision. She extracted something, tossed it into a metal basin behind her, and then swiveled around to show it to them.

"Looks like some kind of a chip," Joplin said.

"Bingo," said Sarah.

"I can't believe I missed that," Carrie said.

"Eff that," said Sarah. "Most people would. In my previous life as an attendant, I spent a lot of time handling bodies, touching the skin as I prepped them. Sam might have discovered it if he'd been assisting you the day you did Gunter's autopsy. It's no big deal."

"It is to me," Carrie said. "And a lesson I won't take lightly. But why didn't the X-rays pick it up?"

"Because I'm pretty sure it's made of plastic or silicon. Hopefully, we can also find out why it was there. Was it to track Gunter or identify him? Or for some other reason completely. But whatever it is, we need to inform the GBI. They have more resources than we do about these things, and we *would* be crossing a line if we kept it to ourselves."

28

JOPLIN AND CARRIE were having a late lunch at the Colonnade when his cell phone rang. He showed the screen to Carrie and cocked his head, not sure she would want him to talk while they were eating. But when she nodded at him, he clicked the phone and speakerphone icons and said, "What's going on, Tullie? I'm with Carrie, having some lunch, and I have you on speakerphone. I take it you're not in a holding cell at the GBI's Appalachian office."

"Hi, Carrie," Tullie said, then they could hear her sigh. "No, I'm not in a holding cell, but I'm on the same short leash you are, Hollis. SAC Pendleton encouraged me to go to Central State and follow up on Jaeger's contacts and buddies there since they don't want to tip their hand with The Cause or Rutledge County, and I have a plausible reason for doing that. So, I'm on my way to Macon. But anything beyond that would probably need clearance."

"That's a good idea," he said. "These are some dangerous people, Tullie. And we're not really equipped to deal with them."

"That's just what my boss said," she replied. "But when did you get so cautious, Hollis?"

"Since he realized he was going to become a father," Carrie said, a little too loudly, in Joplin's opinion.

"I can certainly understand *that*," said Tullie, also a little too loudly, in Joplin's opinion.

For the second time that day, he felt caught between two women with an agenda he couldn't quite figure out. "We looked at Jacob Gunter's body again this morning to see if we missed anything," he said quickly. "Guess what we found implanted in his skin, under a part of the Southern Cross tattoo."

"Well, it'd have to be either a microchip or some kind of a port. My guess is a microchip."

"Good guess," Joplin said, slightly disappointed by her quick answer. "I've notified the GBI, and they're sending someone to pick it up."

"Are they going to tell you what they find out about it?"

"Who knows? But Carrie washed it off, x-rayed it, and I took some high-res photos, which I sent to our CSU lab. I bet BJ can tell us something about it."

"If anyone can, he can," Tullie said.

"I also left a message with your buddy Will Sykes to see if he can help me find out where Gunter might have gotten the tattoo and where he had lunch the day he was killed."

"Good idea. Say hi to him for me when he calls. Listen, do you want me to swing by the ME's Office and pick you up? We could be in Macon by 2:30."

Joplin didn't even need to look at Carrie for the answer. "I think I'll pass on that. But keep us posted, hear?"

"You got it," said Tullie. "Good job on finding that microchip, Carrie," she added, then clicked off before either of them could respond.

"Are you sorry you're not going with her?" Carrie asked.

The server brought their food, and Joplin waited until she'd gone before saying, "Hell, no! I don't like strip searches."

Carrie cocked her head and said, "They don't strip search law enforcement at prisons, Hollis, and you know that."

"Yeah, but they take my phone and my gun, so it sure feels like a strip search to me."

✛ ✛ ✛ ✛

JOPLIN WAS CALLED to a vehicular homicide scene on Ponce de Leon at Juniper Street as he was paying the check. He dropped Carrie off at the ME's Office first, then put his portable light and siren on the hood of his car before heading there. It was only a little after 2 p.m., but traffic was already getting bad in that part of town, especially for a Wednesday. As he got closer to the intersection, he saw why: A black Yukon SUV had t-boned a Camry sedan in the center of it. Joplin made his way between the four lanes of cars as drivers pulled off to the sides to let him pass. He parked next to one of three APD cars, grabbed his bag, and hurried to where officers were trying to shield a female victim from the rubberneckers as two EMTs were carefully easing her out of the Camry. The car's driver could barely be seen behind the crumpled front end of the SUV.

The Yukon's driver was in cuffs, being treated for a gash on his head by a third EMT and loudly complaining about being restrained. Joplin ignored him and went over to a cop standing near the driver's side of the Camry.

The cop looked at Joplin's dark blue ME jacket and said, "The passenger has some serious injuries, but she'll probably make it. Her companion wasn't as lucky. We're just waiting for you to pronounce him. Chief Petersen said she was sending transport." He nodded toward the Yukon driver. "Bozo there 'had a few beers,' as he tells it, and thought he could make it through the intersection before the light turned red. According to witnesses, the light was red long before that, and the Camry had already pulled into the intersection. Musta been some pretty strong beers. He blew a 1.7 BAC."

Joplin shook his head in disgust, then pulled his notebook out of his bag and asked for the victim's name. After writing it down, he went over to the Camry. Out of reflex, he checked for a pulse in the driver's neck, even though the cops or the EMTs had probably already done that. And the man's crushed upper body showed that he must have died instantly. Joplin looked at his watch, and under the man's name, he wrote, "Time of death: 2:10 p.m." Then he took several photos of the scene and walked away, his camera hanging from his neck. Joplin didn't look at the SUV driver as he walked back to his car, afraid he might be tempted to go deck the guy.

His phone rang as he was getting into his car, and he answered since it was Ike Simmons. "Ike. I'm just leaving a scene. You have another one for me?"

"No, this is about the one you processed on Sunday. Kathryn Hampshire? Did David Markowitz already talk to you? He did the autopsy."

"No, but I haven't spent much time in the office the past few days."

"Just wanted to tell you your famous gut is still on the job. David found cotton fibers in her nose and lungs that matched the cover of the pillow behind her head. Ms. Hampshire was definitely smothered. And we're taking a much closer look at her estranged husband."

"Glad I could help, Ike. But I'd also keep the son-in-law in mind if I were you."

He heard Simmons give one of his chuckles. "I jotted his name down and underlined it right after you told me that this mighta been a homicide, partner. Figured he'd benefit if his wife inherited most of her mother's assets. We have a subpoena to get a copy of the will before it's probated. He's also one of the few people she'd open the door to late at night."

"My work is done then, Grasshopper," Joplin said.

"Hey! Who you callin' 'Grasshopper,' cracker? You were as green as grass when you made detective, Hollis. Weren't for me, you'da been busted back to a uniform driving a beat. Or worse. You didn't even know enough to keep a second piece on you when the higher-ups made us partners."

Joplin laughed and said, "Point taken, Ike. I'd be nothing without you."

"Damn straight. Truth be told, I feel the same way. 'Cept when you go all 'second-sight' on me."

"It's not 'second sight,' Ike. It's eidetic memory. And I'm not crazy about having it either."

"I know, I know," said Simmons quickly. "Sorry I brought it up. Fact is, I miss having you as a partner. Ricky is great, but…"

"Same here, Ike. But I also feel like I do more good at this job. And I get to leave work at the office, where it belongs."

This time, Simmons' laughter was explosive, and Joplin could almost see him shaking his head. "You got to be kiddin' me, Hollis. If you think getting pulled into several murder investigations in the past three years is 'leaving work at the office,' you better think again. Like that murder up at Wolfscratch."

"The less said about that, the better, Ike. The GBI and about a dozen other alphabet agents are involved now, so I'm off the case. Even telling you that is saying too much."

"I get it, Hollis. Don't worry."

"Thanks, Ike. Good luck with the Hampshire case. Is Alfrieda going to Carrie's baby shower?"

"Are you kiddin' me? She went crazy buyin' baby girl things as soon as she found out Carrie was pregnant. Y'all have a name yet? 'Cause Frieda wants to get the baby blanket monogrammed."

Joplin let out a long sigh. "Carrie has something in mind, but she won't tell me. Says she has to 'show' me, whatever that means."

"Well, my advice is to go along with whatever she wants, Hollis. She won't be as intense about the name with the second and third babies. I've been there, buddy."

Joplin got into his car and sagged against the seat back. "That really doesn't make me feel any better, Ike."

29

WILL SYKES CALLED as Joplin headed back to the ME's Office. He sounded surprised—almost shocked—at the news that it wasn't Eric Jaeger who had been murdered at Wolfscratch. He also knew who Jacob Gunter was, since he'd arrested him for one of the DUIs on his record. When Joplin told him about the Southern Cross tattoo on Gunter's back and asked to meet with him, Will readily agreed, but suggested someplace further away from Rutledge County this time. They settled on the next day at noon at the same Chick-fil-A in Canton where he and Jesse Waldrup had met.

"The sheriff must be keeping that information about Gunter pretty tight, if it hasn't filtered down to the rank and file," he told Joplin. "Otherwise, I would've heard something."

"Did Gunter have family in the area?"

"I think his wife bailed him out after I arrested him, but they may not still be together, from what I heard. I'd have to check around a bit."

"Well, watch your back, Will. I'll see you tomorrow."

"See you."

Too late, Joplin remembered he had promised Carrie he wouldn't talk to Will in person.

✦ ✦ ✦ ✦

JOPLIN'S OFFICE PHONE rang as he was walking over to his cubicle. Viv was gone, so he hoped he wasn't being called to another scene; he wanted to write up the last one, if possible. Luckily, he recognized the number.

"Hello, BJ. I was hoping to hear from you. Carrie put a rush order on Jacob Gunter's tox report last week."

"We're working on it, Hollis," said the head of the CSU lab. "That isn't our only case, and everyone seems to have a reason why they need their report yesterday."

"I know, BJ. It's just that things are heating up around here. We're trying to find out as much as we can about Gunter before Rutledge County asks us to return the body."

"I'll do my best to expedite it, Hollis. But we need to discuss something else. Namely, the high-res photos and x-ray you sent me of the object you found in the decedent's body. The so-called 'microchip.'"

"'So-called?'"

"Yes. It's cylindrical and made of silicate, like most RFID and NCA microchips, but from what I can tell, it couldn't possibly do what either of those can do. In fact, unless aliens from outer space put it in your Mr. Gunter, it isn't a microchip at all. The x-ray shows it doesn't have any works in it. That's why it didn't show up on the ones Dr. Salinger took during the autopsy."

"Well, that explains that mystery. So, by 'works,' you mean a transmitter?"

"More or less. There are two types of subdermal microchips: Radio Frequency Identification, or RFID, and Near Frequency Chips, called NFCs. The RFIDs have special ID numbers connected to an external database that can provide information. The active ones can be read up to a certain distance—say, a hundred meters—but they have batteries that need replacing at prescribed intervals. The other type, the NFCs, can only be read by a hand-held sensor directly over the implant. Both types have metal parts and can be detected by X-rays and MRIs. But they don't have GPS capability."

Joplin felt his brain dribbling out of his ears, like when Carrie had tried to explain how dominant and recessive alleles controlled various traits in human beings. "So, they can't be tracked?"

"Right. They're just connected to databases or sensors containing information, like an ID number or important medical information. Think of the microchip implanted in your pet or one in a diabetic person, allowing a doctor or hospital to access their medical history."

Joplin let this sink in, then said, "Wasn't there a conspiracy theory floating around when Obamacare was enacted that warned people they'd be microchipped if they signed up for it?"

He heard BJ give a dry chuckle. "Yes, unfortunately. It took a lot of effort and taxpayer money to educate people about the fallacy of that one. They had to push back against what history has shown us our government is capable of doing. Like the Tuskegee study, where 399 Black sharecroppers in 1932 with syphilis were promised treatment by doctors with the U.S. Public Health Service if they agreed to be part of a long-term study. But those government doctors knew there was no known treatment at the time; they just wanted to document the various stages of the disease. And even when penicillin proved effective fifteen years into the study, the patients were still only given aspirin. It wasn't until a PHS investigator leaked the story to a reporter that the public outrage about the study shut it down. By that time, 128 participants were dead from syphilis or related complications, and 40 spouses had contracted the disease, passing it on to 19 children."

"Oh, God," said Joplin. "I'd heard about that study, but didn't know all the details. I still can't believe our government would do that."

"Then I guess you'd find it harder to believe that it sponsored an even worse study in Guatemala from 1946 to 1948, also researching syphilis. But this time, our government deliberately *infected* people with the disease—700 hundred of them—after giving them penicillin to see if the drug could prevent syphilis, not just cure it."

Joplin couldn't say anything for several seconds. "We actually did that?" he said finally.

"We did. And the kicker is that the head researcher, Dr. John Cutler, was rewarded for his work by being made one of the head researchers in the Tuskegee study, which was still ongoing."

"What was it about the oath, 'First, do no harm,' that those doctors didn't understand, BJ?"

Joplin heard the CSU lab director give another one of his mirthless chuckles. "You got me there, Hollis. I've spent a lot of time reading about these infamous research studies since discovering what Josef Mengele did at Auschwitz during World War II. I was in college, taking an elective in applied science at the time, and the professor used Mengele to show what mind-boggling harm scientists and doctors can do in the name of 'science.'" BJ gave a long sigh. "But I've gotten off-topic, Hollis. Sorry. You need to know more about the object you found implanted in Jacob Gunter's body."

"Yes," said Joplin. "But going off-topic was certainly educational, if depressing. I can almost understand why these conspiracy theorists will believe anything that comes down the pike. Anyway, you were saying that the microchip had nothing in it, right?"

"No. Then again, this might be something new, Hollis. Human-implanted chips have been around since the '60s, albeit in rudimentary forms. More recently, some people have had them implanted in their hands, between the thumb and forefinger, for instant access to their work areas, computers, or smartphones. But they're just expensive transponders. You said you'd sent the chip to the GBI. Maybe they can tell you more. And if so, I'd appreciate your keeping me in the loop."

"If they share anything with me, I sure will, BJ."

30

TULLIE HATED THE drive to Macon on I-75 South. Although she didn't have to go to Central State Prison very often, she had spent time—too much—at GPSTC, the Georgia Public Safety Training Center in Forsyth, just twenty minutes north of Macon. "Gipstick" was where she'd gotten through basic training. She'd also attended training sessions and conferences there over the past six years. Like most of her colleagues, Tullie had passed on the free, but depressing, dorm rooms at the facility. Six weeks of basic there had been enough, thank you very much; now, it was up to eight weeks since the two departments had been combined. Thank God she'd been spared that. But staying at economy hotels like the Hampton Inn or the Quality Inn was almost as depressing. And not just because of the rooms.

Tullie had learned not to socialize much with other community supervision officers from around the state on work trips. Too many of them acted like teenagers on class trips once the chaperones had gone to bed. She hadn't been averse to some late-night drinking and a few casual hookups in her younger days, but now she preferred to get together with officers or others in law enforcement who had become friends. Hollis Joplin had been one of those friends.

At one time, Tullie had thought Hollis might become more than that. She'd been attracted to his irreverent sense of humor, broad shoulders, and unusual blue-green eyes. *Cat's eyes,* she remembered thinking when she'd first met him. There was certainly some chemistry between them. *A lot of chemistry,* she thought now, being honest with herself. But nothing had come of it. Tullie had wondered at the time if Hollis thought she was too young for him. Then Carrie, who was only a year or two older than she was, had done a six-week rotation at the ME's Office. And now they were expecting their first child.

Tullie had enjoyed several casual, on-and-off relationships and one serious one since then. She'd remained on good terms with the former—Will Sykes was one of them—but the more meaningful relationship had resulted in a bitter estrangement that had turned into a harassment situation. She shook her head, remembering all the drama she hadn't wanted and how close she'd come to requesting a restraining order. Tullie had seen warning signs after six months with Jim Flannigan, a DEA agent she'd met on a joint task force—pressuring her to get married, not wanting her to spend time with her friends or family, acting jealous over harmless attention from other men, among others—that made her decide to stop seeing him. Getting him out of her life for good took another six months.

Jim had kept the controlling side of himself under wraps for a while, and at first, it hadn't bothered her. Tullie gave as good as she got, and in the beginning, at least, she'd even enjoyed the sparring. Jim could also be charming and persuasive, almost convincing her that she was "overreacting" or needed someone like him to keep her "in line," whatever that meant. But she'd finally admitted to herself that she was slowly becoming someone she didn't like. And didn't want to like. Tullie's concerns were validated when Jim's reaction to her decision to break up with him had led to his drunken, late-night phone calls, unwanted visits, and a scary encounter in the parking lot when she was leaving for the day. Jim had grabbed her wrists, slammed her against her car, and tried to force his tongue into her mouth. She'd kneed him in the nuts so hard he was still writhing in pain on the ground as she drove away.

All of which contributed to Tullie's reluctance to admit that there was a powerful attraction between her and Prez. Not that she was worried he'd harass her if things didn't work out. He was too much of a grown-up for that—caring, intelligent, mature, and comfortable in his own skin. He'd also been divorced for over three years, so there was little chance he'd go back to his wife. But Prez was also her supervisor, not just a co-worker, and the GDOC had rules and regs that could get both of them fired if they started seeing each other. No matter how consensual a relationship between them would be. Even if he weren't her direct supervisor—if Tullie moved to another county, say— the difference in their positions would stay the same. And given the pyramid shape of the Department's hierarchy, it would take years for her to make chief. If ever.

Suddenly realizing that Exit 3 to US 80 West was only a hundred yards ahead, Tullie quickly moved into the right lane, barely making it in time. With a sigh, she turned her thoughts from Vince Randall and focused on her upcoming meeting with Gabriel Benson.

✚ ✚ ✚ ✚

TULLIE PARKED IN the middle of the enormous parking lot in front of the prison. On either end of it, two watch towers rose like medieval turrets guarding a castle. She locked her weapon in the glove compartment, knowing the security officers would take it anyway, and then locked the car. The hot South Georgia weather enveloped her as soon as she opened the door. A humid, unrelenting heat that followed her to the prison's entry and didn't let go until she reached the security checkpoint. Tullie dumped her purse and briefcase on the conveyor belt and watched them go through the sensor, then allowed herself to be wanded before collecting them.

Gabriel Benson was one of five counselors at the prison. His office was on the third floor, at the end of a long hallway. The door was open, and the counselor stood up behind his desk as Tullie walked in. He was tall and muscular with sandy hair, wearing a khaki polo shirt and what looked to be cargo pants. Benson's hazel eyes were warm, as was his smile, and she took the hand he offered and shook it.

"You must be Tullie," he said, ushering her to the lone chair in front of his desk. "I'm Gabe. Welcome to Central State." Tullie noticed there were no photos on the bookcase to the right or any framed diplomas, just a canvas print of a cloud-darkened seascape with the words, "For we walk by faith, not by sight." "Faith" was in the center, the letters four times larger than the other words. He sat down and said, "Is this your first time here?"

"No, but I haven't been here often. How long have you been a counselor at Central State? I've seen your name on release reports several times in the past few years, but it's nice to put a face to the name."

'About three years, so I didn't know Eric Jaeger for the entire time he was here. As I put in my report when he was released," the counselor added, clasping his hands together and putting them on the desk.

There was a whiff of defensiveness in Benson's manner, so she said quickly, "Your report was very thorough, Gabe. I'm just looking for a little more context. Some background information that can't be put in those report forms. Things only a trained observer would notice."

Benson seemed to relax at this and smiled. "Well, he was a model inmate, if there is such a thing. I believe everyone deserves a second chance," he added, gesturing toward the "Faith" poster. "That being said, I've been in this job long enough to know that a lot of guys in here aren't going to take that opportunity or that their newfound love of the Good Book is meant to impress the Parole board. But Eric seemed like he really wanted to change his life. He told me it hit him hard when his Aunt Sally, who helped raise him, died while he was here, and he couldn't go to the funeral."

"He told me that, too, at his first report. And even though I watch behavior instead of listening to promises of good behavior, after six months had passed, I began to think Eric might beat the odds. When he tested positive for cocaine the very next month, I have to admit that my cynicism rate went up."

"I know what you mean," said Benson, nodding. "Kinda set me back, too, when I heard what happened. That you thought he'd been murdered and then found out it wasn't his body. That musta been a trip."

Tullie didn't miss a beat. "Totally," she said. "So, listen, I know your schedule is packed, and I won't keep you. I just have a few questions."

"Ask 'em," Benson said, spreading his arms wide.

"Okay!" said Tullie, smiling her thanks.

✦ ✦ ✦ ✦

SHERIFF HOYT ODUM sat in his county car, an unmarked Buick Regal, and thought about the information he'd just received. He was a big man, tall and broad-shouldered, with much less hair than when he'd first joined the SO and much more girth. His wife and his doctor had been on him to lose weight and quit smoking. But Odum didn't think he could do both at the same time; so far, he hadn't tried to do either. He'd also been drinking a little more than usual. A lot was riding on what would happen in the next few weeks.

Lamar Worthy had almost had a conniption when he'd heard about the pissant death investigator nosing around after Jacob Gunter's death. Odum had calmed him down, told him to focus on his own job and be prepared to answer any queries or orders from that bitch of a judge in Milton County. So, if Worthy heard that the GBI had been called in, Odum was sure he'd shit his pants. Which was why he'd decided not to tell him. Worthy was too much of a Nervous Nellie for his own good. Best not to overload him, especially if they had to take things to another level. And Hoyt Odum was pretty sure they would have to. The reenactment of the battle at Tunnel Hill and everything else they'd planned were just around the corner. Nothing could stop them now. He'd make sure of it.

Odum wished his father could be there to see what he'd accomplished. Not just making sheriff, although that had made Mack Odum proud, given he'd only made sergeant with the Nolan Police Department. His drinking had factored into that, but his talent for beating confessions out of suspects ultimately kept him from becoming chief. Too many cases got thrown out of court or plea-bargained down to nothing because of it. Still, Hoyt wished his dad could have seen the power he'd gathered around himself like an invisible cloak. Nothing could touch him; he had Lamar Worthy and doddery old Judge Danby in his pocket and Harold Danforth to keep the lid on any suspicious deaths. Most of them anyway, Jacob Gunter being one of the few he'd screwed up, thanks to his idiot son.

Mack Odum had tried to control everything with his fists—his family, too. Hoyt and his brother had been on the receiving end of those fists too many times to count. When he was little, Hoyt hated his father for it; then, he began bullying kids weaker than himself and thanked his father for toughening him up. Mack couldn't afford to send him and Donnie to the private Christian school Harold Danforth got his own children into. Still, Hoyt had soon headed up a group of other boys at the local public elementary and high school who took great pleasure in scaring the few Black kids and the children of migrant workers out of whatever little money or possessions they had. Or even just for the hell of it. And if a parent or a teacher complained, Mack Odum would make sure they changed their minds.

But a stint in the Army had been a game-changer for Hoyt. He'd enlisted right after 9/11, and his sharpshooting, aggressiveness, and tactical ability during combat had gotten him recommended for the Ranger Assessment and Selection Program. He'd completed both phases, then joined the 75th Ranger Regiment. Hoyt had thrived in the Rangers, taking part in an unsuccessful raid searching for biological and chemical weapons near Haditha, Iraq, and, later, the successful liberation of Pvt. Jessica Lynch from the Taliban. When he returned home, he was hailed as a hero and had quickly joined the Rutledge County Sheriff's Office. But what Hoyt brought back with him was knowledge— not the academic kind that pussies like Lamar Worthy had—the tactical, strategic understanding of your enemy and the absolute conviction in your mission that was critical to any success.

Part of that knowledge was learning things about people— perps, supervisors, mayors, judges, prosecutors, and coroners— especially coroners, it turned out—and using the information to control them. The iron fist in the velvet glove had become Hoyt Odum's new motto, replacing "Rangers, lead the Way!" His father had lived to see him become Sheriff Odum, but the old man never really understood how he'd accomplished that, or that Hoyt had ultimately seen his father's way of life as a weakness, not a strength.

Hoyt Odum was convinced that a new order was about to be born. A new leader would bring about the changes he and other white men knew were necessary. That man was his *true* father, one who would deal with the minorities and heathens who threatened their way of life. But Hoyt and the men he'd gathered around him had to do everything they could to make sure nothing stood in the way of that new order.

Shaking his head, Odum reached for his cell phone and punched in the contact number for the coroner's office.

31

AS JOPLIN HEADED to his cubicle the next morning, Sarah Petersen opened her door and asked him to step into her office.

"What's up?" he asked, sitting in one of the chairs in front of her desk.

"Don't you have the evening shift tonight?"

"Yeah, but I need to write up a report I didn't finish yesterday before I follow up on some things to do with the Gunter case."

"Speaking of which, I got a call from the Deputy Coroner telling me Rutledge County wants Jacob Gunter's body returned to them."

"Bo called you?"

Petersen shrugged. "He didn't bother to give his name, just his title. But if Bo is condescending, rude, and self-important, then he's the person who called me. He also demanded that *we* transport the body. I didn't object or try to delay things because I thought you might want an excuse to go up there."

"I appreciate that, Chief," said Joplin. "Especially since things are beginning to heat up right now."

"How so?"

"Tullie Fitzgerald called me on my way home yesterday afternoon. She'd gone down to Central State Prison to meet with a counselor there about Eric Jaeger."

"Did she learn anything new?"

Joplin nodded. "Maybe too much. She said the counselor—Gabriel Benson—knew about the body I found not being Jaeger. Only she never said anything about that when she contacted him."

Petersen sat back in her chair and picked up a pen, which she started tapping against the desk. "Huh," she said. "So, who *did* know?"

"Everybody at the meeting at the GBI office in Cleveland when I went there, as well as when Tullie and her chief went there, although I don't think there were any alphabets present then. Plus, you, me, Doc, Carrie, the Hallorans, and BJ. Oh, and, of course, Sheriff Odum had to know. I told Will Sykes when I called him yesterday afternoon to set up a meeting, but that was after Tullie had met with Benson. Will could've been putting on an act, but he seemed very surprised when I told him. Other than that, there's no telling, because I have no idea whom that entire group might have told. But *somebody* told the counselor, and it wasn't Tullie. And that somebody had no business leaking it to him."

"Your best guess?" Petersen asked.

"I *know* it wasn't any of us. Or Tullie and her chief, for that matter. And, by 'us,' I'm including BJ. Certainly, there's a long history of rogue agents in federal agencies, and I'd be naïve if I said the GBI couldn't possibly have a few, but…I don't know; I'm not feeling it. So, my best guess would be Sheriff Odum."

"Which brings us to Will Sykes. And your meeting with him tomorrow."

"Yes," said Joplin at the tail end of a long sigh. "But I really like the guy, and although Tullie had vetted him, I asked her if he could've been the one who leaked the information. She almost bit my head off. Said she'd known Will for ages, and there was no way he could be involved with The Cause."

"Well," said Petersen, "I'd sure be careful what I told him, if I were you. And maybe you can tell him something bogus and see if that gets back to anyone it shouldn't."

Joplin stared at her, then smiled. "It scares me sometimes just how sneaky you are, Chief."

"Wicked sneaky, Hollis," she said. "And don't ever forget it. But tell me: Did Tullie learn anything else from the counselor? She already had his report, so she must have wanted some other information."

"She asked about talking to the three inmates Jaeger was friends with that the deputy warden had told her about. But Benson seemed to steer her away from doing that, saying they were all just 'cell block buddies.' So, she switched gears and pretended she was interested in any gossip about Ray Brent Marsh, because she was fascinated by the Tri-State scandal."

Sarah Petersen smiled. "I guess you got her fired up about that theory of yours, Hollis."

"It's not really a theory, Chief. I just think there might be some connection between Marsh's release from prison and Jacob Gunter's death. So far, the only real connection is Eric Jaeger—that they knew each other in prison and were on friendly terms."

"So, did the counselor have any 'gossip' about him?"

"No," Joplin said, sighing. "He used the same phrase, 'a model prisoner,' as he had when describing Eric Jaeger. Said Marsh never caused any problems or blamed anyone but himself for what happened. And he also got a master's and a doctoral degree in theology while he was there. Pretty impressive, if you ask me."

Petersen tapped her pen on the desk again, frowning. "What about his community supervision officer? Didn't he get probation to follow his prison sentence?"

Joplin nodded. "Yep. But it was just to pay off fines and restitution. Tullie talked to the supervising officer in LaFayette before she called me. The probation order also stipulated that Marsh write letters of apology to the victims and the community at large. The officer said his attorney turned over the victim letters before Marsh went to prison, and he wrote the community letter when he was released. She just monitors his payments, since there were no other special conditions, like drug tests or treatment. She hasn't actually seen him since his initial report. Tullie told her she was trying to locate Eric Jaeger and asked if Marsh might have had any contact with him, but the officer said she doubted that. The general probation conditions prohibit his being around other convicted felons, and she said Marsh doesn't want to do anything that would get him sent back to prison." He paused and said, "She called him a 'model probationer.' Said she believes that all he wants to do is live a good life and help his community."

"Well, at least everyone is consistent in their descriptions of him," said Petersen dryly. "So, the bottom line is that you can't connect Brent Marsh to any of this mess."

"Not yet. And if I do, it might not involve anything Marsh did. Just something someone *thought* he did or might do."

Petersen waved him away. "I'm not even going to ask what that means, Hollis. Just get Jacob Gunter back to Rutledge County, then do what you need to do before you report back here for your *regular* job."

Joplin smiled and gave her a deep bow, then moved quickly into the hall.

✦ ✦ ✦ ✦

JENNA MCALLISTER DID her usual stretches before setting off on her run. Her regular route took her to a nearby park with a playground and a hiking trail. The air felt humid; the temperature had gone up to 80 degrees by the time she'd dropped off the kids at school and put the dog back in the house. She hoped the run would lessen the stress she'd felt lately. Or maybe she was just affected by the stress that came off Andrew in waves. He wasn't sleeping well, although that wasn't new; Andrew had suffered bouts of insomnia for as long as they'd been together. But the tossing and turning and muttering in his sleep *were* new. And his concerns about people—specifically Sheriff Odum and the DA—bugging his office or following him around had now reached a level of paranoia that concerned her.

Several mothers with small children were at the playground, but only a few waved to her. Jenna smiled and waved back as she headed for the trail. She'd gotten used to this over the past year. It had all started when Andrew endorsed Jon Roker, a local attorney and family friend, for judge, when Judge Stokes died of a sudden heart attack. As the wife of a newspaper owner/editor, Jenna had become used to people in town not liking everything

Andrew printed. But those same people also relied on the ads the paper ran for their businesses and the obituaries and church news that were the lifeblood of any small town. So, when they began getting angry phone calls at night, she thought things would quiet down after a few weeks.

But things only got worse when Andrew interviewed Jon for the paper and ran photos of Amelia and the two girls. Letters to the editor competed with the nightly phone calls for Andrew's attention, and he canceled their landline and published only the less violent letters. The sheriff and the DA, without officially endorsing Jeb Starnes, the other judicial candidate, let it be known that they had "grave doubts" about Jon, given that his great-grandfather had been a member of the Communist party. But Andrew hadn't backed down, calling for other, more moderate, voters in the county to elect a judge who would serve their needs rather than be in "lockstep" with certain elected officials. When Jon was elected, she and Andrew had decided to visit Jenna's family in Madison for a week to escape another round of phone calls and angry letters.

It wasn't until then that Jenna regretted the move to Georgia and buying the *Rutledge Gazette*. She'd been happy about being closer to her family and having Andrew at home for dinner most nights. She'd also loved living in Nolan, which was much like Madison, with its stately Victorian houses and a town square surrounding the courthouse, and getting to know her neighbors and the parents of her children's friends. But now, Jenna decided, she'd rather put up with Andrew's demanding job as an investigative reporter for the *Boston Globe* than deal with living in a fishbowl. A very small, roiling fishbowl.

Jenna was so entangled in these thoughts that she didn't notice anyone following her until she was tackled from behind, and a large, calloused hand covered her mouth. The breath was knocked out of her, adding to her panic. A raspy voice said, "Mmm, you smell so good, Jenna. I bet you feel good, too." And then the other hand was thrust into her sports bra, rubbing and squeezing her right breast. Jenna stiffened, terrified by what was happening. What *might* happen. She felt paralyzed, unable to do anything. And then the hand slid into her running shorts, and her mind screamed as fingers probed her. The man groaned with pleasure. Jenna felt herself leave her body, floating upwards, away from what was happening. She could barely hear him when he said, "Tell your husband I'll come back and finish the job if he don't stop talkin' to the wrong people. It'll be the last fuck you'll ever have, darlin,' I promise you."

32

HAROLD DANFORTH, WEARING a gray, summer-weight suit and a black tie that shouted "funeral director," had changed very little since Joplin last saw him. His thick hair was a little grayer and his face a little more lined, but his smile was as warm as ever. If Joplin hadn't known better, he'd think Danforth was happy to see him.

"Well, this is a nice surprise," the coroner said, standing up behind his ornate desk and walking around it to grasp Joplin's right hand. A large brass chandelier loomed over them. "I never figured you'd drive Gunter's body up here yourself."

"The Milton County ME's Office is a full-service agency," said Joplin, giving Danforth his own brilliant smile.

"That's what I've been hearing, Hollis. Good catch your wife made during the autopsy. That Gunter had been murdered, I mean."

Joplin nodded and managed to keep the smile on his face, but it bothered him that Danforth knew Carrie had done the autopsy and that she was married to him. The last time he'd seen

Harold was at GPSTC for training several years ago. "Carrie's a good pathologist," he said offhandedly. "And she'd be happy to talk to you or whatever agency is investigating the murder. Would that be the Nolan PD?"

"I'm not sure," said Danforth, his eyes narrowing. "We coroners don't have much say in things like that."

Joplin nodded again and said, "Been there," although he knew Danforth was lying through his teeth. And then he did a little lying of his own. "Nice set-up you've got here. Very elegant," he added. Though much larger than most of the ones in Austell when he was growing up, the funeral home was filled with the same heavy Victorian furniture and swag draperies that Joplin remembered. Small towns seemed the same everywhere in Georgia, especially regarding their newspapers, churches, and funeral "parlors." These institutions were the social fabric and connective tissue of their residents' lives.

"Thank you," said Danforth, a proprietary smile on his face. "It's been in my family for three generations."

Joplin saw him glance surreptitiously at the grandfather clock in the corner and said, "Well, I know you're a busy man, Harold, and I need to get back to Atlanta, so if you just tell me where to put Mr. Gunter, I'll get going."

"Of course," said Danforth, looking relieved. "If you could bring the van around to the back, I'll help you get the body in."

He walked Joplin back to the expansive entry area and gestured toward the front doors, then turned and walked to the back of the building. Five minutes later, after passing through a large parking area bordered by extensive grounds with benches and sculptures scattered about, Joplin reached the discreet receiving bay. Danforth was waiting for him outside, the huge door propped open, the insincere smile back on his face. He met Joplin at the van's back doors and helped him lift the rolling stretcher holding Jacob Gunter's body onto the ground. By the time they reached the morgue, the funeral director was sweating, whether from the heat or the exertion, Joplin couldn't tell. However, he was pretty sure that Harold Danforth usually relegated that particular chore to an employee.

"You tell that pretty wife of yours I hope to meet her in the near future," Danforth said, mopping his face with a handkerchief when they were back outside.

"Will do," Joplin said. But he felt chilled, even under the midday sun, and it had nothing to do with the cooling chamber into which he'd helped place Gunter's body. What Harold Danforth had said about meeting Carrie felt more like a warning than a polite remark.

Or a threat.

✦ ✦ ✦ ✦

JOPLIN HAD CALLED Will Sykes before he'd left Atlanta and changed the location of their meeting. Despite his usual craving for chicken nuggets and waffle fries, he didn't want to show up at the Chick-fil-A in Canton driving the Milton County ME van. It might blow Will's cover, if he weren't the leaker, and also ruin the lunch crowd's appetites if they thought a body was inside it. Joplin's appetite had already been ruined by Harold Danforth, so he wasn't unhappy about having lunch at the FresqO Wings in the Canton outlet mall. It was far enough away from Rutledge County to be safe, and he could park the van in one of the crowded parking areas. He'd never had time to tell Carrie about the meeting, but this was one of those situations where it might be better to ask for forgiveness than permission. At least, that was what he told himself.

He still wasn't sure what—and how much—he was going to tell Sykes. The deputy had contacted Tullie soon after the discovery of what they all thought was Eric Jaeger's body, which seemed to be a point in his favor. But why? Was it professional courtesy or to expedite her having Jaeger declared dead and off supervision? He was also the first to tell Joplin about The Cause and that the Rutledge County sheriff might be involved when they'd met at Bigun's for lunch. But was that so Joplin would stay in touch and feed him information? But if so, why pave the way for Joplin and Tullie to view the footage from the Wolfscratch security gates?

His mind reeling from being unable to answer any of those questions, Joplin took exit 20 on I-575 and turned into the outlet mall. He was a few minutes late by the time he'd parked and walked a half mile into the mall's food court. Will was already seated at an out-of-the-way table, a big bag of food in front of him. He motioned Joplin to the chair across from him and said, "I got you some wings and fries. Hope that was okay."

"Perfect. Especially since that's about all that's on the menu."

"Hey, I'm sorry—"

"Don't be," Joplin said as he sat down. "I'm the one who had to change things. Besides, you're doing *me* a favor, remember?"

"Right. But catch me up on the Jacob Gunter thing. I still can't believe it. I just busted him a month ago."

Sykes opened the bag of food and parceled out the meals, plasticware, and napkins, then listened intently as Joplin took him through BJ Reardon's revelation that fingerprints on a whiskey bottle at the scene and the body that was autopsied led to the discovery that it was Gunter, not Eric Jaeger. He then gave some of the autopsy results, including the contents of his stomach. After taking a few bites of his wings, Joplin followed this with the sighting of the man in the truck going through the North gate at Wolfscratch who'd looked so much like Jaeger, and Judge Mabry's insistence that they turn the case over to the GBI.

Sykes' sudden pallor under his tan and his shocked expression almost convinced Joplin that he'd had no part in leaking information to Gabriel Benson. But out of deference to Sarah Petersen, he said nothing about finding the microchip hidden under the Southern Cross tattoo. Nor did he mention Gabriel Benson's knowing that it was not Jaeger's body they had found at the Upper Falls in Wolfscratch. What he did add to his narrative, however, was the untrue information that CSU was trying to get information from the handprints on Gunter's body.

"You mean, like latent fingerprints?" Sykes asked.

Joplin nodded. "That and touch DNA, if possible."

"But wouldn't the water have washed away any DNA evidence?"

"Probably. But I've been blown away by what the techies can do with minute amounts of DNA—even if it's degraded. They can harvest mitochondrial DNA from anything, it seems. That's from the maternal line, you know."

"I didn't," said Sykes. "That's amazing."

"It is," Joplin said solemnly. "But we're also trying to find out where Gunter had his last meal and where he got that Southern Cross tattoo. Carrie says his last meal was a chicken burrito with guacamole and sour cream. It might help to know where he ate that meal and where he got the tattoo. Any ideas?"

Sykes' brow furrowed. "Geez, Hollis, that's a tough one. There are about fifteen Mexican restaurants within ten miles of each other—same thing for tattoo parlors. Tats are pretty popular up here."

"I gotcha, Will. It's probably impossible to narrow down either one. Especially the tattoo artist. Given the secrecy surrounding The Cause, it might be someone not even connected to an ink location."

"Well, I'll try to check around, but I figure Sheriff Odum will be on high alert, now that a lot of people must know it wasn't Eric Jaeger whose body was found. Which opens up a whole other can of worms. Like, why did he have Jaeger's wallet on him? And where the hell is Jaeger now?"

Joplin was about to respond when his cell phone rang. He didn't recognize the number and let the call go to voicemail, then said, "Those are the two biggest questions in this entire investigation, Will. But I don't have any answers yet."

✦ ✦ ✦ ✦

JOPLIN LISTENED TO his voicemail as soon as he returned to the van. It was from Andrew McAllister, and within a minute, he understood why the editor hadn't used his cell phone. What he heard made him sick to his stomach. His first thought was of Carrie, because of Harold Danforth's veiled threat about hoping to meet her soon; he needed to do whatever it took to keep her safe—Maggie Halloran and Tullie, too. All of them, in fact, including Will Sykes. Jesse Waldrup was in another state, but Sykes lived and worked near many people who could be part of

The Cause. If the deputy were involved, Joplin wouldn't be compromising McAllister any further, and if he weren't involved, he might save Sykes' life.

He punched in the numbers for the deputy's phone, then explained the situation. Sykes' reaction seemed authentic and as disgusted as Joplin's. After telling him to be careful, Joplin clicked off and called Carrie, but got voicemail. Frustrated, he pulled out of the parking lot and headed for I-575. His thoughts kept going back to what McAllister had told him, and he made a mental note to let Tom Halloran know as soon as he could make a call. These thoughts were interrupted when a medium-sized gray truck cut him off. Joplin quickly moved into the right lane, but when he saw he might cut another car off, he veered onto the shoulder and slammed his foot onto the brake to avoid hitting the guard rail. Nothing happened. Furiously, he pumped the brake, but again, nothing happened. As he slammed into the rail, Joplin saw that it was there for a reason: He had just passed an exit that sloped down from the expressway. But the rail must have been old, because the van hurtled off the shoulder onto the exit ramp, then crashed into a large U-Haul truck.

33

CARRIE SAT IN Bay 4 of the Northside Cherokee ER and read through Hollis' chart. Miraculously, he had only suffered a mild concussion and three broken ribs. The sturdiness of the ME van had probably saved him from worse injuries. But although the nurse who had talked to her assured her his injuries weren't life-threatening, she'd needed to see that for herself.

"I told you I was fine," Hollis said sleepily. "You never believe me."

"Maybe that's because I've spent far too much time in ERs with you," she huffed. "And, besides, you are *not* 'fine,' Hollis. You have broken ribs and a concussion."

Hollis shrugged, then winced. "I'm not dying," he croaked.

"Well, you might *wish* you were dying when you try getting out of this bed."

"Is that any way to speak to the father of your child?" he asked, a pitiful expression on his face.

Carrie stood up and replaced the chart at the foot of Hollis' bed, then came back around and took his hand. "Okay, father of my child, how's this: I'm scared to death for you and our child's future because of your involvement in this Wolfscratch case. I've gone along with it until now because I don't like what's happening in Rutledge County any more than you do. But now I'm asking you to back off and let the GBI handle everything, including Jacob Gunter's death. What happened today might not have been an accident. Dr. Minton and Sarah agree."

Hollis stared solemnly back at her. "So do I," he said.

Carrie listened as Hollis told her about the horrible attack on Jenna McAllister and his suspicions that the brakes on the ME van had been tampered with. He also admitted that he'd met with Will Sykes after taking Gunter's body to the Danforth Funeral Home. She listened to his apology, then waved it off, needing to focus on the situation at hand. Her mind reeling from the implications, she said, "My God, Hollis, those people are not going to give up. Dr. Minton immediately contacted the GBI, but—"

"I'm on it, too, Carrie," said a voice behind her.

Carrie turned and saw Ike Simmons standing at the entrance to their exam room. A nurse pushed her way past him.

"I hope this is okay, Dr. Salinger," she said. "He said it was police business."

"Yes," she said quickly. "It's fine." When the nurse disappeared, Carrie hurried over to Ike and hugged him. "It's more than fine, Ike. How did you know?"

Ike grinned at her. "News travels fast when Hollis is involved, Carrie. You know that. After Dr. Minton contacted the GBI, he called me." He turned to Hollis and said, "The Cherokee County Sheriff's Office has the van now for their accident investigation, but what can you tell me about it? What do you remember?"

Hollis repeated what he'd just told Carrie about the phone call from Andrew McAllister and how the van had ended up on the exit ramp. From Ike's expression, she could tell he felt the same disgust and fear about what the people involved with The Cause had done. And might still do.

"Obviously, the GBI doesn't know about what happened to McAllister's wife," Ike said when Hollis had finished. "That will support our belief that this group might've sabotaged the van's brakes."

"Yeah, but I'm not sure we should tell them," Hollis said.

"Why not?" asked Carrie. "They *need* to know."

"I would agree, if I weren't so concerned that there might be a mole at the GBI, Carrie. Think about it: We don't know who alerted the counselor at Central Prison that it was Jacob Gunter's body we found at Wolfscratch. And we already know that one law enforcement agency is involved in this thing—the Rutledge County Sheriff's Office, not to mention the DA and the coroner. On the national level, the FBI has been connected to leaks to crime syndicates, and the CIA has had spies giving information to foreign adversaries like Russia. Who's to say the GBI is mole-free? And I don't want to risk that possibility where the McAllisters are concerned. Andrew told me they were leaving town immediately, but he didn't tell me where, and I didn't ask him."

"But you told Will Sykes about what happened to Jenna, Hollis," said Carrie. "Even though he works for Sheriff Odum," she added, suddenly furious over his meeting with the deputy despite his promise to her.

Hollis nodded. "I did. I thought he might be next, since he'd just met with me. And although it's true he might have alerted someone with The Cause about meeting with me and where to look for the ME van, so they could tamper with the brakes, I had to go with my gut. Besides, we *know* Howard Danforth is in this up to his neck."

"But, why?" asked Ike. "I get it that he and the DA and Sheriff Odum were controlling what passes as a criminal justice system in Rutledge County, but I don't understand Danforth's part in it."

"Money," said Hollis. "I think Howard Danforth was disposing of people who'd been murdered. Mostly by The Cause over the years, but there could've been others."

"You've got to be kidding!" Carrie said.

"I wish I were. Several funeral home scandals have been in the news in the past two decades. There was one in California involving three generations of a family-owned business— just like Danforth's—where they were doing mass cremations for other funeral homes, then packaging the cremains in individual urns for the bereaved families, which was illegal, not to mention fraudulent. Another one in New York was selling tissue and body parts to biomedical companies."

"But you're talking about murder, Hollis," said Ike.

"Think about it, Ike," he said. "We agree that there's an unholy alliance in Rutledge County between the sheriff, the DA, and the coroner. Unless the coroner flags a suspicious death and sends the body to be autopsied, nothing happens. That's the first and easiest way to cover up a murder. Harold just signs off on a death certificate, stating 'accidental death' or 'natural causes.' And even if a death is an obvious homicide, the sheriff can stonewall the investigation, or the DA can say there's insufficient evidence to prosecute a suspect."

"And they're doing this for money?" asked Carrie.

"Or power," said Hollis. "Probably both. At least in instances where a resident might have wanted to cover up a vehicular death while under the influence or a suicidal death in the family. That would give you quite a hold over someone, especially if they're wealthy and prominent. But I think any murders committed were for two reasons: to get rid of threats to The Cause or to provide an 'escape route' for people who needed to disappear."

"You mean, like an underground railroad for criminals instead of enslaved people?" Ike asked.

"That's a perfect description for it. Which brings us to Eric Jaeger." Hollis shifted his position in the hospital bed, looking extremely uncomfortable.

Carrie went to him and tried to help, then pushed the call button for the nurse. "You need to rest, Hollis. Or at least let me see if you can have some more meds now." Doctors no longer believed keeping a concussed patient awake for 24 hours was necessary, so Hollis had been given a low dosage of hydrocodone, but it hadn't done much for his pain.

Hollis shook his head. "I need to be alert. Too many people are in danger. Tullie especially. They know she's not going to give up on finding Jaeger. Or maybe Jaeger himself will go after her to shut her down. His faked death started all of this, Carrie."

"I know, Hollis, but—" She turned when the nurse entered the room. "He's alert, and his vital signs are stable," she told her. "But the hydrocodone hasn't touched the pain. Could you see if Dr. Montag will order something more?" The nurse nodded and left the room. When Hollis protested, Carrie said, "It's just to get your pain under control, Hollis. I saw the X-rays, and I know it hurts every time you breathe. Just keep telling us what we need to know, so we can get whatever protection everyone needs, okay?"

"Okay," said Hollis. He briefly closed his eyes, then said, "I think some of the people who needed to disappear just faked dying, and Harold Danforth issued a death certificate. But in Jaeger's case, they needed a dead body. He was on parole, so they had to be able to fool the EMTs and Tullie, if it came to that. Jacob Gunter was a gift. He was part of The Cause and looked enough like Jaeger to be his brother. Maybe that was why the militia recruited him in the first place. Because they knew Eric would need to disappear soon after he was paroled."

The nurse came in and nodded at Carrie, then administered the pain med through Hollis' IV.

"But why, Hollis?" Ike asked. "What was Jaeger doing for them?"

Hollis gave a low chuckle. "A lot of things. He had to report back to Harold about Brent Marsh. Tell him if Brent knew anything about some of the bodies he was sending to the Tri-State Crematory."

"Oh," said Carrie. "Now I understand. That's why that old woman you talked to in LaFayette asked you that question."

"Yes," said Hollis, his eyes closing. "'Do they stay dead?' Because she'd seen people who were *supposed* to be dead still walking around." He opened his eyes. "And Jaeger had to get some more meth labs going, because The Cause needed money. And he had to rope Aidan Fitzgerald into the whole thing, but I haven't figured that part out yet." Then his eyes closed again.

After several seconds, when Hollis didn't say anymore, Ike said, "You told him he wouldn't be knocked out."

Carrie shrugged. "I lied. He needs rest. Talking and even *thinking* a lot are just as bad as physical exertion for his injuries. And he's too stubborn to listen to any doctor's orders, mine included."

Ike raised his eyebrows and cocked his head. "You're preachin' to the choir, Carrie."

"I know, I know," she said. "Why would I need to tell *you* that, of all people?"

34

JESSE WALDRUP CAME out of the Piggly Wiggly on East Dickerson, about three miles from his sister's house in Nashville. She'd needed some onions, potatoes, and paper towels, and he'd offered to go to the store for her because he'd needed some beer and cigarettes. Kayla didn't mind his drinking beer—she liked her blush wine—but she wouldn't let Jesse smoke inside the house. That was okay with him, since she was letting him let him stay with her for a while. He'd told Kayla only that he needed a break from work when he'd called her on Sunday.

Jesse also liked being around his sister. She was coming off a rough divorce from Brian, a guy Jesse had never liked, a co-worker at the Enterprise car rental where Kayla had been a secretary. But she was over talking about it, thank God; instead, they discussed old times and friends from high school. Some were still in the area, and Kayla had contacted a few, arranging to meet with them on Friday night.

It wasn't a long drive back to Kayla's house, but Jesse wasn't in a hurry, needing a little more time to himself. And maybe another cigarette before he got there. He was used to living alone, and he'd been there four days now. So, when he saw the sign up ahead for the Country Tavern, Jesse made a quick right into the parking lot. Before getting out of the truck, he texted Kayla that he had to get gas, figuring he could come up with an excuse later as to why it took him so long to get back. Then he headed into the tavern.

It was exactly what its name implied: a small, rectangular building with sawdust on the floor, country music blaring, and patrons wearing jeans and cowboy boots even in the August heat. It was also dimly lit and well air-conditioned. Jesse made his way to the knotty pine bar and took a stool at the right end. He ordered Evan Williams on the rocks, then nodded his thanks to the bartender when he set a bowl of peanuts down in front of him. He was surprised when he felt someone tap him on the shoulder and quickly swiveled around. Jesse relaxed when he saw that it was Ethan Dockery. He'd known Ethan since they were both fourteen, but they'd gone their separate ways after high school. According to Kayla, Ethan had spent four years in the Army and was now a Maury County Sheriff's Office deputy. He was still in uniform, holding his hat in his left hand. A holstered gun rode high on his right hip. Jesse guessed he'd just gotten off shift.

"I heard you were in town," Ethan said, clapping him on the back. His dark hair was thinning, and there were lines around his blue eyes, but he hadn't changed much since their ten-year high school graduation reunion a few years ago. Still in good shape, too.

"I needed some stale air," Jesse said, gesturing to include the bar. Then he grinned and said, "I guess I'm really playin' hooky. I'm staying with Kayla, but I just felt like gettin' out of the house for a bit."

"I hear ya," said Ethan. "Kayla's a great gal, and so is Janie," he added, referring to his wife, "but sometimes we just need to let off some steam, right, buddy?"

"Right," Jesse agreed, relaxing even more. "But I can't let off too much steam 'cause she's expectin' me soon. I got some things she needs for dinner in my truck, so I can't stay long."

"No problem," Ethan said, sitting on the stool next to him. He beckoned the bartender over, then ordered a beer. "You leave whenever you need to."

Somehow, that need faded over the next forty minutes as they swapped stories and ordered another round of drinks. Ethan confessed that his marriage was shaky and he wasn't happy with his job. Then he asked about Jesse's job, and Jesse said he loved it and was also doing some writing for the paper, but was taking a leave of absence. When Ethan expressed surprise at this, Jesse found himself telling him about The Cause and what had happened in the forest. When Ethan seemed shocked, he felt comfortable going a little further, telling his old friend about the meeting with Hollis Joplin.

"Well, that was a good idea," Ethan said, motioning to the bartender for another round. "Because you don't need that kind of shit. How'd you get in touch with this Joplin guy?"

So, Jesse told him about Andrew and all he'd done for him. Said that was why he'd agreed to talk to Joplin in the first place. It wasn't until Ethan asked him if he'd spoken about The Cause to Kayla that a red flag flashed in his alcohol-befuddled brain. He took a last sip of his third drink, set it on the bar, and motioned to the bartender.

"That reminds me: I better get going, Ethan," Jesse said, standing up, then reaching for his wallet in his back pocket. He felt a little unsteady, but tried hard not to let it show. "Kayla will be worried by now. Which is why I haven't told her about any of this and don't plan to. She's had enough on her plate lately, what with the divorce and all."

"I totally understand," Ethan said, standing up, too. "Let me pick up the tab," he added when the bartender handed Jesse the bill. When Jesse started to object, he said, "Let's get together again before you go back to Georgia, and you can get that tab."

"Sounds good," Jesse said, clapping Ethan on the back and trying not to pull away too quickly when Ethan did the same. "See you soon. I'll call you."

Jesse made sure to walk slowly, both because he was buzzed and because he didn't want Ethan to think he was getting away from him as fast as he could. Which was exactly what Jesse wanted to do. Once in the truck, he called Kayla to tell her he was on the way, then said, "Don't let anyone in until I get there."

"Why not?" she asked. "You're scaring me, Jesse."

"Just please do what I said, Kayla. I'll explain everything when I get to your place."

No cars were in his sister's driveway when Jesse made it there ten minutes later, nor any on the street, which eased his mind somewhat. By the time he knocked on the door and identified himself, he'd decided he'd overreacted to Ethan's probing questions. But when Kayla opened the door and took the grocery bag from him, pelting him with questions, Jesse sat down at the kitchen table and motioned for her to join him. It was time to come clean about why he'd asked to stay with her.

✦ ✦ ✦ ✦

IT HAD TAKEN a while for Jesse to convince his sister that they needed to get out of Nashville as soon as possible, giving him some time to sober up. But, in the end, she agreed. An hour later, they'd packed enough clothes for several days and enough supplies to last them two or three days. Jesse had also texted Andy McAllister that his cover had been blown because he'd said too much to an old friend, Ethan Dockery, who might have ties to The Cause. He added that he would call when he and Kayla reached a safe place. They left the TV on, a light in the living room, and one in each of their bedrooms, but killed the outside lights.

They loaded up the car and left the neighborhood slowly and quietly, the headlights off. Jesse hadn't had an answer earlier to Kayla's repeated questions of where they would go, and he didn't have one by the time they reached the interstate either.

"I'm thinkin'," he said as they left the northern Nashville city limits. Jesse was still thinking when they passed the Galettsville exit. But he stopped thinking five minutes later on a lonely stretch of the interstate, just after the White Bluffs exit, when headlights suddenly appeared in his rear-view mirror. Jesse watched, eyes jerking between the mirror and the road ahead, as a small truck pulled alongside them, the driver pointing a gun at him. He sped past the truck, but the driver quickly pulled even with them again, and the gunman took aim.

"Duck!" he yelled to Kayla before making a hard right off the road. In seconds, the car was tumbling down a low, sloping shoulder. The last thing Jesse remembered was the airbag exploding in his face.

35

HALLORAN'S CELL PHONE rang at 9:30 Friday morning. He recognized Joplin's number. "Does Carrie know you're calling me, Hollis? You're supposed to be resting."

"Jesse Waldrup, the stringer for the Rutledge County newspaper, died in a car accident in Tennessee last night," Hollis said. He sounded exhausted.

"Oh, my God, that's terrible! I thought he was in a safe place."

"So did he. He was staying with his sister. She's in the ICU in a hospital just north of Nashville. They're not sure she'll make it, according to Andrew McAllister. He called me last night."

Halloran sighed. "Any chance this wasn't an accident?"

"There's *every* chance it was no accident. Andrew told me he'd gotten a voicemail from Jesse around 8 p.m., saying his cover had been blown, and he and his sister were leaving town. He said he'd be in touch when he got to a safe place. Jesse also warned Andrew that he'd mentioned his name and my name to someone he thought it was safe to talk to, and that we all might be at risk." Halloran heard Hollis sigh. "He was sure right about that, but Jenna McAllister was attacked, and I was almost killed, hours before Jesse talked to this person he thought was trustworthy."

"My God," said Halloran. "I can't believe this, Hollis! This thing is totally out of control. Did Andrew ever make contact with him?"

"No. He tried a few times with no luck. He also tried to get me, but Carrie had turned my cell phone off, and I didn't know till later last night. Then, the State Patrol called Andrew after the crash, trying to locate Jesse's next of kin. They'd found his number on a card in Jesse's wallet. So, Andrew told them about the voicemail he'd gotten and a little bit about why Jesse was in hiding. They said they were going to open a homicide investigation. After that, Andrew called me. I'm not sure it was a good idea for him to say that much, since the friend Jesse talked to was with the Maury County Sheriff's Office, but what's done is done."

"Did the State Patrol give him any details about the accident?" Holloran asked.

"Just that his car had gone off the road and over an embankment. Jesus Christ, Tom! I opened a can of worms that's gotten one, maybe two, people killed if the sister dies, not to mention everything else that's happened. Or *could* happen."

"It's bad, Hollis. I know that. But none of this is your fault."

"I told McAllister that I'd protect Jesse," he said. "I gave my word."

"Yes, but he wanted to stay with his sister, right? Jesse said he'd be safe there, and the GBI didn't think he needed to be in protective custody."

It was Joplin's turn to sigh. "No," he said. "But the real question is how The Cause found out where Jesse was. And how they tracked him after he and his sister decided to leave town."

"Probably the same way they found out you and McAllister were in on this. Have you notified the GBI? I know you were reluctant to earlier, but this is a game-changer."

"Yes, we've had several phone calls about the situation, and they're on it. They also urged us all to move to safe houses with our families."

"I think that's a good idea, Hollis. What does Carrie think?"

"She totally agrees. But that means you and your family, too, Tom. Tullie, as well."

Halloran was blindsided by this; he took a gulp of his coffee as he thought about it. "I think that might be overkill, Hollis. Ike has put a patrol car in front of our house and insists that we stay inside for the next few days. We'll be fine."

"Yeah, but do you want to take that chance? With your family? Think about it, Tom. It's well-known that the four of us found what turned out to be Jacob Gunter's body. And that you and I have worked together on previous cases. They also know that Tullie is Eric Jaeger's parole supervisor, and that she's still looking for him. Also, she's related to you."

"Yeah, I guess so," Halloran said reluctantly. "And I think I'd better talk to Maggie about this. What did you mean when you said, 'safe house?'"

"Somewhere in Wolfscratch. It's the perfect place."

"Have you lost your fucking mind, Hollis? Wolfscratch would be among my top three places for us to avoid right now!"

"Just hear me out. Tom," Joplin urged him. "The GBI will have our backs, according to ASAC Masterson. He's pushing for this because the GBI has had someone undercover in The Cause for a few months. Remember I had a hunch about this? He evidently contacted them, so they were able to open a preliminary investigation, but he's gone silent for some reason.

No new information has been sent out in several weeks, and they can't contact him. They've known the militia is going to do something big, but they don't know what it is. Or when and where it will happen. So, this plan has been approved. We'll have lots of security, and since Wolfscratch is a gated community, they can monitor people going in and out."

"Yes, but it's not an *enclosed* community, as you pointed out. No electrified gates to keep the bad guys out."

"No, but agents will be surrounding the house."

"What house? You can't possibly mean the firm's house! Please tell me you don't mean that."

"61 Blue Ridge Lane, Tom. You got it."

Halloran couldn't talk for several seconds. Then he took a deep breath and said, "Now I know you're absolutely out of your mind, Hollis. I thought letting yourself be drugged with Rohypnol two years ago to catch Blaine Reynolds' killer was bad enough, but this is over the top! You're talking about setting us up as bait for these terrorists, aren't you?"

"Not specifically, but they might think it would be a good time to smoke us out, so to speak."

Halloran was almost rendered speechless again. "I think you mean 'smoke us,' Hollis. And you'd be willing to put your pregnant wife in that kind of danger?"

"No, of course not," Joplin said quickly. "Or Maggie and Tullie, either. What kind of person do you think I am?"

Halloran almost slapped himself. "The kind," he said slowly, "who needs to speak clearly and transparently. Tell me *exactly* what you and the GBI have in mind, or I'll hang up."

He heard Joplin sigh into the phone. "You're right, Tom. I got ahead of myself. And I know you need things to be all logical and planned out. My fault entirely. So, here goes: Tullie has opted to stay with her parents; she insists she'll be safe there. But if you and Maggie sign on, the four of us will drive to Wolfscratch later today in your car and go through the North gate, just as we did before, getting a two-day pass. Then we'll all have dinner at the Clubhouse, but instead of returning to 61 Blue Ridge Lane, Maggie and Carrie will go to another house with two GBI special agents."

"And we'll be sitting ducks," Halloran said. "I like the part where our wives are out of the picture, but not the rest of it, Hollis. Besides, what do we say when Moira and Ryan hear that we're up there? And without telling them?"

"That's the beauty part, Tom: We're going to tell them. And invite them and Tullie to join us at the Clubhouse tonight. But we'll be busy after that if the Fitzgeralds want to get together. Tullie plans to go to Fox Run on Saturday with her father to find out what Aidan is up to—remember you thought his excuse for not going to St. Kitts with his wife didn't add up? So, you and I can hike or play golf; we just won't have our wives with us. And there'll be some female GBI agents at the house taking their places in case anybody's watching."

Halloran took his time mulling this over. Then he said, "And you're telling me Carrie is okay with all of this? I'm finding that hard to believe. Not only is it inherently dangerous, but you're also recovering from a concussion and broken ribs."

Joplin cleared his throat. "Not *all* of it, I'll admit that. I'm still working out the details with the GBI."

Halloran laughed out loud. "You're one of the bravest men I know, Hollis," he said, "except when it comes to telling your wife something she doesn't want to hear. I'll bet my membership at the Driving Club that she doesn't know a thing about the two lady GBI agents."

"Did I tell you we want you and Maggie to be the baby's god-parents, Tom?"

"Don't try to bribe me, Hollis. Besides, I thought you were raising her in the Jewish faith. There won't be a baptism, right?"

"Right, but there'll be a baby-naming ceremony, and there are godparents for that. Sort of, anyway."

"Does that mean you have a name for the baby?"

He heard Joplin sigh. "Not yet, but we will by the time she's born. I promise."

"Okay, Hollis. I know I'll regret this, but I'll talk to Maggie. And if she agrees, so will I. But there's no guarantee that Carrie will. In fact, I'm counting on it."

✢ ✢ ✢ ✢

HALLORAN CALLED MAGGIE after he got off the phone and filled her in on Jesse Waldrup's presumed murder. She was shocked and furious at the callous ruthlessness the white supremacy group had shown in trying to destroy two people—three, including Hollis—and that they might have contacts, if not members, in Tennessee law enforcement. She was also shocked by what had happened to Jenna McAllister and afraid for everyone else they might target. But to his great surprise, Maggie agreed to the whole crazy scheme Hollis had outlined after asking a few questions of her own. Most of them involved the specifics of the GBI's protection strategies for him and Hollis after she and Carrie left for the safe house. Others had to do with where Megan and Tommy would be staying and what they'd tell the Fitzgeralds about going up to Wolfscratch again.

"I figured the kids could stay with your parents again, if that's okay. And I guess we could tell Moira and Ryan that Healey and Caldwell had to cancel another client golf weekend, so the house was free. They won't really care, will they?"

"I doubt it. But what if they mention it to Aidan? We still don't know what his involvement might be in Jaeger's disappearance."

"Letting people know who might be associated with The Cause seems to be the whole purpose of our going up there, Maggie. Maybe I didn't make it clear: It's a fishing expedition, and we're the bait."

"No," Maggie said, sighing. "You were very clear. And I want these people caught just as much as Hollis does. As *you* do, Tom. We have an opportunity to help prevent whatever violent acts the people in this group are contemplating. And whether we like it or not, Aidan might be part of that group, as well as my aunt and uncle."

"Exactly."

"But what about Healey and Caldwell? Should you notify David Healey? They probably won't want the firm's house involved in this."

"That's a valid concern, but I'll only talk to Alston Caldwell, not David."

"So," said Maggie, "I guess we're all just waiting to see if Carrie signs on."

✛ ✛ ✛ ✛

"ABSOLUTELY NOT!" CARRIE Joplin said later that morning. They were sitting on the loveseat in their bedroom, the cats beside them, and his ears hurt as she let him know, in detail, exactly how she felt. The uniformed officer was downstairs, and their bedroom door was closed, but he doubted that muffled much of his wife's outrage over the "absurdity of an idea like that" or what he was "possibly thinking." Did he even remember, she asked him, that he'd almost been killed not 24 hours earlier? And even though the people with the Cherokee County Sheriff's Office weren't positive the van's brakes had been sabotaged, given its age and maintenance history, didn't he remember that they thought it was 'likely'? And didn't he realize he was going to be a father soon?

Things went on like this for several minutes, then Joplin put his arms around her, ignoring a loud complaint from his ribs. "You're absolutely right," he murmured into her hair. "I wasn't thinking. I'll tell Masterson that we're not on board. Tom and Maggie can go up there alone or change their minds, when I tell them we're not going."

"Tom and Maggie are going?"

Joplin nodded. "Yes, I just heard from Tom. He even got permission from Alston Caldwell to use the firm's house. But their situation is a little different from ours."

"Oh," said Carrie. "I guess so, even though they have children. So, maybe I should just call Maggie to make sure she understands what the risk is. Even to them, I mean."

"That isn't necessary, sweetie. We're all grown-ups. And no matter what the Hallorans decide to do, you and the Bump are my priorities."

36

JOPLIN WAS FIXING lunch for three, which included Jackson Denning, their police protection, when he heard Carrie come downstairs. He looked up as she walked into the kitchen. "Are you hungry?" he asked her.

"Always, but you should have let me do that," she said, eying the tuna salad he'd just made. "You're supposed to be resting, remember?"

"I'm not dizzy anymore, and making sandwiches isn't hurting my ribs, sweetie. Besides, I could say the same about you. You had to take care of me yesterday, and then we were both up half the night after the phone call from Andrew McAllister."

Carrie pulled three plates out of the cabinet and bent to gather paper napkins from a drawer. "I'm too upset about all this right now, Hollis. Have you called Masterson yet?"

"Yep. Right after we talked. He understood."

"Oh," she said, sounding a little surprised. "I didn't think you'd do it so quickly."

"Don't tell me you've changed your mind just because the Hallorans are going to Wolfscratch."

"Not really. I mean, that's not why."

Joplin set down the spoon he was using to spread tuna salad on the bread slices. "Carrie, you laid out some very logical and compelling reasons why going up to Wolfscratch would be extremely dangerous. And I agree with you. What's going on?"

"I know, Hollis, and all those reasons are still true. It's just that I did go ahead and call Maggie. And I think I hadn't looked at the whole picture when I said we shouldn't go."

"And what is the 'whole picture?' Because I meant it when I said you and the baby were my highest priorities. And you were right. This is the GBI's job, not ours."

"And I genuinely appreciate that, Hollis." Carrie took a deep breath, then said, "It's just that you were also right when you said we had a unique opportunity to help the GBI prevent what could be the deaths of many people. I don't know if I could live with myself, if we didn't try. And you said that Masterson could keep us safe afterward."

"Yes, but there are no guarantees, even under the best circumstances. And we'd be going up there blind. We don't know who in Wolfscratch might be involved in Jacob Gunter's death or with The Cause."

"Isn't that why we'd be going up there? To try to find out if there's a connection? You told us how the ATF kept those two militia guys from spreading ricin in Georgia back in 2011, remember? So, we have to trust that these federal agencies and the GBI know what they're doing. And I also trust *you*, Hollis. And Tom. The two of you have solved some pretty difficult cases in the past, when you finally started working together instead of keeping things from each other. At least this time, we're all on the same page."

"You and I *think* that, Carrie. But I'm never sure with Tom. And who knows what else Tullie might be holding back? She's still very protective of her family."

"I guess that's a chance we'll have to take. But how can I complain about the world we're bringing our daughter into, if I don't try to help keep it safer, Hollis? It's everybody's responsibility, and I shouldn't get a free pass because I'm pregnant."

Joplin closed his eyes and gave a long sigh. Then he looked at Carrie and said, "Okay, but we'll follow the original script: We have dinner at the Clubhouse with Ryan, Moira, and Tullie tonight, and then GBI agents will move you and Maggie to a safe house. Agreed?"

"Agreed."

✦ ✦ ✦ ✦

WITHIN AN HOUR, GBI agents were discreetly in place in and around their house. A man and a woman dressed in street clothes informed them they were there to take photos of Carrie and gather some of her clothes for the agent who would be standing in for her that weekend at Wolfscratch. He could tell that the magnitude of what they'd agreed to do had hit Carrie, but she cooperated fully. The agents' visit lasted about forty-five minutes.

Afterward, they spent a little time calming the cats down; Banshee and Quincy weren't used to strangers moving around the house. After coaxing them out from under their bed and brushing them, Joplin and Carrie gave them some catnip treats and collapsed on the sofa. Joplin took some Extra-Strength

Tylenol for the headache building behind his eyes and the broken ribs he'd neglected all day. Then he made a quick call to Tom Halloran and discovered they'd just had a similar experience, albeit without having to calm cats.

"I guess there's no turning back now," he said.

"Was there ever?" Tom asked.

✚ ✚ ✚ ✚

HAROLD DANFORTH PACED up and down his office. He needed to prepare for a viewing later in the afternoon, but was too keyed up. Everything would be coming to a head soon. Everything they'd been working for and praying for. And paying for, God help him. Harold shuddered to think of all the money that had passed through their hands. His hands, really, and *only* his hands, because Hoyt Odum said his books and accounts would be subject to auditing and periodic checks. And that pussy, Lamar Worthy, said the same thing, of course. So, it had been up to him to open a checking account in another county under another name to handle the money. Although he'd done that before when he'd sold body parts to medical schools back in the Nineties. Which was how Odum had gotten his hooks into him.

Danforth sighed and stopped pacing for a few minutes. It was all because of his leeching relatives. No, make that Mayellen's leeching relatives. They knew a good thing when they saw it, God help him. So, when Mayellen got pregnant the first time she'd let him have sex with her, her Mama and Daddy had hustled him into marrying her before he knew what was happening.

They'd been living off him ever since. Even when he had to borrow against the business, something his father and grandfather had never done. Then, a medical supply salesman told him he could have a lucrative side business dealing in cadaver tissue and parts. And he'd been right. Right up until Hoyt had told him he knew all about it and threatened to arrest him unless Harold started "helping" The Cause. Reluctantly, Harold had agreed, even though he didn't give a hoot about all that Confederacy crap.

But helping The Cause by declaring certain suspicious deaths accidental and using Tri-State to dispose of the bodies had ultimately resulted in his business insurance rates being tripled when the scandal hit. Then, Odum had roped him into drug trafficking by using his mortuary van and limos to transport meth concealed in caskets around the state and across state lines.

"It's a perfect cover," Odum had said. "Who would ever think to look inside a casket? Or want to?"

But Harold would do it all over again, because that was how he'd met the love of his life. And all that nonsense about the Lost Cause mattered to *her*. Maybe it was the only thing that mattered to her.

Harold Danforth wondered at times if he meant anything more to her than a means to an end, but he didn't care. She was so far above him in every way that mattered: looks, intelligence, class—anything he could think of, she had it over him. And he knew he would never refuse to do whatever she asked of him. Which was why the whole crazy idea, from what little he knew about the Mission, had to work. Hoyt had agreed to cut him loose afterwards. Then they could both leave lives that they didn't want anymore and be together.

She had promised him.

37

THEIR GROUP WAS seated at a table overlooking Lake Sconset. Halloran was certain that was due to the Fitz-geralds' high profile at Wolfscratch. Getting a reservation at the last minute for seven people for the Friday night seafood buffet was almost impossible; getting one with a lake view was unheard of. He knew this because of complaints from other partners when they'd tried it themselves, for hastily arranged golf weekends sponsored by Healey and Caldwell.

And it was Labor Day weekend.

It was also a lovely evening. With very little wind to ruffle it, the lake looked like a mirror reflecting the cloudless sky above. And although it wasn't leaf season yet, the dogwoods dotting the surrounding mountains were already turning red. Halloran might even have enjoyed himself, if he and the Joplins weren't up there offering themselves as bait for some unhinged back-woods militia.

They'd all been unusually quiet on the drive from Atlanta, especially after Joplin had received a call from ASAC Masterson telling him agents had secured the area around the house on Blue Ridge Lane. But when Halloran had pulled into the driveway thirty minutes later, there was no sign of anyone, neither agents nor, hopefully, people out to kill them. Despite this, they'd wasted no time depositing their weekend bags and freshening up before heading to the Clubhouse where, Masterson had assured Joplin, security was already in place. Now, as his eyes moved from the lake to a room packed with diners shuttling back and forth from the buffet area, Halloran wondered whether the GBI had coordinated these measures with Wolfscratch Public Safety and what they might have told them.

"So, what are we doing the rest of the weekend?" Moira asked, returning him to another stressful aspect of his current reality. Her right hand went up to finger the turquoise and silver necklace at her throat. She was wearing a long denim skirt and a white shirt belted by even more turquoise and silver. All purchased on their last visit to Taos, she'd said earlier, when Maggie had complimented her on her outfit.

"Mother, I'm sure they all have plans for the rest of the weekend," Tullie said quickly. "Tee times and hiking and stuff."

Halloran sipped his Martini—Grey Goose with a twist—and smiled broadly. "Well, Hollis and I do have a foursome set up with two clients of mine who are here on their own dollar for a change, but we could all take in a vineyard tomorrow afternoon. Maybe Fainting Goat? I love that place."

"That sounds wonderful," Maggie said. "Carrie and I are going to relax around the pool for most of the day, but we'd love to go to a vineyard."

That was the story they'd agreed to give the Fitzgeralds, if Moira insisted on getting together again. The plan was that Maggie—from the safe house—would call early Saturday afternoon and say that Carrie wasn't feeling well, but they could all spend some time together on Sunday. Another lie.

Halloran, still a Catholic at heart, if not every Sunday, silently prayed to St. Jude, the saint who handled impossible requests, that Moira wouldn't insist on taking chicken soup to Carrie. But at least Tullie would be on hand to run interference.

Hollis lifted his own Martini, also Grey Goose, but with blue cheese olives, and said, "Here's to golf and goats. May they never be on the same grass at the same time that we are."

✠ ✠ ✠ ✠

TWO FEMALE GBI special agents, who would look like Maggie and Carrie from a distance, were already in place when they returned to the house on Blue Ridge Lane. The Carrie looka-like wore a pregnancy prosthesis; both women wore some of the clothes taken the day before in Atlanta. Two other agents, both male, appeared and explained that they would remain inside with them. They said several others, including ATF agents, were stationed around the house. Within minutes, Maggie and Carrie were whisked into a dark sedan and off to the safe house. All of their phones had been confiscated as soon as they returned from the Clubhouse— for "safekeeping," said Master-son, since they could be tracked through them. Halloran and Hollis were instructed not to sit outside by the pool, because that area couldn't be secured, given the density of the trees sur-rounding the house on that side. But otherwise, they were free to move around the main floor.

The two female agents gave their names as Laura Fielding and Gabby Waters, impersonating Maggie and Carrie, respectively. Although Laura's facial features were nothing like Maggie's, Halloran marveled at how she—or whoever had prepped her—had captured his wife's look and short, pixie hairstyle. His surprise must have shown, because Laura smiled and said, "I'm wearing a wig. And we tried to find something that resembled what your wife was wearing tonight. We have some people at the GBI who work with undercover agents, doing make-up and clothes."

"Were they the ones who came to our house?" Halloran asked.

"No, those people were there just to gather things for them and take photos. The people I'm talking about were hired because they're experts in their field, which makes us all feel safer when we go undercover."

"Well, they certainly did a good job," he said, forcing himself to smile; the overall effect was a little disturbing. From the expression on Hollis' face, Halloran thought he might be feeling the same way. The GBI stylists had managed to find a prosthesis that matched Carrie's baby bump perfectly. Or maybe they just had one that could be shaped to the proper size. Gabby also wore a long, dark wig and an outfit similar to Carrie's that evening.

"I need a drink," Hollis said abruptly, heading for the small bar in the kitchen. "Ladies?"

"We're on duty," said Laura Fielding. "Just tonic and lime, if you have it."

"Same for me," Gabby said, patting her stomach.

"I'll fix my own," Halloran said, moving in Hollis' direction.

✛ ✛ ✛ ✛

AT HOLLIS' REQUEST, they watched a recap of the news on CNN. Hurricane Hermine had hit the Florida coast, and Georgia was preparing for flash flooding over the next 48 hours. Elon Musk's Space X rocket had exploded at the Kennedy Space Center two days before its scheduled launch. And Hillary Clinton's campaign reported that she had raised $143 million in August, her most significant monthly haul for the 2016 election. Hollis clapped his hands, cheering loudly. Gabby looked at him sharply, then laughed.

"You're not for Trump?" she asked him, when the show went to a commercial.

"Hell, no!" Joplin said and would undoubtedly have said more on the subject, if Halloran hadn't stood up and suggested they play cards instead.

They played poker on the kitchen table. Hollis got up around 9:30 to make himself another drink and glanced at him, but Halloran shook his head, too tense to drink anymore. He was concerned that the alcohol might affect him more at this point. The fact that four GBI agents and several other law enforcement agents surrounding the house were there to protect them didn't make him feel any easier. Jesse Waldrup's "friend," a sheriff's deputy, had evidently shown up at the bar to find out if he'd talked to anyone about The Cause, shortly before Jesse and his sister had been run off the road. And Will Sykes had told Joplin he was concerned that some Rutledge County deputies—and the sheriff himself—were members of The Cause. Or sympathetic to it, at the very least.

So, when Gabby gave a big yawn and said she needed to go to bed, Halloran was almost relieved. Almost. Because, of course, the two agents would be in the bedrooms with him and Hollis. At least, he thought so; the arrangements hadn't been discussed earlier. Maybe they would leave and join the other two agents once the lights were out.

Either way, he thought, *I won't be getting much sleep tonight.*

Laura stood up and took his hand, then bade the others good-night. Hollis and "Carrie" were staying in the master bedroom, while he and "Maggie" were in an upstairs bedroom, just like the first time they'd all been there together. After turning out the lights, they all went their separate ways.

As soon as Halloran and Laura were in the bedroom, she closed the drapes, then turned to him. "Are you carrying a gun?" she asked him.

"No," he said. "I don't even own one."

"Well, do you know how to shoot one?"

"Yes, although it's been a long time."

Laura pulled a smallish-looking gun from her back waistband and showed it to him. It was a revolver. She cocked it, putting a round in the chamber, then handed it to him. "I'm going to join Ted, Marty, and Gabby for a bit, but I'll be back."

"Okay," said Halloran, but he really wasn't. Had she given him the gun because she, too, had doubts about her fellow law enforcement agents? Or was it simply insurance, if all else failed? After Laura left the room, he didn't have long to wonder, because the door opened again, and Hollis rushed in.

"What the fuck is going on?" he asked. "Did Laura ask if you had a gun?"

"Yes, and she gave me one, when I said I didn't."

"Give it to me."

"Why?"

"Because I need to see if the ammo is real."

38

THEY SLIPPED OUT of the house through the French doors leading to the pool area. Joplin had listened carefully at the end of the bedroom area hall to the buzz of conversation from the kitchen and determined that an emergency meeting had been called. The GBI agents seemed concerned about an ATF agent who was part of the outside surveillance team. While they were busy calling for backup, Joplin had motioned for Tom to follow him down the stairs at the end of the hall.

"How are we going to get past the surveillance team?" Tom whispered. The only light came from the full moon reflected in the pool.

"Not sure. Stay close behind me and hug the house while I figure it out."

"I thought you had a plan."

"I did. It was to come up here and be protected by the GBI and various federal agents. That's not working out."

"But the threat seems to be coming from the ATF, Hollis."

"Maybe. But there could be more than one threat."

"What does that mean?"

"Be quiet, Tom. I can't strategize and answer questions at the same time."

After a few more minutes, during which Joplin mentally measured the distance to the bamboo on the other side of the pool, then from the bamboo to the forest beginning at the house's boundary line, he signaled for Tom to follow him to the back of the house. "I'm going to make a dash for the diving board and squat down behind it. If no one shoots at me, wait 30 seconds and follow me."

"What if someone shoots at *me*?"

"Shoot back at them. Don't you still have Laura's gun?"

"No. I left it on the dresser after you finished checking it out. I didn't want her to get in trouble for giving it to me."

Joplin shook his head and said, "Then I guess if anyone shoots you, *I'll* have to shoot back and go for help, since I still have my gun. But relax, Tom. If anyone is watching us, he'll shoot me first."

"That doesn't make me feel any better," muttered Tom.

"Then go back upstairs and play happy couple with Laura. Just don't say anything about my escape."

"And explain to Carrie that I might have let you get killed? Or to Maggie that I trusted some strange woman over you? Not a chance."

"So, shut the fuck up and do what I said," Joplin hissed. He darted away from the house, then ducked down when he made it to the diving board unscathed. Thirty seconds later, Tom crab-walked over to him.

"Now, what?" he whispered to Joplin. "And don't tell me you need to think about it."

✦ ✦ ✦ ✦

TWENTY MINUTES LATER, they were creeping along Blue Ridge Lane, taking cover behind trees when cars passed them. Joplin's ribs were killing him from the exertion. After ten more minutes, however, they'd reached Wandering Deer Pass, and he decided it was safe to try to catch a ride.

"Stay out of sight while I check things out, Tom. The last thing we want is to get picked up by a member of our so-called 'security team.'"

"Maybe I'd rather just take my chances with them instead of *you*, Hollis. This whole thing is ridiculous. I mean, what are you going to say to someone who stops to pick us up, anyway? Our car broke down? We decided not to take our cell phones with us when we left the house at ten o'clock at night? Which brings us to my favorite question: Where were we going, Hollis?"

"Don't worry, I'll think of something."

"That's exactly what I *am* worrying about."

"Next time I'm trying to smoke out a right-wing militia, I'm not bringing you, Tom."

A few minutes later, aided by the full moon, Joplin was able to make out a red Mercedes convertible with the top down heading toward them, a blond woman at the wheel. As it got closer, he saw that the woman was Betsey Cunningham. Quickly, he waved his arms to attract her attention and called out to Tom to join him.

The car slowed to a stop, and Betsey gave them a delighted smile. "Need a ride, boys?"

"We sure do," Joplin said. "Our car broke down, and we didn't want to call the house because the girls have already gone to bed." He ignored Tom's poke in his lower back, even though his ribs began to complain again.

"Well, I don't have any jumper cables, so do you want me to take you back to where you're staying or over to Public Safety? They can probably jump-start your car."

"Actually, if you could just drop us off at the Fitzgeralds' house, we'd appreciate it," Tom said. "I'm sure they've got jumper cables."

Betsey didn't ask why they hadn't just called the Fitzger-alds for a ride—or even seem to wonder where their car was. Joplin mentally slapped his head for not explaining that, but it evidently hadn't occurred to her. Maybe all those blonde jokes were accurate, he decided.

"Sure, no problem," was all she said. "But I need to drop some-thing off at a friend's house first. It's just down the street on Wild Turkey Run. Hop in."

Joplin was about to get in the back, but Betsey smiled again and patted the seat next to her. Reluctantly, he went around the car to the passenger side. Tom got in the back seat behind Betsey. They made small talk, Tom telling her how they'd decided to go to the Clubhouse bar for a nightcap after Maggie and Carrie went to bed, and that neither of them had thought to take their cell phones.

"Drinks at a bar are always more fun than at home," Betsey said, sounding as if she were talking about something com-pletely different. And although he'd only known Betsey Cun-ningham a short time, Joplin was certain that was her intention. As if confirming this, she put her right hand on his left thigh and squeezed it. She turned to give him another delighted smile, then veered left off on Wild Turkey Run, leaving her hand where it was. Joplin began to wish he'd taken Tom's advice and stayed at the house. He was better with a gun than handling a woman like Betsey.

"Here we are," she sang out, pulling into a long circular drive in front of an imposing, almost contemporary, house. It was built with cedar shakes but had vast expanses of glass, and Joplin wondered why anyone would build a house like that when most of Wolfscratch boasted handsome Craftsman-style houses. Evidently, he decided, it was owned by people oblivious to their surroundings. But they'd managed to make a lot of friends anyway; there were several other cars in the driveway, plus a few on the street.

"Is there a party going on?" Tom asked.

"There sure is, sugar," she said, getting out of the car. "It's Labor Day weekend, after all. And y'all can help me take in the bags of ice, if you don't mind. Then I'll get you to Moira and Ryan's house. It'll just take a minute."

Betsey popped the trunk, which was packed with bags of ice. They each grabbed a couple and walked up to the house. The sound of music reached them before they made it to the broad stone steps.

But what awaited them wasn't your average Labor Day weekend party.

✦ ✦ ✦ ✦

THE INTERIOR WAS lit by hundreds of candles and perfumed by pot and patchouli. Donna Summers' "Love to Love You, Baby" pulsated loudly, accompanying about ten people as they gyrated in the middle of a sunken great room. Several others were draped over each other and the two white leather sofas they were lounging on. Each wore some kind of uniform or identifiable outfit; there were nurses and doctors, police officers, firefighters, and construction workers, complete with hard hats. As he stood transfixed in the expansive entry hall, holding two heavy bags of ice, it occurred to Joplin that either all the guests had just gotten off from work with no time to change clothes, or Betsey Cunningham had brought them to the Wolfscratch Swingers' Club, complete with a Labor Day theme.

The latter possibility was confirmed when he followed Betsey through the dining room—which held a large, glass-topped table covered with platters of food—into a ginormous kitchen with gleaming appliances, a massive granite island, and a bare-assed woman in a French maid's uniform bent over one of the barstools. A bare-assed man wearing a John Deere cap and a plaid shirt was plowing her south forty.

Without breaking his rhythm, the man turned his head and said, "Hi, Hollis. Glad you could come."

"Well, I can't really stay, Jack," Joplin said, glancing nervously at Betsey to see if she had noticed that it was her husband pumping away at some woman right in front of her. He knew very little about swingers; he had always assumed the "activities," for want of a better word, took place behind closed bedroom doors. But Betsey sailed by her husband and his consenting adult and headed for the Sub-Zero off to the right, then dropped her ice into the freezer. Joplin handed her his bags, then turned to look for Tom. Anything to keep his eyes off Jack Cunningham, who, by the sound of things, was nearing coitus completus. But Tom either hadn't followed them into the kitchen or else had backed out when he saw Jack and his... housekeeper. Joplin wished he'd done the same.

"I'll wait for you in the car, Betsey," he said as he rushed from the room, too late not to hear Jack Cunningham's apparently unending groan of appreciation.

"Hollis, wait!" she called after him, but he was running like a panicked deer to get out of the house. He'd reached the entry hall when he realized he hadn't actually seen Tom since they'd entered the house. Reluctantly, Joplin stepped down into the living room and waded through the sweating bodies still dancing to "Love to Love You, Baby." Soon, he was sweating, too.

A woman handed him a bottle of Dasani water and said, "Here, honey, you look like you need this more than I do." She had glitter on her eyelids and a pom-pom tucked into the waistband of her cheerleader skirt, which barely covered her sis-boom-bah. Gratefully, Joplin took it from her and gulped down most of it, then moved across the room, searching for Tom Halloran. When he realized Tom wasn't on the dance floor, he kept going, coming to a door he hoped led to a powder room, because he desperately wanted to splash water on his face. It did, but three people—none of them Tom—occupied the tiny space, being creative with the pedestal sink and the low toilet. Joplin stared at them, then impulsively decided to get into the room with them. They all seemed extremely attractive, and he wanted to hug them.

"No room, buddy," said the man being serviced by a waitress in a pink uniform with a white apron and a nameplate that read "Madge." His friend was sitting on the toilet, trying to pull Madge's uniform up to her waist.

"No problem," Joplin said. "Would anyone like to dance?" he added, but they were evidently too intent on getting to know each other better to answer. Reluctantly, because he really wanted to get to know *them* better, Joplin eased out of the room. He was suddenly feeling a little strange and wondered if the two drinks he'd had earlier at the safe house were catching up with him. Or maybe it was just the vestiges of yesterday's concussion. He didn't have much time to ponder this, however, because Betsey called his name, then wrapped her arms around him from behind.

Surprisingly, his ribs didn't hurt when she hugged him, but now Joplin felt like his head was in a fishbowl. Everything seemed distorted. And, yet, he had a great desire to go back and dance with the people in the living room. "I'm feeling a little weird, Betsey," he said.

"I think you feel *wonderful*, Hollis. But maybe you need to lie down." She took his arm and started to walk him down the hall.

"But I'd really like to dance," Joplin said.

"Okay, but first, tell me who gave you that bottle of water?"

"I don't know, but she was pretty."

Betsey chuckled and said, "I bet she was. And I also bet her name was Molly."

"Maybe. Can we go dance now? I really feel like dancing."

"Let's just go lie down for a few minutes, and then we can dance, okay, sugar?"

"Okay. Did I tell you you smell wonderful, Betsey?"

39

HALLORAN STOOD BETWEEN a white Porsche and a red Corvette, waiting for Tullie. As soon as he saw the "guests" dancing in the living room, he'd wondered what was going on. Actually, it had looked more like vertical sex than dancing, and they were all in costumes. But it wasn't until he turned and saw the pineapples decorating the dining room table that he'd realized what was happening. Hollis had already disappeared into the kitchen, so Halloran had grabbed a cell phone from a table in the entry hall and quickly exited through the front door. Then he'd called the Fitzgeralds' landline, not knowing if Tullie still had her cell phone. Luckily, Tullie had answered and said she'd be right there when he'd explained the situation. But ten minutes had passed, and Halloran was getting anxious.

Why hasn't Hollis come out by now? he wondered. *Hadn't he seen the same crazy scene?* Halloran waited a few more minutes, then headed back to the house. Car lights suddenly enveloped him, and he turned to see a blue Jeep Cherokee pull into the driveway. He rushed over to it.

"Where's Hollis?" Tullie asked.

"I don't know, but I think we need to get him out of there."

"Why aren't you at the safe house, Tom? What happened?"

"I'll explain later. Let's just get Hollis out of here."

He could see Tullie start to ask another question, then she nodded and quickly got out of the car.

"Just follow me once we get inside."

There weren't as many couples dancing in the living room, but the music was still as loud and pulsating. Halloran replaced the borrowed cell phone on the table in the entry hall, then motioned for Tullie to follow him Figuring most of the action was taking place in the bedrooms, he headed down a hall to the left. Several doors lined it; all were closed tightly. Hoping they weren't locked, he tried the first one on the right. Two dark-haired men were on either side of a gently moaning blonde woman, clamped tightly to her breasts, heads bobbing up and down as she fingered herself. Halloran quickly shut the door.

"He's not in there," he said tersely. "You check the rooms on the left. I'll finish these."

The next door was to a bathroom. Jack Cunningham was thoroughly soaping up a woman standing under the shower-head. He turned and said, "Tom! Want to join me? I've got a really dirty lady here. I mean nasty." They both started giggling.

"Maybe later, Jack. I'm looking for Hollis. Have you seen him?"

"Not for a while."

Halloran shut the door without responding. The last door on the right was occupied by two nude women passionately kissing and touching each other. He stared at them, mouth open, and one of the women looked up at him and winked, but didn't stop what she was doing.

"Tom!" he heard Tullie say in a stage whisper. Halloran quickly shut his mouth and the door.

"Is he in there?"

"No," said Halloran, embarrassed by his reaction to what he'd just witnessed. "Let's check the kitchen, then see if there's another bedroom on the other side of the house. Did you ask anyone you saw about him?"

"I didn't want to spend that much time in those rooms. And, frankly, it'll take me a long, long time to unsee what I've seen tonight."

"Tell me about it. I'll need to go to confession for my impure thoughts when I get back to Atlanta."

"You still go to confession?" Tullie asked as she followed him back down the hall.

The kitchen was mercifully empty. They hurried back into the living room, where only one couple was left; the party had moved outside to the swimming pool. Halloran asked the remaining couple if there were any other bedrooms. "The ones back that way are pretty full," he said, motioning to the left. "If you know what I mean," he added, raising his eyebrows.

"Oh, we know," said the woman. She wore a Delta uniform with a name tag stating, "Fly me." "There's a bedroom down that hall," she said, nodding to the right.

Taking Tullie's hand, Halloran walked toward a hall leading off the living room. They passed a door that was probably a powder room and headed to another at the end. Halloran took a deep breath, glanced at Tullie, and opened it.

Hollis was in bed with Betsey Cunningham. They were under the covers, but obviously naked. Betsey looked up at them and said, "Hey, y'all. Hollis and I were just getting started, so it's not too late to join the party." She turned and smiled at Hollis. "Is it, sugar?"

"The more, the merrier," he said, smiling up at them. "You're beautiful, Tullie. Have I ever told you that?"

"What the fuck," said Tullie. "Did you give him molly, Betsey?"

Betsey Cunningham raised her arms, causing the sheet to slip down and expose her breasts. "Not guilty, Your Honor," she said, still smiling.

"Well, someone did. His pupils are as big as saucers."

Betsey shrugged. "Not my fault."

"Cover yourself up, Betsey." Tullie turned to Halloran and said, "Could you please help Hollis get dressed, Tom?"

"Wait a minute, Missy," Betsey spat out, tugging the sheet over her breasts. The smile was gone. "Who the hell do you think you are, Tullie? We're all consenting adults here, just having a little Labor Day party, and I don't think you were invited."

"Then, by all means, call the police," Tullie said. "No, wait— I'll do it myself. The house reeks of pot, and Hollis doesn't do drugs, much less fool around on his wife. So, I'll bet you several of the verified *guests* at the party are in possession of some other illegal substances, *Missy*."

Betsey leaped out of bed and started pleading with Tullie, who was impervious. She began throwing articles of clothing at her as Halloran attempted to dress Hollis. When Tullie pulled out her phone, Betsey sat down on the bed and started dressing herself.

"What do you want, Tullie?"

Tullie's thumbs remained poised over the phone. "Tell me what 'someone' gave Hollis and how much."

Betsey motioned toward the Dasani bottle on the bedside table next to Hollis. "I think there might have been some molly in that bottle, but he'd already drunk most of it when I found him." When Tullie glared at her, she added, "I have no idea how much was in the bottle, but if he's not a regular user, whatever he consumed must've really affected him."

"I'm sure you loved that, Betsey. You were all over him at my parents' house last weekend."

"What are you going to do, Tullie?"

"What I should do is call the police. I know you call this kind of thing a 'wife-swapping club,' but it looks more like an unlicensed sex venue to me. Especially if people are paying to be able to do some of the stuff Tom and I saw back in the bedrooms,"

"No!" Betsey shrieked at her. "It's not like that! People don't pay to get into the club—not even a membership fee! Whoever hosts the evening provides the catering and the alcohol. And as for some of the things you've seen tonight, well, it's just that we've had to change with the times and sort of *expand* the membership to include different types of couples with different... interests, shall we say."

"So, I guess that would explain the threesome doing golden showers or the hot-dogging and bondage going on behind Door Number Two," Tullie retorted. "Clean-up after one of these 'club meetings' must be a bitch, Betsey. I heard about the pineapple on Tom and Maggie's car, by the way. Did you actually think they'd be interested in something like this?"

Betsey shrugged. "You never know. You'd be surprised by some of the people who've joined us from time to time. As I said, there's nothing illegal about it."

"Yeah, but marijuana and molly and whatever other drugs you've been offering your 'club members' are," Tullie said. "How are you doing with Hollis, Tom?" she added, her eyes still on Betsey Cunningham.

"You can look," Halloran said. "He's decent. I would've had him dressed sooner, but he kept hugging me. How long does it take for that stuff to wear off, anyway?"

"About four hours, depending on how much he ingested. And he has no tolerance."

"I would hug you, too, Tullie, if you were closer," said Hollis, beaming. "You're just beautiful. I've always loved your hair."

"Thanks, Hollis, that means a lot to me. I think."

"Oh, and just for the record, Betsey," said Halloran, "Maggie and I would *not* have been interested in any of this." He remembered his reaction to the two women in the last bedroom he'd checked and hoped that lightning wouldn't strike him.

"Let's get this show on the road," Tullie said.

"So, what are you going to do?" Betsey asked, panic in her voice again.

Tullie turned to look at her, but didn't say anything for several seconds. "I might regret this, Betsey, but I've decided not to call the police. Wolfscratch is a great place. A scandal like this would hurt a lot of people who don't deserve it. But I'm going to be watching you. If I get even a whiff of any more clubs like this in the area, you're toast. And I also know several people who can put eyes and ears on you. Am I clear?"

Betsey nodded, then hurried out the door. They all followed her down the hall. No one was left in the living room, but they heard music playing in the pool area behind the house. Through the wall-to-wall windows, they could see skinny dippers in the glow of colorful lanterns on tiki poles.

"Pool party!" Hollis shouted, and before they could stop him, he rushed outside and jumped into the water, clothes and all.

40

IT TOOK TEN minutes to get Hollis out of the water and another five for Betsey to find a beach towel in which to wrap him. By the time they made it to Tullie's car, she and Halloran were both exhausted. Hollis, however, was still going strong.

"That was a great party, wasn't it? Wasn't that a great party? Are we going to another one? Because I'm not tired, y'all. And I never got to dance!"

"Where *are* we going, Tullie?" Halloran asked. "We can't go back to the firm's house. According to Hollis, our cover's been blown by someone in law enforcement. So, we can't trust anyone."

Tullie put her head on the steering wheel for several seconds, then said, "I get that, and it's freaking me out. We also don't know where Carrie and Aunt Maggie are, and we can't call anybody to find out."

"Don't be sad, Tullie," Hollis said, patting her shoulder. "Everything's going to be fine."

"I guess you don't remember that you decided we couldn't trust our security detail at the firm's house, Hollis," Holloran said, fed up with the whole evening.

"We also don't know if we can even trust my parents," said Tullie. "Or my brother, Aidan. Which is what started this whole investigation in the first place: My family might have been involved in what turned out to be Jacob Gunter's murder. Look what I've gotten y'all into!"

Hollis patted her shoulder again, saying, "You were just trying to do your job, Tullie. And we wanted to help you, because we found the body."

"That sounds pretty rational, Hollis," Halloran said. "You think the molly is wearing off?" he asked Tullie.

"I have no idea what you're talking about, Tom, but I'm absolutely fine," Hollis said. "Everything's fine. But if you're upset, Tullie, maybe you should call your chief. He's a good guy. And, Tom, if you're worried about Maggie, why don't you just call her?"

They both turned around to look at Hollis, who stared back at them as if they were the ones who'd lost their minds. "What?" Hollis asked.

"We had to give up our phones before we left Atlanta, Hollis, remember?" Halloran said.

"Oh, right," he said, frowning. "But maybe Tullie still has her phone."

"I left mine at my apartment," she said, then reached across Hollis and opened the glove compartment, "But I did buy a few of these on the way up, just in case."

"Burner phones!" Hollis said. "I sure wish I'd thought of that. But then we might've missed the party."

Halloran closed his eyes, and Tullie groaned. But although Hollis was still somewhat impaired, he seemed to remember what had been going on that night. "Tullie, I think calling your chief is an excellent idea," Halloran said. "But first, let's get out of this driveway. For all we know, a few swingers might be making out in the backseats of some of these cars."

＋　＋　＋　＋

MAGGIE ANSWERED ON the second ring. "Tom! Where are you? We've been frantic over here!"

"Thank God you're okay," he said. "And where is 'here?'" I mean, I assume you're at the safe house."

"Of course we are. But all hell broke loose about an hour ago. The GBI agents with us got a call from *your* agents that you were missing! And then, ASAC Masterson called about 20 minutes ago to make sure we were okay. So, where are you, Tom? And I sure hope Hollis is with you, because Carrie is going nuts."

Without going into too much detail—especially about their side trip to the wife-swapping party—Halloran explained what had happened. Maggie interjected several "Oh, my God!" exclamations, but otherwise stayed calm. When he'd finished, they were both silent for several seconds.

"I can't believe this," she said finally. "What are you and Hollis going to do, Tom?"

Halloran sighed. "That's the big question. The only reason I was able to call you is that Tullie had some burner phones and called her chief, who got this number from ASAC Masterson. We're hoping the two of them can come up with a plan that will keep us all safe, although Hollis was against contacting anyone at the GBI."

"But from what we heard, it was somebody with the ATF who leaked information about where you and Hollis were staying, and he's been taken into custody. Tom, I think you two should come here. Tullie, too, if she wants."

"Right now, we're just waiting to hear back from Tullie's chief. But I have a feeling Hollis won't want to go anywhere the GBI suggests. He says our cover's been blown, and he'll probably want you and Carrie to leave where you are, even though the ATF agent is in custody."

"Maybe Carrie can convince him. Can she talk to him?"

Halloran turned to look at Hollis, who smiled brightly back at him. His pupils weren't as dilated, but he still wasn't himself. "He's tied up right now, Maggie. Could you just explain everything to Carrie and tell her Hollis is fine? Right now, he's just worried about her. Okay?"

"Sure," Maggie said, but Halloran knew she wasn't happy with the explanation. However, he also knew he could count on her to say the right things to Carrie.

"I'll call back when I know something," he said.

After several phone calls back and forth between Vince Randall and ASAC Masterson, with both Tullie and Hollis chiming in at times, they reached an agreement: He and Hollis would join their wives at the house on Blue Ridge Lane to discuss the situation. Tullie would sit in on the discussion, but she insisted on returning to her parents' house after that, no matter what the rest of them decided to do. And Randall insisted on joining them as soon as he could get up to Wolfscratch. Halloran made a mental note to mention this to Maggie at an appropriate time, wondering if Tullie and her chief might have more than a professional relationship. Everything he'd heard about Vince Randall was good, but a personal relationship might end both their careers.

Deciding he had enough on his plate without worrying about Tullie's love life, Halloran prepared himself for what he was sure would be an unpleasant reunion with the various members of the GBI. Also, not enough time had elapsed for the molly to leave Hollis' system. So, even if the agents didn't know Hollis well enough to realize he was under the influence, Carrie certainly would. And Hollis was still soaking wet from his dip in the pool. So was the gun Halloran had found in his pants pocket while helping him get dressed. He was hopeful they'd be able to explain what had happened at the house on Wild Turkey Run with a bit of... understatement. In his legal career, he'd learned that outcomes often depended upon narratives that relied heavily on emphasis, nuance, and direction. But Halloran also knew that juries were far more susceptible to misdirection than law enforcement or wives. Especially wives.

41

TULLIE WASN'T SURPRISED to see that there were almost as many cars parked in the driveway of the house on Blue Ridge Lane and the adjacent cul-de-sac as there had been at the wife-swapping party. But there were no Jaguars or Porches or Corvettes among them. Instead, dark-colored sedans and SUVs lay in wait, much like their owners ensconced in the house. She knew they'd all be pissed as hell, out for blood, and looking for ways to cover their butts.

Tullie parked her car behind the last one in the driveway. "Hollis," she said sharply, turning to look at him in the back seat. "Tell me again how you're going to handle this. What we talked about, remember?"

The same goofy smile played across his features. It had been less than two hours since he'd ingested the molly, not enough time for it to have left his system. But she and Tom had drilled into his drug-addled brain how potentially serious the situation was. Maybe, Tullie hoped, Hollis' usual savviness would be sort of like mental muscle memory and get him through this.

"I need to let you and Tom do all the talking and only answer questions if they're directed at me," he said solemnly. "And then, with only a few words." Hollis smiled again and cocked his head to the side. "Did I get it right, Tullie?"

"Perfect," she said. "Just follow the playbook, and we'll be fine."

"From your lips to God's ears," said Tom, shaking his head slowly.

They exited the car and walked single file to the front door, Hollis' shoes making hideously noisy squishing sounds. The door opened before they reached it, and Carrie rushed out and down the three stone-covered steps, more gracefully than her advanced pregnancy should have allowed. She threw her arms around Hollis, hugging him soundly before pulling away and saying, "Why are you all wet?"

"I fell into a swimming pool," he said. "Why did you stop hugging me? You smell so good!"

"You fell into a swimming pool? How did that happen, Hollis?"

He shrugged and grinned and said, "That's my story, and I'm sticking to it. Oh, God, baby, you smell so good!"

Carrie turned and glared at Tullie, then turned to Tom and did the same thing. "What the hell is going on? What has he taken?"

Tullie heard boots coming down the steps and said under her breath, "If you could just play along for a while, we'll tell you the whole story. I promise you."

Carrie continued glaring, then nodded and took her husband's arm.

✚ ✚ ✚ ✚

MAGGIE HALLORAN WAS waiting for them in the entry area of the house and gathered them all in a big hug. When Tullie moved away and looked around the great room at the GBI agents gathered there, it was clear that her earlier assessment of what their attitudes might be had been grossly underestimated. There were ten in all; Special Agent Tim Nugent had escorted them in, and the rest—five men and four women—were standing rigidly inside the sofas or seated on them, arms crossed in unyielding, defensive positions. The diplomacy ASAC Masterson had used to maneuver the three of them into this meeting would be sorely missed if they started it without him. Luckily, Carrie took matters into her own hands.

"My husband needs to change his clothes," she said, guiding Hollis toward the hall leading to the bedrooms without waiting for anyone's permission.

Special Agent Nugent, who seemed to have appointed himself interim leader, said, "Well, while we're waiting on them and ASAC Masterson, why don't we—"

"Not a chance," Tullie said quickly. "This situation is above both our pay grades, so let's just wait until our supervisors get here."

"That might take a while," Nugent said.

"No problem. I'll just let my parents know I'm okay." She headed into the kitchen.

"Mr. Halloran, would you--?"

"I don't think so," he said. "I'm a civilian. And a pretty pissed-off one, I might add. Just so you know."

And so they waited, Tullie on the phone and Tom and Maggie whispering to each other at the kitchen table. Fifteen minutes later, Hollis and Carrie came out. Hollis was now dressed in tan shorts and a light blue polo shirt, and his smile wasn't as wide as before. Tullie prayed to St. Anthony—whom she'd ignored for years—that Hollis had found his lost mind. Carrie dashed her hopes, however, by shaking her head. If Special Agent Nugent noticed, he didn't mention it.

ASAC Masterson must have used his blue light and siren from wherever he'd been to get to Wolfscratch, because he arrived ten minutes later. The tension in the air intensified to DEFCON 3, then ratcheted up to DEFCON 2 when another man dressed in civilian clothes followed Masterson into the house. Tullie glanced at Tom, who just shrugged, but she saw Hollis' expression change to a more serious one. Unless all the molly had suddenly left his brain, she assumed the second man was Special Agent in Charge George Pendleton.

Shit! Tullie thought grimly. The situation had just gone from bad to worse. She hoped Hollis would follow the plan and keep his mouth shut.

"I'm Special Agent in Charge George Pendleton," the man said, confirming her fears. He had white hair, but his skin had very few wrinkles, and his authoritative air left no question about who was in charge. Pendleton looked pointedly at her, then at the Hallorans and the Joplins, and said, "I'd appreciate it if you'd all join me and ASAC Masterson in that dining room I just passed to discuss this situation." When they'd all nodded, he turned to the group of agents in the great room. "We'll widen the discussion in a little while," he added, making that sound more than a little ominous.

Tullie didn't look to see if the agents nodded or saluted, just followed the group into the dining room. She made sure to sit next to Tom so they could try to signal each other under the table, then wondered if the wiser choice would have been to sit next to Hollis instead. With another prayer to St. Anthony, Tullie smiled at Carrie and signaled with her eyes that controlling Hollis was all on her. Then she turned her full attention to SAC Pendleton. The first words out of his mouth made her like him, despite herself.

"First, let me say that I'm well aware of what a cluster-fuck this operation has been so far. Mistakes have been made that have compromised your safety, as well as the agents who were protecting you, and I've made GBI Director Winslow aware of everything that's happened. But I also want to promise you—and try to assure you—that we've taken steps to remedy those mistakes. The ATF agent responsible for leaking information to people outside this mission has been arrested and is being questioned. We have no reason or evidence to believe anyone else here tonight is involved, but replacements for these agents have been requested."

It was Tom who responded. "While I appreciate your assessment of the situation, SAC Pendleton, I think I speak for the Joplins, Tullie Fitzgerald, and my wife when I say that there isn't anything you can do to assure us that we'd be safe under your care. I have a great deal of respect for the GBI and the agents who were guarding us tonight—Laura Fielding and Gabby Waters put our safety above theirs. But I find it hard—no, impossible—to believe that one ATF agent was responsible for all the leaks and for sabotaging this mission."

"What other leaks are you talking about?" Pendleton asked.

"Well, for one," Tullie interjected, "the counselor at Central State Prison knew that it was Jacob Gunter who was murdered at Wolfscratch, not Eric Jaeger, and he could only have gotten that information from someone present at the meeting with Hollis at your regional office or someone directly connected to The Cause. I certainly didn't tell him when I contacted him about wanting a meeting."

"There are also the attacks on Hollis and Jenna McAllister and the murder of Jesse Waldrup," Tom added.

"Yes, but those could all be attributed to illegal surveillance by phone tap or electronic bugs in Andrew McAllister's office and home by members of The Cause," Pendleton said. "And you and Investigator Joplin found Gunter's body and made certain his death was autopsied, so you may have been watched very closely by members of law enforcement up here who are allied with The Cause. Which is why you were given protection and agreed to be used to smoke out others involved with The Cause."

"Yes, but we didn't know those 'others' might also be part of our protection," Tom insisted.

Pendleton started to answer, but the front door burst open, and Vince Randall strode into the entry area, followed by the GBI special agent who was posted outside. Tullie was more relieved than she wanted to admit to herself.

"I'm Vince Randall, Ms. Fitzgerald's supervisor," he said to Pendleton.

"Glad you could make it, Chief Randall," Pendleton responded. "Thank you for your help arranging this meeting. Now, maybe you can help me convince these good people to stay under our protection."

Randall took a seat across from Tullie. "I agreed to help get them here to discuss the situation, but that's as far as I can go, sir. It's not my life on the line."

Pendleton nodded. "I understand. But maybe if I focus on other lives—maybe a lot of them—that are also on the line, it might make a difference."

"We already know about your contact within The Cause," said Tom. "And that he—or she, for that matter—hasn't been heard from in several weeks. Also, that 'something big' is going to happen that may kill a lot of people. That's what got us up here, more than anything else. But unless you can expand on that, my wife and I can't agree to continue being bait. The Joplins—"

"Can't agree either," Carrie said quickly. "We'd rather take our chances with security of our own."

"What security, ma'am?" Masterson asked. "You can't tell me that—"

"I don't think we need to tell you anything, sir." Carrie's chin rose. "And it's Doctor, not ma'am."

You go, girl! Tullie mentally urged her on. *He's a chauvinistic, misogynistic sack of shit!*

ASAC Masterson's face reddened. "I beg your pardon, ma'am—Doctor. I mean, Doctor Joplin. I just can't believe any security would be better than ours, with all due respect."

Carrie inclined her head in acknowledgment. "Ordinarily, I'd have to agree, but this is an extraordinary case, given the law enforcement wild card. So, I guess we'll just have to see, won't we?" And, with that, she rose, in all her pregnant glory, and said, "I'm extremely tired and need to go home. We'd appreciate it if you could have our things from the other safe house packed up and brought to us here. We're leaving."

42

THE REST OF the weekend was a blur of comings and goings, urgent phone calls, and intense discussions. Ike Simmons headed a crew of Atlanta Police Department officers providing security for the Joplins and the Hallorans; they rotated through both houses in 8-hour shifts. Ike also had a tech expert sweep their house for bugs; he found three downstairs and one in the master bedroom, presumably planted by the GBI after they'd gone to Wolfscratch. Another tech swept the Hallorans' house and found the same thing. They'd decided to leave them all in place and act accordingly. Using their burner phones, Joplin, the Hallorans, Tullie, and Vince Randall were in constant contact. SAC Pendleton also called him on his cell to give him updates, always urging him to reconsider accepting protection. All of which engendered the intense discussions.

The *most* intense conversation, of course, was the one out on the back terrace between Joplin and Carrie on Saturday morning concerning What Happened When He And Tom

Left The Safe House. Joplin told her his memory was fuzzy, but Carrie had nixed that escape route.

"'Fuzzy' isn't a proper medical term," she'd said firmly, brooking no dissent. "I'm reasonably certain, from what Tullie told me and what I observed of your behavior last night, that someone gave you molly, probably in a bottle of water. Does that ring a bell?"

"A faint one," he said, scrunching his face into a perplexed expression.

"Molly is the street name for MDMA, a crystal powder form of methylenedioxymethamphetamine." Carrie continued. "It's a supposedly 'purer' form of Ecstasy, which got a bad rep because it was frequently cut with other drugs, like cocaine, ketamine, and ephedrine. Fentanyl, too, sometimes. Which made it extremely dangerous and often lethal. But while still very dangerous, molly doesn't usually have any of those ingredients." She took a breath and said, "So, I don't think you have a memory problem, Hollis. I think you have a problem with whatever you do remember that you don't want to tell me."

Realizing that being married to an extremely intelligent woman prevented any reasonable extrication from his predicament, Hollis threw himself upon her mercy. "You're absolutely right, Carrie," he said. "I do remember feeling like I wanted to hug and kiss everyone. I also wanted to dance. A lot. And when Tullie and Tom tried to hustle me out of this strange house where we ended up, I couldn't keep myself from jumping into a pool full of naked people."

Carrie's eyes narrowed. "I sense that I'm not getting the full story."

Ignoring some images of himself in bed with Betsey Cunningham, Joplin said, "Blame it on the drinks Tom and I had before we escaped from the safe house and before I was given the molly. And after a lot of stress about thinking The Cause might know our location. But the bottom line is that you don't have anything to worry about, Carrie. I promise you."

She stared at him for several seconds, then nodded. "Okay. I believe you. Now, tell me how you're feeling."

Instead, Joplin gathered Carrie in his arms and gave her a long, lingering kiss that he hoped would *show* her how he felt. Feelings were much harder for him to express than for Carrie. Joplin never seemed to be at a loss for words, but humor and glibness came more easily to him than translating his emotions. They'd been married for almost two years, and he hadn't thought he could love his wife more than he already did, but now Joplin realized that was wrong. It wasn't just relief that Carrie had accepted what he'd told her because she trusted him. It was much more than that: They were partners as well as lovers, bound by friendship, intimacy, passion, and the knowledge that they had each other's backs.

Joplin was confident that he would never knowingly—*willingly*—betray Carrie. But some part of him had worried that the molly had taken that control away from him. He'd been naked under that coverlet with Betsey Cunningham, and no one had put a gun to his head. *What if Tom and Tullie hadn't come along at just the right moment?* he'd asked himself over and over during the past twelve hours. And, his heart, like the Grinch's, had grown several sizes bigger when he'd looked into Carrie's eyes, realizing that *she* knew he wouldn't cheat on her. And Joplin trusted her judgment more than his own.

"Well," she said, when he finally let her go, "that was more of a clinical question, but your answer addressed part of it."

"I will love you till I die, Mrs. Joplin," he told her solemnly. "But God willing, that won't happen anytime soon. And, except for feeling a little tired and nauseous, clinically, I think I'm okay."

"Good deal," she said, giving him a playful fist on his chin, which told Joplin that she was feeling a little emotional herself. Although she would probably call it *verklempt*.

Around two that afternoon, Tullie called, also sounding a little verklempt. "I just got back from Fox Run," she said. "Aidan wasn't expecting me to come with Dad, and it showed. He was as nervous as the proverbial cat on a hot tin roof. Which is not like my brother, believe me."

"I believe you," Joplin said, stepping outside onto the back terrace again. "What do you think is going on?"

"I'm not sure. The Dutch Warmblood—the jumper he wanted to buy for Brooke that he told Tom about showed up, but so did a bunch of horses that couldn't get near a show ring if their lives depended on it."

"You mean they were nags?"

"Not quite that bad, but they were…ordinary. Like farm horses. Certainly not horses any of the parents who have daughters riding there would want for them. And Aidan clearly wasn't happy that I saw them."

"So, why do you think they were there, Tullie?"

She sighed into the phone. "I have no idea."

✦ ✦ ✦ ✦

THAT NIGHT, JOPLIN fell asleep with both cats hunkered down at the foot of the bed and his arm cupped protectively around Carrie's baby bump. As he was falling asleep, he could feel his daughter moving around, like a large koi swimming in circles in a garden pond. It was an enjoyable sensation, making him feel closer to her, getting to experience a little of what Carrie felt throughout the day. But as he fell deeper into sleep, Joplin saw the horses Tullie had described, their heads low as they were led into a large paddock. He sensed their thirst and weariness and fear. Joplin tightened his arm around Carrie, who murmured something unintelligible, waking him.

"Sorry, go back to sleep," Joplin whispered, gently pulling his arm away so he wouldn't startle her again. He drifted back to sleep a few minutes later, but his dream wasn't filled with horses this time. Instead, he watched two men in dusty uniforms load a large iron ball into a cannon and light its fuse. They did this four more times, the explosions battering his ears to the point of pain. Joplin could smell the smoke billowing out of the cannon and heard people screaming from a distance.

Chaos dominated, with men rushing around a field surrounded by hills and trees, carrying rifles with attached bayonets and stabbing each other when they weren't shooting. He walked among them, apparently unseen, stopping to help a young man who lay on the ground, calling out for his mother. A bayonet had ripped through his abdomen, and Joplin was sickened by the smell of blood and open bowel. He knelt by the man and took his hand; it was all he could do for him. The young man's eyes opened at the touch and focused on him, then faded, like a light being dimmed.

Joplin jerked upright in bed, bathed in sweat and breathing heavily. Another piece of the puzzle snapped into place.

43

ON SUNDAY MORNING, Gary Summers called as he and Carrie were eating breakfast. "You asked me to contact you if we found Jacob Gunter's truck," he said, after identifying himself.

"I did. Thank you. Where was it?"

"It was in one of the Clubhouse parking lots. The first one after you enter the area. That's why it took us so long to locate it."

"That was pretty clever of whoever put it there," said Joplin.

"Yes," Gary said, sounding relieved. "Means it was probably put there by someone who lives here."

"Exactly. Clever of *you* to observe that."

"Just trying to help," Gary said, but there was pride in his voice. "Is there anything else I can do? To help, I mean."

"Nope," Joplin said. "You've already done enough, and I appreciate it."

A few minutes later, Joplin called Gary back on his burner phone from the terrace. "Sorry to bother you, but I did think of something right after we hung up. Do you have time to take some photos of the truck, particularly the wheels? And maybe the inside, too? I know you need to turn it over to the Rutledge County Sheriff's Office, but it would really help."

"Sure thing. I think I know what you want."

"Thanks, Gary. Anything I can ever do for you, just ask."

Joplin joined Carrie back at the kitchen table and picked up his bagel, but he must have been staring into space as he mulled over what Gary had told him, because Carrie said, "Penny for your thoughts?"

"Oh. Sorry." He took a bite of bagel and chewed slowly.

"I take it that was the security guy at Wolfscratch with an update on Gunter's truck," she prompted him.

Joplin put the bagel down and looked at her. "Yes, and I was trying to figure out how Eric Jaeger got in and out of Wolfscratch," he said, not bothering to speak cryptically. He intended to report Gary's call, even though the GBI probably knew about it, if the phones were tapped. "The truck was found in one of the Clubhouse parking lots, so Jaeger didn't drive it out. And I doubt he was on the backseat floor of it going into Wolfscratch, because Gunter would have gotten suspicious about going to the Upper Falls with somebody who looked so much like him. But there isn't a shot of him coming through the gate with anyone else."

Carrie delicately forked more nova onto her bagel, then shrugged. "Maybe he was on the floorboards of someone else's truck. Or even a car."

"Yep," Joplin said. "But, whose? Well over two hundred or so other cars and trucks went in and out of Wolfscratch that Thursday."

Carrie shrugged again. "Does it matter? I mean, in the scheme of things? We know he was there, because he traded clothes with Jacob Gunter. But does it matter *how* he got there?"

Joplin pinched the bridge of his nose. "I keep thinking that if I know how Jaeger got to the Upper Falls, I'll know who's behind this. But you're right. I probably won't find out, so I need to move on."

"I'm all for it. How do you propose to do that?'

"By working on the nursery. I want to get it painted before the baby shower. We won't even be able to get in the room after all those presents are unloaded."

Carrie beamed at him. "That's a wonderful idea! I'll put my maternity overalls on."

"You have maternity overalls?"

"Of course. I wear them on my days off, before you get home. They're not very sexy."

"I'll be the judge of that, Mrs. Joplin," he said.

✚ ✚ ✚ ✚

AFTER DINNER THAT night, Joplin received another phone call on his cell, followed by a text on his burner phone. The call was from SAC Pendleton, informing him that Kayla Hibbard, Jesse Waldrup's sister, had died without regaining consciousness. The State Patrol had questioned Sheriff's Deputy Ethan Dockery, since he was allegedly the last person to see Jesse alive. Dockery, however, had professed great shock and sadness over his friend's death, but asked for a union rep to be present when they began to ask more pointed questions. With nothing more than Jesse's frantic call to Andrew McAllister before he and Kayla were run off the highway, however, they had no probable cause to arrest or even detain the deputy.

Joplin thanked Pendleton for calling, then relayed Gary Summer's information about Gunter's truck. They briefly discussed whether the GBI should take possession of it and risk alerting Sheriff Odum of their involvement. Pendleton opted not to; Joplin opted not to tell him about the photos Gary had agreed to take. But he did decide to ask about the "microchip" found on Jacob Gunter.

"Funny thing about that," Pendleton said. "It was a dud. Nothing in it to track Gunter or transmit data."

"Then what was the point of implanting it?" Joplin asked, also opting not to tell the SAC that he'd already heard this from BJ Reardon.

"We tossed that around the table, but other than the possibility that that particular implant was defective, we decided it was all for show—to make the militia inductees *think* they were being monitored. These groups are very similar to cults and use a variety of things to control their followers—ideology, propaganda, and fear tactics, to name a few. They offer to protect them from a world that's out to get them, but also create a stressful atmosphere within the group that makes members feel like they're always being watched."

"And killing people like Jesse and his sister sends that message big time."

"Exactly," said Pendleton. "It also means the stakes must be pretty high. Whatever they're planning is something they'll go to any lengths to keep secret."

They ended the conversation, and Joplin immediately received a text on his burner phone from Maggie, letting him know she'd had a chance to review the photos she'd taken at the Upper Falls and would like to show him what she'd discovered. He turned to Carrie and said, "Wanna have the Hallorans over for Labor Day drinks tomorrow afternoon?" When she grinned and held up both thumbs, he texted Maggie back.

✚ ✚ ✚ ✚

ON MONDAY, AT 4:45 p.m., Kevin Masterson walked into Pendleton's office and asked if they could talk. Pendleton motioned to the chair in front of his desk, but didn't say anything. He was letting his deputy stew in his own juices a little longer. Pendleton hadn't been kidding when he'd described the Lost Cause operation as a "cluster-fuck." In his opinion, Masterson was a self-important prick whose star had begun to fade. He evidently knew where some bodies were buried within the GBI, or he wouldn't have risen this high up. Pendleton had been saddled with him for the past two years and was determined this would be the last one. He only hoped he could salvage the operation before it was too late. Too many lives depended on it.

"Report," he said curtly, without inviting the ASAC to sit down.

Masterson swallowed and said, "The Hallorans are on the move, sir. We're pretty sure they've all discovered the bugs, because Joplin's been seen going out to the back terrace several times in the past 24 hours and talking on his cell phone, but nothing important has come through the tap. Except for the conversation with the security guard at Wolfscratch."

"Which he made sure to tell me about."

"Exactly." Masterson cleared his throat. "Anyway, we think they've all got burner phones, because the Hallorans haven't communicated with the Joplins via their cells, but they seem to be heading to Garden Hills."

"Where the Joplins live."

"And, of course, we're tailing them."

"I'm sure they're expecting that," Pendleton said. "Ike Simmons, an APD detective, is coordinating their security. I checked him out. He's first-class, and he and Hollis Joplin go way back. They were partners when Joplin was a homicide detective. I'm confident he found the bugs, and they've got their own agenda going on now. Simmons will see to that. So, what's your Plan B?"

Masterson was back to swallowing hard. "Maybe it's time to take one or more of them into custody as material witnesses, sir. Or even charge them with obstruction."

"A fool's errand," said Pendleton. "To what end? Until they're ready to share information with us, you won't get a thing out of them."

"Not even if we—"

"Especially not, Kevin. Given the gravity of the situation, Director Winslow okayed wiretapping both houses and got a judge to sign off on it. But these people are not suspects. They're fellow law enforcement officers and innocent civilians. And we're not the CIA, thank God. Try to remember that."

✚ ✚ ✚ ✚

JOPLIN SET UP tiki torches on the back terrace for the mosquitoes and put appetizer plates and plenty of cocktail napkins on the table for four people; Ike couldn't join them because of a family barbeque. A cocktail cart held various libations and mixers, and Carrie had whipped up some dips and a cheese platter. The GBI might have some sound-amplifying equipment to overhear their conversation outside, but if what Maggie had to show him fit in with what he'd learned over the weekend, Joplin would have to contact Pendleton anyway. What The Cause might be planning to do was information he—as well as the FBI, the ATF, and maybe even Homeland Security—needed to know ASAP.

The Hallorans arrived a few minutes after 5 p.m. They all filed out to the terrace, and after drinks had been fixed and plates filled, Maggie pulled a manilla envelope from her tote bag.

"I took several photos of the picnic area while you and the EMTs were down by the Falls, in addition to the ones I'd already shot of the body. So, I developed all of them myself in my dark room, then enlarged these so I could see things in better detail," she said, handing Joplin four of them. "Tell me what you see."

Two photos were of the ground near the drop to the water below. Joplin studied them carefully, then turned to the other ones. They showed the area to the left of the previous photos leading to the parking lot. In each, he observed some clear shoe prints and other scuffed ones, as well as some U-shaped marks. More importantly, however, were some tell-tale blobs next to a tree near the overhang to the water.

"Horseshoes and road apples," he said, passing the photos to Carrie.

"Exactly," said Maggie. "And, yet, there are no stables within Wolfscratch, and I don't think people can ride horses into it. Besides, wouldn't someone have spotted a person on horse-back?"

"As I've said before, Wolfscratch is a gated community, but it's not enclosed," Joplin said. "So, we can assume that this was how Eric Jaeger got in and out of it without being caught on camera at either of the gates. And he could have stuck to forested areas on his way to and from the Falls. Anyway, this is the last piece of a very complicated puzzle for me, although I can't understand why I didn't notice that a horse had been up there at the Falls. I can understand missing the tracks, but not the manure."

"I didn't notice them either at the time," Maggie said. "It wasn't until I went over the photos again that I saw them. We were looking around the recreation area at first, then I saw the body through my distance lens and called you over. After that, things got pretty chaotic. And we didn't eat our picnic lunch there after the body was taken away, for obvious reasons. We went down to the Lower Falls."

Tom frowned as he looked down at the photos. "Do you think Jaeger got the horse from Aidan, Hollis?"

Joplin shrugged. "It looks that way, especially after what Tullie told me yesterday, about seeing those unknown horses at Fox Run. And after some online research I did today. But if so, Aidan is up to his neck in this whole thing. I only hope he didn't realize what The Cause is planning on doing."

"And what is that?" Maggie asked, looking concerned.

"First, let's get Tullie on speakerphone. She has a right to know this, too."

A few minutes later, Joplin had gotten through to Tullie and announced who was present on the terrace and why he'd contacted her.

"Okay," she said, sounding apprehensive. "I have a feeling I'm not going to like what you tell me, Hollis."

"You won't, but there might be time to keep the situation from getting worse." Joplin took a deep breath, then said, "You asked us to investigate what you thought at first was Eric Jaeger's murder and what, if any, your parents' and your brother's involvement might be. Because your mother is a prominent member of the local Daughters of the Confederacy, and at autopsy, it was discovered that the body had a tattoo of the Confederate Medal of Honor on his back, tying him to The Cause. And also, because you'd seen Eric and Aidan arguing in Aidan's truck just before he disappeared, right?"

"Right," said Tullie.

"Then, we discovered that it was Jacob Gunter who'd been killed, wearing Jaeger's clothes and carrying his wallet and identification. But that didn't clear your family, especially since, according to Tom, Aidan seemed to have an ulterior motive for not going to St. Kitts with his wife that wasn't about a horse he was planning to buy for her. And yesterday, you went with your father to Fox Run to see for yourself if Aidan was telling the truth."

"I know all this, Hollis," Tullie said, sounding impatient. "Where is it leading?"

"I'm getting there, Tullie. You were relieved that the Dutch Warmblood that Brooke wanted actually showed up, yet puzzled when a large group of other horses did, too. But they weren't show horses like the ones trained at Fox Run. I think you described them as 'ordinary, like farm animals.' Right?"

"Yes."

"So, just before I called you, Maggie showed me some blow-ups of the photos she took of the Upper Falls when we found Gunter's body. And there were horseshoe tracks and manure in the picnic area that none of us had noticed that day."

They all heard Tullie take a quick breath. "I've never heard of horses being allowed inside Wolfscratch before, Hollis, but I suppose it's possible. Are you implying that Aidan was up there with Gunter and Eric Jaeger?"

"No, I don't mean to imply that. I think it was Jaeger who brought that horse."

"Then why bring up the horses I saw yesterday?"

"The Cause is connected to a white supremacy militia, and Jesse Waldrup told me that several members participate in Civil War reenactments. So, what do these reenactors need besides guns and cannons and people?"

"Horses," said Tullie, after a long silence. "Lots of ordinary horses. Like farm animals."

44

HALLORAN TOOK A large sip of his Jack Daniels, trying to process what he'd just heard. "We all agreed to help the GBI try to find out what The Cause was up to and why they've been targeting people like Jesse Waldrup and the McAllisters—and us—who know about them," he said to Hollis. "But all anybody seems to know is that 'something big' is going to happen. You're saying they're going to use their militia to do that. So, do you know what that is?"

"Not exactly. But I think it's going to happen this Friday. That's all I know for sure. I did some internet research, and there's going to be a reenactment of the Battle of Tunnel Hill in North Georgia on September 9th. Confederate troops held Union soldiers off far longer there than anyone thought possible. They ultimately lost the battle, and Sherman made Tunnel Hill his headquarters, but it still has a lot of meaning for the South, especially among white supremacists. Jesse Waldrup told me he was part of a group training for that battle before he left town. And given all the chatter about something happening soon, I think it'll happen during that reenactment."

"Okay. Tullie, how many horses did you see at Fox Run on Saturday?"

"About twenty or so, Tom. But I have no idea if that's enough for a reenactment."

"But there might have been other transports, right?" Hollis asked.

"Sure, although I think Aidan waited until Brooke would be gone to arrange this one. But Hollis, buying and selling horses to a reenactment group isn't illegal, so why would Aidan try to cover it up? Even if The Cause is behind it."

"I don't know. However, if The Cause is using them for something illegal—like a terrorist act—that could be construed as aiding and abetting them. But that might have nothing to do with why Aidan and Eric Jaeger met that day when you saw them."

"Terrorist groups—and this is a domestic terrorist group—like to make a big splash," Halloran said. "To inspire terror in the people they're trying to intimidate. So, how will they do that through a Civil War reenactment?"

"Again, I don't know," said Hollis. "The only thing I can come up with is that they plan to use real ammo on the field and kill the people playing the Union soldiers. But there might be a number of Southerners playing those roles along with reenactors from above the Mason-Dixon line, so why would they do that?"

"For the symbolism of it, I guess," Tullie said.

"What about the spectators?" Maggie asked. "Maybe there are some important people who'll be there."

"Good question," said Halloran. "So, maybe now's the time to contact the GBI."

✚ ✚ ✚ ✚

GBI DIRECTOR JOHN Winslow was an imposing man. He was almost as tall as Halloran, but had broader shoulders and a thick, bodybuilder's neck. His gray eyes were flinty, and his handshake was firm. Winslow didn't shake the women's hands, just inclined his head toward them, something Halloran was sure they didn't appreciate. SAC Pendleton followed him into the dining room, where they'd all moved twenty minutes earlier, once they heard Winslow intended to come to the Joplins' house. Two aides were close behind the director, with two more at the front door. Just before they'd arrived, Hollis had placed his burner phone, still connected to Tullie, on the table.

Winslow motioned for them all to take seats, declaring himself in charge. Halloran wondered how long it would take Hollis to set him straight. Not long, as it turned out.

"Gentlemen," said Hollis, not sitting down. "You're all here at the invitation of my wife and myself. That can change very quickly. We have information to give you, but we won't be interrogated or intimidated."

"What makes you think that's our intention?" growled Winslow.

"Just about everything, from the bugs you put in our houses and on our phones to, respectfully, your attitude when you came into this house, sir."

Winslow stared at him, seemingly nonplussed. Pendleton smoothly inserted himself into the situation. "I may have been too intense in my assessment of the situation, Investigator Joplin," he said. "My fault entirely."

306

Halloran could tell Pendleton was witnessing a different version of Hollis than the one he'd seen on Friday night.

"Your assessment was accurate, SAC Pendleton," Hollis said, "but we didn't care for the surveillance tactics. I'd also request that only you and Director Winslow be present right now."

Winslow didn't look happy, but he nodded assent, and all four aides left the house. Hollis finally took a seat at the table. "Now that we've gotten the playbook clarified, I need to tell you a few things. "

Halloran listened as Hollis repeated everything they'd discussed earlier, including his belief that violence would occur at the Battle of Tunnel Hill reenactment on September 9th. Neither Winslow nor Pendleton interrupted him during the fifteen minutes this took, but their facial expressions showed their reactions all too clearly. When Hollis finished, Director Winslow began firing questions at him.

"How many horses has Aidan Fitzgerald procured for The Cause?"

"As I said, sir, Tullie only saw around twenty this past Saturday, but there might have been others before that or since. And we don't know that they were meant for The Cause. But it's a plausible assumption based on what's happened in the past few weeks."

"Did she ask him why he bought the horses?"

"Yes. Aidan told her it was a favor for someone on a neighboring farm, but he didn't give a name, and she thought he might become suspicious if she asked. She did bring it up to her father, Ryan Fitzgerald, when they left Fox Run, but he didn't seem concerned about it."

"You said you've done some research on the Tunnel Hill reenactment," Winslow said. "We have, too, since it's been on our radar for some time. It's the only reenactment performed annually in Georgia for the past 30 years, and it hits the timeline. Around 500 to 600 men are involved, comprising the Union and Confederate battalions' infantry, artillery, and cavalry. On Friday, as every year, around 400 schoolchildren from around the area will be there for an 'educational day,' learning about the battle and its historical significance. It's a pretty big deal, especially in North Georgia."

"Thanks to The United Daughters of the Confederacy, I'm sure," Halloran said dryly.

"Oh, yes," Winslow responded. "There'll also be a contingency of the Sons of Confederate Veterans, who proudly trace their lineage back several generations to actual Civil War veterans. The reenactors belong to the Georgia Division Reenactors Association—the GDRA—which has about 2,000 registered members. We've monitored that organization, but now we'll pay closer attention. Unfortunately, it's a pretty loosely organized group, formed by dozens of units all over the state."

"I'd be surprised if they even know about The Cause and its militia," Hollis said. "Jesse Waldrup told me only a select group of reenactors were invited to that week-long indoctrination several weeks ago. But he didn't recognize anyone. They were from different parts of the state and were instructed not to give out their last names."

"That's what we heard from our insider," Pendleton offered.

"Tom," said Hollis, nodding in his direction, "said earlier that domestic terrorist groups, like their international counterparts, want to inspire terror in the people they're trying to intimidate. But who would that be, in this case? Most of the participants will be supplied, I assume, by this GDRA group, and though some might be people who've moved here from Northern states, most are Southerners. Or is there a group of Northern reenactors playing Union soldiers?"

Director Winslow shook his head and sighed. "We're still trying to find out about other participants. As for the motive and the target behind any violence being planned at this reenactment, that's a valid question, but I can't answer it. Unfortunately, since 9/11, everyone, including Homeland Security, has been more concerned about international terrorism than the homegrown variety. We think that's a mistake."

"Maybe the targets are in the audience," Carrie offered. "Do you know of any prominent people who'll be attending? Maybe some politicians or activists who are against Civil War reenactments?"

"We're looking into that," Winslow said.

"A member of Homeland Security was present at the meeting I had with SAC Pendleton at the Appalachian office. What does he think?"

"He's taking this seriously, as far as I can tell. But I'll press him. See if he's followed up on the Tunnel Hill battle. I'm also going to bring the FBI in on this. We need all the help we can get."

Hollis nodded, then looked at Winslow and Pendleton in turn. "What can you tell us about the 'insider' you mentioned? That was one of the reasons we all agreed to act as bait up at Wolfscratch—because you hadn't had any communication from him in several weeks. So, I think it's time for you to tell us who he is."

Winslow shook his head. "We think he's dead, but on the off chance that he's still alive, I can't tell you his name. As you've pointed out to SAC Pendleton, in no uncertain terms, there's a leak somewhere, and I agree that it probably wasn't just with the ATF agent who was part of your surveillance team at

Wolfscratch. At this point, it's better not to have you involved unless you remember anything else that might help us." He turned to Pendleton, then added, "George will be your direct liaison, but you can also ask for me at any time. We'll still keep an eye on all of you for the time being, but feel free to get rid of the bugs we planted before you got home Friday night and accept our apologies for the inconvenience you might have incurred." Winslow looked at each of them, then added, "And our thanks for all you've done."

✚ ✚ ✚ ✚

THEY SAT AROUND the dining room table long after the GBI group had departed. Hollis got more wine and liquor, and Carrie and Maggie retired to the kitchen to see what they could rustle up for dinner. Still on speakerphone, Tullie said she was good and shook her glass, making the ice tinkle.

"Good old Jack Daniels, as fine a Southern whiskey as you'll ever find," she said. "But I'll be disappointed if Maggie and Carrie make pizzas, since I'm not there."

"We'll try not to make yummy sounds," said Hollis.

Tullie gave a long sigh, "Actually, I'm more worried about what the fuck Aidan has gotten himself into. I mean, besides whatever The Cause is going to do. I think the GBI will be on him like white on rice, if they haven't been already."

"I have to agree with you," said Halloran. "At the very least, they'll be monitoring any horses brought to Fox Run and where they go after that. But whatever Aidan's done, Tullie, that's on him, not you. Have your mother and father mentioned anything about him? You said Ryan didn't seem bothered by the horses you saw in the corral, but did he or you mention it to your mother?"

"I did. I asked if Dad had told her about the horses, and she said he hadn't. She was definitely more curious about it than he was, but then the conversation quickly switched to Brooke's new horse, Black Jack. That, and whether or not Brooke might be pregnant, are about all she can talk about these days."

"Well, I bet she was curious about why your boss followed you up to Wolfscratch, right?"

"Not really. He slept in his car Friday night, but she didn't know that, and I insisted that he go back to Alpharetta Saturday morning. They did meet him, though, and Mom said he was 'good-looking' and reminded her of President Obama, just like everyone else, but that was it."

Halloran decided to jump right in and said, "You mean she didn't suspect that the two of you have feelings for each other?"

"WTF, Tom!" Tullie sputtered. "What are you talking about?"

"It's apparent not only to me, Tullie, but Maggie, too. Are you and Vince Randall the only ones who don't know?"

There was a long silence, then Tullie gave another long sigh. "I honestly have no idea how he feels, Tom, but I know that it would impact his career if there *were* anything between us, so, bottom line, there isn't *going* to be anything going on. And you tell that to Maggie, you hear?"

"Loud and clear, Tullie."

"And that goes double for you, Hollis. I know you heard all this."

"Even louder and clearer, Tullie."

45

THE NEXT FEW days were as stressful to Joplin as anything that had happened in the past few weeks. He felt helpless in the face of a nameless, shapeless, violent event that he knew was coming, despite everything they'd all tried to do to prevent it. In the past, Joplin had always known what he was up against as he tried to find justice for the victims in his care, whether as a homicide detective or a death investigator. But now, the type of evil that saw mass murder as merely a means to an end could be anywhere—in a forest full of assault weapons, a patrol car, or an upscale, gated community.

Against Ike's advice, he and Carrie had gone back to work at the ME's Office. A security detail was posted at the front and near the rear admitting door, and Sarah had placed Joplin on office duty. Bits and pieces of information reached him from time to time. They added a few more pieces of the puzzle, but not enough to show what the whole thing would look like.

On Tuesday morning, Gary Summers sent the photos Hollis had requested of Gunter's truck. The mystery of where he'd gotten his last meal was solved by a bag from Taco Bell on the passenger seat, with a receipt for a chicken burrito and a Coke. There were also two empty cans of Bud Lite and an almost empty fifth of Southern Comfort on the floor. In keeping with his construction job, various tools were in the truck bed, covered by a tarp. A Confederate flag decal was on the lower right side of the back window, along with a sticker that read, "Southern Born & Raised." One on the lower left side read "Mama Tried."

Mama didn't try hard enough, Joplin thought, shaking his head. *Maybe Gunter's wife and kids were better off without him.* Will Sykes had gone to see his wife after she'd been notified of his death and had told Joplin that she'd kicked Gunter out after his last DUI and hadn't seen him since. She'd looked tired and a little sad, but didn't express any interest in how or why he had been murdered.

BJ Reardon called Carrie a little later to say Jacob Gunter's tox report was in. His blood alcohol level had been 2.03; he was also full of THC and cocaine, probably from a blunt, she told Joplin after the call, since the histologist had found both drugs in his lung tissue. Joplin asked her if she wanted to have lunch together; Sarah had offered to bring them back something from Fat Matt's Rib Shack. Carrie agreed, but only after stipulating that she wanted a salad and that he should order one, too.

"It's called Fat Matt's for a reason, Hollis," she'd said. "You need to come down and observe the next autopsy I perform on a grossly overweight man and see the visceral fat surrounding his organs that causes inflammation and clogged arteries."

He closed his eyes and made a face. Feeling virtuous for not mentioning her recent craving for the Buckhead Diner's chips with blue cheese dip, he said, "I believe I'll pass on both the autopsy and lunch from Fat Matt's. How about a turkey sandwich on whole wheat bread from Subway? No mayo."

After lunch, Joplin spent two hours sorting through vehicular homicide photos and labeling them for the insurance companies that had requested them. He hated that part of his job, especially when the accidents involved kids. He was wondering how he could keep his daughter from ever driving or even being a passenger in a car driven by one of her friends, when Tullie called.

"You are not going to fucking believe this!" she said.

"Probably not. What happened?"

"I talked to my mom again about Aidan—at least I *tried* to. She not only brushed me off—again—she asked me why I was so *jealous* of my brother! Jealous! Can you believe that, Hollis? Aidan is probably up to his neck in this whole militia thing and maybe drugs, too, and she doesn't think I'm worried about him, she thinks I'm jealous of him!"

"Whoa, there, Tullie!" Joplin said. "You didn't bring up the militia or anything about drugs with your mother, did you?"

"No, of course not! I was just trying to find out if Aidan is in over his head with Fox Run. He might have taken on too much debt expanding the indoor arena and adding the café and bar. That might explain why he's gotten involved with The Cause."

"We still don't know that, Tullie. There's no evidence that Aidan's selling drugs, and, as you pointed out, it's not against the law to procure horses for a group of Civil War reenactors. Were you able to find out anything from Moira?"

"Just that she and Daddy are going to the Tunnel Hill reenactment on Saturday, like they do every year. She wants me to go with them."

"And what did you tell them?"

"No way, just like *I* do every year."

"Is Aidan going?"

"He said he'd try to make it after he picks up Brooke and her friend from the airport on Saturday. I just hope the fucking GBI figures out what The Cause is up to before I lose my entire fucking family at Tunnel Hill, Georgia."

Joplin sighed, then said something he would later regret. "I understand why you're so upset, Tullie, but I have to ask: Do you eat with that mouth of yours?"

"Three fucking meals a day," she said, then hung up on him.

✠ ✠ ✠ ✠

"WELL, YOU SHOULDN'T have asked her that," Carrie said while they were driving home that night, their APD escort in tow. "I admit she cusses too much for my comfort, but since when did you become so sensitive? From what you've told me, Tullie has always been a hard-drinking, tough-talking sort of person. And she's also pretty stressed out by everything happening with her family right now, too. Or might be happening."

"Might be?" he asked, turning his head to look at her.

Carrie looked at him sideways. "I just mean, as you pointed out to her, that we don't know that any of them—Moira, Ryan, or Aidan—are involved with The Cause. In fact, Tullie's the only one saying that's a possibility."

Joplin almost swerved off Cheshire Bridge Road. "What? What are *you* saying?"

Carrie shrugged. "Think about it, Hollis: Tullie brought you and Tom and Maggie into this by saying she saw Aidan and Eric

Jaeger arguing in Aidan's truck just before Jaeger tested positive for cocaine. We only have her word for it that happened. Add that to the fact that Tullie claimed she didn't know it wasn't Jaeger on my autopsy table that day and, well…"

"I can't believe this," he said, turning to stare at her. "That means she would have to be the one who murdered Jacob Gunter and is a ringleader in The Cause. So, why in the world would she want to have us investigate his death? That's how we learned about the militia and what they're planning."

"I know," Carrie said. "And I haven't figured that out. We're obviously missing some parts of the puzzle, as you like to say. But I do think Gunter's murderer was a woman, Hollis."

"What do you mean? Why? How?"

"I decided to look at the photos from his autopsy after you told me about the false lead you gave Will Sykes. That we were trying to get DNA or prints off the body where the killer had pushed him. And I noticed for the first time that the index fingers on both handprints were almost as long as the middle fingers."

"And this means…?"

"That, in all probability, the prints were made by a woman. Everything's on a continuum, of course, but research shows that, in general, most women have longer index fingers in comparison to their middle fingers than men do." She held up her left hand. "See? Now look at yours."

Joplin glanced at his own left hand on the steering wheel and saw that she was right. It was something he'd never noticed before or would've thought important if he had. "Okay," he conceded. "But why haven't I ever heard about that? You'd think there'd be a lot of attention given to that research on the news."

Carrie sighed. "Yes, but after the initial research, people started to read too much into the discovery and extrapolate the findings into a broader application about sexuality and gender. It generated a lot of controversy that's had negative, unintended effects. So, the scientific community backed off. And as I said, it's all on a continuum. Lots of women don't have that trait."

Joplin took some time to process this, then said, "Okay, so you think the handprints were made by a woman. I'll buy that. And you're right that we only have Tullie's word for it that she saw Aidan and Eric Jaeger together, but—" He shook his head, unable to say more.

"Just allow for the possibility, Hollis."

"No," he said emphatically. "I've known Tullie for years. This is not her." Joplin looked at her. "And what possible motive could she have?"

Carrie looked right back at him. "One as old as Genesis," she responded. "And one her own mother gave: jealousy. And a need for revenge, if we believe that her parents gave Fox Run to Aidan without even discussing it with her."

✦ ✦ ✦ ✦

IT WAS A quiet evening. Carrie seemed to be giving him space. Neither brought up the subject of Tullie again, but it was all Joplin could think about. He wavered between believing that what Carrie had told him was hormones and some jealousy on *her* part to actually considering what she'd said. The latter gave him no joy. What Carrie had said could be true: Everything she'd used to support her outrageous theory was, in fact, correct. There was no evidence—forensic or corroborative— to rule it out.

Joplin's brain sent him images of every contact he'd had with Tullie: Her sudden appearance at her parents' house at Wolfscratch, telling him about Eric Jaeger, discussing her fears that her mother and brother might be connected to Jaeger's death at the Hallorans' house, the meeting at their house to discuss Joplin's visit to the GBI regional office. Then there were all the phone calls pulling him into the case, wanting information from him, giving him information. But if she, not Aidan, was connected to Gunter's death, why focus attention on it? Rutledge County was treating it as an accidental death, so she'd be off scot-free. It made no sense.

They went to bed, both cats beside them, as if sensing their restive moods. At one point, possibly getting bad vibes from Joplin's twisting and turning, Banshee began to howl. He got out of bed and picked her up, whispering to Carrie that he needed to go calm her down. Carrie mumbled something and turned over.

Joplin carried the cat to the couch in the den and sat her on his lap, stroking her fur and murmuring stupid things. He'd had to do that a lot when he first got her a few days after Blaine's death. Banshee had been inconsolable, something Joplin understood. Before Carrie, Blaine had been his only serious relationship after his first wife left him, and when she'd broken up with him with very little notice or much of an explanation, it had hurt. It had hurt even more when he'd discovered, while investigating Blaine's murder, that when she'd dumped him, she'd been pregnant with his baby and had decided to get an abortion. Joplin had understood Blaine's reasons for doing it, but he still wished she'd been able to tell him.

As he stroked the cat, Joplin took some deep breaths and tried to release the tension from his shoulders. Carrie was the most important person in his world. He trusted her with his life and his heart; nothing could change that. Like Tom, she was fiercely analytical and could zoom in on a small detail or pull back to see the bigger picture in ways Joplin couldn't fathom. And he knew Carrie believed what she'd said about Tullie; it had nothing to do with hormones or jealousy. They both had once been betrayed by someone they'd cared about and trusted; she was trying to remind him of that without saying it.

But belief, even when informed by analysis, wasn't always true. Joplin had seen the truth of *that* too many times in his life. As his eyes began to droop, and Banshee began to snore, a solution came to him: He would have to figure out something to disprove what Carrie believed. Or confirm it.

46

WEDNESDAY, SEPTEMBER 7TH, dawned clear and hot. Joplin and Banshee had been awakened at 6:30 by a kiss and a head pat from Carrie. He looked around at the light coming through the tall windows and couldn't believe he'd fallen asleep on the couch.

"Rise and shine, you two. Quincy and I are toasting bagels."

Banshee rose and shone more quickly than Joplin did. "Really?" he said. "You've trained him to push down the lever on the toaster?"

"I have to hold him up to it because I don't like animals on the counter, but, yes, of course. Now, come over to the island and have one. I didn't let him put cream cheese on anything."

Whether Quincy had helped make it or not, it was still delicious and a sign that everything was okay between them. Joplin's subconscious hadn't told him how to decide if Tullie had been playing them all, but he had faith it would. Not belief, not even certainty; faith would have to do.

.

✚ ✚ ✚ ✚

NOTHING MORE WAS mentioned about Tullie as they drove to the ME's Office, accompanied by their security. Sarah's office was dark, which was strange. The voicemail button was flashing as Joplin sat down at his desk.

"I decided to take a sick day since you're there to hold down the fort, Hollis," Sarah's voice said. She sounded very congested. "My doctor called in a Z-pack, but It hasn't started to work, and the bronchitis is really kicking my ass. I know a lot is going on, though, what with this situation in North Georgia and the GBI, so don't hesitate to call if I need to come in or if you need to talk."

Sarah hadn't taken a day of sick leave since she'd been made chief investigator two years ago, so Joplin didn't begrudge her that. It *was* coming at an inopportune time, however. No news from the GBI might be good news if they'd figured out what was happening, but not knowing was getting on his last nerve. He took a call from APD about a possible suicide on 14th Street and assigned it to Viv, who was walking in from the break room, coffee mug in hand. She took the Post-it note with the address, then poured her coffee into a hot/cold cup.

"Chief must be pretty sick, if she's staying home," she said. "You talk to her?"

"She left me a voicemail. Sounds like she coughed up one lung, and the other's not far behind."

Viv clucked and shook her head in sympathy as she walked out the door. Joplin turned on his computer and pulled up a few daily news outlets to get his mind off Tullie. He learned that a federal judge in D.C. had ruled that construction on the $3.8

billion Dakota Access pipeline could continue on sacred tribal burial sites where the company's security forces had deployed attack dogs and pepper spray on protesting Native Americans. Taylor Swift and Tom Hiddleston were no longer a couple. On the political front, Joplin saw that 88 retired military leaders, including Lt. Gen. William Boykin, leader of an anti-LGBTQ group, were endorsing Donald Trump. The *New York Times* revealed that Trump had been fined several times for exceeding campaign contribution limits; one $250,000 fine was the largest ever imposed by the New York state lobbying commission. The FBI stated it had been unable to recover 13 cell phones used by Hillary Clinton during her stint as Secretary of State, and that at least two of them may have been "smashed." Clinton was also in the news for a campaign rally at the Johnson C. Smith University in Charlotte, North Carolina on September 8th.

His need for current news and caffeine sated for the moment, Joplin decided to do more pertinent research and found several entries for reenactment videos of the Battle of Tunnel Hill. The reenactments had taken place every year on the weekend after Labor Day since 1993. He chose the latest one from the previous year. Winslow had said that it was one of the few reenactments that took place on the actual battlefield where it had occurred. It had been an essential battle in May of 1863, marking the beginning of Sherman's campaign to capture Atlanta, his "March to the Sea." The Clisby Austin House had served as his headquarters as he planned the campaign. Before Sherman's victory there, the house had been a hospital for wounded Confederate soldiers. The nearby Chetoogeta Tunnel, completed in 1850 to allow the Western and Atlantic Railroad passage between Atlanta and Chattanooga, had also been the site in April of 1862 of "The Great Locomotive Chase," in which Union soldiers set a W&A locomotive called "The General," on fire in an attempt to destroy the tunnel.

The video opened with a shot of the Clisby Austin House and two women dressed in bonnets and period dresses coming down the steps. Several white canvas tents had been erected in front of the house. The action then moved to the battlefield, with reenactors dressed in Union and Confederate uniforms on opposite sides of the field. Officers on both sides sat stiffly on horses, their swords at the ready as they oversaw cannon fire, interspersed with charges by rifle-toting and bayonet-holding soldiers. Several soldiers on each side dropped to the ground amid puffs of cannon smoke; microphones amplified the noise level. It was an impressive presentation that aroused a certain amount of pride, even in Joplin's anti-antebellum soul. And the irresistible framework was a lively regional festival, complete with popcorn, cotton candy, and homemade root beer sold by "sutlers" in period clothes, as bagpipers filled the air with military tunes.

But two things struck him after watching the solemn carnage: (1) No limbs were shot off or blood actually shed, although some reenactors wore bandages dotted with crimson. (2) the Rebel soldiers were too clean and well-fed—overweight, in some cases—to have been part of the rag-tag, underfunded, underfed Confederate army. Joplin had great empathy for the real soldiers; they were likely poor, white sharecroppers like his ancestors. But he had only contempt for the politicians and wealthy landowners who pushed for secession. The war had torn the nation apart and decimated a South willing to sacrifice its citizens in a doomed effort to maintain a way of life that couldn't exist without slave labor. This particular battle had resulted in thousands of casualties.

Joplin shook his head, overwhelmed by the losses on both sides and by his beloved South, which couldn't accept the outcome of a war that almost destroyed America, nor the part it had played in starting it. History was usually shaped by the winners of a war, not the losers. But the United Daughters of the Confederacy had done an excellent job of rewriting history and making every schoolchild learn it by heart.

He clicked off the video and closed his eyes. A phone call spared him from further rumination on the subject. Joplin welcomed the diversion, then saw that the number was the one SAC George Pendleton had given him should he need it.

"Joplin here," he said.

Pendleton identified himself and said he wanted to update Joplin on what they were all calling "the Situation."

"I hope it's good news, sir."

"Not really. We've kept a pretty close watch on Fox Run, but the horses Ms. Fitzgerald saw aren't there, and there haven't been any more deliveries. We can't get close enough to the house to plant bugs, because Aidan Fitzgerald hasn't left it since we learned about the horses. We've got high-tech equipment that shows him clearly in the place, often talking on a cell phone, but it's not the one registered to him. Must be a burner. We were able to get eyes and ears on the stable after he went to bed Monday night, but that's a no-go so far, what with the holiday weekend. If he's doing something illegal, it's a good time, since there haven't been many riders there."

"Any visitors?"

"Just his mother. We knew her from your little party at the Wolfscratch clubhouse last Friday."

"Have you been able to get into his financials?" Joplin asked. Tullie's story wasn't holding up so far.

"Still working on that."

"What about the militia?"

He heard Pendleton sigh. "We've had drones and heat-seeking devices covering the area. Nothing. We did find an abandoned meth lab about two miles from the special training area in Gordon County that Jesse Waldrup talked about, but it was a bust. Looked like it had been utilized fairly recently, but they'd cleaned it out. No prints, no DNA, and no identifiable clothing or objects. Pretty fortunate for them, huh?"

"Yeah, somebody got the word out that you were on their tail. Have you talked to Gabriel Benson, the counselor at Central State?"

"First thing we did after our meeting yesterday. We have him on ice as a material witness in an ongoing investigation, but he's not talking, and we can't hold him indefinitely. Something needs to give. And soon."

"How about any of the principals? The sheriff or the coroner?"

"We don't have enough probable cause to get surveillance on them or charge them, but we're keeping an eye on them. Danforth hasn't left his house, and Sheriff Odum is "on vacation," from what we've managed to discover. That was from your buddy, Will Sykes. He did say that was unusual for him, though."

Now it was Joplin's turn to sigh. "Any further intel on high-profile people attending the reenactment?"

"The Lt. Governor will be there for part of the day, which is no surprise. It's a good photo op for the good ole boy crowd. Also, the usual group protesting it as a racist event. It's a little bigger this year, given the growing drive to eliminate Confederate statues and memorials. But I just don't see The Cause opening fire on the bystanders. It would be an excellent example of shooting yourself in the foot. Who would want to go to any more reenactments? We're missing something, but I'm damned if I know what it is."

"What about the town of Tunnel Hill? Could the horses and weapons be there under cover of setting up for the reenactment?"

"We've observed several trucks in the area unloading canons and wagons. The reenactors usually bring their own vintage rifles and swords. But they've also been staking out places for tents. And from what we've heard, the so-called 'sutlers' who sell food, Civil War crafts, and period clothes won't start setting up their tables until Friday. So far, it seems like a typical reenactment weekend."

Joplin wracked his brain for anything else to suggest. Like Pendleton, he knew there was something they were all missing, but he had no idea what it could be. He was tempted to bring up Tullie and Carrie's suspicions about her and the narrative she'd gotten them to believe. But he had no proof that it was a false narrative. Yet.

"I'll keep my thinking cap on, sir, and let you know if I come up with anything. I promise you."

Pendleton sighed again. "You do that, Investigator. We're open to anything at this point."

Joplin clicked on the video again and saw a scene labeled "Campfire." It showed men dressed in Confederate uniforms sitting around a blazing fire, glasses raised, then panned to a motley crew of musicians with fiddles and flutes playing for the troops. Another scene showed what was evidently an officer and his lady under a tent, relaxing in canvas camp chairs on an oriental rug. Joplin was grateful when his cell phone rang.

"What's up, Tom?" he said.

"Has Tullie called you?"

"Not today. I think I ticked her off yesterday."

"How so?"

"She called me and told me about an argument she had with Moira. She said she tried to find out whether Aidan might be in over his head with Fox Run—as a reason for his unholy alliance with Eric Jaeger, which, of course, she didn't mention. But Moira went ballistic and accused Tullie of being jealous. I guess I wasn't sympathetic enough, and I also implied she cusses too much."

"Well, that would do it, especially since the argument has gone viral. It seems Moira decided to let Aidan know about Tullie's 'concerns,' and now he's up in arms and insists on meeting with her. Wants her to go to Fox Run."

"That's a terrible idea," Joplin said.

"Which is what I told her."

Joplin thought for a minute, then told Tom about Pendleton's phone call. "The GBI is desperate for any kind of lead, and they've got Fox Run under surveillance. Maybe Tullie should keep that meeting."

"Another bait situation?" Tom said. "Are you out of your mind, Hollis?"

"Probably. But the stakes are pretty high, and Tullie might not be in any danger. Things might not be what we thought."

"What does that mean?"

Reluctantly, Joplin explained Carrie's suspicions about Tullie and his inability to prove her wrong. "I'm not saying it's true, Tom—I have trouble believing that Tullie has been leading us on, for whatever reason. But I can't dismiss the idea either. Just think about it. You're a logical, analytical person. The only counter to this theory is that if Tullie killed Jacob

Gunter, why would she want his death to be treated as a possible homicide and drag us into it? Or connect us with Will Sykes, if she's involved with The Cause? It only makes sense if she killed Gunter, but has no connection to The Cause."

"Or if she's not involved with either, the murder or The Cause," Tom said. "Which has my vote. Hollis, I'm not just saying that because she's Maggie's cousin. I've known Tullie for almost twelve years, and she's not capable of this."

"I've only known her for six years, but I can't believe it either. But you can't prove a negative, Tom, so maybe this is an opportunity to rule that theory out. A safe opportunity, because the GBI has eyes and ears on Fox Run."

Tom gave a long sigh. "What do you want me to do?"

"Let me run this by Pendleton and get back to you."

47

PENDLETON WENT FOR it in a big way. He assured Joplin that they had enough surveillance cameras on Fox Run to see if any bad actors were around, and agents stationed nearby to rush in and rescue Tullie if there were. Joplin conveyed all this to Tom and also nixed his idea of driving up to Wolfscratch to accompany Tullie to the meeting with Aidan.

"If anything happens to her," said Tom, almost growling, "I'll hold you—"

"Personally responsible," finished Joplin. "So will I. Hold me responsible, I mean. And if she doesn't want to go to Fox Run after you tell her about the plan, I'll talk to Pendleton. You can also tell her I said I was a jerk on the phone yesterday, and I'm sorry, okay?"

"Yes, I can go along with that, but it's still up to Tullie."

Carrie was beyond concerned about the plan, telling Joplin her suspicions about Tullie were just that—suspicions—and that he shouldn't have acted upon them.

"I haven't 'acted upon them,'" he insisted, knowing he sounded defensive. "I'm taking Pendleton at his word—that the GBI has Fox Run and Aidan under surveillance. This could be a major break in the case, Carrie. Proving that Tullie isn't involved with Gunter's death or The Cause is secondary."

Joplin could tell she wasn't convinced. He'd almost decided to scrap the plan when Tom called back and said Tullie had agreed to it. He said she wasn't happy about it, but she also thought meeting with Aidan might move things along. She'd also agreed that Joplin was a jerk.

So, they all waited throughout the afternoon, hoping to hear good news. But when news finally arrived, it wasn't good at all.

✦ ✦ ✦ ✦

SAC PENDLETON SOUNDED the first alarm. According to the special agents placed around Fox Run, Tullie never made it there; they were out scouring the area. Then Moira called Maggie, wondering if she'd heard from Tullie since, per Aidan, she'd never shown up for a scheduled meeting with him. And Ryan, who had immediately left Wolfscratch to look for Tullie, could find no trace of her.

"Maggie knew about your brilliant plan and wasn't thrilled about it," Tom told him. "Now she's incensed, so I'm going up there."

"Wait a minute," Joplin insisted. "Just hold on there. If anyone should go up there to look for Tullie, it's me, Tom. And I will, I promise you. I just need to come up with a plan."

"That's what caused this debacle, Hollis," said Tom. Joplin could almost hear his teeth clenching.

"Fine. Let's both go. We'll come up with a plan on the way there."

Which is what they did, over the protestations of Maggie, Carrie, and Pendleton. Their wives extracted promises that they would keep the lines of communication open and not do anything stupid. SAC Pendleton insisted on having an agent meet them at the Hallorans' house to attach a tracking device to Tom's car; the GBI would also track them through their cell phones.

Tom Halloran's teeth were still clenched as they headed north on 400. "So, what's the new plan, Hollis?" he asked.

Joplin refrained from telling him that Tullie's disappearance could mean that she was, in fact, a part of The Cause. That it might have been a ploy to get them up to Wolfscratch, and his plan would have to take that into consideration. Instead, he pulled out his cell phone and said, "First, we're going to talk to Gary Summers and see if Tullie actually left Wolfscratch."

Tom turned to glare at him. "You still believe she's part of this insane plot?"

"No, Tom. I'm a trained investigator, and that's what we do: start with the last known place the missing person was known to be. If she's still inside Wolfscratch, that's where we'll begin our search."

As they left the interstate and turned west, Gary called. He confirmed that Tullie had left the property at 1:05 p.m. in her dark blue Jeep Cherokee and hadn't returned. Joplin thanked him and turned to Tom. "Now, we go to Plan B."

"Which is?"

"We go straight to Fox Run and talk to Aidan."

"And say what, exactly, Hollis?"

"I'm not sure, but something will come to me. Maybe even the truth for a change."

✚ ✚ ✚ ✚

HALLORAN WASN'T SURE what Hollis meant by "the truth," but decided it was better not to know. He was clearly along for the ride; his only real option was to try to minimize the fallout. Given his career, that was something Halloran knew he was good at doing. Hollis' forte was plunging headlong into the fray, no matter the danger or cost to anyone else.

So, they drove past both entrances to Wolfscratch and headed to Fox Run.

The iron gates were closed when they arrived. Halloran punched the "talk" button and said, "Hi, Aidan, it's Tom Halloran and my friend, Hollis Joplin. Can you let us in?"

There was a long pause before Aidan said, "Hi, Tom. What's going on?"

"Your mother called me and is worried about Tullie."

"You're kidding. You drove all the way up here from Atlanta because of that?"

"You're family, Aidan, you and Tullie and your parents. And I'd like to think I'm part of that family because of Maggie. She's worried, too."

There was no answer, but the gates slowly opened. Halloran drove on to the main house; Aidan's truck was parked in the circular driveway. He met them at the door, his eyes bloodshot and his beard three days past the fashionably scruffy look. There was a crystal glass with three fingers of a brown liquid in his right hand and a scowl on his face. The scowl tightened as he gazed at Hollis.

"You must be that death investigator everyone's talking about," he said, not moving back to let them in.

"Who's everybody?" Hollis asked.

Instead of responding, Aidan turned and began walking through the two-storied entry hall to the back of the house. Moira and Ryan had remodeled it a few years before they moved to Wolfscratch into an enormous open floor plan, with a gourmet kitchen to the right and a den filled with rustic antique furniture and leather sofas on the left. Halloran observed that if he'd been expecting Tullie, Aidan sure hadn't cleaned up for her. The sinks and counters were littered with dirty dishes, fast food containers, and empty beer cans. A half-gallon bottle of Wild Turkey—down by a quart—was on the granite island.

"Have a seat," Aidan said, gesturing toward the den with his glass. He looked at the glass and added, "Want a drink?"

"No thanks," he and Hollis said together, as they made their way to one of the leather sofas.

Aidan sat down on the other one and said, "So, what's all this fuss about Tullie?"

"You tell us. You had something to discuss with her, but she never arrived at the appointed time."

"So? She probably just blew the whole thing off. That's what I told my dad when he came rushing over here. There's no explaining what goes on in my sister's mind sometimes."

"What did you want to discuss with her?" Hollis asked.

Aidan glared at him, his All-American good looks distorted by anger. "Why do you want to know, Death Investigator Joplin? Do you think she's dead?"

"I sincerely hope not, Tullie's brother," said Hollis, leaning forward and clasping his hands between his knees in a classic interrogation pose. "But she could be soon if you don't tell us about your involvement with The Cause. Two people who knew about that group are dead, and I was run off the road by one of the members last Friday. Another member sexually molested a woman to get her husband to stop talking about it. Do you think they won't hurt a community supervision officer who's called attention to a parolee on the lam? A man who violated his parole and created a meth lab in the North Georgia woods to help them pull in money to fund their terroristic intentions? A parolee you were seen talking to—no, make that arguing with—in your truck in a Home Depot parking lot just before he absconded parole?"

Aidan's face had turned pale under its tan. "Who said I was arguing with Eric Jaeger in my truck?"

"A very reliable witness. So, what were you arguing about?"

"We weren't arguing!" Aidan insisted, then shut his mouth, evidently realizing he'd just admitted to being with Jaeger.

"Okay," Hollis said, smiling. "I stand corrected. So, what were you *talking* about?"

"None of your goddamn business!" Aidan said vehemently. "I don't have to talk to you."

"Fine with me. But the GBI has had you under surveillance for the past few days, so I imagine they'll have a lot to talk to you about."

"They said they wouldn't hurt her!" Aidan blurted out. "They're just going to get her out of the picture until they can—" He abruptly shut up and gulped down some of his drink.

"Until they can do what, Aidan?" Halloran said.

He took a deep breath, then said, "Until their 'mission' is accomplished. And I swear, I don't know what it is."

"You didn't want to know," Halloran said, disgusted by what he was hearing. "Because it might make you feel bad about what you were doing, Aidan. About your part in this whole thing."

"No!" Aidan insisted, jumping up and lurching to the kitchen island, where he poured himself some more Wild Turkey. He took a hefty swig and turned back to them. "All I did was sell them some horses and—I just sold them some horses. That's all, I swear!"

"That and lure your sister over here so they could grab her," Hollis said. "Your own sister! And I don't buy your story, Aidan. Anyone with a brain can see that you've over-extended your-self with everything you've done at Fox Run. And selling some horses to The Cause wouldn't bring in the cash you need. What kind of a deal did you strike with Harold Danforth and Sheriff Odum? Are you selling meth for them? Maybe to your students?"

Aidan turned even paler and began to shake his head vigor-ously. "Good God, no! I would never do that! Did Tullie tell you that? I can't believe this!"

"Tullie was *worried* that that's what you were doing, Aidan," Halloran said, trying to de-escalate the situation. "She came to us because she was concerned that you were somehow involved with Eric Jaeger. Either in what we thought was his murder or Jacob Gunter's murder when we discovered that the body we found at the Upper Falls was his, not Jaeger's."

Aidan moved back to the leather sofa and sank into it.

"Just tell us who has Tullie," Halloran pleaded. "Before some-thing happens to her. That's all we want from you right now. Everything else can be worked out, I promise."

"Harold Danforth has her," Aidan said, looking and sound-ing defeated. "He's keeping her at the funeral home. But he's known us all our lives, Tom. He would never hurt her."

"Maybe not," Hollis spat out. "But there are plenty of fanatical Cause members who would. Think about that, Brother Aidan, while you're rationalizing whatever you did for them, including betraying your sister." He stood up and said, "Let's get out of here, Tom. I've had about as much horse shit from this guy as I can take. Pun intended."

They left Tullie's brother still sitting on the sofa. He didn't bother to get up. But once outside, Halloran said, "Should we take Aidan with us, Hollis? I'm afraid he might tip off Danforth before we can get to Tullie."

"He won't want them to know he's ratted them out, I promise you," said Hollis. "No matter what he said, Aidan knows what they're capable of doing." He patted his jeans pocket. "Besides, I've had my cell phone recording everything since we got here. I'm sure Pendleton has heard everything Aidan told us, and the agents positioned around Fox Run will be picking him up as soon as we leave. What I do want to do is check out the stables before we leave, though. I don't think the horses Aidan bought for The Cause are the only things missing."

48

HOYT ODUM STOOD in front of the three horse vans they'd borrowed from Aidan Fitzgerald, hands on his hips. Everything they needed for the Mission was already stowed away, even though they wouldn't leave until midnight. There was enough tactical gear for ten men, including Kevlar vests. There were also seven AR-15 rifles he'd purchased for the Sheriff's Office five years ago from Primary Arms and three DDM4ISR rifles he'd bought a year ago from Daniel Defense. These, Hoyt had packed himself. They were special, in more ways than one.

Not only had the DDM4ISRs cost twice as much as the other AR-15s, they'd taken much longer to obtain. Hoyt had needed to get NFA tax stamps for each one. Like regular AR-15s, they were 16 inches long, exempting them from NFA taxes, but these babies had built-in suppressors. The tax on each one was $200, and it had taken eight months to get the necessary certificate to send to Daniel Defense. Hoyt had justified the extra expenses by telling the county commissioners that he needed them for raids on the meth labs that had begun popping up in Rutledge County over the past year.

"We need to be able to take out their security people without letting the perps inside know we're coming," he'd told them. "Suppressors aren't what you think of as silencers—those are illegal. But suppressors cut down on audio emissions. So, when the rifle is fired, it sounds more like a paintball gun being fired than a rifle, see?"

And they *had* seen. And been anxious for Hoyt to buy them, in fact. What was rich was that he and other members of The Cause were the primary controllers of most of the meth labs in the county; the ones they hadn't created, they'd taken over when they'd found them. It had been rough for a while, keeping them running with only a rag-tag group of Cause members. Then Eric Jaeger had been paroled, and the rest, as they say, was history.

Or it would be, after tomorrow.

Hoyt tapped a cigarette out of the pack he took from his shirt pocket and lit it. He took in a deep, satisfying breath and blew it out, his mind going over the plans once again. Originally, they'd had something else in mind for the Tunnel Hill reenactment weekend. It would've been good, he had to admit, but a month ago—almost to the day—The Cause had received a call to arms from someone they couldn't refuse. It was as if he were speaking directly to them, urging them to protect their country from a traitor who would take away their rights as free white men. One right in particular, the right to bear arms. And if that happened, there'd be no America as they knew it. It would be overrun by niggers and kikes and spicks and ragheads. Real Americans would be totally outnumbered and without any way to protect themselves.

Shit, Hoyt Odum thought with disgust, throwing his cigarette butt on the ground and crushing it. *We shoulda done something when Obama was elected. The Nigger-in-Chief.*

Hoyt shook his head, trying to clear it so he could focus on the Mission. They planned on taking I-75 North to Chattanooga, then 74 West to Charlotte. The three horse vans wouldn't attract attention up to that point. Still, they'd need to leave them in the Charlotte-Douglas International Airport parking lot, until it was time to head for a designated vantage point on the route their Secret Service contact had given them. His men would follow in the three cars that would be part of their caravan; they'd already be dressed in their uniforms. The tricky part would be after they reached the designated spot, but Hoyt had planned for that. Their capes might attract attention since it would be 90 degrees on a sunny day, but they would conceal the rifles. The agents in the entourage would be on alert, but that was already taken care of. The Cause had members everywhere.

And then, they could execute their target: a traitor of the worst kind, at the highest level.

✦ ✦ ✦ ✦

"DO YOU KNOW where Harold Danforth's funeral home is?" Halloran asked as they passed through the Fox Run gate and turned onto the apple road.

"Yep. I had the pleasure of returning Jacob Gunter's body to him last week."

"Oh, right, I remember now. You were going back to Atlanta from there when you were run off the road."

Hollis nodded. "And I guess we can safely say that it was Harold who let The Cause know that I'd be a sitting duck after I left him. We can also probably eliminate Will Sykes as a source of information for The Cause."

Halloran glanced at him. "And maybe Tullie as Gunter's killer?"

Hollis sighed. "Yes, Tom. But I understand how Carrie came up with that theory, and you have to admit it was a possibility. "

"Given that you and Carrie were once both betrayed by someone close to you, of course. I can admit that. But possible and probable are two very different things. Maggie and I could never see it."

"Got it," Hollis said. "So, can we focus on rescuing her? That'll make me feel a whole lot better."

Save for Hollis' directions, they passed the rest of the journey in silence. Thirty minutes later, Halloran pulled into a large parking lot in front of a white, columned building with a large, tasteful sign in black script that read "Danforth Funeral Home."

"Pretty elegant for a small-town funeral home," he observed.

"The inside still shouts funeral *parlor*," said Hollis. "Queen Victoria would feel right at home. I suspect his wife has more aspirations than taste."

✦ ✦ ✦ ✦

HAROLD DANFORTH ANSWERED the front door buzzer himself this time. He was smiling broadly, full of bonhomie and goodwill toward men, but Halloran suspected it was all for show. Even if Aidan hadn't alerted him, Danforth didn't seem surprised by their appearance.

"To what do I owe the honor?" he asked.

"We came to get Tullie," Hollis said, also smiling broadly.

"Tullie Fitzgerald?" Danforth said. "Why in the world would you think she'd be here?"

"Because her brother, Aidan, told us so, Harold. Now, cut the shit and let us in. And if I don't see Tullie immediately, I'll call the GBI. They know we're here."

Harold Danforth turned pale, but he ushered them into a wide entry hall dominated by heavy Victorian furniture and an enormous chandelier, then into what Halloran assumed was his office. Another imposing chandelier loomed over them. "Have a seat," he said. "I'll see if she wants to talk to you."

Neither of them sat. Hollis patted the bulge at his waist, indicating he was armed; Halloran had never doubted it. A few minutes later, Danforth appeared at the door with Tullie, who looked more angry than afraid. She was pointedly rubbing her wrists, which negated what she said next.

"What's the big fuss? I'm a big girl, you know."

"We know," Hollis replied, smiling. "But your mother doesn't. She asked us to find you. You know how mothers can be."

"Do I ever," said Tullie. She turned to Danforth. "Gotta go, Harold, but don't think it hasn't been swell."

Harold Danforth suddenly seemed at a loss for words. Then Betsey Cunningham appeared in the doorway, carrying a Glock like the one Hollis had. She smiled brightly and said, "Hi, boys. I thought maybe I should join the party."

"BETSEY?" SAID HALLORAN, thinking she was there to help them. "How did you know we were here?"

"Because she's running the whole show, Tom," said Hollis. "She's the one who sent Harold to pick Tullie up. Didn't you, Betsey?"

"The girl just can't keep her mouth shut," Betsey said, waving the gun at Tullie.

"You don't seem very surprised, Hollis," Halloran said, amazed at how calm he seemed.

"Well, Carrie told me she was pretty sure Gunter had been killed by a woman," Hollis responded. He turned to Betsey. "From the bruise prints you left on Jacob Gunter's back when you pushed him over the cliff at the Upper Falls. The index finger was as long as the middle finger. But I didn't focus on you until I realized it couldn't be Tullie."

"What the fuck are you talking about, Hollis?" Tullie said.

"I'll tell you later," he said.

"You probably won't get that chance, Hollis," said Betsey, turning the gun on him. "And I'm not curious enough to ask what you're talking about. What I do want is for you both to put any weapons you have on the floor. Very gently. That means you, too, Tom."

Hollis retrieved his Glock and laid it on the floor. Halloran patted his pockets and said, "I'm not carrying a gun, Betsey, but I wish I were."

Without responding, Betsey kicked the gun out of reach. "Okay, everyone, let's head downstairs. I don't think Mayellen Danforth would want me getting blood all over her pretty carpets."

Harold held up his hands. "Now, wait a minute, Betsey. I didn't sign up for this."

Betsey shrugged and said, "Fine, Harold. I'll shoot them, and you bury them. Will that keep your hands clean enough?"

"But you said we were just going to keep Tullie here until… afterward. And Hollis said the GBI knows they're here!"

"And you believed him?" she said. "You're an even bigger fool than I thought you were, Harold."

"I have to agree with her, Harold," said Hollis. "At least on that point. Because she was never going to let Tullie leave here alive. And you're next, buddy, right after she plugs us."

"She wouldn't do that," he said, shaking his head. "We love each other, and we're going to be together once this is all over." He turned to Betsey and said, "Tell him, Betsey."

Instead, Betsey Cunningham sighed and said, "I don't have time for this, Harold. Just get over there with the others, and let's get a move on."

"She's just been using you, Harold," said Hollis. Halloran knew he was trying to buy time until the GBI got there, but he was worried that Betsey would get so angry she'd shoot him even sooner than she'd planned. "You and your funeral home were just a way to funnel cash and drugs out of the county and dispose of a few bodies now and then. All for The Cause, right, Betsey? I bet those little sex parties you arrange every month are a part of the fundraising, both because of the blackmailing opportunities and the drugs you sell there. And, of course, there's big money from all the meth houses you got Eric Jaeger to manage once he got out of prison. Plus, there's Aidan Fitzgerald and his access to horses and vans. I bet he gave you a good deal."

"You bitch!" Tullie spat at her. "You fucking cunt!"

Betsey's lip curled, but her eyes danced. "Such language, Tullie! Your mother would be appalled. Then again, she spends *most* of her time being appalled by you and your pitiful job. But you'll be happy to know Aidan didn't help us out just for the money; he knew how thrilled Moira would be when she found out what we're doing. And he was also *very* relieved that Sheriff Odum wasn't going to arrest him for being a little too hands-on with some of his underage clients at Fox Run. He was *happy* to help us!"

"So, all of this has been done so you and Sheriff Odum could form a militia to terrorize people, right, Betsey?" Hollis said. "Cause a big, red splash to call attention to how the South was wronged during the Civil War and that it's not gonna take it anymore, hallelujah! Is that what you have in mind? Maybe parade around on the field at Tunnel Hill and shoot the reenactors playing Union soldiers with real ammunition? Or maybe mow down some of the more prominent spectators in the crowd?"

The lip curled even more. "I can tell you're grasping at straws, Hollis, and it's not attractive. I liked you a lot more when you were naked and under the influence of molly. Have you told your wife about that?"

"You bet. We both got a kick at the thought of me having sex with somebody who could be my mother, if my mother had been a racist, power-hungry bitch."

Almost in slow motion, Halloran saw Hollis move toward Betsey Cunningham as she gave a guttural scream and raised her gun with both hands, aiming at him. Then he saw a man who looked like Jacob Gunter rush into the office, grab Betsey, and wrench her arms toward the ceiling as she fired the weapon. The bullet hit the enormous brass chandelier and sent it crashing down on all of them. They lay in stunned silence for several seconds, then Hollis roused himself and pulled the gun from

Betsey's hands. Dazed and confused by what doctors would later diagnose as a severe concussion, Halloran could only watch as men in GBI SWAT uniforms burst into the room and began to secure it, then check on the injured.

49

IT WAS A long afternoon. They were taken to the same Northside Cherokee hospital where Joplin had been treated the week before. Once he was placed in a room, he asked a nurse if he'd get a frequent flier discount or an upgrade, but she told him he had to lose a limb for that.

"Touché," he said and didn't even mind it when she jabbed him to insert an IV line, although he added, "I'm fine. There's nothing wrong with me. How're my friends, Tom Halloran and Tullie Fitzgerald?"

"Afraid I can't give you that information," she said. "I can tell you that you have a pretty bad gash on your head that needs attention. That's in addition to the three broken ribs you sustained last week, according to your records. And we're observing you for concussion. That enough for you?"

Joplin grinned and said, "I like a woman who doesn't pull her punches. If I weren't happily married, I'd ask you out."

"And if I weren't happily single, I still wouldn't take you up on that," she replied, then left the room.

Joplin was still trying to figure that out when SAC Pendleton entered the room. "How are you?" he asked, moving to the right side of the bed.

"I'm fine, but Nurse Ratchett wouldn't tell me anything about Tom and Tullie."

"Ms. Fitzgerald has a broken collar bone, and Mr. Halloran is severely concussed. As you may be."

"Nope. I'm still working on last week's concussion, sir. My insurance won't pay for a new one for six months."

Pendleton almost cracked a smile. "Do you ever stop joking, or is that your way of handling stress?"

"Very rarely and probably yes, to answer your questions. And now, please, answer mine, sir: Have you gotten anything out of Bonnie and Clyde?"

"If you mean Harold Danforth and Betsey Cunningham, the answers are quite a bit and nothing at all. Mrs. Cunningham, who has a broken nose, immediately asked that her lawyer be called, even when we revealed that your phone had recorded everything she said before we arrived on scene. Mr. Danforth, on the other hand, couldn't *stop* talking when he heard the recording. He insisted he knew nothing about what Odom called the 'Mission,' and I'm inclined to believe him, based on your recording.. I don't think he wanted to know, and the ringleaders assumed he'd talk too much, if he did. "

"And I'm assuming they were blackmailing him, in addition to Betsey offering her considerable charms."

Pendleton nodded. "He told me Sheriff Odum had discovered that he was selling body parts to various medical research companies and hospitals, something quite a few funeral home directors have been caught doing. So, he agreed to 'look the other way,' as he called it, when he was called to the scene of a death that was obviously a homicide."

"Which probably happened a lot while Ray Brent Marsh was managing Tri-State Crematory and panicked Harold and Odum when the scandal hit the papers. And that's where Eric Jaeger comes in, right? Your mole who infiltrated The Cause?"

Pendleton gave him a wry smile. "Yes, on both counts. The sheriff had eyes and ears at Central State Prison, and when his lackeys couldn't find out anything from Marsh, they told him that Eric had gotten to know him over time. So, when he was paroled, Odum was one of his first visitors, demanding to know whether Ray Brent had ever talked about Tri-State or any of the bodies Harold sent him. But even when Eric assured him that Ray Brent was oblivious to anything illegal going on—that he'd only talked about how he'd let those families down—Odum wouldn't let him off the hook. He told him about The Cause and said Eric needed to go to work for them and manage their meth houses, or he'd find a way to send him back to prison. Eric knew he wasn't kidding, but he really did want to go straight. Ms. Fitzgerald was right about that."

"So, he contacted the GBI and agreed to infiltrate The Cause," said Joplin.

Pendleton sighed and rubbed his forehead. "Yes, and we did a piss-poor job of protecting him. That's when we formed the task force with the ATF, the DEA, and Homeland Security. Eric managed to let us know about some 'mission' The Cause was planning and about the cache of military-grade weapons they'd amassed, but then he went off the grid. He was under constant surveillance and couldn't contact us, and we couldn't get to him."

"Was that before or after Tullie saw him with her brother in the Home Depot parking lot?"

"After. Betsey Cunningham had negotiated with Aidan over finding horses for the Tunnel Hill reenactment, but she told Eric that Aidan insisted he needed more money than that would bring him. Told her he knew about the drugs she was selling at the wife-swapping parties and wanted in. So, they sent Eric to meet with him in the Home Depot parking lot, and Aidan was angry about his cut for helping to move the meth around. That was evidently when Sheriff Odum stepped in and told him the Nolan police had received a complaint about his overstepping some boundaries with one of his riders at Fox Run. Said he'd talk to the parents and make it go away, if Aidan cooperated."

"God," said Joplin. "This is going to kill Tullie. Did Aidan admit all this?"

"No. We arrested him right after you and Tom Halloran left Fox Run, but he refused to talk, even when we informed him of your phone recording. His parents got him a high-priced attorney, and Mrs. Fitzgerald threatened to sue us for false arrest. But between what's on your phone and what we've learned from Eric Jaeger, we're not worried about that."

"So, right after that, Eric went off the grid."

"Yes," said Pendleton. "The next day was Thursday, the eighteenth. Betsey told him to borrow a horse from Aidan and sneak into Wolfscratch, to the Upper Falls that night. She didn't want to risk being seen with him or having his face recorded by the security gate cameras. But she didn't tell him what was going to happen, just said to 'play along,' that she and Odum had figured out a way for him to 'disappear' and keep Community Supervision off his back. But when Eric saw Gunter, who looked so much like him, he realized what the plan was."

"Was Gunter spooked, too?"

"Not right away. Eric thought Gunter was already pretty drunk when he got to the Falls and didn't have a clue about what was happening. Then Betsey suggested they party and gave Gunter a blunt filled with cocaine and pot, and he seemed totally compliant, even when she told him to exchange clothes with Eric. She made it seem like they'd enjoy a kind of kinky three-some. Evidently, she and Gunter had been sexually involved in the past."

"Is there anyone Miz Cunningham *hasn't* been sexually involved with in Georgia?" Joplin asked.

"Just you, from what I heard on your phone recording," Pendleton said dryly. "Anyway, by then, Eric had had enough and tried to intervene, but Betsey suddenly produced a gun and told him to back off. Then she ordered Gunter to the edge of the cliff, and he finally understood what was happening. When he refused, Betsey clocked him with the gun handle, then pushed him over the edge."

"It never occurred to her that her handprints would show up on Gunter's back," Joplin said. "Or that Bo might be called to the scene instead of Harold, who evidently hadn't been told what Betsey had planned."

"Or that someone like you might find the body," Pendleton added. "Anyway, after that, Eric was under constant supervision and had no way to contact us. He told us they made him get a Southern Cross tattoo a few days later and said they'd microchipped him so they'd know wherever he was, which freaked him out."

"So, how did he end up at Danforth's funeral home?"

"We're not sure, but Eric said he thought they intended to get rid of him. One of Odum's deputies told him he'd done a good job and he'd be free to go after he helped Mrs. Cunningham with something at the funeral home. He didn't buy that, of course, and she made the mistake of leaving him alone in the embalming room when she went upstairs to find out where Tullie was, since she wasn't downstairs. So, Eric followed her and decided he'd better do something when he heard her arguing with you and ordering everyone to move downstairs."

"Well, thank God he did," Joplin said. "Have you found Sheriff Odum yet?"

"No, he's still in the wind and so are the three horse vans from Fox Run, which bothers me. Most of the horses Aidan purchased for The Cause are at Tunnel Hill, but not the vans."

"Not to mention all the military-grade weapons Jesse Waldrup saw in the woods."

"We're pulling the snitch chain, but no one wants to give us anything."

Joplin sighed. "So, to sum up: Aidan and Betsey Cunningham have lawyered up and aren't talking, Harold sang like a bird but doesn't know what the 'Mission' is, Eric Jaeger filled in a lot of missing pieces and, like Harold, can testify against the others at trial, but he doesn't know what the 'Mission' is either. And Odum has disappeared, presumably to carry out the Mission, which most likely involves military weapons, horse vans, and maybe some horses."

Pendleton nodded, his expression even more concerned.

"What about Jack Cunningham? Is he in custody, too?"

"After we had him listen to your recording, he claimed to be in shock. Said he knew nothing about The Cause or the Mission or his wife's involvement. We have nothing on him, except his participation in the swingers' club and all the drugs that involved. Betsey never mentioned him on the recording, so he could be telling the truth. Anyway, you've summed every-thing up pretty well. The bottom line is that time is running out. We have no clue what the Mission is, but if it's connected to the Tunnel Hill reenactment, we only have two days to find out."

As it turned out, however, they had less time than that.

50

JOPLIN WAS FINALLY discharged from the hospital around 6 p.m. Carrie also insisted on taking Tullie with them; her parents weren't speaking to her, having decided that Aidan's legal troubles were all her fault. Joplin wasn't sure whether Carrie's insistence was because of her guilt over thinking Tullie was a murderer or empathy because Tullie's parents had abandoned her, but Carrie wouldn't let her refuse.

"I'll fix some of that pizza you missed on Labor Day," she promised.

"Deal," said Tullie, looking at the sling holding her broken collarbone together. "I don't think I could even open a can of soup tonight."

The drive home was silent, none of them ready to broach the day's events. The cats greeted them warmly at the door, purring and rubbing up against their legs. Even Tullie's legs. Joplin fed them, then made himself and Tullie stiff drinks; they'd both refused pain meds at the hospital. While Carrie made pizza, they settled into chairs.

Joplin spoke first. "I can't imagine what you're going through, Tull. Betrayed by your brother, kidnapped by Harold Danforth, almost murdered by a family friend, and then abandoned by your parents. How are you even on your feet?"

Tullie shook her head. "Just let me get some more of this Jack in me before I start the pity party, okay, Hollis? I'm just not up to processing it yet. Besides, you were almost killed, too."

"Yeah, but I'm used to it. And it didn't come with a side of betrayal."

Instead of answering, she took a long sip of her drink and shook her head again, eyes brimming. They sat there, drinking and thinking in silence, until Carrie brought the pizza, plates, and napkins into the den, setting them on the large coffee table. They ate and talked about the Hallorans, who were staying on at the hospital due to Tom's concussion. After a while, Carrie announced that she was going to check on the guest bedroom and bath for Tullie, then going to bed.

"Tomorrow's another day," she added, "and it might be just as long as today. I'm recommending bed rest for both of you."

Tullie helped Joplin clear off the dinner things, then said good night. Joplin joined Carrie and the cats in the master bedroom, but knew he wouldn't get much sleep.

✦ ✦ ✦ ✦

JOPLIN'S PHONE TOLD him it was 2 a.m. Carrie was on her back, snoring softly, with Banshee snuggled close on her right side and Quincy at her feet. His brain flipped through image after image like a slide show: Jacob Gunter's body nestled in the crook of a tree branch. Jack Cunningham looking perplexed as he discussed Betsey's "Gone with the Wind" litmus test. The Southern Cross tattooed on Gunter's back after he and Carrie turned him over during the autopsy. Donald Trump smiling broadly at a rally as his followers chanted, "Lock her up! Lock her up!" when he mentioned Hillary Clinton and her damning emails.

Joplin held that image for several seconds, something stirring in the back of his mind. Then it faded away. More images took its place: Betsey Cunningham smiling as she stopped to offer him and Tom a ride after they'd fled the house on 61 Blue Ridge Lane. Betsey's face distorted by rage as she pointed her gun at him when he provoked her at Danforth's funeral home. The empty spaces where three of Fox Run's vans had been.

Joplin knew his subconscious was trying to tell him something, but he wasn't getting the message. With a sigh, he began his sleep meditation, relaxing various body parts, beginning with his feet. By the time he reached his rib cage, his brain finally let go.

✦ ✦ ✦ ✦

JOPLIN FELT MOVEMENT on his side of the bed and slowly opened his eyes. Monica Lewinsky was smiling down on him. She looked like the more recent photos of her that he'd seen from a 2014 televised TED talk, but she was wearing the infamous blue Gap dress with Bill Clinton's semen stains that had caused such a media feeding frenzy in 1997.

"What are you doing here?" he managed to say.

"I'm not really here," she answered. "You just have a very overactive mind, even when you're asleep."

"Tell me about it. But why am I imagining you?"

Monica shrugged. "I think I'm supposed to remind you of something. Something important."

"Well, it hasn't worked."

Monica Lewinsky stood up, the smile fading from her face. "Well, don't blame me. Then again, why should you be any different? Everyone blamed *me* for what happened with Bill Clinton, remember? I was just a 22-year-old intern, and he was the most powerful man in the world."

"I remember," said Joplin, feeling a wave of pity for her.

"Do you?" Monica asked, turning and walking away.

✦ ✦ ✦ ✦

LIGHT WAS STREAMING through the slats of the plantation shutters in their bedroom when Joplin awoke. His phone showed that it was now 8:35 a.m. Carrie and the cats were not in the bed with him.

Neither, thank God, was Monica Lewinsky.

Joplin sat up abruptly. He knew what he was supposed to remember. Couldn't believe that he hadn't realized it earlier. Now, it might be too late. Sheriff Odum might already have his militia members in place.

He pulled up SAC Pendleton in his contacts list and jabbed the name as hard as he could.

51

IT'S HILLARY CLINTON," Hollis Joplin shouted into the phone. "She's speaking at a rally at the Johnson C. Smith University in Charlotte, North Carolina at noon today. That's where Odum and the horse vans will be. You need to alert the Secret Service."

"What the hell are you talking about, Joplin?" Pendleton said.

He heard Joplin take a deep breath and blow it out. "Donald Trump has been focusing on Hillary Clinton's emails—the ones containing possible classified material on her private server— at his last few rallies, provoking the crowds to chant, 'Lock her up! Lock her up!'"

"Yeah, I've seen that on TV. It's over the top, but that's just Trump. Nobody takes him seriously."

"Well, they should, especially the Secret Service. I'm sort of a news junkie, and I've noticed a lot of hate tweets in the past few weeks. Some people are even calling for her death, saying she's a 'traitor,' but no one's been flagging that or trying to defuse the situation. Like you, everyone just thinks that's Trump's rhetoric. But he's got a huge base with a lot of fringe followers, including David Dukes, the former head of the KKK, and militias like The Cause. More importantly, Charlotte is only 133 miles from Tunnel Hill, sir."

Now, Pendleton took a deep breath. "And you think that's where Sheriff Odum and the horse vans are?"

"Yes, sir! I think Odum has been keeping them out of sight since he picked them up from Fox Run. But the trip to Charlotte would only take about two hours, and it's horse country up there, so they wouldn't look out of the ordinary. They're probably carrying a mixture of horses, men, and weapons. But the vans would draw attention if he drove them onto the campus, so I think he'll park them somewhere along the route the Secret Service is taking Hillary and try to get to her while she's still in the car. "

"I see," Pendleton said, beginning to understand Joplin's intensity. "And you think we should contact the Secret Service?"

"Yes, but only someone who can be trusted. Remember the ATF member who was connected to The Cause? I'd bet my life that most members of law enforcement follow the rule of law, but there are too many who don't, especially when racism is involved. Someone on Hillary Clinton's security team might be compromised, sir."

Pendleton sighed. "I think the whole thing sounds crazy, but everything we know about this militia shows they're crazy as hell—and lethal, too. I hear you loud and clear about the Secret Service, but I need to confer with Director Winslow about this. We can't just go charging up to Charlotte, you know. We have no jurisdiction."

"What about the North Carolina Bureau of Investigation?"

"Same problem. The Cause might have people there, too, like Tennessee, and we'd be letting them know we suspect what they're doing."

Joplin went silent again for several seconds. Then he said, "I can go. I don't have any jurisdictional problems, sir. I work for the ME's Office. Strictly speaking, I'm no longer in law enforcement."

"Out of the question," Pendleton snapped. "So, don't go getting any ideas, Joplin. I've talked to some people about you. You've had two life-threatening experiences due to going *way* outside your job description. I don't doubt your courage or abilities, but you need to leave this in my hands. I promise you we'll figure something out."

✚ ✚ ✚ ✚

SO, JOPLIN WAITED, but it was the hardest thing he'd ever done. His impulse-oriented, hot dog genes urged him to take things into his own hands and charge up to Charlotte, loaded for bear. Instead, he went out to the kitchen, where Carrie and Tullie sat at the island, drinking coffee and tea. Tullie was wearing one of Carrie's non-maternity nightshirts, her sling draped carefully over it. Carrie was dressed in a pantsuit.

"I sure hope you're not thinking of going to the ME's today," Joplin told her.

"Why not? Some of the major perpetrators are in custody, and the others are focused on whatever the 'Mission' is."

"That doesn't mean they won't be tying up loose ends, and I think all present here—except for the cats—are in that category."

Carrie set her teacup down with a sigh. "And I think you're overreacting, Hollis. I've taken too much time off from work as it is."

Tullie looked from one to the other. "Should I call Dr. Phil?" she asked. "I can go with either perspective at this point, but it's really beyond my expertise. I've never been married."

Luckily, Joplin didn't have to answer; the doorbell rang, and the door cam showed that it was Ike Simmons.

"Did I get you out of bed?" he asked, eyeing Joplin's pajamas.

"No, Carrie let me sleep in," Joplin said, stepping back from the door. "Come on in, Ike. You can help me convince her not to go into the ME's Office today." Without waiting for Simmons' response, he marched back into the kitchen.

"I brought reinforcements," he announced. "Ike doesn't think you should go to work either, Carrie."

Simmons held up both hands. "Wait a minute, Hollis. I never said that."

"Well, you will when I update everyone about what's happening in Charlotte, North Carolina."

Joplin reiterated what he'd told SAC Pendleton earlier, slowly and calmly this time, careful not to sound like a conspiracy theorist. At first, the narrative met with the same skepticism Pendleton had expressed, but by the time he'd finished, he could tell they were beginning to believe him.

Simmons was the first to speak. "What did Pendleton say he was going to do?"

"Talk to Director Winslow. He promised they'd figure something out without tipping our hand to whatever Secret Service agents might be involved. But I don't see how that can happen, frankly."

"Beyond our pay grades, Hollis. I agree with Pendleton. We need to let them do their jobs."

"Fuck," said Tullie. "Then we all need better pay grades."

Simmons looked at her. "She always talk like that?" he asked.

"Always," said Carrie, looking defiantly at Ike Simmons, who was her dear friend. "Any problem with that?"

Simmons raised his hands again. "Sorry, that was sexist. Alfrieda would bite my head off, too."

Carrie's expression softened. "One of the many reasons I love your wife, Ike."

"So," said Joplin, trying to bring the conversation back to what was important, "do you now agree that Carrie should stay home today, Ike?"

"I think you should all stay here—especially you, Hollis. Don't go getting any ideas about hot-dogging it to Charlotte. And I'm gonna put a security team back on this house for good measure."

✦ ✦ ✦ ✦

IT WAS 11 a.m. The men were ready, dressed in Confederate uniforms proclaiming them members of the 23rd Georgia Infantry Regiment from Bartow County. Each wore an insignia declaring them to be "Bartow Yankee Killers." In January of 1865, that group had fought at the Second Battle of Fort Fisher in Wilmington, NC, led by Capt. Benjamin G.P. Poole under Col. Marcus R. Ballenger. After a bloody, two-day battle, Wilmington had been lost to the Union, depriving the Confederacy of a port for receiving supplies and access to the Northern Rail.

But today, Odum knew, Charlotte, where Jefferson Davis had received word of Abraham Lincoln's execution, would once again belong to the South. The real South.

Odum knew the men were hot in their gray capes, but they didn't complain. They were all on high alert, yet didn't seem nervous, even to Hoyt Odum's observant eyes. The men knew they might not survive the day, but they were patriots on a mission to save their country.

Odum was proud of them. Like any good general, he would stay behind the lines, sending strategic information by a burner phone and urging them on. Part of him wished he could be among them; the other part knew he needed to stay alive and free to continue the war on another front. But this battle was the most important one: It would not only take back ground lost in 1865, it would also send a message to a country allowing itself to be taken over by mongrels.

And a traitor would soon be dead.

Their caravan was parked on a quiet, tree-filled lane off Beatties Ford Road, about fifty yards from the entrance to the university. Their Secret Service contact had chosen the site because Hillary's entourage would pass right by it at a precise time, with a text sent to him just before that happened. All around them were subdivisions peopled by students and faculty at the university and graduates who had decided to live and work in Charlotte. Johnson C. Smith University was the top-ranked private HBCU in Charlotte; it was in the top 30 of the 102 Historically Black Colleges and Universities in the nation.

But in just a few minutes, Odum thought with satisfaction, *it would be forever known for the blow struck by The Cause on behalf of all God-fearing white men.*

Odum signaled for the men to mount up. The horses were nervous, even if the men weren't, tossing their heads and bucking a little. They wore blinders, and his men knew how to calm them when necessary, but they'd soon be moving, which would help. At precisely 11:17 a.m., Odum received the text he was waiting for and gave the signal for them to begin moving toward Beatties Ford Road. He stayed behind them, able to see the university's entrance with his high-powered binoculars. At 11:20, Odum observed three unmarked black cars turn into it: Hillary, he'd been told, would be in the middle one.

The men charged down Beatties Ford Road, urging the horses at a fast clip. Odum watched as they barreled into the university grounds and tried to surround the Secret Service cars. They were stopped by a barrage of fire from several men dressed in black tactical shirts and helmets and carrying M4 Carbines who seemed to appear from nowhere. Odum saw his men fall from their horses almost simultaneously. Before waiting to see if any of them had survived the deadly volley, he raced back to his car, jumped in, and fled through the subdivision.

52

IT WAS 12:03 when Joplin got the call.

"It's over," was all Pendleton said.

Joplin took a deep breath and swallowed hard. "How? When? What happened?"

"Director Winslow thought your theory was just crazy enough to be possible, so he called the director of the Secret Service. Evidently, they go way back—the Naval Academy, I think. Director Barnstead was pretty skeptical about it and, of course, convinced none of his agents could be part of a conspiracy to assassinate Hillary Clinton. But out of an abundance of caution, he got the FBI and Homeland Security involved. They already had drones in the area as backup for the Secret Service. Within minutes, they'd pulled up real-time aerial footage of the three horse vans and three accompanying cars on a side street right off Beatties Ford Road, near the entrance to the university. Then Barnstead had a SWAT team sent there immediately from the FBI's Charlotte field office."

"Damn!" said Joplin. "Did they take them all into custody?"

"Not then. No probable cause at that point. Anyone observing them would have thought they were part of some Civil War reenactment group. They were dressed in period uniforms and wore capes that concealed their weapons. The team had to wait until the group made a move, which they did at 11:20 a.m., just as what would have been Mrs. Clinton's entourage was entering the university."

"Would have been?"

"The official entourage had been diverted to the other side of the campus. The one Odum's men tried to attack was filled with more SWAT team members."

"Jesus!" Joplin said. "Did any of the militiamen survive?"

"Four of the ten are in critical condition at the CMC Sammy Ross, Jr. Trauma Center. The others died on scene."

"Was Sheriff Odum among either group?"

"Unfortunately, no. The FBI aerial surveillance team was covering the militia by then, and Odum wasn't among them when the attack happened. But one of the three cars accompanying the horse vans went missing, and they think he was able to get away through the subdivision that abuts the area while the SWAT team was securing the crime scene. They hadn't been able to get anyone close to that area before the attack, because several regular agents were busy diverting traffic from it. But they're tracking Odum's car, so it shouldn't be long before he's in custody."

Joplin took a deep breath and blew it out. "So, it's finally over," he said.

"Yes, thanks to you, Hollis. If you hadn't put this thing together and figured out what the 'Mission' was, a lot of lives would have been lost. And the presidential election would have been turned on its ear, to say the least. You'll be happy to know that Mrs. Clinton still intends to give her speech once the Secret Service okays it. You'll probably hear from her and a few other people later today. Oh, and according to Winslow, Director Barnstead already has a lead on the identity of the Secret Service agent who was Odum's contact."

"Well, that's good news."

"It's all good news, Hollis. From our perspective anyway."

"Except for Hoyt Odum still being in the wind."

Pendleton sighed. "Right. Except for that."

✦ ✦ ✦ ✦

AT 2:37 A.M., Hoyt Odum, wearing black fatigues and night vision goggles, silently approached the patrol car parked outside Hollis Joplin's house in Garden Hills. The front windows were rolled down, and he could hear the two officers, a male and female, talking to each other. The male officer asked his partner if she was going to their Lieutenant's retirement party that Friday. Before she could answer, Odum pointed his Ar-15 with the built-in suppressor into the right front passenger side and blew off her head, then did the same to her partner before the man even registered what had happened. He then quickly moved behind a tree in the front yard and waited for any signs that the occupants had awakened. Satisfied that that didn't seem to be the case, Odum headed for the back of the house. He intended to use the rifle to blow the lock off the back door and gain entrance. Joplin probably had an alarm system, but Odum knew it would take police at least ten minutes to arrive.

And he only needed five to take out fucking, meddling Hollis Joplin and his wife.

✦ ✦ ✦ ✦

JOPLIN LOOKED AT his digital clock; it was 2:39 a.m. Something had awakened him, but he didn't know what it was. However, his subconscious seemed to know because his body and mind were suddenly on high alert. He moved quietly out of bed, not wanting to awaken Carrie until he figured out what was going on. The plantation shutters were half-opened, and he peered through the slats. The patrol unit Ike had insisted on was parked at the curb, but there was something off about it. Joplin squinted, trying to figure out what it was. A streetlight was on, but it was about twenty feet away. Then he saw that Officer Hill was slumped over on her partner, who was slumped against the driver-side door.

He wondered if they had fallen asleep on duty, but even as part of his mind knew that couldn't be true, another part registered that Hill was missing her head. Then Joplin heard a sound coming from downstairs, and now he realized that the reason he'd awakened was because he'd heard a suppressed rifle being fired. He grabbed his Glock from the bedside table and, even more quietly, eased out of the bedroom and crept down the hall. The guest room door was open, showing a wide-eyed Tullie; she had evidently heard the sounds, too.

"Tell Carrie to call 911, then get my second piece out of the bedside table drawer," he whispered. "Wait on the stairs until I signal you."

Tullie nodded and followed him out into the hall, then headed for the master bedroom. Joplin held his weapon in both hands and positioned himself near the top of the stairs. He was certain that the intruder was either Hoyt Odum or one of his minions; he hoped with all his heart that it was Odum. This confrontation had been a long time coming, and it would be finished soon, with Odum dead or in custody.

Light coming from the kitchen allowed Joplin to see a shadow extending into the entry hall. He watched as a tall, heavy-looking figure in black followed it, looking cautiously forward, then to the right, a rifle extended before him. Joplin knew he'd have to let the intruder get much closer before he could down him with the Glock. He held his breath and waited as the figure began to climb the stairs. Tullie emerged from the master bedroom, and he nodded toward the stairs. She acknowledged this and held his side piece up with her left hand.

When the figure was halfway up the stairs, Joplin aimed at its center mass and fired. The figure reeled and clutched the banister, but wasn't downed, and he knew then that the person was wearing a Kevlar vest. But as Joplin aimed again, the AR-15 was pointed at him. Joplin jumped back into the hall and fell, his Glock dropping from his hands. He saw Tullie moving backward for some cover, and then he was staring upward into the intruder's face.

"You fucking son of a bitch," the man said, and now Joplin was sure it was Odum. "Most of my men were killed today while performing their patriotic duty, and I hold you personally responsible, you nigger-loving, Jew-loving excuse for a white man. So, after I kill *you*, I'm gonna kill your wife."

"The police are on their way, Odum. You won't get away from here alive."

"The fuck do I care?" he said. "I'll die happy knowing I put you away, and there'll be a shit ton more just like me to carry on our mission. "

As Odum raised his arms slightly to take aim, Joplin scooted forward and kicked the sheriff's legs out from under him. The gun went off, shooting a hole in the ceiling, but Odum hung on to it and started heaving himself up. Joplin body-slammed him, then began searching for his Glock as Odum sat up. But instead of trying to stand up, Odum simply pointed the AR-15 at Joplin's chest and said, "It's over, fuckhead."

Two shots were fired in quick succession behind him; Odum toppled forward onto Joplin's legs, half his head blown off. Some of the sheriff's brains had splattered on Joplin, but Tullie quickly moved forward anyway and kicked the rifle away from him. She held Joplin's Beretta Nano in both hands, although her right hand could only steady it. "You okay, Hollis?" she asked.

"I will be as soon as I get this bastard off me." The sound of sirens encouraged Joplin as he struggled to push the body off of him. "Nice shooting, Tullie. Is Carrie okay?"

"I'm fine," she said, appearing behind Tullie. She looked a little shaken despite what she'd said. "I called 911. Are *you* okay?"

"Never better," he said.

✚ ✚ ✚ ✚

BY 9:30 A.M., three CSU techs had left the house; others were still working outside where the two uniformed officers had been killed. Sarah Petersen, still sounding congested, had called to see how they were and offered to help in any way she could. She was devastated that she'd been on sick leave while they were all in danger. Maggie and Tom had also checked on them from the hospital, where Tom was still being observed due to his concussion. Maggie assured them that the doctors hadn't discovered any long-term problems. Like Sarah, they'd seen the news about the attempt on Hillary Clinton's life and Hoyt Odum's subsequent home invasion and attack on Joplin, Tullie, and Carrie on TV, and were full of questions. Joplin talked to them for a few minutes, then turned the phone over to Carrie. Despite the phone calls from President Obama and Hillary Clinton the night before and similar calls from Secret Service Director Barnstead and GBI Director Winslow, Joplin felt himself on the brink of a Blue Funk.

"Are you sliding into a Blue Funk?" asked Carrie a little later, sitting next to him on one of the sofas in the living room. She was still in her nightgown, but had put on a bathrobe when CSU arrived.

Joplin had showered away Hoyt Odum's brains and was wearing khaki shorts and a polo shirt. Tullie, sitting across from them, had changed into another pair of jeans and a shirt that Carrie had loaned her. Vince Randall was on his way to pick her up and take her to her apartment, she'd told Joplin earlier. There was still no word from her parents.

"What's a Blue Funk?" Tullie asked.

Carrie stared at her. "You've known Hollis for several years and don't know what a Blue Funk is?"

"We haven't worked together in a long time," Tullie said. "Is it like a depression?"

Carrie rolled her eyes. "It's like a depression on steroids," she said. "The last time it happened, he holed up in his apartment for three days. Never showered, never answered his phone, and ordered the most disgusting take-out food imaginable. It was pitiful, and we were in the middle of a big case."

"That was over two years ago, Carrie," Joplin huffed.

"So?"

"So, two police officers just died protecting me. They were each married, with children."

"And that's your fault?" Carrie asked. "They died with honor, doing their duty, and they were protecting Tullie and me, too. And we will talk to their families and go to their funerals and honor them all our lives, even though that will be poor comfort for their families. So, we'll also do what we can for them, however we can. I promise you that, Hollis. But this is not about you."

"I know," he said. "I just need a little time to process the whole thing."

"Hey!" Tullie interjected. "I'm the one who's gotta go through an Internal Affairs investigation for a righteous shooting of a white trash psycho, Hollis! With counseling to follow, remember? If anyone's entitled to a fucking Blue Funk, it's me, not you,"

"Oh, God, Tullie," Joplin said. "Have I even thanked you for saving my life?"

"Relax, Hollis. You've thanked me several times, and Carrie's promised to give me your next child. I'm good."

Joplin cracked a smile at that, then looked up as the front door opened, and a CSU technician came inside, followed by Ike Simmons and SAC Pendleton. The technician went upstairs, and Ike and Pendleton entered the living room.

"Hope you don't mind, Mrs. Joplin," said Pendleton.

"Not at all," Carrie said. "We were hoping you might stop by. You, too, Ike. I can't tell you how devastated we all are about

Officer Hill and Officer Ramirez. It's all we can think of right now."

"Thanks, Carrie," said Ike. "I went to each of their families and told them that in person."

"Thank you," said Joplin. "We'll be paying our respects soon, too."

Simmons nodded, then took a deep breath and said, "We thought you might want to know what's happening on the case." He turned to Pendleton.

"All four of the surviving Rutledge County deputies are going to pull through," he said. "But none of them has agreed to make a statement. Yet. I think once they hear that Odum is dead, that might change. But even without their input, we have enough incriminating evidence—including forensic and cell phone data—to piece together the conspiracy to assassinate Mrs. Clinton. That's exclusive of what we've learned from Harold Danforth and Aidan Fitzgerald," he added, nodding at Tullie.

She jerked her head up. "Aidan agreed to talk?"

Pendleton nodded. "And against the advice of his attorney, I might add. He's fully cooperating. Insisting he had no idea what The Cause was planning and was horrified when he found out. That remains to be seen, but I think he might be telling the truth because of corroborating information from Harold Danforth and Eric Jaeger. Your brother, however, was still involved in the drug trafficking that supported The Cause, Ms. Fitzgerald, so he's looking at a fairly lengthy prison sentence."

Tullie sighed. "I know."

"But what you did this morning does credit to the Fitzgerald name, Tullie," Ike said. "Don't forget that. You and Hollis kept the situation from getting even worse. I don't even want to think about what Hoyt Odum might have done if he were alive."

"Thank you for that, Ike," she said.

"You can leave me out of it, Ike," Joplin said. "I was flat on my ass, with him ready to kill me until Tullie plugged him." When Simmons started to protest, Joplin said, "Just tell me about Betsey Cunningham. Is she cooperating?"

"Not at all," Pendleton responded, his mouth twisting into a wry smile. "She wants her day in court. I suspect she'll use the trial as a forum to expound on her white supremacist beliefs. Her attorney is calling her a member of a 'patriotic' group supporting the 'New Confederacy.'"

Joplin sighed. "It's not new," he said. "It's the same crap being recycled by the Neo-Nazis and the white supremacists in this country, but it all goes back to Hitler and every other monarch or dictator in history who thought ethnic or religious cleansing was a brilliant idea. And rooting out groups like The Cause won't end it."

"I know," said Pendleton. "But we have to keep trying."

"Tell that to the families of Officers Ramirez and Hill," Joplin said, lowering his head.

"Listen here, Hollis," Ike Simmons said, and Joplin heard anger in his voice. "I'm the one who assigned them to protect y'all, and I'd do it again despite what happened. And Ramirez and Hill would respond the way they did, even though they knew they'd be in danger. Because that's what we do: We serve and protect. And even though there are bad apples like Sheriff Odum and his militia, most of us want this job for the right reasons. So, please don't take that away from two people who were heroes in my book. Don't do it."

Carrie and Tullie turned to Joplin, who said, "I won't. I can't, when you put it like that."

EPILOGUE

ON A BRIGHT, chilly October Sunday, Joplin and Carrie jogged to Frankie Allen Park. Six weeks had passed since the terrible events surrounding the attempt on Hillary Clinton's life. The presidential election was only a few weeks away, and most polls were giving her a substantial lead over Donald Trump. Joplin felt exhilarated at the thought that America would be electing its first female president. Another first, after Barack Obama's victory eight years ago.

They were using his favorite route to the park: Winslow Drive to Peachtree Way, then Acorn Avenue, past the Garden Hills swimming pool to Brentwood Terrace. Carrie was pushing the new jogging stroller she'd received at her baby shower. There wouldn't be a baby in it for another month; today, it held their picnic lunch, which probably weighed what their daughter would at birth.

"What've you got in there?" Joplin asked, nodding toward the covered basket.

"Just some tarragon chicken salad sandwiches, a fruit salad, bottled water, and a couple of chocolate caramel brownies," she answered. "We're meeting the Hallorans for dinner tonight, so I didn't want to make too much."

Joplin groaned. "I've gained ten pounds since you got pregnant, sweetie. I love everything you make, but my love handles are growing love handles."

"And I've gained twenty-five pounds," she snapped back at him. "So, be quiet and just enjoy the day."

"Yes, ma'am," he said contritely.

They made their way to the small African-American cemetery next to the old church. The first thing Carrie did was take a small potted plant of mums out from under the cloth napkin that covered their lunch. Walking up to one of the decaying headstones, she carefully placed it on the ground, then plucked at a few weeds around it. Light dawned in Joplin's clueless mind.

"You're the one who's been tending to the graves!" he said.

"Not just me," Carrie said, turning around to look at him. "There are others. And soon, there'll be even more. The Atlanta Historical Society's getting involved."

"But why didn't you tell me?"

She gestured toward the rest of the cemetery and said, "I knew you'd feel guilty about living here if you knew the history of all this. I mean, I felt guilty once I found out. So, I decided to do something about it and got involved with some groups dedicated to restoring it. And I come here a couple times a week and bring flowers for the graves."

"I've seen them," Joplin said quietly." And I *do* know what happened here—that residents in Garden Hills complained about the Black residents living here, and Fulton County bought or zoned out property owned by freed slaves and their descendants to turn this into a baseball park for white kids."

"But you never said anything!"

"I didn't want *you* to feel guilty. You loved the house so much, Carrie! But I called the Atlanta Historical Society and sent some money when I found out they had started a fund to care for the graves. I still feel guilty, but it's a start."

Carrie walked back to him and gave him a big hug. "Yes, it is. And so is something I want to do. If you agree, I mean."

"Anything," said Joplin.

Carrie pulled him over to the grave where she'd laid the flowers. "This one belongs to Savannah Barnes, a descendant of slaves, who got a college degree at Morris Brown University and became a teacher. She died of influenza in her early thirties, but her life had a huge impact on her community." Carrie turned to Joplin. "I want to name our daughter after her, Hollis. So that every time someone asks about her name, we can honor Savannah Barnes. It's the only way I can keep living here." Her eyes searched his face for some kind of unspoken answer.

"Savannah Barnes Joplin it is," he said, gathering her in his arms. Then, he kissed her forehead and added, "Savvy or Barney, for short, right? Or maybe Vanna? I love that game show."

She swatted his left arm. "You'll never change, will you?"

"Probably not, sweetie. But you and Savannah are welcome to work on that."

END

AUTHOR'S NOTE

AS MENTIONED IN the previous books, there is currently no Milton Count in Georgia. But up until 1932, it did exist, having been created in 1857 from bits and pieces of Cobb, Cherokee, and Forsyth counties. It was then merged with Fulton County to save it from bankruptcy during the Depression. My Milton County extends much further south than the original but, in my opinion, reflects the current racial, political, and financial concerns of many of its residents. My main intention in bringing it back to life, however, was to have more creative control over the medical examiner's office where Carrie and Hollis work, as well as to differentiate it from the ME offices in Fulton, Cobb, Dekalb, and Gwinnet Counties.

Rutledge County and Nolan, Georgia are also fictional, as is the resort community of Wolfscratch. Although the setting of *Southern Cross* may resemble a beautiful area where I live, all of the characters, streets, lakes, etc., are also fictional. As are the events that form the story that I've told in this book.

In each of my books, I like to include historical events in Georgia that add to the plot. In *Southern Cross*, I've touched on the Trail of Tears in North Georgia, the origins of Frankie Allen Park in Atlanta, the Tri-State Crematory scandal of 2001, and a failed militia attack in 2011. There are also references to various government conspiracies in the past and political coverage. As always, I thoroughly research actual events to ensure that what I'm weaving into my fiction is accurate. This research comes from newspaper articles, Wikipedia, medical and legal records, and news videos, among other sources. There was so much research that I thought of annotating it, but came to my senses and decided that was a bit pretentious for something meant to entertain. I invite readers to do their own research if they have trouble believing some of the historical content.

I do want to emphasize, however, that although the description of the Tri-State Cemetery scandal is accurate, Ray Brent Marsh's "appearance" in the book is purely fictional. I was careful to use only accounts of how he acted and what he said or was said about him that were in news accounts. Although there's been much speculation over the years as to why Mr. Marsh didn't carry out his duties at Tri-State, no one really knows, except for Marsh himself. Some of the probation officers I supervised in Atlanta volunteered to help with the investigation at the crematory, and it was an event that has stayed in their minds—and mine-- for many years.

Southern Cross is more "political" than my previous books, but it's one I needed to write. It began as a narrative about a resort community impacted by local law enforcement and judicial corruption. And then, the January 6th riot happened. I was horrified by what I saw on television that day and afraid of what it meant for our country going forward. I've lived in the South most of my life, and images of Confederate flags carried by some of the protesters haunted me, especially those of a man who took one into the Capital, resting it on his shoulder as he strolled around the Rotunda. He also brandished it at a Black police officer who had told him to leave the premises.

Since my novel's timeframe was already set in the months leading up to the 2016 presidential election, I decided to use it as a way to explore how words, actions, and our history as a nation, as well as conflicts, both long-simmering and newly-ignited, had resulted in the chaos of January 6th and its aftermath. The seeds of this chaos were planted long before Donald Trump ran for president, but I believe that if we don't try to understand what has happened to us as a nation, our country will remain as divided as it was during the Civil War. And more chaos will follow.

I also believe that crime fiction lends itself to this kind of exploration. Every mystery novel or short story is a narrative of how human pathology, in its many forms, impacts society. I hope Joplin and Halloran have been able to lead readers through this one in an entertaining and provocative manner.

ACKNOWLEDGEMENTS

FICTION WRITERS TODAY have so many resources because of the internet. We can subscribe to medical and legal search engines, view geographical areas and landmarks through MapQuest, and research just about anything that comes up while creating a novel or short story. We can also use programs that check our spelling and grammar, saving us from certain embarrassment when we finally turn our creation over to an editor or publisher. All without leaving our desks.

But nothing compares to the human touch. I'm fortunate to have several "beta' readers who take time out of their own busy lives to offer me the objectivity needed to create the best book I can: Tom and Nicole Armentrout, Sue Crawford, Bill Donovan, and Eric Copeland, a new addition to the group. They are all knowledgeable, perceptive, meticulous, and honest— qualities that can't be found in writing apps. They can also examine a book up close, finding minor errors that detract from the overall quality, to more global ones involving character development or plot holes. And they've still managed to approach my books as readers who love crime fiction, giving me a heads-up about how other readers will react to them.

John Martucci, of Martucci Designs, is the creative human touch who has designed all my book covers. These covers not only attract readers, but also set the tone of the books themselves. The *Southern Cross* cover does this in spades, capturing the Atlanta skyline, night-sky constellation, and the Medal of Honor images that run through the book. I will count on him to work his magic for all those that follow.

Many, many thanks to Jane Ryder of Ryder Author Resources and Caerus Kourt of Bookery for their amazing work on the formatting, interior design, and publication of the book. Thanks also to Mandy and Gabe Kendrick for their contributions to the formatting process.

Arnie DePetro, who retired as the Georgia Department of Corrections Divisional Director, allowed me to pick his brain about certain aspects of the parole process. Any mistakes or use of poetic license are mine alone.

My thanks to the members of Wine and Crime, a local book club that has been the source of many pleasant evenings spent discussing crime fiction. They also hounded me into finishing this book. And our monthly hosts were kind enough to let me use their house as the model for the one the Joplins and Hallorans stay in at Wolfscratch. I hope it comes across on paper as beautiful as it is in real life.

Thanks also to all the book clubs and various other groups who've invited me to be the guest author at their meetings. That's the fun part of writing. The members consistently provide me with thoughtful questions, excellent critiques, and much-appreciated reasons to keep writing. The food and wine aren't bad either.

To all my readers, thank you for choosing my books and giving me your feedback. I hope you'll take the time to review this one. Stay in touch at **PLDOSS.COM**. I'd love to hear from you.

www.ingramcontent.com/pod-product-compliance
Lightning Source LLC
Chambersburg PA
CBHW020637030726
47498CB00002B/255